THE HORIZON EVENTS
A VEIL IS TORN

LUKE A. WINTER

Ark House Press
arkhousepress.com

The Horizon Events: A Veil is Torn is a work of fiction. Names, characters, businesses, places, events, locales, and incidents are either the products of the author's imagination or used in a fictitious manner. Any resemblance to actual persons, living or dead, or actual events is purely coincidental.

Cataloguing in Publication Data:
Title: The Horizon Events: A Veil Is Torn
ISBN: 978-1-7642308-2-7 (pbk)
Subjects: [FIC042080] FICTION / Christian / Fantasy; [FIC002000] FICTION / Action & Adventure; [FIC028010] FICTION / Science Fiction / Action & Adventure.

Edited by Eddie Albrecht
Cover art by Jussea Sutton

Design by initiateagency.com

To my King

ACKNOWLEDGEMENTS

I could not have written this book without many amazing people supporting me. Anushka, thank you for insisting I had no good reason not to write a book. Thank you Mum, Zac, Liam and Abbi, for reading what was bad so that something good might come of it. Exactly zero thanks go to Dad for "motivating me" by refusing to read my book until it was published. Thanks go to Eddy for editing my manuscript and Dax for her amazing cover artwork. Thank you to the team at Ark House for taking me on board. Thank you to everyone else who checked in, advised, or supported me along the way. But my highest gratitude and praise, as always, goes to Jesus. You are the original world-builder, storyteller, and author of salvation. May my words always point to yours.

PROLOGUE

"Ground to Dirk Leader. Ground to Dirk Leader."

"This is Leader. What's our target?"

"Evac Transport *Naba's Hope* is outbound from Mari City. It can't make it to the Runner alone, Commander."

"Copy, Ground. We're on our way."

Sunlight brushed the edge of Tachillah's atmosphere, glazing the higher clouds in a fiery glow. The thick bands of mist blushed pink and orange as the planet rotated, its capital city crawling slowly towards a new dawn. From space, the world looked peaceful and serene. As Tomas watched, a starship broke through the clouds and shot towards the heavens, leaving wisps of displaced vapour in its wake.

"There she is. Keep it tight, Dirks. We're going in."

The reality of the moment was, of course, far from serene.

"Dive!" Tomas pushed forward on his yoke as an explosion bloomed overhead, gritting his teeth as the compression wave rocked his QW-12 Wasp Starfighter. Shrapnel pinged off his shields in a shimmer-crackle of blue light as he pitched down, keeping the shuttle in his forward view. His engine surged behind him, forcing him against his seat.

On all sides, the void was alight with plasma and steel. Squadrons of Ebon clawcraft swarmed like innumerable insects around him, spewing needles of azure fire from their quin cannons. A cruel metal talon curved around each side of the pentagonal starfighters, ever reaching towards their prey.

But their prey was fighting back. Tomas performed a snap roll that took him out of the path of a pair of rising Wasps, throwing a mental salute as they passed by. The Core Star Fleet had assembled every space-worthy ship for this battle—the last battle, it was thought—for one way or another, the Great Invasion would end today.

"This is suicide, Lead!" Tomas' helmet buzzed with Dirk Three's cry. "The fighting's too thick!" Another set of explosions punctuated the comment as two starfighters collided to his left. Tomas strafed clear, sparing a glance to the radar on his dash. Seven blue indicators kept a tight formation behind him, surrounded by a hurricane of blips in both blue and red.

Tomas keyed his mic. "There are a thousand civilians on that shuttle, Dan," he said, "and this is what they're headed into. If it's too thick, start thinning!"

Putting actions to words, Tomas angled from his path and hammered down on his firing studs. Blue-purple bolts of plasma lanced out from his Wasp's forward mandibles, spearing through the clawcraft that had been chasing one of his allies. The Ebon craft's hull buckled and melted under the assault, and then its engine detonated, tearing the ship apart.

As one, Dirk Squadron drove a spearhead into the cauldron of battle, swiftly reaching and securing themselves around the shuttle *Naba's Hope*. It was the last evacuation craft to leave the planet. The others had already reached the distant *Remnant,* the System Runner that waited in high orbit to begin its harrowing interstellar escape.

"Commander, my port cannon's fried!" Dirk Six's panicked voice lit the comm. "Commander, it's not responding!"

"Six! Power down, take a breath." Tomas' heartbeat skipped as he looked over his shoulder and saw that his friend's left mandible had been completely blown off. The death around him he could tune out, *needed* to tune out, to keep himself alive, but even the minor peril of one of his own sparked a cold and personal fear in his gut.

As one, the Dirks and the *Hope* rose out of Tachillah's pull. Now that Tomas faced away from the planet, the full scope of the battle was revealed to him. Plasma bolts streaked past his cockpit from every angle, prompting his canopy to tint itself to protect his eyes. Capital ships thousands strong were warring above him, drawing alongside their targets and ravaging them with sheets of energy and missiles. Shields flared and burst, hulls blackened, peeled and cracked. Innumerable starfighters wove, tumbled, rose and fell through it all, most too distant and fast to see with Tomas' bare eyes. A furious and fleeting inferno marked each pilot's death. They were the briefest of stars, joining for a moment with the constellations of the star cluster that surrounded them in a distant curtain of light.

A trio of clawcraft dropped towards the shuttle, their plasma fire a concentrated stream upon *Hope's* starboard shields. Tomas depressed his studs, taking out the lead fighter even as Dirk Two took the second from behind him. The third clawcraft veered off.

"Ha! That's four already!" The squadron frequency was a tumult of chatter and cries as the Dirks carved upwards through the deadly fray.

"Kech-dung it is! You stole that earlier one from me!"

"A kill's a—Scourge-spawn! Two more coming in!"

"He's on you, Eight. Roll out of it!"

"My shields can't take it. I'm—"

An indicator winked out. Tomas felt his stomach twist, and he closed his eyes despite the risk. In the moment of darkness, unable to hear the roar of engines or the shriek of folding metal through the barrier of space, he could almost imagine he was dreaming. That this was just some horrible nightmare he would wake from and forget.

"All fighter squadrons to intercept and eliminate Kaldean shuttle *Getorah* immediately! Repeat: all squadrons to eliminate Kaldean shuttle *Getorah* immediately!"

Tomas' eyes snapped open. A small blip had been highlighted on his radar, launching from Tachillah's surface and making swiftly for higher space. *Green: an independent vessel.* Tomas keyed his mic over to the command frequency.

"Admiral, this is Dirk Leader. We're in the middle of an escort." *What in the Four Pits is going on?*

"This takes priority, Commander. Ben-Eloah has stolen a weapon critical to the war effort and intends to barter it for his life. He must be stopped!" The rage in the speaker's voice was tangible, and Tomas felt his own anger flicker in response.

"A spy?"

"A traitor, Commander. A Human."

By the sixth sun ...

"Dirks, on me! Prime missiles and keep forward shields at full. Transfer all remaining power to engines." Two mechanical thuds sounded from behind his shoulders as the Wasp's missile racks primed the first pair of warheads.

"But Lead, the civilians!"

"They're on their own, Two. We have orders." Tomas brought his Wasp into line with the fleeing shuttle, which was headed straight for an Ebon dreadnaught.

A traitor, when the entire Cluster balances on a wingtip! Tomas felt every heartbeat drum against his ribcage as he closed the distance to *Getorah*, only marginally aware of the fight still raging around him. *How could he condemn all free species to die?*

"Ben-Eloah?" Dirk Three remarked. "Wasn't he that crazy cultist on the surface, claiming he could save us all?"

"Stow it, Dan." Tomas leant forward against his restraints, willing his Wasp to be faster.

"Lead, they're coming in from the side! We need to break off!" Tomas looked at his dash, at the wedge of allied fighters racing after their new target. The Dirks had the lead for now and were closing fast on their objective. Behind them, Ebon clawcraft cut through the formation from all directions, mercilessly striking at their prey.

"Admiral?"

"Take that shuttle down, Commander, or we are all lost! *Take it down!*"

A scream cut across the comm, and Tomas looked in horror as Dirk Two exploded off his right wing, a clawcraft blasting through the midst of the fireball. *Getorah* was in sight now, a small, battered shuttle climbing desperately towards salvation. A high tone rang out from the computer as Tomas locked onto the fleeing traitor, but he wouldn't be in firing range for several seconds. Ahead, the Plague-class dreadnaught loomed, its rows of guns sending wave after wave of light slamming into the closest CSF vessel.

Ten seconds.

Getorah continued to drive straight towards the enemy. It should have been trying to evade the missile lock, but it never altered course. Was Ben-Eloah taunting him? The thought only fanned the fury and disgust Tomas felt burning inside.

Four seconds.

Behind him, the other squadrons began to break off as the clawcraft ran pass after pass against their charging ranks. Dirk Seven disappeared as a salvo cut across his stern, slicing white fire straight into his engines. Tomas' hands were a vice upon his yoke.

Two seconds.

You have betrayed us, Ben-Eloah. I give you your just reward. The shuttle did not flinch.

The tone lock jumped a note, and Tomas squeezed the trigger.

"Missiles away! Break and dive!" Two blazing blue-white projectiles shot over his head as Tomas threw his acceleration lever into reverse. He watched the twin lights streak across the dark expanse towards *Getorah's* stern.

Time seemed to slow and all action cease as the universe stopped to orbit a single moment, every far-flung star a shining witness to the passage of one instant. Tomas breathed out.

The missiles struck, and *Getorah* was engulfed in a fiery explosion swiftly overtaken by a second, brighter radiance that tore through space. It rushed over and through Tomas' Wasp, filling his ears with the sound of a hurricane, blinding him even through closed eyes. An inexorable force pressed against his chest until it felt like every bone was being driven into his heart.

Terrified, he cried out, but the sound was swept away with everything else until suddenly—

Tomas' vision cleared, and he stared at the empty space where Ben-Eloah's ship had been, a space that was the next moment filled with a torrent of plasma fire and missiles.

Tomas jammed his thumbs on the firing studs and flew into the wave.

1

Tomas Amets woke with a start, eyes straining against the sweat and tears that filled them. He drew from the air in gasps, hands reaching for the pilot's yoke that wasn't in front of him as he dove, his thumbs depressing triggers that no longer existed.

Then it was over, and he was in his bed.

"Lights!"

A clean white-blue poured from the illumination strips in the ceiling, banishing the shadows from the small cabin he'd been lent. It was simply furnished: a low plastic desk, two fold-down chairs under the viewport, and a small hydroponics basin between them. Red-stemmed ferns crept over the basin's lip, the only bright colour in the room.

A mirror was set into the closet door opposite the bed, and Tomas caught sight of himself in its reflection: a pale, sweaty Human twisted half out of his bedsheets, brown buzz cut darkened with moisture, eyes staring.

That dream … that memory …

He shook the last images from his mind. He hadn't dreamt of the Battle of Tachillah for years. It had been a good dream once—a memory of the greatest victory the Cluster had ever known, ending forty years of merciless invasion.

Then it had become a nightmare, and he had cast it from his mind lest he find himself staring every night into the eyes of all the pilots he had watched die.

Peeling his covers off the rest of the way, Tomas stood up, stretched and turned to the viewport that dusted starlight across the floor. His face was a phantom upon the glass, reflecting the half-life he felt inside. He stared at it for a moment, then focused beyond.

Far beyond, to the planet Jerassh that drifted eighty million kilometres away. Looking barely larger than a star, the pinprick glittered softly, joining with the radiant surrounds of the Globular Cluster. To either side of the viewport, the shift station stretched outward and downward, a landscape in its own right. But the lights that snaked and gridded the hull were only a timid comparison. Turning away from the glass, Tomas stripped off his damp nightclothes and headed into the shower.

The water quickly washed the worry of his sleep away. It had been a dream, but he was awake now, and the universe had moved on. They had defeated the Ebon, and Tomas had survived. Only a few of the pilots who had been there could say the same.

Stop it. Stop thinking about it. Tomas forced a smile to his lips, pushing his mind onto a different path. *You honour them by moving on, by doing your duty.*

The thought calmed him as he dressed, not in his usual pilot's flight suit but in a grey blazer and pants. Taking a last look at the stars outside the window, he headed down the hall. His duty would be slightly different for the next few days, but he would do it all the same.

The mess was empty as Tomas passed through the automatic doors. All shift stations operated under Universal Time, which copied the twenty-six-hour day of the Cluster's capital planet, Kaldea Prime. That starlight might take a hundred years to reach Jerassh, yet the day shift would still start when dawn struck the Hall of Council on Kaldea's frozen surface.

Tomas ordered a mug of jolt and some Nutri-Light at the terminal and waited. Before long, a server bot wheeled out from behind its rubber curtain, a fresh meal on its polished head tray. He downed the beverage on the spot, relishing its warmth, then snatched up the bowl and headed towards the hangar.

Eight battle-worn Quad-Wing-12 Wasp Starfighters rested on their landing struts inside Hangar 11E, facing the stars. A shimmering mag-screen glazed the outside view in a hazy electric blue, but it was no less breathtaking. The tightly packed stars of the Cluster were bright yet cold as they caught in the canopies of the watching fighter craft. And beyond those stars, somewhere, lay the Eye of Urim: the four-armed spiral galaxy the Cluster orbited as a distant child.

A Wasp's fuselage was high and wide at the back and accommodated the powerful engine block. From there, the hull tapered downwards and inwards, past the weave-glass canopy, ending in a thin, flat nose. Pilots often joked that it resembled a duck's bill.

The gun-metal paint job was interrupted by two bright orange strips that ran from the front backwards, ending inside the shoulder mounts that sported three powerful missiles each. The same orange covered all four wings and nicely complemented the 'wasp' namesake.

Tomas set his bowl down atop the port mandible of his fighter and ran a hand along the sleek, angular surface from the inbuilt plasma cannon up towards the wing's elbow. It wasn't really a wing—the two affixed further back did a much better job stabilising in-atmosphere flight and housed the port and starboard attitude thrusters—but they were certainly useful. Reaching past the fighter's bow like the mouthparts of some giant Gazam, they looked menacing even without the azure plasma salvo that could spew from their guns.

"Still mad about being stuck on terminal security, Lead?"

Tomas shook out of his momentary lull, turning towards the slender Human female entering the hanger with her hand raised in salute.

"I've been given better placements, Quil." Tomas returned the salute as Falaquil Caron finished her approach. "A pilot should feel no gravity but his ship's and his own." He prodded his boot into the metal floor for emphasis.

"Fighter jockeys—you always think everything revolves around you. Now I know why." His wingmate grinned mischievously. She was outfitted in a security blazer the same as Tomas, but on hers there was not a crease or fold out of line. Her braided terracotta hair fell like an arrow down to the small of her back.

Her brow furrowed. "Are you okay? We missed you in the mess."

Quil, twenty-five years old, had been with Dirk Squadron all four years since she left the academy. She had faced uncountable dangers and trials, but Tomas could see the inexperience, the innocence, that still lingered in her storm-blue eyes. Tachillah had taken that innocence from him.

"I'm fine," Tomas said, and it was almost true. "Just needed some time to myself."

Quil placed a hand on her hip, an eyebrow raised. "Don't you always say the Dirks are strongest together?"

"I ... well ..." Tomas tried to scowl, but a grin broke through. "You've locked me again, Two. Being in charge is no fun!"

Dirk Two laughed, and the sound put the last of the night's upset behind him. She was right, of course; they were strongest together. That was why every pilot had his wingmate.

"Come on," Tomas shifted his bowl, then hoisted himself onto his fighter's mandible. He motioned for Quil to sit next to him. "I still have to eat, but I'd rather avoid Dan and Gerad's antics for as long as possible."

That earned a second laugh. "As ordered, Commander." Quil shook her head as she joined him. "Some battles aren't worth facing, eh?"

"Not while there's fuel left to avoid them," Tomas agreed. He would tell her about the dream, he decided, once Tachillah had faded back into the distant memory of victory it was supposed to be. Until then, well, he had a job to do.

Jerassh Station had numerous bulletins advertising it as a 'station like no other'. Tomas had heard and seen similar proclamations at every shift station he had visited, as if the lie were a crucial subsystem installed in every port as it was built.

For when it came to shift stations, they were all the same. At the core of every station was a superstructure of connected decks, rooms and corridors, layered and pressed together in pyritic asymmetry. Every beam and hull plate was made of kuwrium—'sun steel', it was commonly called—a metal alloy as strong as it was bland and grey.

Out of this core protruded a large, curved transport rib that traced out the station's orbit some five thousand kilometres above the shift gate's enigmatic surface. On this rib sat four docking modules, each a feat of engineering in its own right. Highly populated systems would have an extended transport rib, with more modules along it to accommodate the constant ferrying of passengers. But four modules sufficed for Jerassh and its native population of three billion.

As Tomas and Quil rode the transport tube towards Module B, he couldn't help but think the core structure looked like a cluster of crystal, some sort of salt perhaps. The architecture was almost certainly Yiishi in origin, so perhaps the inspiration had come from ancient Yiishi miners prospecting for minerals across the stars.

The thought kept him occupied as they slowed to arrive at the port module. As with each module, the hangars and bays on one side handled passage to and from the system's planets, while the other concerned itself with travellers headed inter-system through the shift gate.

A chime sounded as the tube stopped at the module's tenth floor, and Tomas stepped into a bustling hive of noise and colour. Garish tapestries of lavender, violet and orange were draped across the white polyplex walls, advertising local tourist destinations in every writable language. Strings of humanoids wove towards the terminals and security checkpoints, herding offspring and pushing cargo sledges as they sought the quickest route through the chaos.

Tomas had no fear of tight spaces—flying in a starfighter didn't allow him that luxury—but if ever he were to develop claustrophobia, it would be within this clamouring crowd. It felt like oxygen was being inhaled from his lungs as he squeezed and pardoned his way forward, and he was ever aware of an urge to climb over those before him, just so his head might breach the surface of the throng.

"There's Klord," Quil shouted and waved at someone ahead. Tomas looked but could see nothing. He followed her until, pushing through a group of lumbering Gitorians, they came upon a line of roped stanchions. Behind the line, the remaining members of Dirk Squadron were talking quietly amongst themselves. One of them gave Tomas a hearty slap as he unlocked the rope.

"A little late, aren't we, Lead?" Daniel Pandyne jeered. He was a Human slightly younger than Tomas, yet his eyes sparkled with the energy of one half as old. His head was bald save for a silver-black goatee and a moustache that curled like a second smile.

Quil nudged Dirk Three in the side. "Is our instructor here yet?"

"No."

"Then you're all just early," she teased as she pushed past to talk to Dirk Six. Dan looked back to Tomas, who shrugged.

"You *are* early. Back at base we're always waiting on you or Gerad."

Dan grinned along with his moustache. "More women here than on Gerduk," he said, his eyes dancing. "Wandering, searching, waiting until I oblige them with my charm ..."

A rattle-hiss escaped from over Dan's shoulder. Teliac Sfeze—Dirk Four and the squadron's resident Gazam—snapped his mandibles together in laughter.

"Does your—tch—charm increase with your—tch—crash reports?"

Dan whirled. "Hey! I haven't hit anything in at least a month!"

"So you must be due," Teliac clicked-laughed again, staring his wing-mate down with his vertical compound eye. The eye visor was sunk between two teardrop faceplates that were the same umber-black as the rest of the warrior's exoskeleton and prevented any peripheral vision. The insectoid predators allowed no distractions when stalking their prey. Tomas was just glad he'd never been that prey.

Three and Four faced off in silence, a mock battle of wills.

The silence didn't last long. "Scourge-sucker!" Dan jeered.

"Tch—coward."

"Kech-brain!"

"Please, both of you, we're representing the fleet." Holding a hand up, Tomas dared to edge between them.

"Of course, Commander," Teliac snapped his gaze around, and Tomas flinched. "This assignment agitates me."

"I know it does. But *you* know the local team has been put into quarantine for the week, and you know our orders."

Teliac hissed, yanking his stun pistol from its holster and holding it up. "This weapon dishonours me. I am a pilot, not—tch—a cattle herder."

"I know," Tomas repeated, his hands still held to ward off a coming blow. With Gazem, you never felt totally safe. "But it'll be a long week if we don't come to terms with it now, so I need both of you to work with me. Please?"

There was silence for a moment as Tomas slowly wilted beneath Teliac's unreadable visor.

"Yes, Commander." Dirk Four turned away, and Tomas straightened, relieved.

"And you too, Dan … *Dan?*"

But Dan's attention had moved on sentences ago, and he pressed against the rope, beckoning into the crowd.

"Hey! You! Yeah, hey kid!" He waved to a small boy running between bodies with a hexagonal prism in his hands. It was a model System Runner, Tomas realised, nearly as long as the boy was tall, and the roar of its large engines spit-spluttered out from the child's pink lips.

The boy froze at Dan's call, the starship suspended mid-climb. He drew it to his chest protectively.

"What's that you've got there, pal?"

"It … it's mine!"

Dan crouched low and beckoned once more. "It's so big! Can I have a look?"

Realising he wasn't in trouble, the boy brightened and waddled over. Dan widened his eyes.

"*Wow.* She's amazing, true as core! What's she called?"

"It's the *Remnant,*" the boy said proudly. "It kept my mum safe at the big battle!" He went to pass it under the guiding rope, then thought the better of it and hugged it back to his chest. "Mum says it's ten kilo … kilomers long and *really fast*! They had to fly it cos … cos the Ebon had the shift gate."

The kid's knowledge was impressive. Tomas tried to spot his mother amongst those nearby, but no one was paying attention to the exchange. Dan puffed up his chest.

"That's right! I was at that battle, can you believe? Look." He tugged his collar forward, presenting a metal pin. On it, three ribbons of metal wove around a tongue of flame. The ribbons represented the three governments of the Cluster. The Central Systems, called the Core by most; the Chammuah Crescent, and even the ill-reputed North Wilds had banded together to face the Ebon threat.

The pin's value was not lost on the boy, who looked somewhere between swooning and exploding. "You're a *pilot*!" He said the last word with special reverence.

Dan's pride was as bright as a nova. "You bet! Me and my friend here—" without looking, he reached back and yanked Tomas into view "—were on the front lines. He shot down fourteen ships all by himself!"

The boy's jaw struck the deck.

Tomas felt himself redden and held his hands up. "One of them wasn't even armed …"

"It counts!" Dirk Three insisted, flashing Tomas an irritated look. "Don't ruin the story!"

"What story?" A young woman appeared from the crowd, and the boy bounced up to her. "Mummy! Mummy! I met a pilot!"

"Did you?" The mother glanced admiringly at Dan, who rose and offered his hand.

"Daniel Pandyne, CSF, at your service. I saw your boy here and thought to keep him safe until you …"

Tomas turned from the conversation with a roll of his eyes. So that had been the plan all along, had it? He should have known better. Dirk Three had few motives.

A soft sadness crept from his gut: hollow, grey. Tomas sighed, looking at the pin on his own blazer. Twice today, he had been reminded of the Battle of Tachillah, and while his mind was ever conscious of the victory—of how many lives had been saved—his heart forever lagged, sobered by the memory of death.

Yet he was still a pilot. Why? Tomas looked back to the young boy beaming from ear to ear, still cradling his spaceship, and found his answer. The Cluster still needed protecting, and he, Tomas, would continue to protect it.

And if the sadness remained, that would just have to become part of the cost.

2

Even before they arrived at their guard post, Tomas could see Quil was sick of the assignment.

"So, who's going to snap first?" she said as she fingered her stun pistol restlessly. They were stationed in a small clearing beside the departure terminals, surrounded by pressing queues of people. Quil began to lean on a flimsy barricade separating two lines, then thought the better of it. "My money's on Seven."

Their instructor had arrived a full hour late, barely stopping to assign the Dirks around the floor and explain their jobs before speeding away on another errand. Tomas hadn't even caught a name from the silver-furred Daban and was left feeling more than a little unprepared.

He scanned the crowd, overwhelmed with the prospect of spotting any rule-breakers amongst the chaos. It wasn't just the sight or sound; the smell also assaulted him. The odours of a thousand worlds mixed in a salty vinegar as lifeforms pushed and pressed through the gates, the air humid with perfumes and pheromones. He tried to spy the other wingpairs split across the floor but failed.

"I'll take that bet!" Gerad Belte's indignant voice boomed through the earpiece, too loud. Tomas took a moment to adjust his settings. "Four is easily the trapped hoonish in the room, and that's core. Why would you choose me?"

"You're stuck by the information desk," Teliac was quick on the reply. "Nothing happens there. And I don't—tch—snap. My foes snap, as I invert their skeletons."

"Power down, Four," said Tomas. "We've got a long day of meaningless conversation ahead of us, so let's start it mildly, shall we?" He thought for a moment. "Sorry, Seven, my money's on you as well."

"Well I protest! I'm as resolute as a Sun Guard, you'll see!"

"Sun Guards don't talk, Seven," Dirk Six cut in, earning laughter from everyone except Gerad.

Tomas continued to keep a close eye on the travellers approaching the exit gates. As was expected, most were Human or Daban; unless you were in a homeworld system, those two races were always the most common. Both were remarkably similar in appearance, and yet equally distinct. Thin fur covered the Daban everywhere except their head, and their arms were webbed to their torsos with a leathery gliding membrane, though underneath a shawl or cloak the difference was hidden away. Indeed, many of the patrons shambling up to the terminal clerks and getting their palm-chip scanned wore such coverings. Both the poor and the rich had reasons to travel unseen, or unremembered, at the least.

The skin on a Daban's head was also drawn much tighter to the skull than on a Human, an unsettling appearance, as the sunken cheeks and prominent jawbone made the large white-less eyes seem much larger. Tomas had heard they wore huge goggles when gliding through the canyons of their homeworld, Torinne.

He took a small step backwards as a litter of Yiishi pups ran past him, chittering excitedly in their native language and ducking through and around the legs of the crowd. There was a startled yelp, and he caught sight of the last one tunnelling through a group of touring gentry. One of the mistresses had bumped into the cargo sledge next to her, toppling some of the luggage. Red-faced, she turned and shouted at the fleeing children, but the rest of her company laughed her off.

Two figures stooped to collect the fallen cases, soundless in their action, all but ignored by the group. Their skin was bare and dark, but not dark in any reasonable use of the word. Their bodies absorbed all light, rendering them as unnerving silhouettes. The result was a depthless blot on one's vision, like someone had cut a humanoid hole in reality and exposed the shadow beneath. Only the presence of thick, glowing slave collars spoiled the effect.

Void. Husk. *Ebon.*

Tomas looked away, settling his focus back onto the terminals. Disgust thickened his blood to soup, first at the slaves, then their mistress, and finally at himself.

"Don't worry about it, Lead," Quil said. She had also been watching the slaves. But she hadn't been there when the last Ebon warriors had powered down their ships in surrender, still thousands strong but beaten at last, the merciless destroyers of countless worlds now begging for mercy.

Chief of Council Duidain had issued the command himself: "For their crimes, all Ebon are now enslaved. For each of the forty years they slaughtered us, they shall serve us four hundred."

That had been the Capital's order, but the Capital was a long way from Tachillah, where dead allies formed a floating graveyard, and the enemy ships lay exposed and weak.

So they had stormed the ships, Tomas among them, culling their prey until fury and grief were spent. Deep down, he had known the act was wrong, but in a universe of a thousand cultures and laws, what was truly right? No punishment could return what had been lost. In the eyes of a grieving husband, mother, or orphan, the Ebon would never finish paying for what they'd done.

That memory had quickly soured, and Tomas let it remind him that he fought no longer to kill or avenge, but to protect.

Only to protect.

The luggage was once again settled on the cargo sledge, and Tomas continued to watch despite his better judgement. Both Ebon shrank back to the rear of the gentry, silent and servile. The need to dominate had been driven from them by force.

"Do you think they deserved this, Quil?" Tomas couldn't help but ask as he drew his attention back around the rest of the bustling floor. He was still on the job, after all. The Yiishi children had rejoined their mother at the terminal gate and pushed up against each other as their paws were scanned. The mother, whose head came just above Tomas' waist, chittered loudly as she tried to keep them still enough to count.

Quil tapped on her holster as she thought. After a minute, she shook her head. "No, but I don't think we got what we deserved either," she said. "No one did. When the news of the battle hit the academy, we didn't believe it was over. It was a week before we were confident enough to celebrate, and the day after we did, the major overseeing our division told us we would all have to stay in school three more years."

An ancient Chamisib plodded out of the crowd and signed at them with cracking leathery hands; a simple well-wishing as it entered the nearest line. Quil smiled up at the ageing anneloid, signing her thanks before continuing.

"The Great Invasion was all we knew growing up, but you at least had proper training. By the time I was old enough, they'd compressed the program in an effort to boost ranks. As soon as we could fly straight and hit the trigger, they shipped us off to die. I was two weeks away from graduating when the war ended, and I didn't even know how to land, true as core," she laughed at the memory, but the sound rang slightly hollow. "Docking procedures don't matter to dead pilots."

Quil stopped herself, as if she'd delved too deep into her past and touched something cold at the bottom. She reapplied her smile and shrugged. "We didn't win the war, Commander: we just came second last. But hey, now we're a rockrat's tail away from galactic peace, so go us."

"That's a mighty big rockrat," Tomas sighed, then mentally scolded himself for it. "I'm sorry, that was negative. I ..." He looked his wingmate in the eye. She looked back, and he saw nothing but the care and friendship he'd always known from her. "Last night, I dreamt I was there. Back at the battle. That's why I haven't been myself this morning."

Quil pressed her lips together as she contemplated the new information. True as core, if there was a friend in need or distress, Falaquil Caron would be the first to help. It was who she was.

Having ordered her thoughts, she said, "Have you ever been back?"

To Tachillah? The idea had never crossed his mind before. "No ... not yet. Do you think I need to face my ghosts or something?"

"You never know. I just thought you could look at the planet, at the debris, and tell yourself that it's in the past. But I can only guess what it was like being at that battle. I don't think I'd want to know."

"Well ..." Tomas stopped as a prickling sensation stood his hair on end. Despite the mass of bodies bumbling around, the air felt cold. Something was wrong.

"Lead?"

Training lured his hand towards the butt of his pistol as Tomas scanned the crowd. Nothing suspicious jumped out at him, but an enemy could be anywhere. He glanced at the closest gate, where a figure wrapped in a desert native's scarf was approaching the clerk for palm scanning. The being stopped short in a sudden coughing fit, doubling over.

It was the perfect position from which to pull a hidden weapon. One sidelong glance at Quil told Tomas she had drawn the same conclusion.

He switched on his mic and started towards the gate and the bent native. The rasping hacks sounded Human, female, and genuine, but Jerassh Station wouldn't have requested security if everyone here was genuine.

"Dirk Lead here. I've got a suspicious person at the departure terminals, possibly armed. I'm heading over to—" Tomas spun around as a large crash silenced everyone nearby. His hand snatched his gun from its holster, a brief jolt tensing his muscles as the I.D. chip in his palm unlocked the weapon's trigger.

He followed the startled faces and saw that the laden cargo sledge from earlier had been completely overturned. The mistress was on the floor, scooping up spilt clothes and jewellery from a damaged suitcase, shrieking and cursing. It was much the same as last time.

Except last time, the Ebon had been there to clear the mess. Quil began moving through the crowd with a purpose, and Tomas looked past her to see the ordinarily timid slaves clawing and shoving their way through the crowd towards the lift tubes. They looked terrified, though without expressions it wasn't easy to tell. Shouts started to ring out as they continued to force their way past the onlookers.

Tomas had been filtering out his squadron's conversation, but now his ears listened as they began to call in.

"Lead; Six. Some Ebon have gone crazy near the terminals. Moving in now."

"Two here. They're aiming for the tubes. Intercepting."

"What in time and space is going on?"

"Silence, Seven, and calm this crowd! Something started this."

Klord was, as usual, on the right page. Tomas was all too eager to paint his sights on the Ebon slaves, as was the rest of the floor. People scrambled over one another as they tried to get out of the way of the rampaging silhouettes, and those nearest the gates began surging forward, desperate to pass through.

Quil shouted at the Ebon to freeze, but both pushed on oblivious. One of the pair glanced back over its shoulder and, catching sight of something, redoubled its efforts to reach the waiting tubes. Tomas tried to follow its gaze as screams ricocheted around the room but saw only the cargo sledge.

"I'm boxing them in," Ernn Galoot, Dirk Eight, had managed to reach the transport tubes ahead of the black aliens. "This scorching mob! I can't get a clean shot. *Clear out, you kech-lumps!*"

The Ebon saved him the trouble by breaking through the far edge of the crowd. Eight snapped his stun pistol up. The Ebon stopped short, studying the Kilya pilot that barred their way. Two black chests rose and fell in time to soundless breaths.

Tomas took advantage of the reprieve and scanned over the gentry, the toppled luggage and the staring crowd, determined to find the true cause of all this. A Taphuun crept slyly towards a dropped necklace, only to be put to flight by a hurled shoe and a burst of cursing. The act drew all nearby stares save for one cloaked female.

Tomas' eyes locked onto the woman, but his brain didn't immediately process what he saw. She was beautiful, and unlike any creature he had ever seen. Her skin was a shimmering, ghostly white, and light passed through it as through a fog. A clay-white scar ran down her cheek beneath the surface. The strands of hair that escaped her hood were like mist as she brushed them aside, fixated on the Ebon slaves. Her eyes were blazing rays of illumination that lit the space before her, and as Tomas watched, she raised a hand from beneath her robe and muttered a single word.

At once, a high shriek pierced the clamour, drilling a molten needle of sound into Tomas' skull. The Ebon death whistle. The surrounding travellers dropped to their knees and covered their ears, and it took all of Tomas' willpower not to do the same. As he turned, however, he saw that Ernn hadn't been as strong. Dirk Eight's aim dipped. The lead Ebon launched forward with a fist, flooring the pilot and rushing past him.

Tomas expected the fear of the crowd to double, but as Ernn hit the ground it was like a wire snapped, and those who were fleeing were suddenly raging forward, bloodlust in their eyes. The death whistle cut off as the Ebon were buried in a stampede. Ernn disappeared, and Tomas saw Quil struggle momentarily before her head was swept under the wave of beings.

"No! Stop!" The words might as well have been challenging gravity itself. Tomas tried to shove those closest to him away but could make no progress to the centre of the mob. An alarm began blaring through the overhead speaker. "Quil!"

Abruptly he turned, searching again for that alien woman. She had caused this, he knew; had commanded the Ebon into some kind of frenzy. Where had she gone?

There—pushing towards the security terminals and the freedom beyond them. Tomas started after her, carving his own path through the masses. His finger itched on the trigger of his pistol, but he kept the barrel low, eyes straining to pick out her simple robe as it rose and fell through the waves of people.

"He's clear! Ernn's clear!" Quil's voice came through his earpiece, and he glanced back. He saw nothing, of course. "Lead, how do we get this crowd to stop?"

Tomas keyed his mic. "Stay clear until backup arrives. I'm chasing down the …" Tomas faced forward again, but it was already too late. He'd lost sight of her. He bit off a curse.

"Repeat that last. Lead?" Tomas ignored Quil and picked up speed, shoving people out of his way, ignorant of their protest. The screeching alarm hammered into his thoughts from above. He couldn't let the woman escape. He *wouldn't.*

He began to notice a parting in the crowd to his right, some sort of new commotion that people were trying to avoid. It was the only clue he had. After a beat of hesitation he ran towards the parting, nearly stumbling as he came through the edge of the circle.

Two others shared the space. The first was the woman, a shining dagger in her hand, the muscles under her cloak coiled for flight. She looked at him as he entered, catching him in the light of her eyes. It was a light both pure and white, and at the same time a kaleidoscope that danced in hues and shapes; ribbons of colour in liquid crystal, or solid cloud.

Then the gaze left him, and he followed it onto the second figure. This man, Tomas saw by the silver-white uniform, was a CSF officer. A narrow visor of black metal hid his eyes, and a wicked smile played across his lips. He held a sword of red steel in his hands. Before Tomas had time to wonder at the weapon, the woman launched toward the man, her dagger cleaving through the air towards the officer's face.

Tomas yelled out and brought his pistol to bear, but he was too slow. The officer, though, was up to the challenge. He sidestepped the first wild swing, and the second. On the third, his hand lashed out like a snake, catching the woman's arm. She pulled free with a spin, coming around for the next attack.

It never fell. As she turned, the officer plunged his sword through her back and into her heart. Ivory liquid burst out the front of her cloak, and her body crumpled to the ground as the blade withdrew. The officer watched the body as it fell, then stepped back into the parting crowd.

For the next few seconds, Tomas just stood, his hands shaking as he stared down the sight of his gun. Then his arms fell and he ran to her, dropping to his knees, placing his hands to stem the bleeding. He knew as he did that there was no hope. There was no light in the creature's eyes.

A scream of utter, soul-rending torment swept across the crowd, and silence rushed in behind it. It lifted Tomas from his task, but he could only see the blank faces of the crowd pressing close around him once again. The officer was gone. The alarms, too, had stopped blaring, but he could still hear a senseless amalgam of noise in his ears. The noise resolved into voices.

"What was that scream?"

"Dan, focus! I've got more gate jumpers over here!"

"Does anyone have eyes on Lead? He's still not responding!"

"Two, it's Six. Another security team has just arrived."

"Lead? Lead, please respond!"

Tomas knew he should say something, but he felt numb. Why was he numb? Something clattered to the ground, and he jerked back down.

The woman was gone, leaving only her tattered cloak in his bloodied hands. A small disc lay on the ground beside him, fallen from one of the cloak's pockets. He picked it up.

"Lead!" Quil's voice came not from his earpiece but from behind him. "What ... what happened here?"

What *had* happened?

A hand touched his shoulder. "... Lead?"

Tomas looked up at her. "I don't know," he said.

"I don't know."

3

... the tone lock jumped a note, and Erae squeezed the trigger.

"Missiles away! Break and dive!" Two blazing blue-white projectiles shot over her head as Erae threw her acceleration lever into reverse. She watched the twin lights streak across the dark expanse towards Getorah's stern.

Then she realised what she had done, and horror rose in her like a wave, not of water but of filth thick and rotten. In her mind, she dug her heels in, fighting against the inevitable march of time as the watching stars averted their gaze.

The missiles struck, and Getorah was engulfed in a fiery explosion swiftly overtaken by a second, brighter radiance that tore through space. It rushed over and through Erae's Wasp, filling her ears with the sound of a hurricane, blinding her even through closed eyes. An inexorable force pressed against her, crushing bone and flesh alike into the singularity of her mistake.

Terrified, she cried out, but the sound was swept away with everything else until suddenly—

Erae's vision cleared, and she stared at the empty space where Ben-Eloah's ship had been, a space that was the next moment filled with a torrent of plasma fire and missiles.

Erae jammed her thumbs on the firing studs and flew into the wave.

Erae Tamah woke with a start, on the ground beneath her sleeping cocoon. Pain rippled through her back and thigh, bubbling and mixing with the adrenaline that propelled her senses from rest. Panic brought her legs beneath her even as she deciphered her surroundings in the darkness and saw there was no danger.

She was in her cabin on the *Silent Empress*; the arrhythmic rumbling of the engines was information enough. It was the turbulent snore of a wondrous metal beast, breathing just enough to keep itself alive as it drifted through the heaven between planets and stars.

How terrifyingly peaceful inertia can be. Standing up fully, Erae reached to the light panel on the far wall and felt for the switch.

With a delayed flicker, the halogen tube hugging the corner of the ceiling came to life, casting odd shadows around the cramped cabin as it sought to sneak some light past the wads of electrical tape that covered its cracked glass. Sickly sulphurous yellows stumbled around, elbowing out the darkness and the fears that came with them. It was light enough to see by and not much more.

Not that there's anything worth seeing. Erae sighed inwardly as she performed a slow spin in her compact lodging. Without a step, she could reach from the two sleeping cocoons on one wall to the fatigues hanging from a snaking water pipe on the other. The third wall sloped towards her, forcing a crouch if she wanted to see clearly through the porthole.

Through the porthole and to the stars beyond, where rivers of white fire wove through a world of black silk and void, life and death intertwined on a scale far greater than any mortal war.

War ... the battle! A barrage of images collided inside her mind, and Erae found herself caught by her sleeping cocoon as her vision greyed, her breath suddenly weighed by all the fear and pain that had vanished when she awoke.

It had been a dream, a nightmare imprisoning her in a cage of her own thoughts. She'd been in a starfighter, flying in some momentous battle she had never known. There had been courage, and darkness, and a hideous betrayal. The tar-thick feeling of it choked her throat.

But who had she been? The name was lost in the mist of her thoughts, the memories fleeing even as she laid eyes on them. Why it mattered so much, she couldn't say, but as the dream slipped away, an urgency took her, begging her to grasp for some last piece beyond her reach. In the end, she only knew that she had not been herself.

Anxiety of an unknown breed shivered up and down Erae's ice-blue arms, setting her hands to action. One ran through her raven hair, catching on the sleep knotted there. The other reached for the sapphire pendant hanging from a chain around her neck. It was carved to resemble a diving ginah hawk from Nava, her homeworld.

"Siro?" The comm panel by the door crackled to life, startling her. "Ganna tyippli mi ilyt na nyit. Siro?"

She padded over to the panel and keyed the mic. "Say that again, Driz? I just woke up."

[I was asking, Captain,] the speaker chittered, and this time Erae was ready to translate the Yiish words, [are you sure we have the right time?]

"You know as much as I do. Why?"

There was a pause. [Well, the *Comet* is late to the rendezvous. More than usual, I mean.]

Erae's eyes shot to the sleeping cocoon that hung above her own, the one belonging to her best friend, Amarie Gayyam. The young woman was a highly skilled infiltrator, often away on some mission Erae wasn't privy to. Such was life with the Defiant.

She had been late before, on purpose even, just to get a kick out of seeing Erae worry. Erae liked to believe she could be calm—at peace, even—with the constant uncertainty inherent in their way of life. She said the rule better than she followed it, as was the case now.

"I'll be right up," she said into the comm, her mind sorting through the possibilities as she turned to dress. Amarie should be fine. She *would* be. Epieta was with her, and that was a great comfort. Both were capable warriors if the matter came to it.

Although … Epieta wouldn't have been sent if the mission wasn't dangerous. Erae huffed as she threw on her coat, frustrated at her lack of knowledge. A stealth-op, a retrieval mission of some kind, but that was it. She didn't even know the star system.

Please … just hurry up and get here. Erae muttered a quick prayer, then pressed the door release for her room. The mechanism slid the door open halfway before giving up, and Erae huffed again. The *Empress* had seen better days, most of them before Erae had inherited her. Shouldering through the gap, Erae headed for the ladder up to the cockpit.

The *Silent Empress* had initially been built as a cargo freighter and had served that purpose for many years under the captaincy of Erae's grandfather. Pa Jacob Tamah had loved the craft as a member of the family, and tinkered with it until its original model and shape were impossible to recall. The same passion had passed to Jacob's son, and then to Erae, though she found she spent more time repairing than upgrading the old thing.

She reached the top of the ladder and pulled herself through the opening, steadying herself as gravity shifted around her body. Most of the ship was oriented in one direction, with a person's feet facing the engines and their head towards the bow, but the cockpit was offset by ninety degrees. The transition could be unsettling if you weren't ready for it, but Erae had no trouble exiting the hole in the back wall and getting her feet under her. She leant over the co-pilot's chair.

"Anything yet, Driz?"

Pakt N'Drizo arched his squat head back and blinked at her with four beady black eyes. [Still nothing, Captain,] he squeaked. He pressed a button on the board in front of him, then typed a quick command with his small, furry paws. [I've pushed our sensors as far as they can go. She's never been this late before.]

"She does enjoy setting new records," Erae replied, trying to sound positive, if not feeling it. She patted Driz on the head, then slid into the seat beside him. The viewport stretched in front of and above her, full of the misted lights of the Cluster. She focused on an orb of tenebrous, violet gas silhouetted against them, searching it for motion of any kind. No matter where Amaire and Epieta had been sent, they would have to come through the shift gate to make this rendezvous—*if* they were still coming. Just how big of a record was Amarie trying to set?

Erae checked the time on her monitor, then started. "Three hours?" She whirled back to Driz. "They're *three hours* late? Driz!"

Driz raised his paws in defence. [That's why I thought we might have the wrong schedule. I would have woken you, but, well, it's Amarie! Even the king wouldn't know how often she's been late. She's—]

"Not this late, Driz!" Erae cut the Yiishi off, any pretence of calm truly gone from her. "She's reckless, not incompetent … and not while Epieta's with her."

Her eyes strained towards the shift gate, as if by increasing her effort she might penetrate its surface and find her friends within. Her hand hovered over the ignition controls, but where would she go?

She went for the microphone instead. "Driz, hook into Fal-Comm and send this recording back to base. They'll know where we need to go. Then send a second packet to Rahga and tell them to proceed without us."

[But Captain!]

"They'll be fine," Erae insisted. The Rahga mission was hers to lead, but Amarie was part of her crew. It was an easy decision to make.

She keyed to record.

"Base, this is Captain Tamah reporting an emergency change of orders. I'm requesting full disclosure of—"

"Drillyb!"

"Enough, Driz!" Erae scolded him before her mind finished translating the word. *Contact.* "Where?"

Driz punched in a command, and a digital grid snaked its way across the glass viewport. A sensor alert formed a red box over one edge of the shift gate.

"Driz?"

[It's the *Silver Comet,*] he answered without looking up from his own monitor. [Putting you through now.]

An indicator on her side lit up, and Erae was on the mic in an instant. "Amarie? Amarie, can you read me?"

A soft background static hissed out of the cockpit speakers.

"Amarie? Epieta? Can anyone respond?"

In her peripherals, she saw Driz shake his head, his ears flat.

Amarie?

[Their ship reads fine, no damage.] He paused for a moment. [Visual contact in six, five, four …]

He finished the countdown, but it was a little longer before Erae spotted the two-man starfighter approaching them, growing steadily larger. Erae tried the mic again, but the static-silence remained.

"Driz, what's wrong?" She rose from her seat and pressed a hand to the viewport. "Are they not receiving us, or are we not receiving them?"

[I can't tell, Captain, but the *Comet* just accepted the slave request. Amarie must be inside.] As he said this, he reached for his yoke and began making small turns and pulls.

Erae forced herself from the glass long enough to look at her monitor. On it, a glowing outline showed the elegant silhouette of the *Empress*. A triad of large engines surrounded the cargo hold at the ship's rear and took up nearly half its length. From there the hull swept in curving fins towards the bow, uninterrupted save for the dorsal gunwell and the plasma cannons in the bow's chin.

A second silhouette entered the screen, much smaller and with sharper lines. Erae watched Driz fly the *Comet* into frame remotely, drifting towards the airlock on the *Empress'* underside. The visual did nothing to quell the storm that had risen inside Erae's gut.

"I'm going down," Erae said, quickly reaching the back wall and swinging her legs into the hole. "Keep trying the comm."

She didn't bother with the rungs, but let the ladder's sides slide through her gloves as she dropped to the deck below. Her boots struck with a crash.

"Marpe! Crisp! Get out here!" she shouted towards the bulkheads, then picked up her feet and slid the rest of the way down. The ladder ended at the same level as the airlock, where the main part of the freighter ended. Below that was the cargo hold and engines, accessible by a hatch in the floor that Erae paid no mind as she raced to the airlock door. This inner door had a window, but all that was revealed was the airlock itself—a small white room with a door direct to space on the far side. Erae activated the intercom attached to the wall.

[Hook engaged. Extending the cofferdam now.] Driz dutifully updated her. She heard a mechanical whir as the extendable docking tube reached across the void, creating a path from the airlock to the *Silver Comet*'s cockpit.

[Seal is good. Pressurising.] The whirring was replaced by a rush of hidden air, expanding the cofferdam and permitting passage inside the airlock. Erae's anxiety inflated along with it. She shut her eyes, embarrassed by the weakness. She was stronger than this.

Her breath was fogging up the window. She wiped it clean as the far door slid silently open and a helmeted woman floated inside. The visor was down, but it didn't matter. Relief flooded and buried her doubt. She stepped back from the airlock with wet eyes.

The inner door opened, and Amarie stepped through—her friend, her sister in arms. She was dressed in wrappings of tawny cloth and leather, and pauldrons of animal hair that scratched Erae's face as she pulled her friend in and squeezed hard.

Amarie returned the embrace with equal force, but it wasn't long before Erae pulled back and checked her over for signs of injury.

"What took you so long? Are you okay? Driz said the *Comet* was fine, but ..."

"I'm so sorry." The words were a whisper barely caught through the helmet.

Erae allowed a wry smile to her lips. "Apologies aren't as good as actions, you know. I may not go on spy missions like you two, but I can ..."

She slowed, then pulled back. "Where ..." her mouth froze with her heart.

Amarie pulled her helmet off, releasing a mop of red and purple curls as vibrant as plasma fire and a rich, brown face stained with tears. Fresh drops fell from blinking, emerald eyes.

"Epieta's dead, Rae. They killed her. We failed."

Erae reached out again, but this time there was no strength in the embrace. Beyond Amarie, the empty airlock waited with open doors.

Amarie whispered. "She wasn't supposed to die."

4

The planet Kaldea Prime hung in space before Tomas like a shining beryl-blue gem. The surface was a pristine vista of ice, not broken by the rise of mountains or the brushstrokes of cloud and snow. The frozen plain glinted softly in the pale light of Marduk, Kaldea's distant yellow-white sun. There was little heat in that pallid disc, and the thick constellations of the Cluster nearly drowned the star out with their enveloping glow. In such conditions, life was a far hope.

Yet there was native life on Kaldea Prime; in fact it abounded. The planet's interior, while cooling slowly but surely towards inevitable death, was still warm. Heat meant energy, and energy a chance. In a universe of possibilities, sometimes a chance was all you needed.

Large numbers of fish and marine reptiles writhed through the chemical soup that circulated under the planet's frozen lid, sluggish and light in the low-energy environment, predator chasing prey with all the apparent enthusiasm and haste of a cooling white dwarf. Luminescent corals clung to the underside of the immeasurably thick roof, chandeliers of colour feeding the kelps and grasses of the ocean floor. Crustacean colonies fought wars atop lumbering beasts the size of star cruisers, sending the slain bubbling up towards the ancient oils that pooled in reservoirs above.

It was these biochemical liquids that had interested the long-forgotten founders of Kaldea Prime, as they had materialised from the Shift at yet another system barren of intelligent designs. And now, as Dirk Squadron decelerated towards the Cluster's capital, Tomas couldn't help but wonder what those founders might have thought had they seen the planet today.

Two ring superstations encircled the planet around its equator, dusted with innumerable sparkling lights. Here was the literal crown of the Cluster: two fifty-kilometre-wide circlets decorated with spires, docking bays and complexes as if with thorns. Artificial gravity, shielding, projected breathable atmosphere star-side as high as two klicks—it was all there. The political centre of the Core required no less.

Tomas sighed deeply as he disengaged his point drive, slowing his Wasp to manageable speeds. His team in tight formation behind him, he skirted the crowded spacelanes and made towards Gerduk, the military moon that waited above.

It was good to be home.

There had been a few minor incidents throughout the rest of their week at Jerassh, but they had been lost in the general tedium of the assignment. Patrolling the sector afterwards—the pilots back in their cockpits at last— had been equally bland. This was, when Tomas thought about it, a good thing. Even if it made Teliac antsy.

No, there had been nothing at all like that first day, when the Ebon slaves had caused a riot. And the white alien woman … she had kept on Tomas' mind like a pressing hand. Her appearance baffled him, though it probably shouldn't have. The Cluster was home to fifteen pure-blood sentient species, but their mixed offspring were as varied as they were countless. One of the pure-blood species, a race of ursine technocrats called the Otrei, even sported translucent skin. It was reasonable to think she was descended from them.

If not her appearance, then perhaps it was her disappearance that unnerved him so. His brain looped over the mystery as Gerduk grew against the background of stars. His hands moved on autopilot, guiding his craft and the rest of Dirk Squadron towards the launch tunnels nestled in the cratered shell of the moon.

Her body had vanished in his arms. Where had it gone? Ghosts, Jeqon, Spirits and all such absurd creatures filled his mind. They were the myths that populated children's storybooks and spacers' nightmares alike, but to even consider that such tales were real ...

Tomas shook himself, proclaiming the absurdity of the idea and the need to focus his thoughts elsewhere. Quil's suggestion of visiting Tachillah sounded better with each passing hour. A vacation might be the break he needed to get his head back on the right vector.

He entered the launch tube and came out the other side in an expansive hangar full of Starfighters. The moon base's recycled air shimmered underneath the Wasp's thrusters as he eased towards the ground, his hand steady on the yoke. He landed with a muted clunk and unstrapped his webbing. With a hiss, the canopy seal popped open, washing him with familiar sounds and smells.

Like a lubricated machine—and not just because they were covered in lubricants—a team of mechanics dragged a refuelling junction to the middle of the hangar and led a hose over to Tomas' Wasp. Taking a breath that filmed his lungs in grease, Tomas unbuckled himself and climbed down off the craft's nose.

The aches of body and mind rolled off him as his feet touched the deck, and he smiled as he watched the rest of his squadron land.

Falaquil was next out of her cockpit, sliding off the side of her craft with ease and grace. Her earthy hair was mussed from being under a helmet, and her fringe was plastered to her forehead with sweat. She waved his way, then began to stretch the stiffness out of her back and limbs.

Daniel and Teliac were the pilots of Flight Two. They landed simultane-ously, smoke puffing out from under Dan's fighter craft as the thrusters cut off. The mechanics quickly swarmed it, complaining loudly. Dirk Three warded off their accusations with low bows and soft words, but it had little effect until Teliac came to his wingmate's side, all four arms folded across his chest. One glance at the Gazam had the mechanics very interested in their work.

The leader of Flight Three was Klord Yyert, Dirk Five. His Wasp touched the deck with barely a sound, and Tomas could see the Daban dou-ble-checking every system was off before he popped the canopy. Memeile Sercard, Dirk Six, was the other Daban of the squadron, and both wore custom loose flight suits to accommodate their gliding membranes. Black fur poked out from their neck seals as they removed their helmets.

Then came Seven and Eight.

"It's there for a reason, Ernn! Go bother someone else."

"There for a reason! What's the scorching yoke there for then?"

"Are you serious? Fine! How's about the fact that you're an avian that *flies in a ship*!"

Tomas rolled his eyes as he turned towards his last two pilots. Gerad Belte and Ernn Galoot both hailed from the binary planets of the Kilayim System and were more similar for it than they would ever dare admit. Young Gerad was the Dirk's rookie—the newest member—and the other pilots were quick to remind him of it. The dusty blond Human found most jokes and pranks pointed his way.

Ernn was just as crude and vain as Gerad, but much older. The Kilya veteran had sea-green feathers and an ivory casque that ran down from the top of his head to his beak. The fleshy wattle under his chin had been dyed white to match, and cut in crisp, jagged lines.

The oldest and newest Dirks stalled their argument as they realised the others had already gathered by Tomas. One simmering and one sullen, they headed over.

"Thank you, gentlemen," Tomas said with a patient smile. "What was the issue this time?"

Gerad looked up first, indignance in his green eyes. "He's mad 'cos I landed on autopilot."

"You're soft enough without it!" Ernn snapped back.

"You wanna bet?"

As the pair initiated round two, Tomas looked around. Dan and Teliac stood together, chuckling. Memiele was shying away from the conflict, while Klord stood ready to receive orders. Quil caught his searching eyes and winked, knowing his mind.

For this was his family, and he loved them. Sure, his parents were still alive, and he had a younger sister, but his parents were off prospecting on Kazloc, and Delphea was off at the organics embassy in System D1108. He hadn't seen them in person for years.

No, these seven were his family, as were those who had risen and fallen before them. Punch-and-kick as they were, they always had each other's backs.

Tomas cleared his throat. "That's enough, team."

Silence fell, albeit begrudgingly.

"Alright then. I want my rack time as much as you do, so listen up. Dan?"

Dirk Three looked at his toes. "I have to give General Niyott a detailed report about why my port-wing thrusters have been replaced by asteroid dust."

"You *need* to give General Niyott a detailed report on how to fly straight and check your scanners," Tomas returned the grin his squadmate was trying to hide. "But we'll go with your approach. Klord?"

"I will download flight telemetry from Gerad's and my Wasps and transmit it to Major Laaev for future training simulations, as per her official request."

Tomas nodded. "Exactly. Have these tasks done before brief at seven hundred, then it's ringside for some R and R." He paused to receive some nods. "As for me, I'll submit my report to the General, then I'm out like a light. Dismissed."

The Gerduk military base was, in a word, efficient. If Tomas had used an additional descriptor, he surmised as his boots echoed in muted steps down the off-white polyplex tunnels, it would be 'labyrinthine'. As a recruit during the Great Invasion, it had been an easy task to get lost amongst the winding levels full of engineers, janitor-bots and thundering platoons double-timing towards their waiting dropships. Every footfall had drummed courage along the corridors, and every breath had cautioned fear.

Tomas headed deeper into the moon, passing barely a soul. So many had died in those years, and there was little hurry to enlist now that the war was over. The CSF had been left a husk, like the moon it laired within, and the remaining forces were pressed thin to keep the order so many took for granted.

Taking a left at the next junction, he passed through the sliding doors into a carpeted lobby. The small space was ringed with doors to various general's offices and was furnished only with a white receptionist's desk on one side. There weren't even any waiting chairs. *Efficient, true as core.*

A cycloptic orange dome poked around the desk's computer. "Commander Amets. It is good to see you." No movement accompanied the bright, chirping voice, but the construct's eyepiece flashed a warm lemon-yellow.

"Hey, Sigsby, how's life?" Tomas approached the desk. "I like the new paint job. It suits you."

6BHH704 "Sigsby" raised a mechanised arm in salute. Its eye sparkled pink. "Oh, Commander, you make me blush. Existence remains a daily excitement."

The eye switched back to its mirthful yellow. "Life, on the other hand …"

"Remains a concept you eagerly avoid," Tomas finished the joke. "Is General Niyott available?"

"She is engaged but knows you are here." The Shell turned back to its work at the computer terminal. "Please, have a seat."

Tomas snorted and looked around the room. "Sure, thanks." He paced around for a minute, but when the door to Niyott's office showed no signs of opening, he opted to lean against the back wall instead.

Sigsby was a Shell, which was distinct from a regular robot in the same fashion that sentients were distinct from mere beasts. How they came about was lost to time, as were many of the atrocities committed in the war that followed.

But that had been aeons ago, and the Shells were more respected as people than even the off-breeds were. The name 'Shell' suggested a being devoid of character and substance to some, but when Tomas had asked Sigsby about it, the reply had been profound.

"I am a Shell, sir, because just like a crustacean, someone calls this metal body a home."

After the last of the Automaton Wars, three laws were passed down as a sign of trust. By them, Shells could only live in humanoid constructs, and standard robots were forbidden from such forms, so one could always tell them apart. A Shell was also only allowed to live for a thousand years, no matter how many bodies it had been in. Tomas briefly wondered how many years Sigsby had left.

The door began to shift, and Tomas stood at attention. His eyes widened as a tall warrior stepped out, plated from head to toe in shining gold armour accented by scarlet cloth. The helmet's faceplate depicted a beautiful Human man, but as the head turned to scan the room, the eyeholes were dark, hidden behind black glass. Its gaze rested on Tomas.

This was a Sun Guard, the highest order of the military elite, answerable only to themselves and the Chief of Council. They were the shield of the Cluster: fearsome, unknowable, stalwart. To be in the same room as one meant you were either incredibly safe or incredibly dead.

Tomas' spine stiffened as a second guard stepped from the room, then both parted to allow passage of a third figure, and Tomas' back just about snapped in two.

"Yes, yes, and you too!" Chief of Council Rekkuul Duidain called cheerfully over his shoulder as he entered the lobby. He turned to smile at the room, sweeping his head in a shining echo of the stoic guards beside him. Tomas snapped a hand to his head in salute.

Duidain laughed, waving the salute away. "Put that hand down, please, please. I'm no military officer." His eyes sparkled as he walked up to Tomas. He glanced at Tomas' rank slides. "I don't believe we've met, ah …"

"Commander, sir. Amets. Dirk Squadron." Tomas lowered his hand awkwardly, and Duidain seized it in a firm shake.

Duidain was a man of over eighty, Tomas knew, but not by looking at him. He had a head of thick black hair combed back; smooth, fair skin and a jawline to rival the golden sentinels behind him. The cosmetic work alone must have cost a fortune twice over, but the energy the councilman exuded hinted that cosmetics might be a mere start to the sandworm.

"Ah, Amets," he said. "Yes, yes, Layla mentioned you."

Tomas was at a loss for a moment. Duidain slowed, then laughed again and slapped his thigh.

"Oh forgiveness, please, haha! I meant Niyott, of course. The good General."

"Right ... of course," Tomas said. This was not how he imagined having a brush with greatness. "Speaking of which ..." He took a small step to the side.

"Of course, you must have lots to discuss." Duidain winked, his smile never slipping. "It was a pleasure to meet you, Commander. Farewell!"

And with that, the whirlwind left. Tomas felt his shoulders drop, and he resumed breathing. The reprieve was brief, for he couldn't keep the General waiting. Still, the Core's Chief of Council, and he knew Tomas' name! He was glad to see Duidain was as kind in person as on the broadcasts, but he had not known the sheer *life* of the man to be so ... *lively.*

General Niyott stood from her desk as Tomas entered, and he snapped off a salute. This time, it was returned.

"Sit down, Commander."

Tomas did so, looking briefly around the office. The walls in this room had been painted a paling blue, and a green throw-rug covered the floor. This, combined with the sun lamp in the ceiling, gave the office a light, outdoor feel. The General had grown up on the vast hunting plains of Chtepiek, and a cabinet to one side boasted the horns and ivories of her hunts.

The room might have been warm, but General Niyott was its frigid centre. Her desk was simple and clean, her poise rigid. Her eyes were the colour of copper and just as hard, and while she could smile, it wasn't common. Tomas wondered what a conversation between her and the councillor must have been like.

"Your team is all safely back from Jerassh?"

Tomas nodded. "Yes ma'am."

"Getting some rest?"

"Yes ma'am. They're looking forward to knowing how long their shore leave will be."

Niyott paused. She clasped her hands in front of her.

"Let's discuss the report you sent through."

Tomas nodded, eager to get his answers at last. "The event is as my report states, but my chief concerns are the identity of the assailant and her manner of interaction with the Ebon. I haven't viewed it yet, but amongst her effects I found a …"

He trailed as Niyott held up a hand.

"I know the report, Commander," she said, "and that is enough. The matter has been resolved."

Tomas tilted his head. "The matter—"

"Has been resolved." Niyott finished. "The operative you mentioned, the one who dealt with the attacker; he also reported the event to his superiors."

"Oh, right. Who was he?"

Niyott shrugged. "An intelligence operative. Counter-insurgency, that sort of thing. He doesn't report to me, and I don't report to him. That's all I need to know."

She leant forward. "And all you need to know is he is dealing with the situation. He says he has all he needs, and further assistance on our part will only frustrate his plans." Her lip curled. "Sounds like the plot for a pictolog, but that's spy-work for you."

Tomas felt himself sink into his chair. Was it over, then? "But I might be able to help. I found a disc—"

"I said it was handled!" Niyott said sharply, slamming her palms into the desk. The trophy cabinet rattled, and Tomas jumped upright. "This isn't your area, Commander. Anything you've found is something our people already know. Dispose of it and forget it. They'll have us both if you don't!"

Niyott sighed, and her hands relaxed. "These orders protect everyone, Tomas. You acted properly while at the station—the operative praised you in his report, you know—but your part in it is done now. Let your questions lie."

Tomas nodded, resigned. "And the strange woman?"

"Dead, I'm told. A half-blood mongrel and nothing more," she smirked. "What else would a criminal be? She was probably a Partisan, too."

Tomas nodded again. It seemed he had been right in the end.

Niyott sighed again, her brow furrowing. "Before you go, there is one further matter. Your squadron is needed back in the field right away. Leave, I'm afraid, will have to wait."

"Yes ma'am." Tomas felt his throat lump up like he might cry, and his cheeks reddened at the thought. The last deployment had exhausted him, he realised. He was tired, but there was no time for rest. The hope of vacation was entirely driven from him.

The General offered a small smile, and Tomas realised she was more worn out than he was. They were in this fight together, and that was a comfort.

Tomas stood and saluted. "I'll see you in the morning, General."

"In the morning, Commander. Get some sleep."

He left for his quarters with mixed emotions, but fatigue overrode all thoughts save one. His squadron was *not* going to be thrilled come the morning.

5

The morning arrived, and with it a fresh mind full of worries.

Tomas sat on the edge of his bed, frowning. His quarters on Gerduk had no viewports; the installation was buried too deep into the moon for that sort of thing. The room was designed for sleeping in and storing personal effects, and it would provide no more. Though considering the quality of the sheets and the thin, unforgiving mattress, one could argue that even sleep was a tall order.

Tomas was used to the accommodation, yet here he was in the darkness, awake hours before reveille, stuck between a stubborn duty and a quiet, almost giddy rebellion. His left heel bounced a constant rhythm on the floor.

He turned the disc over in his hands. *They have all they need,* Niyott had said. *Dispose of it and forget it.* Tomas was happy to oblige.

But … he flipped the disc over again, studying its blank surface. Did he have to destroy it now? The operatives and spies might already have their answers, but Tomas didn't. The half-breed woman, her alliance with the Ebon, the reason for the attack—*something* in all this was important, enough so for a CSF operative to become involved. He had found himself a bystander to adventure, and it excited him more than any mission had in a long time.

He picked up his tome-tile from the nightstand, holding the disc over the slot. This was insubordination, he knew, but it was also harmless. He needed to know.

"And I *will* destroy it," he reasoned aloud. "As soon as I'm done." He pushed the disc in, and the tile started to whir. Both of Tomas' legs were bouncing now.

It'll be text files and numbers, he cautioned his excitement, *and chances are you won't know port from starboard.*

The load finished, and a list of files filled the screen. They were video recordings, periodically dated, all exactly four hours long. Tomas' pulse quickened and, his curiosity now far stronger than his caution, he selected the first one.

The list disappeared, and a dim room showed on the screen, walled in grey stone and lit by gas flames. Patrons sat at round tables, leaning into chairs of cattle hide as they drank and ate. A kind of tavern, then. Was this on Jerassh or somewhere else?

From the tome-tile's speakers, he could hear the muted hum of conversation, accompanied by intermittent bursts of laughter. An empty table dominated the foreground, clearly the focus of the recording. Tomas waited at first, then skipped forward, but while the tavern was alive with movement and people, the table remained empty. The recording ended.

"Riveting." Tomas selected the second recording, but it was more of the same. He tried a third, then a fourth, skipping to random points. Nothing.

He massaged the back of his neck with a hand. Going through the disc properly would take forever, and his sense would cut in long before then.

Tomas quit the log and scrolled to the last recording. It was less than an hour long. Interrupted, perhaps? Rapping a knuckle on the bedframe for luck, he accessed the file.

A woman reclined at the table, a pipe glass in her hands. A red dress followed her curving figure to the floor, stark against her black skin. Tomas' breath caught.

This wasn't the void-black of the Ebon but a darkling smoke, its internal shadows curling and writhing as the gas flames flickered on the wall behind her. Silky wisps of hair fell around the creature's shoulders, and a curving horn of coal black adorned her head. And her eyes ...

They were rainbows of white light, their thrill dulled through the camera's lens. But they were the same kind as Tomas had seen at Jerassh; he was sure of it. *She* was the same kind, and just as beautiful.

A second spectre entered the frame and approached the table. He was the same species as the woman but much larger, dressed in grey trousers and nothing more. Ten small, blood-red horns crowned his head, and he snarled as he pulled up a chair and sat across from the woman. His translucent skin and muscles were punctured by ribbons of the same red, running across and under his flesh.

"Charon, dear brother," the woman crooned. The voice was melodious and wonderful, but as Tomas heard it, it made him feel cold. He leaned in. "I've been worried so. I expected you to appear long before now."

"Far be it from me to keep you waiting, my *dear* Remiyyah," the male growled back, and if the first voice had been ice, then the second was fire. "But I hold no memory of your appointment over me. I come as I choose."

Remiyyah smiled: a fiendish grin that revealed a pair of wicked white fangs.

"A wise choice demands wit sharper than yours," she said.

"Yet I am here."

"Hmm, yes indeed." Remiyyah relaxed further into her seat. "For kinder company I could not have hoped."

Charon spat onto the table. "You gild words, and waste time." He thrust a finger at her. "Look at you! Surrounded by vermin; cavorting, gracing them with the hunt when your scar-less hide but watches. The *Mortal Shroud* indeed!"

"And what of your title?" Remiyyah snapped, her voice sharpening. Charon snarled, and Tomas noticed that the rest of the tavern was in a hush. Charon's hatred penetrated the screen, and the room seemed darker around him. If the woman at Jerassh was one of these, her death was well-earned.

"Why am I here?" he demanded. His hands were fists on the tabletop.

"To kill a rat," Remiyyah said, the venom in her tone replacing all previous mockery. "Can you not smell it?"

Charon sniffed the air, and his eyes widened. "Celah Neiru? Here?" His head snapped upward and to the left, tracking.

"In this very city," Remiyyah scoffed. "Trying to spy on me, I don't wonder. Such disrespect! I would handle it myself, of course …"

Charon's lip curled in derision. "But you don't know who it is, do you? You aren't strong enough to face him."

"And you are?"

"I have always been," Charon stood, light catching on the scars across his chest. "Time shall hide that truth no longer."

"Time … yes." Remiyyah sipped her drink, and her venom faded. "That brings me to one more thing. The Kin Lord calls us to counsel. One month, on Shbiy's ninth moon."

"Shbiy? The groon farms? Is not Abaddon our seat?"

"I do not question the order," Remiyyah replied. "But I have my guess. The bargains of old are ending, brother."

A shift occurred in both creatures, some untold fervour that passed between them. Perhaps it was a new light in their eyes, but this light did not brighten so much as it made everything else appear dark.

"Do you lie, sister?" Charon had lowered his voice, causing Tomas to press closer to the speaker to hear. "I have suffered an age for this and will not now suffer jest."

Remiyyah nodded, and a smile touched her face once more. "The war begins at Shbiy, and from there to all stars."

She rose from her seat. "Kill the Celah. Do not fail." Black smoke grew around her, and when it cleared, she was gone, dress and all. The torches leapt and sputtered from their valves.

Charon growled, smelling the air again. His eyes tracked the roof above him for a moment, and he summoned smoke of his own. The shroud rose in a column and splashed against the ceiling, and when it cleared and the flames had taken breath, there was only the table.

Tomas shut the tome-tile off, plunging his room back into darkness.

It was instantly unbearable, and Tomas fought with himself, struggling to remain seated and give his eyes time to adjust. He closed them but fear manifested shadows behind his lids.

"Lights!" The room lit up, and he exhaled. His hands were shaking. But why?

These creatures unsettled him. Their smiles, their eyes. And to vanish in smoke? Was it a trick of appearance, designed to intimidate those around them? The woman at Jerassh had disappeared, but not in smoke.

Spirits, his mind reeled. *Spirits of hate and death.*

"But it's absurd!" he declared to the nearest bulkhead. "Is that what we believe now? Life after death, and vengeful souls! Get a lock on, Tomas!"

He shouldn't have woken up early for this. Tomas put the tile down and ran his hands across his face. His mind was making a child out of him.

It could be a perfectly normal, natural thing. Chamisi could project their thoughts in waves of neural electricity, and Ebon skin absorbed all light, even infrared. Was it so much of a jump to think a mongrel species might change its density or turn invisible?

My hull plates are warping.

He clenched his fists, and the shaking subsided. A bitter laugh escaped his lips.

"I really needed that vacation," he sighed. "Not another mission."

He stood up, once again in control. Was there anything else to that recording? Remiyyah had spoken of war, probably between them and the Celah characters they hunted. Perhaps that was what they were recruiting Ebon for.

From there to all stars, she had said. An exaggeration, surely. The beings had demonstrated a knack for grand words. The greatest threat to the Cluster had been the Ebon Invasion, and while it had devastated millions, it had failed. The Ebon were shattered, and even if these people managed to recruit every Ebon slave, it would amount to little. The Core would never fall.

"But that would be why C.I. got involved," Tomas muttered. "Even a small army of Ebon will cause a panic, no matter how brief." He laughed again, shaking his head.

This had been an exercise in curiosity, and it was over. It had been as interesting as he had hoped—more even—but the day moved on, and he had a squadron to lead.

"Gate-Ghouls and spies indeed. It's time to get dressed." He turned to his closet, then paused. He still had more than an hour before reveille. He moved back to his bed.

"Lights off!" Darkness fell once more, but this time around a commander instead of a child. A commander who would get what little rest he still could.

The briefing room was half full when Tomas arrived, with many more people filing in through the doors. Tomas recognised few faces and remembered even fewer names, but gave himself no grief for it. As long as he knew his pilots and superiors, he could complete the mission. The Dirks that had arrived were currently towards the back, talking amongst themselves.

Tomas stumbled as an arm fell hard across his shoulders. "Morning, Lead," Dan said.

"Three." Tomas grinned and nodded. They made their way to the others.

Dan smoothed his moustache with his free hand. "Before we begin, I'd like to formally log that I could be three drinks down in a ringside bar by now."

Tomas looked sideways at him. "The day's only just begun."

"Ah, but that's the thing about planets," Dan grinned. "It's always night somewhere. Ain't that right, Four?"

"Pardon?" Teliac lifted his head, and the group shifted to accommodate the newcomers.

"That's my wingmate."

Teliac stared.

"He's got a point," Gerad said. "Not about drinking, but the leave. We've barely had time to rest."

"Rest?" Ernn snapped his beak. "Does the babe need rest, ha! This is the military, Scourge seal it, and you'll rest in ash or not at all. *Rest!*"

"Power down, Eight," Quil put in, giving Tomas a quick look. "We can't be on duty indefinitely."

Tomas knew the comment was meant for him. He shifted out from under Dan's weight.

"I know you're tired, all of you," he said. Ernn crossed his arms and huffed. "I'm tired too. I could have fought for our leave and changed Niyott's mind, but I didn't."

He glanced around the group. "If I fight for shore leave, I fight to prolong oppression and to see innocents killed. That's dramatic, I know, but I'm just adding a little perspective.

"We've a little fuel left yet, and I won't put us through anything we can't handle. But I need you with me."

Quil softened. "We're not going anywhere, Lead."

"Yeah," Dan chimed, "that's called desertion. Although—"

"Enough, Three." Memiele hushed him with a hand, then pointed. "Not every ear appreciates your humour." Tomas turned to see Niyott enter the room, followed by two captains. The first was a ginger Yiishi he didn't recognise, but the Human was Herald Liuwayu, captain of the Liberator-class frigate *Might of Gaph*. The two took seats in the front row as Niyott ascended to the stage.

"You should get down there," Quil nudged him. "We'll catch you on the way to the hangar."

"Copy," Tomas walked briskly to the front as the attendants took their seats. He saluted all three officers, then sat beside Liuwayu.

"Captain," he said quietly.

"Commander," Liuwayu returned. He was old but unbent, his hair a fine silver, and his voice crackled like dry leaves with every syllable. "I trust you've kept well since Citrine."

"Well enough, though if I close my eyes I can still hear those gulls screeching."

Liuwayu wheezed, a rattling inhale, and winked at Tomas. "You're lucky you were only there two months," he said.

"Good morning," Niyott's amplified voice broke from the speakers, and the remaining chatter died down. "Let's begin. I want this briefing to be over as much as the rest of you."

She tapped her tome-tile, and a red planet appeared on the wall behind her, rotating slowly.

"Rahga, of the Rahgese System, was colonised by miners for its tungsten, iron and copper ores. There are thirty-one colonies, most no larger than a hundred men. All recovered material goes from these to the capital, Madhebah, where the largest mine is."

The image changed to a layout of a small city that bordered a snaking ravine. The terrain was elevated towards the fissure, littered with pinnacles and crags. Out on the plateau, the buildings were sparse and unprotected.

"Madhebah is the only port on the planet and supplies all the mines with food and equipment. Refined metals are hauled from the surface to an orbiting station, then out-system. It is a small but essential cog in the Core's machine, and it has been incited against us.

"According to our report, local malcontents hired a mercenary force and used them to overthrow the city. They've pillaged and plundered everything outside the ravine itself, which is defensible against incursion and houses the city's leadership. The workers on the surface aren't as fortunate and are barricaded in their homes. Those who refuse to join the insurrection are being shot on sight."

A murmur rippled through the seats. A violent bid for independence was one thing, but executing civilians? Soldiers reserved little mercy for scum like this.

"Your mission," Niyott continued," is to reclaim the city and capture the insurgents alive, if possible. Captain Forn has been chosen to lead this taskforce. Captain."

The Yiishi stood and saluted the General before joining her onstage. The smaller sentient's ears were pricked straight up, and he scowled at the room as if he were addressing his enemy, not his own men.

"*Boundless* and *Might of Gaph* will work to achieve a safe orbit above the Capital," he said. His voice was low for a Yiishi's, which turned his rapid chitters into a rumble of words too quick and fearsome to argue with. "Commander Amets and his fighters will assist with this. Once secured, targeted strikes will take out the city's defence systems. These are concentrated around the refineries, so civilian casualties should be minimal."

He inclined his head to Niyott, and several parts of the city were highlighted. Forn began gesturing to these areas, but with his small reach it wasn't always clear which marker he was pointing to.

"*Might of Gaph*'s dropships will secure these zones here and here, forming an evacuation corridor for those trapped in the ravine. My forces will descend upon the opposite side of the city here and sweep in upon the mercenaries, liberating trapped residences as they go. Some of the Scourgespawn will undoubtedly try to escape. Dirk Squadron will intercept these and disable their engines." He stepped back.

"Thank you, Captain," Niyott retook the centre. "This should be a simple assignment, but take no chances. You outnumber these insurgents, but do not hope in intimidation or surrender. They will likely fight to the last man."

"But why?" an officer asked from somewhere behind Tomas. "Aren't these just mercenaries? Won't they have already taken their Draik and run?"

Niyott pressed her lips together. "Unfortunately not. These mercenaries are devoted, fanatical even. They only hire to select parties, usually involved in seceding from the Core."

"Partisans?" someone called out.

Niyott shook her head. "This is a small group who call themselves *the Defiant*." The display changed to show a symbol: two concentric circles intersected by three lines. Two lines came from the top left, the third from the bottom right, just passing inside the inner circle.

"Closer to pirates than rebels, so I wouldn't be surprised if you haven't heard of them. They are ruled by a geriatric despot with more power than sense, and we have reason to suspect they supported the Ebon Horde during the invasion. The leader's son, at least, was a confirmed agent."

Several officers yelled out in anger, some jumping to their feet. Captain Forn's basso curses outdid them all in both volume and variety. Tomas kept his anger inside, though it was no less than his fellows'. How could anyone, no matter how criminal, side with the Ebon?

"*Silence*," Niyott barked. Order returned. "The traitor is long dead, and these mercenaries will follow, by your hand no less. Justice is better carried by actions than words, do you understand? Commander Amets knows this well."

Tomas felt his face warm at the compliment. "Me, General?"

"Of course," Niyott said. "After all, you were the one who killed him."

Tomas blinked. "Who?"

"Ben-Eloah, the leader's son. Now you get to help finish the job." Niyott looked back to the crowd as a whole. "If there are no more questions, your enemy awaits. Boarding shuttles begin ferrying in three hours. Officers, see to it your men are in line before then. Dismissed."

Ben-Eloah, the traitor. Tomas remained seated for a moment as the others filed past him. That man had nearly cost them the war, nearly cost the Cluster its freedom. He couldn't understand how anyone would follow such a man.

But he didn't need to understand. These mercenaries were slaughtering the Rahgese. Niyott was right; justice was found in action.

It was time to take action.

6

"This is our home! You can't take it, and we'll fight to the last of us to reclaim it! Eeyah!" The declaration echoed up the ravine, followed by a resounding cheer. Looking down from the surface, Erae could just make out the man who had uttered the cry, standing proudly at the entrance to the mine where the last of the local militia had blockaded themselves.

Gathering her breath so her shout might reach past the increasing wind, she tried again. "Please, Sergeant, your hold over Madhebah is over, but your life doesn't have to be! Lay down your arms and ... and come speak to us. We stand by to receive your wounded from the warrens."

Erae's team did not dare flush the survivors from the tunnels, not even with Rahgese rebels guiding them through the maze. The nobles of Madhebah were as stubborn as the rock they delved, and it would take many lives to break through their defences.

"We do not speak with mercenaries or those who hire them," the Sergeant shouted back, his voice carrying on the cheers of his company. They had exalted every line so far, sucking up their superior's favour like tarill bats in a field of flowers. The walls of the mine echoed with every 'eeyah', and after hours of impasse, it was finally beating Erae's resolve.

"If I die, I die in glory. There is courage in this ground, Eeyah! On what do you stand?"

Erae turned away, looking in exasperation at her escort. Marpe and Ruth were waiting behind a perimeter line, safe from harm while Erae pleaded with the sergeant for parley. As she headed towards them, Ruth stepped forward.

"Let me try, Captain," the Kilya said, her azure wattle bobbing as she approached. Ruth, or Leader Bronze-beak as the rebels called her, was the figurehead of the Rahgese independence effort. The avian was old, but there was a fire in her still, and she had inspired many over the past days.

Ruth stopped as Marpe, the colossal Qua'seth coral-being who served on Erae's crew, placed a firm hand on her shoulder. His fingers, woven from bright orange and red corals, left a damp patch on Ruth's weathered wind parka.

"The moment your casque crests the chasm edge, you will lose it." Tubular beard corals the same colour as his arms carried the voice from his core: a deep resonating gurgle as if Marpe was underwater. "They haven't shot the Captain in the hope you will appear to them."

"A bit harsh," Erae added, "but unfortunately he's right. You'd have more luck finding the Gazem Queen than you would talking to this kech-brain." Erae waited until she was sure the local leader had stopped moving, then trudged back to the ravine and its insufferably stubborn residents. Perhaps a mention of their dwindling food stores would help. *It's worth a try,* she decided as she leant over the drop.

"Sergeant—" She broke off as a plasma bolt grazed the edge of the ravine and rocketed past her face. The air fizzled and cracked before her, and Erae backpedalled in shock. For a moment, the world was encapsulated in the idea of a broken body at the bottom of a ravine. The next: a paper-moth sky, the cold desert sand and an embarrassing pain in her legs and rear.

Erae threw a curse first up at that sky, then down at the ravine.

The Sergeant's yell drowned out both. "Back to the rock that birthed you, mongrel!" he snarled. More plasma blasts shot skyward, superheating patches of sand into glass as they grazed the ledge. "Half-breed freak! By your blood will Rahga be cleansed of your foul stench, Eeyah!"

The insults were hurled like sand on the wind; not damaging, but sharp enough to sting. It didn't matter that she'd heard them countless times before. Erae rolled over and pushed herself upright, and her gaze locked onto the sea-foam hues that swirled and marbled her arms, onto the darker blue calcium enamel that formed glossy, hard blotches running up from her elbows and under her sleeves.

Impure. Abomination. Beast. So they'd been called, and so they'd become. It didn't matter that off-breeds were as common as pure species. It didn't matter how many people were kind and loving at heart if there were still those stubborn few who hung on to the hatred of their old ways, like this kech-brained sergeant who refused to surrender.

Erae got back on her feet and marched away from the ravine. Sensing her frustration, Ruth and Marpe let her pass and followed at a distance as they walked along the main road. Madhebah city was spread low and wide on the surface: ore processing plants and housing districts for the poor that worked them. Everything rich and influential was carved into the walls of Madheb ravine, high enough to not be disturbed by the mining at the bottom of the deep rift.

The worst part was it was all too easy to believe them—the lies. On her good days, Erae couldn't give a fifth limb about what people thought of her. Beauty, fame, race; none of that mattered when she was on a mission. At that point, it was down to instinct, skill and faith. On her bad days though, the lies sat on her shoulder, slipping their breath into her ears. Or they curled up under her tongue and rotted away. Or they itched under every patch of her entirely blue skin.

"Scorching sergeant," she grumbled as she stormed on. "Him and all his scorching men!" She had never thought herself cut out for diplomacy. That had been Epieta's job on this mission, but now she …

Erae stopped, grief interrupting her anger. It was too soon. It was too
… *wrong.* And now what was Erae supposed to do? Everyone was looking
to her for answers she didn't have.

She forced herself to resume walking. She didn't want to restart the tears
now.

Ochre sandstone houses hemmed her way, the street quiet and empty.
The locals were waiting inside, just as Ruth had asked them to. Sometimes
eyes could be seen gleaming between the sheets of rusted tin that boarded
the windows.

They were all waiting for her.

Eventually the houses were replaced by rocky crags and low dunes. The
Defiant had set up camp outside the city to prevent civilian casualties in
the event of an ambush. It was a motley collection of shuttles, starfighters,
and a few dozen polyplex instant-up buildings, or 'stups'. The ivory habi-
tats were auto-erecting boxes with airtight seals, and were the cheapest the
Defiant could pilfer or trade for. Soldiers and pilots milled around on the
sand, tinkered with their spaceships, or sat talking with some of Ruth's local
rebels. She nodded to them as she passed by, returning salutes when they
were given.

They were all waiting for her, too.

The largest stup sat in the centre of camp as an ersatz staging post, and
as Erae approached it, Driz poked his furry snout out of the door, then
hurried towards her.

"Gwa ilyt canobbo mi eniigiw, Siro," he chittered off in Yiish. [We've
had a report, Captain!]

"About time, Driz. Let's hear it," Erae replied, then instantly regret-
ted the harshness of her tone. She was still sore from the ravine, but she
couldn't take it out on her crew. "Sorry," she amended, "Please go on."

N'drizo nodded, unperturbed, then continued. [Gabriel says the CSF will arrive within two days. The worst-case scenario is three frigates and two squadrons, but he'll have proper details and times by nightfall.]

Erae's heart sank. "We … we don't have the firepower to take on frigates." She looked around, aware that nearby ears might be turning towards their conversation. But she was telling the truth. This had been a ground mission, her Defiant troops training and leading the locals that Ruth had mustered together. They didn't have much in the way of fighter craft and nothing that could match a frigate.

Not without Epieta. But she wasn't here, and Erae was still the mission leader.

Marpe and Ruth came up to join them, and Erae repeated what she had been told. Ruth's eyes went wide at the mention of the coming attack force, and she clapped her beak open and closed a few times. Under different circumstances, it might have seemed comical. Eventually, she got some words out.

"I always knew the Core would come for us, but in our zeal for freedom, we never hoped to consider what happens now. Are we really worth the attention of such an army? This is a small world, surely nothing to the capital."

"It seems someone disagrees," Erae tried to keep her despair under the surface. "Driz, did Gabriel have any orders for us? Anything from Remiel?"

[No, Captain. Just the information.]

"Not even when you mentioned …" Erae couldn't say it.

Driz took her hand in his paw. [Gabriel said *you* must decide whether we stay or flee.] His snout twitched. [He said the king's strength is our own.]

Marpe gurgled a wordless agreement, and Erae sighed. How was it that she stood on the planet's surface, yet at the same time that planet rested on her shoulders? She glanced at the horizon, the sky already dimming into evening.

"All right," she said finally, "Let's get inside. We've got a lot of planning to do."

"You'll stay?" Ruth asked hopefully.

"Don't worry, ma'am, we're not bailing just yet," Erae assured both the avian and herself. "This won't be pretty, but we'll think of something. We always do."

Her gut churned as she said it. Death was a natural part of war, and she hated it. Some of her men had already died, on her orders, for her ideas. The sole consoling fact was that they had succeeded, and Madhebah was theirs.

Now they would have to fight all over again. Erae knew they would get through this trial—that assurance she would never doubt—but at what new cost?

Erae knew she was once again sending some of her friends to die.

Night swiftly fell upon the world, showing no mercy to those who still laboured, giving no time for thoughts to find their course. It was as if the universe caught wind that conflict was approaching and now bent its will to speed it here. And so the planets, stars and wheels of time spun ever faster.

At least, that's what it felt like. The day's strategic debate had taxed Erae, and she would not find relief in the decisions they had made. They had a plan, one that made efficient use of their resources and considered all the known information. Pilots had been briefed and volunteers selected. Now they could do nothing but wait.

Most of her mission team was inside the stups, drinking and singing, celebrating the friends they were sure to lose. She should have been with them, but how could she? It was one thing for two doomed soldiers to drink and be merry together. It was completely different when one of the two had doomed the other.

Besides, she had different company tonight, and a different task. Erae's gaze swept the distant dunes; the hazy outlines of a hundred imaginary behemoths, or perhaps the ridged tail of just one, its full grandeur hidden by the darkness. Rivers of starlight dripped from one horizon to the next, intimately visible thanks to the low population of this desert world. The mist of a thousand silver suns seeped through the air and wind, perching beside her as she and Amarie stood atop the remains of a weathered, rust-stained batholith.

Her pessimism forgotten for the moment, she let out the slightest breath of air, a wordless symptom of infinite beauty funnelling into a pair of eyes. It was a familiar phenomenon, and yet Erae too often forgot to search for it, or even to notice it when it found her.

A gust of wind sprinted across the dunes and up the rock formation, slapping at Erae's ice-tinted face and neck. She drew her weather jacket tighter and shivered, and the dunes paused to shiver with her.

"I can see them there," Amarie said softly. Her eyes were also on the stars. Erae turned to her.

"Starfighters, dreadnaughts. Symbols of hope and victory." The young woman clenched a fist. "Reapers bending down to cut the wheat. And we are the chaff."

Erae took a step back. "Those aren't your words," she said.

Amarie shook her head. "They were my father's." She lowered herself to a crouch, still staring out. "I thought he meant the Ebon at the time."

Erae moved forward and placed a hand on her shoulder. "The Ebon were always the bigger threat."

"Then why does the CSF hurt more?"

Erae had no response to that. She thought about the strange dream she'd had recently— being in the cockpit, surrounded by light and sound, Ebon and CSF ships swarming in every direction, and her in the midst of it all. Names echoed in her ears as she launched a twin streak of white towards a fleeing shuttle, and then horror filled her, but the battle did not end.

She still felt that something was meant by the vision, but that alone couldn't help her. She needed to talk to Remiel, or Syllebeth, perhaps.

"Erae?"

"… Yeah?"

"Do you think they're already on their way? Somewhere out there, waves of them in the Shift?"

Erae shook her head. "Not if they're coming from the capital. Gabriel has never led us wrong." She felt Amarie shift beneath her hand. Her shoulder muscles tensed.

"We'll be waiting," she said. "And we'll teach them. They'll know who the real reapers are."

Erae sighed and shut her eyes. *She's nineteen,* she told herself. *And she's in more pain than you.*

And yet you will inflict more still, said a second internal voice. *You are a true friend indeed.*

"None of that tonight," she said aloud to both friend and voice. "The air is still enough. Let's begin."

Amarie tensed again. "I … don't know if I can."

Erae crouched down, feeling the swell begin in her heart. The day's tears were arriving at last. She turned Amarie's face with a trembling hand.

"It's time, Am."

Tears, like drops of starlight, ran between her fingers and fell to the parched ground.

Amarie leant into her hand, then nodded slowly. The two women helped each other stand. Amarie took a small cylinder from her belt and clasped it in both hands.

"Epieta …" She broke off and tried again, her words choked.

"Epieta, I'm sorry. You were my sister, my friend. You taught me so much …" She wiped at her nose. "You taught me so much, and I'll never forget it. I love you. I'll … I'll avenge you, I promise."

Erae hung her head, and her own tears fell.

"I promise," Amarie repeated, her voice hardening. "They're coming, but I'll kill them. All of them."

No, you won't, Erae thought sadly. *And very soon you'll know, and you'll hate me for it. But I can't see you throw your life away for revenge.*

"Epieta," she said, her mouth full of more words than she could bear to say. "You were too good for this world, and left it too soon. We'll …" She shook her head and retreated to ceremony.

"Farewell, daughter of light. We release you. Join the stars, and shine forevermore."

Amarie took a step away, holding the cylinder above her head. There was a click, then a dart of white plasma shot out the top, fizzing against the night as it reached for heaven.

Erae watched it go but closed her eyes before the flame died. In her mind it flew on, joining with the constellations above.

"Goodbye, dear sister," she whispered, and the two women silently embraced.

7

There was something undeniably invigorating about the rising hum of a plasma engine as it came online. It was a call of mission, an announcement of power. Tomas could be anyone outside the cockpit, but inside he was Dirk Leader, CSF pilot. It didn't matter that his squad mates were still badgering his eardrums over skipped leave. He was alive and ready to go.

"Dirk Leader is green across the board. Launching."

Flipping the activation on his thrusters, he revelled in the glorious moment when the landing gear fell away and he was once again held up by the powerful machinery around him. Nursing the throttle so as not to blast the hangar with ionised particles, Tomas guided his craft towards the launch tube and into space. As the ready calls from Dirks Two through Eight made their way over the comm, the dusty moon fell away beneath him, leaving an open expanse of glittering void.

Tomas let his Wasp hang in place for a minute as the rest of the starfighters cleared the tunnel and formed a rough cruising formation. As one, Dirk Squadron navigated towards the assigned outgoing spacelane and aligned directly towards Port K and its shift gate, where the rest of the assault force was waiting.

"Engage point drives on my mark." Tomas prepped a timer on his console and watched it trickle down. "Mark."

The Wasps jumped forward, though the pilots felt barely a twitch as their inertial sinks absorbed the force of their acceleration. Flying at a tenth of lightspeed was a crawl compared to the vast distances of space, but it would more than suffice to reach the gate. Kaldea Prime and its gate both had the exact same orbital path, a remarkable phenomenon which meant the gate was only ever an hour away. Tomas disengaged the drive once the violet-clouded shift gate filled his view. Port K sat against it, a silver talon reaching around its prize. The station was designed similarly to Jerassh's port, but the sheer demand for inter-system travel meant Port K comprised hundreds of modules.

The gate itself was easy to take for granted despite the true marvel it was. In this case, it was a marvel of mystery. No sentient race knew how the planet-sized spheres of purple gas had come to be. But as far back as the earliest documents could reach, people had been awed by the unknown planetoid travelling across their night sky. Every system in the Cluster had one, just as every system had at least one star.

The scrutiny of these gates was limited at best. The sphere itself was an excited argon plasma, writhing and contorting in uneasy equilibrium. Repulsion and gravity and gas all balanced in a standing war, orbiting the sun just like a planet. Yet this was merely a mask to the true mystery: a curtain veiling a much grander sight.

It wasn't until the churning sphere had blocked out the entire forward starscape that Tomas could see the waiting Liberator-class frigates with his eyes. *Boundless* and *Might of Gaph* drifted in a high orbit around the gate. Over a hundred metres from bow to stern, the hulls resembled a rectangular prism with a trench ringing the transverse axis in the middle, giving some the impression of an 'H' flying through space. The outer blocks were a cheerless light grey, and each housed two beefy, vertically stacked engines. An impressive line of plasma turrets ran in a diagonal down each side.

The centre prism tapered at the front to form the bridge and was painted in the fleet's favourite flavour colour: orange. Unlike the burnt orange of the Wasp starfighters, the central section of each frigate was a washed-out orange-grey—much easier on the eyes when looking at a large vessel.

A ping of light on Tomas' control board told him he was being hailed. He took a moment to check the conversation was encrypted before opening the line. "*Boundless?*" He queried.

"Commander Amets, you're making us late." The crackled basso reply was swift and unkind. "Get your squadron of kech-brained egotists into escort formation now!"

Tomas winced. Forn seemed to have a replica of Ernn's unsavoury vernacular, only Tomas didn't have the authority to reprimand a captain of the fleet.

"Sorry, sir," he said. "The techs were finalising repairs on one of my Wasps. We're forming up now."

"I didn't ask for your excuses, Commander; I gave you an order. Get it done." There was a click as Forn disconnected.

"Sounds like someone skipped the sugar in his jolt," Quil said over the comm as soon as the call ended.

Tomas frowned. "You weren't supposed to be listening in, Two."

He imagined her innocent shrug and smile. "Yeah, well wingmates look out for each other, and I can't do that deaf, can I?" she snorted. "*Egotist.*"

The Dirks eased their craft into a routine box formation, one flight in each corner of the transverse plane of their charge. Micro-adjustments from his thrusters edged his craft into an orbit matching the powering up Liberators, and then his engines switched to idle. A quick check over his shoulder assured him Quil was right where she was supposed to be. The purple pulsations of the shift gate reflecting off her fuselage forced a squint to his eyes.

The comm popped again, this time over a general channel. "If you're *finally* ready, Captain Liuwayu, Commander Amets, we'll begin entry procedures. Transferring the necessary nav telemetry now. Shift embarkation in nine minutes and counting."

Both officers acknowledged, and then they were underway. "Eyes open, Dirks," Tomas said on the squadron frequency. "Work starts now." The thick silence of vacuum filled with a steady hum as he kept his starfighter a hundred metres ahead and left of Forn's frigate. Tendrils of evanescent violet curled out to graze the convoy. Tomas felt his grip on the yoke tighten as his mind anticipated the awe he was about to experience, even if he'd seen this next view countless times before.

Gas clouded his viewscreen, filtering the usual white-dusted starscape into dull purple motes on a black canvas. Static confused his sensors for a moment as he switched them to high-frequency mode, and he kept an eye on the rising external temperature. He ensured his path was clear of other spacecraft, then twisted to look over his shoulder. Dirk Two was visible through the fog, but the further ships of the assault force had been completely obscured. The sun was no more than a faint lamp of purpled light.

And in the next second, heralded by a sharp triple tone from his dash, it was all gone. The suffocating veil withdrew, replaced by constellations of magnificent lavender stars glinting mutely all around. Quil's ship had also vanished, as if Tomas had fallen from his plane of reality to a truer universe beneath.

It was a mere second, and then his wingmate erupted out of the backdrop of purple stars and entered the shift gate. She waggled her wings up and down as if she knew he would be watching. "You're drifting, Lead," she said. "Skybus at ten o'clock."

Tomas pushed himself around in his chair and corrected his position, the blocky commercial vessel still harmlessly far away. Now that he faced forward, there was more to see than just stars. Star cruisers and ship formations flickered in and out of existence, arriving from one edge of the noticeable curtain of mist and moving through the planet-sized void to leave from some point else.

Mentally shaking his head, Tomas arced into a turn and brought his craft onto their intended embarkment vector. The greatest mystery of the universe, he mused, now harnessed for simple travel and communication. How far sentients had come! For it was the Shift that allowed, somehow, for faster-than-light travel. The Kaldean Astronautics Academy had described it as "a network of dimensional holes in space-time leading to a shadow universe operating on the far side of relativity's light-speed asymptote". As if describing it well meant anyone knew what was going on.

The genuinely confusing aspect, Tomas knew as the convoy neared their target, was the way the gate worked. More than a simple doorway into another realm, every trip was one-way. When you entered from reality and saw the Shift, it was into the Shift you had to go. If you turned around and tried to fly out from the same point, you would blast off, many times faster than the speed of light, towards whatever distant shift gate was in your way.

And if you embarked into the Shift blindly, you had better hope you hit an exit gate, or you might never see real stars again. As far as explorers could tell, only the Cluster's stars had shift gates. The distant Eye of Urim had none, and as such had never been reached.

When a pilot disembarked from the Shift into a gate, he was met with the opposite phenomenon from entering. He would only be able to see and enter the normal universe.

Faster-Than-Light-Communication, or Fal-Comm, worked around these principles by placing an omnidirectional transmitter inside the gate and a rebound satellite outside. As the team passed by the transmitter sitting in the centre of the void, the kilometre-wide sphere blinked its lights merrily, as if it had nothing to do with an inter-dimensional solution that had united star systems and species lifetimes away.

All sentient cooperation and progress, all space-age development and sustenance, critically relying upon an unsolved enigma. Though he'd used it a thousand times and would use it a thousand more, Tomas had vowed to never see the experience as mundane.

"Seven; Three. How do you plan to spend the next eight hours?"

"Retrieving my stolen slumber, Three, and perhaps a pictolog. Why?"

"Oh, how nice. Which pictolog, perchance?"

A smile crept onto Tomas' face. He knew where this was going. A typed message scrolling over one of his monitors told him Quil and Memiele were on the same thought vector. The ships approached the murky purple veil once more, still in excellent formation as they arrowed towards the current location of the Rahgese System.

"*War on Agonak*, I suppose. Why, though?"

Dirk Six cut in. "What did Dan pay you Klord? You know you've sold your integrity."

"Hush, Mem, I'm busy. And *Agonak*, Seven? *Pal*? I thought you'd much prefer … *Little Freighter*."

"Wait," said Gerad, then after a pause, "No, no, no! I'll have your head for this!"

Tomas keyed his mic. "He's replaced all your pictologs with *Little Freighter*, hasn't he?" The faint thumps of a fist against metal could be heard through his headset, along with a thin Human wail.

Dan's belly laugh rolled across quasi-space. "It's stuck playing," he cried. "He can't even mute it!" He tried to bite back a second bout of laughter but quickly failed.

"Thirty seconds to embark. Make your final checks." Forn's sudden bark on the overriding channel was enough to quiet Dirk Three. Tomas took the opportunity to get a word in.

"Shut it off, Klord; we need to be mentally stable when we arrive at Rahga," he said, then thought for a moment. "Dan, if you ask me *really* nicely, I might let you reactivate it for the trip home."

Gerad's cursing was cut off as Tomas' Wasp breached the edge of the gate and launched off with sudden, intense acceleration. Faster than the comm chatter trying to reach him, Tomas sped off amongst the false stars, his heart lodged in his throat despite not feeling any movement at all. An endless void surrounded him, for all approaching light was being compressed beyond the visible spectrum.

Tomas pressed close to his viewport for a moment, taking the sight in: a complete isolation from the universe, enveloped by nothingness on all sides, an absorbing dark that might have convinced him he was sleeping if not for the presence of his ship.

Well, catching up on sleep was the next item on the agenda, and perhaps the only void more complete than the Shift. Leaning back in his seat and closing his eyes, Tomas welcomed the prospect.

"Lead, they're coming in from the side! We need to break off!"

"… we are all lost! Take it down!"

"Missiles away! Break and dive!"

Erae jerked awake, whacking both knees against the pilot's console.

"Ah!" she cried, more in surprise than pain, struggling to separate sight from vision. She was on her back in the pilot's chair, the front viewport facing directly up into a sky of fresh dawn. The artificial gravity was off while the ship berthed, which put the console above her and the back wall below.

Erae closed her eyes, letting her head flop back into the headrest. She had been dreaming again, the same terrifying sequence as a week ago. The memories were as blurred as ever, but the emotions that accompanied them, the fear and horror and hate, these had never been sharper.

"Peace of the King," she muttered. "*Pit-scum.* What's the worth of it?" She had never had two identical dreams before. Did this mean it truly was a vision, and not some random plot of her inner mind? If so, what was its purpose? The answers were lost to her.

She forced her eyes back open. A light on the console told her the calculations she'd been running were complete. The central monitor displayed a news broadcast coming through the Fal-Comm; it looked like the Chief of Council was making an address. The feed was muted, but Duidain's smile and gestures were so large and enthusiastic that he almost didn't need words.

Erae's eyes strayed to a second screen, and the message on it. It was part of the communique Gabriel had sent them two days ago. The white letters sat innocently on the display, ignorant of the weight they carried.

Two Liberator-class frigates. One fighter squadron. Noon, local time.

The force was smaller than they had feared, but no less dangerous. Those frigates would be packed with hundreds of the Core's armed and armoured soldiers, each with years of quality training. The Defiant didn't have resources like that, and the Rahgese definitely didn't. Their victory depended on the success of the plan Erae had devised.

That was the notion eating at her, the question that had pulled her from her room in the middle of the night to lie beneath the weave-glass, watch the distant stars and wait for her doom to arrive.

Have I sent them all to die?

The panic fell swift upon her, lurching her forward and stealing her breath. Reason was overridden; her arms tensed and shifted as she sought some corporeal foe to strike. A timid moan crawled from her throat.

The fight lasted less than ten seconds, then she was back in control. Reason resumed its position in her mind, and the world that had been closing upon her released its tension, stars springing back to their place beyond the horizon. The Defiant had done all they could, short of abandoning Rahga entirely. And *that* was not going to happen. Erae had done all she could.

"Eladdiyr, remind me," she whispered, "remind me that you're in control. It's not my … it's not my strength that will win this battle. It can't be, for I have none left."

That was the truth, the promise she relied on. Victory *didn't* depend on her plan alone. If it did, they had already lost. She needed to trust that her king would keep his people safe.

Erae needed to believe that.

"Alright then," she breathed. "Let's see what nonsense you're spouting today." Reaching up, she unmuted the broadcast. Duidain's energetic voice quickly filled the cockpit.

"…en and women of all species who have served so valiantly, in not just this fight but all fights throughout time! Let us remember—yes! Remember—next month we celebrate the seventh anniversary of the greatest battle of our history: the Battle of Tachillah. Remember what this glorious day means."

The councillor slowed for emphasis, pressing his hands together in front of his chest. "Together, there is no battle we cannot win. We are the masters of every field! The stars and galaxies are ours to mould so long as we *work together.*

"That is, yes *that is* my pledge to you all. I tell you, do not settle for anything less than everything you deserve! And as I tell you, so our government works every day to deliver. That is why—"

Erae shut the console down, shaking her head. Duidain seemed so kind, but he had to know his government was corrupt. Freedom, truth, victory; they were all lies from the lips of a smiling serpent. On some worlds, it was the oppression of half-bloods or conscription into the armed forces. On worlds like Rahga, the miners and workers slaved all day just to get by, and every year they were taxed more and more to support a capital planet that cared less and less.

But now they had thrown the yoke off, and the Core's justice was coming.

Rahga's suns were rising, washing new light over the desert and banishing the last of the stars. Ouhn, the white dwarf, had nearly finished its transit across the surface of Rahn, its red giant partner, and was visible as a fierce prick of light towards one edge of the larger star. What would they witness today, before Madhebah turned its face away once more?

Erae finally mustered the effort to roll from her chair, landing on her feet with a soft thud. Of all of the day's witnesses, Erae knew Amarie was the most unwilling. The young woman was desperate to get back in the *Silver Comet* and avenge her fallen friend. Grief had turned to anger, which was precisely why Erae couldn't let her fly.

But Amarie still felt betrayed, and Erae still felt like her betrayer. She peered through the hatchway down to Deck Two. The thought gave her one more reason for the Defiant to win today.

It was a silly assurance, but Erae latched onto it with all her heart. She would *not* die while her best friend was angry with her.

Which meant that for a good while longer yet, Erae knew she wouldn't die at all.

8

Eight hours after he embarked, Tomas watched the final seconds count down on his monitor. On cue, the unfocused fabric between dimensions exploded back into void and stars; Dirk Leader had successfully disembarked at the Rahgese shift gate. There was no inertia to throw him hard against his crash webbing—or, more realistically, to turn him into an atom-thick jelly—as he returned to sub-light speeds. This had nothing to do with his Wasp's inertial sink either. The sink absorbed and dissipated the force of most flight manoeuvres, but the Shift was an entirely different magnitude. It was yet another point to the unending mystery, but Tomas had other matters on his mind. His eyes darted between his monitors and his canopy, alert for any nearby threats. As of this moment, Dirk Squadron had entered a system at war.

The vicinity was clear, though Tomas kept up his search as the rest of the team materialised through the veil. The view to one side was dominated by the radiant presence of Rahn and Ouhn, only a light-minute away from the gate and painfully bright even through the purple filter of the shift gate. Rahn was an incredible sight this close; a wall of fierce energy stretched out like some vast infernal plane.

One last check of the scanners yielded the same emptiness Tomas was expecting, and he relaxed his search. Rahga was a terrestrial 'cold desert' world, skimming just outside the prime habitable range. At point-one, it would take over three hours to reach it, so it was unlikely the insurgent movement would risk the few fighters they had on staking out the gate.

A voice popped over the comm, its irritated tone leaving no question about the speaker. "Disembarkation successful; all forces accounted for. Proceed to Rahga at standard speed, reporting all sighted spacecraft. Commander Amets, I needn't remind you to deploy your fighters now."

"No sir," Tomas acknowledged, offering a mental roll-of-the-eyes before keying the squadron frequency. "Time to make something of ourselves, Dirks. Flight Three, assume scout positions one hundred klicks forward of the frigates. Flight One will trail at fifty klicks. Flights pending: ten klicks at leisure. Weapons charging, forward shields at maximum. Point drives on the captain's mark."

"Yes sir." All eight pilots responded as one, holding off on senseless chatter for the time being. Tomas cranked his acceleration lever forward and let the slight g-force hold him against his chair. A good pilot never dialled his sink to remove all inertia; you needed to *feel* the twists and turns as you made them. When he and Quil were fifty kilometres ahead of the main force, he reversed thrust until his Wasp matched their velocity, then cut his engines. The buzz-hum of his warming plasma cannons became the only sound as his fighter soared through the heavens on the arms of its own momentum. Tomas smiled.

True as core, he loved being a pilot.

Klord and Memiele jetted past as they headed to their assigned position, and Forn called the mark. Point drives activated in unison, and the assault force was off. Not much later, the comm came alive with the familial banter of his teammates. The audio traffic was against regulation, but it was doubtful Forn would eavesdrop on the squadron channel. Tomas himself was happy to let the offence slide. He knew his Dirks well enough to trust that they could keep an eye on their radars as they talked. He also knew they'd rather ten-to-one odds in a dogfight than spend even one hour without heckling each other.

He chuckled. The best of the CSF indeed. He kept his eyes on his console, ready for the enemy to appear. At this speed, he might only have seconds to react.

"Lead, Six," Memiele spoke into a lull in the chatter. Her voice was even quieter than usual.

"Go ahead Six. Spotted something?"

"Not yet. I, uh … I don't have a good feeling about the mission."

Tomas frowned. "What's on your mind?"

Memiele took a moment to respond. "You won't believe me … but I saw a Jeqon."

Everything seemed to go cold and quiet. It was as if Tomas' canopy had blown outward and sucked the atmosphere into space. He worked his mouth to say something.

"Uh … you're right, Six, I, uh, that doesn't scan." He tried not to sound too concerned and took an internal moment to thank Dan and Gerad for keeping their mouths shut. They would mock Memiele as insane later, to be sure, but they at least had the integrity to stay focused before a fight.

And they *would* mock her, for the notion was insane. The Gate-Ghouls were a myth, spun from a culmination of the unknowns of the universe. They were the fantasy-fuelled embodiment of everything sentients were scared of: something they didn't know.

But they did know. Nothing could live in the Shift.

"What did it look like, Mem?" Quil spoke next.

"Just … like the stories, I guess. Sort of like an Otrei, transparent and pale, but also bright and shining. But it had chains and … and I can't remember anything else."

"When did you pass it?" Tomas asked.

Memiele said, "I saw it about an hour after we embarked, but I didn't pass it. One moment it was there, and then … it wasn't. Only, I can't remember seeing how it went."

Tomas keyed his mute and sighed, running his hands across his face as much as his visor would let him. He did not need this now. The team did not need this now: an omen of bad luck uttered from probably his most level-headed pilot. But how to deal with the situation?

Biting back another sigh, he flicked the comm. "I'm sure it was nothing, Six," he said. "Just pre-battle nerves. None of us were thrilled when the General gave us this mission."

Memiele's voice turned hurt in his earpiece. "You think I'm making this up as protest to skipping leave?"

"That's not what I meant—"

"What he *means*," Falaquil interrupted with a tone that suggested Tomas would be receiving a lesson on social skills later, "is that we're all tired. You could have been dropping in and out of sleep. I've had my fair share of Jeqon dreams."

Dirk Six sounded unsure. "It was too real to be a dream, Two. It could be an actual warning."

"And thanks to you, we've been warned. But we need to focus now, copy?"

"… I copy, Two."

Listening to Quil take over, Tomas felt a relieved and knowing smile smooth his furrowed brow. Quil, as she often reminded him, had his wing. His, and everyone else's. Exhaustion poked its way behind his eyes, and he blinked twice to refocus on the readings before him. Omen or no omen, they would face the next few days as a team.

He let some energy re-enter his voice. "We've got some hours to go yet, Dirks; let's keep those scanners hot for trouble. The local militia reported twelve ret-fit starfighters with no missiles, so we're expecting twenty, and with. Last kill buys first kill a drink."

From a distance, the planet Rahga appeared red and withered, like a fruit dried by the suns until it was wrinkled and small. The ochre sands covered to the poles, trapping treasure troves of water and ammonia ice under metres of packed sediment and rock. It was hard to distinguish features like mountains or dune fields; everything was brushed over by the gravel and rust. The only relief from the endless shades and streaks of red were the thin white clouds drifting across the sky.

Madhebah was too small to be seen from space, carved into the Madheb gorge and spilling out onto the neighbouring plateau. If Niyott was correct, civilians and soldiers were trapped in those mines while the terrorists had free reign over the surface. These Defiant goons had stopped all ore exports, which would usually form a slow trickle of hauliers from the city to the station in geosynchronous orbit above. As Tomas' Wasp drew around the side of the planet, the station came into view. It was a dated model: an axial cylinder supporting a collection of rotating rings. The dock was dark and silent, its rings stationary. Even it hadn't escaped the insurgent's attack.

Tomas disengaged the point drive, slowing his Wasp to twelve klicks a minute, his eyes ever straying to his radar. Apart from the derelict station, there was no sign that anything was out of place. A passerby might not realise the world was under siege until they landed in the city.

"The scanners remain clear, Lead," Klord said. He was still a few kilometres ahead, cruising alongside Memiele. "Securing an orbit should not be a problem."

"Can't be very good rebels if they don't know to leave a lookout," said Gerad.

"Just because we haven't seen any doesn't mean they aren't here, Seven," Tomas replied, though he was equally doubtful. Perhaps Niyott had over-sold the Defiant's capabilities. A rebel group apt enough to take and hold the colony city *should* have been smart enough to post a scout ship along the shift-bound route. They would want to know when reinforcements were arriving.

He peered at his sensors again. Six blue identifiers showed the two frig-ates and four remaining Dirks behind his Wasp. They were headed back into their escort box formation, guiding the ships as they made a wary approach into low orbit. Once secure, the dropships would begin their assault on the planet.

The lifeless orbital platform continued to unnerve him, seeming more alive now than if it had been blinking and moving as it should. Then it would have been a space station, useful and knowable. Instead it was a beast waiting to pounce, watching the convoy's every movement.

What if the Defiant haven't checked for our arrival because they already knew when we would be here? The notion sent a chill snaking down his spine, and he thought briefly of Memiele's omen. Real or imagined, it was never unwise to be prepared.

So long as you didn't get spooked in the process.

Tomas' heart thudded beneath his skin, drumming a beat to his grow-ing unease. *Enough of this.* He keyed the comm.

"Dirk Leader to *Boundless*: Captain, they should have responded by now."

"Our enemy is the lazy derivative of useless scum, Commander," Forn's grumbling sounded less sharp than before, as if the Yiishi was convincing himself as well as his subordinate. "Don't be surprised if they've fled at the sight of us."

Cautious of being reprimanded, Tomas tried again. "Wouldn't the city have hailed us if they'd been freed?"

Captain Forn snapped back. "Not if they're still holed up in—" he broke off, and Tomas could hear a conversation in the background. The uneasiness in his chest grew.

"Commander Amets," Forn addressed him again, his tone cooler but no less intimidating. "We're receiving a low-power radio signal from the station. It could be the enemy or surviving station forces. We need your squadron to investigate."

"Sir, it could be a trap."

"*As ordered*, Commander. We will proceed to pre-set orbit without you; twenty minutes till power down and counting. I want that docking station cleared." A muffled click told Tomas that Forn had closed the channel.

First Niyott, now Forn. When did I get so comfortable back-talking my superiors? Tomas mentally and physically shook himself up, wringing out the frustration. *If there's a trap, I'll know soon enough,* he thought. "Dirk Squadron form up on me. We'll do a fly-by on the dock and see what we notice. I want scanners open for hails that might not be strong enough to reach us until we're close. Two teams; Five will lead the second split. Let's go."

Tomas led Falaquil, Dan and Teliac in a bank that swept the copper-coloured planet around and under their vision. Klord and the others executed a sharper bank that tracked them towards the other side of the station.

Hanging in otherwise empty space, the station's motionless rings and impressive axial pylon remained as lifeless as the void around them. Or so it seemed. Burying the still inexplicable feeling of doubt and warning, Tomas tilted forward on his yoke and dove towards the pock-marked hulk before him. No shields were active, allowing the Dirks and their Wasps to approach the derelict structure safely, shallowing their dives and slowing to glide along the central hull.

Cerulean light from Tomas' engine danced off the portholes, sensor blisters and kuwrium plating as he flew by, scanning for any indication of the mysterious transmission's source. The signal strength had increased as they'd approached, but it still wasn't powerful enough for the starfighter's sensors to gather specific information.

"Heat readings are normal, Commander," Quil said after a while. "If there are lifeforms on this station, they must be very spread out." Which meant it was unlikely there was anyone at all, as both survivors or ambushers would stay as a group.

"Acknowledged, Two." Tomas kept cruising along the pylon's length, occasionally shifting position to dodge one of the support beams that ran from the central mass to one of the outside rings. The central ring loomed up ahead, eerie in its stillness, not a single blinking service light on its hull. Chances were someone had left a passive scanner online when the attack on Madhebah had started, but it had been worth it to make sure.

Tomas sighed and spared a look through the top of his canopy at the earthy marbled hues of the planet and the two shrinking ships cruising dutifully towards it. It was time to head back. "Dirk Squadron," he said over the comm, "we're done here. Regroup and—"

"Lead, I have something!" Dan shouted, and Tomas swore the cry was loud enough to cover the small void between their ships, however impossible that might be. "My ship just passed through a tight-beam transmission, true as core. Came from a communications blister."

"Send me your coordinates at the time of intercept, along with the position of that blister." Tomas received both within the second and punched commands into his computer until it drew a straight line from the blister, through Dirk Three and out to deep space. Not to the planet, the shift gate or even the CSF frigates; nothing was along the transmission line. What was out there, and how far away was it?

The confusion added to that still present seed of worry. Tomas keyed for *Boundless'* bridge, gazing up at the empty space and the stars beyond it.

"Amets. Have you found anything?" Captain Forn managed just one sentence before all chaos broke loose.

A needle-thin streak of light shot out from the nothingness where Tomas had been looking and lasered towards the distant frigates. In less than an instant, the object jetted across space and crashed through the shields and then the hull of *Might of Gaph*, sundering the frigate in a tremendous explosion as detonating fuel and combusting atmosphere refracted off millions of pieces of debris. Molten alloys that had once been girders and plating drizzled and froze in shapeless tendrils, spinning outwards as the ship was ripped in two. The flames abated as all the available oxygen was consumed, and after ten seconds of shocked silence, the two halves darkened, still speeding faithfully towards the planet that would now be their tomb.

Boundless' bridge, still coming through Tomas' helmet, was a pit of chaos. Voices both quiet and loud bounced in his ears, though his mind barely registered them.

"It's gone! They're all gone!"

"Was that an asteroid strike?"

"All those men … did the pods launch?"

"Drop starboard outer shields. Cannons to bear."

"Drop shields?"

"I said drop shields, you incompetent vark maggot!" Captain Forn's bellow brought a halt to the disorder. "That was a starfighter collision, flying cold at point-one! The station must be sending targeting data. I need those shields dropped so we can fire at the approaching fighters *is that clear men?*"

"Yes sir!" An encouraged response made its way over the comm, and Tomas blinked out of his horrified stupor. They had been caught out, yes, but the battle wasn't over yet. There was an enemy to face.

A second streak flashed across space and into being, only to explode amidst the screen of blue-purple plasma fire erupting from *Boundless'* right side. The barrage chewed the remaining debris so that by the time it hit the frigate's inner shields, no piece was larger than a rivet. While basic starfighter and ship shielding could be polarised to allow projectiles *out* while blocking anything from getting *in*, larger military craft had a second auxiliary shield layer. This stronger outer shield absorbed much more damage but had to be lowered if you ever wanted to fire back.

"Commander, get your scorching squadron over here immediately. They might have more surprises for us." A third starfighter sliced through the void and was enveloped in the azure fire.

"Yes sir." He returned his hands to his yoke and away from his mouth, where they had drifted. Looking ahead, he saw he had reached the central ring, which was also the largest. Tomas accelerated forward, keeping his eye on the unfolding combat scene until the underside of the ring structure obscured his view.

He turned to face the front of his Wasp, then doubled back. There above him, several dagger-shaped starfighters were hugging the inner hull of the ring.

He could only see them because they were powering up.

9

"On the ring! Evasive manoeuvres!" Tomas snapped a quick roll to port before yanking back on his yoke, craning his neck against the sudden force shoving him into his chair as his Wasp pivoted away from the station core. The next five seconds were excruciatingly slow, the upward turn exposing his full silhouette to the new threat. Each of those seconds he imagined the sudden, brief inferno of pain that meant he'd been hit by the enemy's cannons.

"My scan indicates fourteen new energy signatures have appeared. I am flagging them as hostile now." Klord's voice was unhurried as numerous red indicators blinked to life on Tomas' monitor. "Engaging at will."

Tomas' climb finally brought his guns in line with the ring, and the first ship detaching from it. Evidently, the terrorists had been powering up to finish off the frigates and weren't ready for the half-squadron underneath them. He could see four of the sleek ships from his position, but the flare of engines further along the ring assured him of the others.

They were a narrow, aerodynamic design with large swept-back wings fabricated for atmospheric advantages, painted in a pattern of reds and browns that matched the scheme of the planet below. Adrenaline surging through him, Tomas finished angling towards his still sluggish target and hammered down on his firing studs.

Ballistic blue-purple incandescence streamed from his Wasp's mandibles, lighting the void before him. Each dual release of energy was accompanied by a metallic cracking sound that reverberated through the cockpit, but the energy projectiles made no transferable noise as they raked across the ring in pairs, tracing their fleeing target. Tomas pulled harder into his inversion, tightening his turn, and was rewarded when his fire clipped the tail of his prey. The pilot of the jet—Tomas' monitor had identified the ship as an outdated SpaceJet-400—swung his craft to the side in a desperate escape attempt, but it was too late. Shields flared and died as round after round of plasma splashed against them, and then the entire craft exploded in a small ball of blue flame as fuel and air combusted.

The spectacle died as quickly as it started, leaving nothing but partially melted chunks of hull. Grain-sized fragments fizzled against Tomas' shields as he ploughed through the remains. A glance at his monitor showed six red indicators speeding towards his position, with the rest headed towards the frigate still blasting away in the distance.

"Flights Three and Four, get after the runaways before they start strafing the frigate." Tomas forced his yoke to the side as he oriented towards his next target. "Missiles first; let's even the odds a bit." Numbers on his monitor started scrolling down, indicating the distance between him and the enemy SpaceJet. He started his missiles priming, dimly aware of the frenzied chatter around him.

"I've got one on my tail!"

"Hold tight, Two, I'm nearly there."

"I cooked one but he's still drifting!"

Twin points of light grew in front of Tomas, hammering at his shields, blinding his forward vision until the canopy's electronic tinting activated. Kicking his attitude thrusters to full, Tomas dropped his Wasp below the stream of fire, then rolled to starboard as his foe shifted aim.

The two fighters were still far enough apart that the manoeuvre only bought him a second of time, but it was all he needed. Shifting all available power to his forward shields, Tomas pivoted his remaining momentum back at the dagger-craft, meeting the incoming line of plasma bolts head-on. It was a risky plan, leaving his stern vulnerable to a stray shot or a second enemy fighter. Alarms bleated out their warning as his target pummelled his shields, his ship's cry of terror as the two starfighters barrelled towards each other.

Numbers continued to dwindle, both the distance and his shield strength, but it only took a couple of moments of staring down the face of death before a new tone, solid compared to the warbling sirens, informed him of his missile lock. It hadn't jumped to the tone indicating a good range, but with both ships speeding towards each other as they were, that wouldn't be an issue.

Cutting to the side so his payload wouldn't get hit the moment it left his shields, Tomas squeezed the trigger. With all the noise around him, he felt more than heard the *clack-whoosh* of the missile release and watched two blue-white fireballs rocket forward, blazing over his head and towards their prey.

There was nothing the other pilot could do. Dual-fired missiles were intentionally desynced by a fraction so that a shield barely powerful enough to absorb the first impact might collapse before the second. The SpaceJet's shields weren't even close to being up to the task, and the first explosion had already torn apart the starfighter before the second arrived to eviscerate the remains.

Chalk another one on the resume. Tomas breathed a sigh of relief. It had been a bold tactic, relying on his craft's superior capabilities compared to his opponent, but it had worked. Slapping at his dashboard until all the alarms trickled into silence, he spent a moment equalising his shields, then paid attention to his radar.

Eight blue indicators were still shining strong, dancing around the nine remaining red marks. Then one of the reds winked out, blasted through by

Teliac's Wasp. *Boundless* had ceased firing, having dealt with all the ballistic fighters, and was scraping the planet's outer atmosphere. Forn appeared to be ditching the prearranged orbit in favour of a safe landing.

What kind of an operation is running here, that they would throw away life to achieve victory? Following the hull of the station's axial cylinder, Tomas headed towards his next target: a starfighter sticking tight to Dirk Eight's rear. They were battling just out from the orbital dock. Tomas goosed the throttle and tried to find a suitable vector towards the pivoting duo.

"Eight; Lead. I'm coming on your tail." He tracked forward as Ernn banked sharply, then changed direction mid-loop in a fervent attempt to throw off his pursuer. Despite his less manoeuvrable craft, the enemy pilot held on through the twists, sending plasma volleys tearing through the space Ernn's Wasp had barely vacated.

"Can't shake the rat," Ernn grunted, concentrating too hard on surviving to think of a more vulgar description. "Shields holding at twenty per cent. Which side are you on?"

"Portside." Tomas spared a glance to check readings and make sure his stern was still clear. "Swing towards me on my mark and set up for a head-to-head. Pull up on the second mark." Tomas primed his second pair of missiles, hoping he wouldn't need to save too many for the ground assault. *Boundless* might have some in her stores. Either way, it was better to survive now and regret later.

"Mark." Dirk Eight curved hard to the left, levelling out in a collision course with Tomas' speeding fighter. Ernn's tailing opponent matched the turn, too intent on claiming the kill to realise his mistake. If either Ernn or the SpaceJet turned away, Tomas would have a clear shot.

"Mark!" Tomas pre-fired two missiles as Ernn's nose shot up towards the planet, exposing the enemy fighter. The SpaceJet had no option but to keep to its course, firing passionately. Tomas' missiles had nearly made it to the starfighter when the first got struck by a plasma bolt, detonating them both. The jet couldn't dodge the explosion in time, however, and came out the other side with its shields crackling and its front half scorched black. A burst of fire from Tomas' Wasp pierced through the cockpit and hit the fuel cells, sealing the ship's fate.

Ernn gave a half-shout of exhilaration, and Tomas leant back in his seat. Sweat stung his eyes, so he let himself drift while he wiped them and slowed his ragged breathing. There was, he admitted, a repressed pleasure in defeating a foe in battle. After every kill, the body swarmed with a mixture that was five parts relief at surviving the encounter, four parts pride in being the better pilot, and one part elation in the incredible power he held, that he could take another life.

It was an ugly truth, but a truth nonetheless. Ernn had come back around and formed up behind Tomas as his wing, and as a pair they banked towards the planet. The enemy count had dwindled to three starfighters, all retreating to Madhebah as fast as possible. Without giving the order, Tomas knew the closest of his squadron would give chase until they hit the upper atmosphere, at which point the aerodynamic form of the SpaceJet-400s gave them the advantage.

A job well done, he thought, and went to say as much into his mic when Ernn cried out in alarm.

"Taking fire from behind! Shield's—" A burst of static cut him off, and Dirk Eight's indicator winked out. A soft yellow glow swept over the top of Tomas' canopy, the only sight or sound that reached him through the horrible isolation of space.

"Eight? Eight do you read?" Tomas felt himself fly forward against his restraints as his thrusters fired in full reverse, decelerating his craft. His mind whirled as it tried to fit the pieces together. There had been nothing on the radar, nothing at all.

"Eight?"

Two seconds passed. Tomas twisted his head, wishing the back of his ship could suddenly turn transparent so he might see what had happened. He was about to bank hard to the right when the first piece of debris came into view.

The remains of Ernn's Wasp sped past him on its course to Rahga, a hundred jagged fragments drifting as if still connected to each other, locked into the inertia of Ernn's final commands.

Dirk Eight was gone.

Tomas had no time for anger or grief as a sudden pounding on his shields threw him into his restraints a second time. It lasted for just a moment before a large grey shape shot past overhead, coming so close that its shields scraped Tomas' with an awful crackle and forced an involuntary duck out of him. It was a triangular starfighter, modified beyond recognition, and its pilot had not been expecting Tomas' rapid deceleration.

A cloaked ship. Rage clouded his disbelief. *These blazing Scourge-spawn filths have a ship with radar-cloaking.* Letting out a scream he didn't know he had in him, Tomas jammed his thumbs hard on his firing studs, pouring the emotions of this sudden loss into every twin burst of fire that left his Wasp's mandibles.

Violet bullets splashed off the craft's rear particle shields, and the enemy fighter tried to juke out of the withering barrage. Tomas matched the movement, adrenaline surging through him, heightening his precision. His ears picked up the exclamations of his approaching squadron, and his peripheral vision noted their convergence on his location, but only one thought penetrated the red haze in his head.

I've let another one of my friends die. Tomas could feel hot tears forming behind his eyes as he watched the shields in front of him shimmer and flare, sputtering on the brink of failure.

A turret slung under the back of the fighter swivelled around, firing before Tomas had time to react. Ionic energy struck his Wasp's bow and washed over his shields, electricity arcing onto his hull and sending blue light snaking across his vision. Sparks shot out from the dashboard as the entire console shorted out, and with a shriek and a jerk, his engines followed suit. The comm dissolved into static, then silence. This time it was a complete silence, without even the hum of the engine to accompany the kilometres-a-second plunge Tomas' Wasp took towards the nearing planet.

Loosing a string of curses, Tomas moved his hands along his controls, fighting for any sort of reboot. The grey starfighter dove out of vision and lost itself against the blackness of space. Tomas' fingers scrambled around as he initiated the restart sequences, and he balled them into fists to keep them from shaking. There was no hope of catching the stealth fighter now. There was no hope in avenging Ernn Galoot's death.

Tomas gave a final shout and threw his fist at the unlit monitor. Of anger and horror, anger was the easier emotion. Another friend lost, and not even in a fair fight. It was an injustice.

But no matter how loud Tomas protested, the universe would never hear. He was trapped in a bubble of sound and sorrow that would never penetrate the void and reach the outside world.

Mourn later, an internal voice prodded, stalling a second strike of his fist. *Your people need you now. The planet needs you now.* He held the fist in the air, shaking, before letting it sink to his side. Tomas closed his eyes, breathed, then resumed bringing his starfighter to consciousness. He soon had it running and pulled off from his uncontrolled vector onto a safer course. Emotionally drained, Tomas let his hands do their job while he sat, detached, and watched. No words were exchanged over the comm.

In formation, Dirk Squadron drifted towards *Boundless'* landing site. Below them, *Might of Gaph*'s two halves had reached the atmosphere and began to break up as the chains of gravity dragged the vessel to its fiery destination. Streaks of light drew Tomas' eye, and he watched the brief and brilliant bursts journey across the orange-brown background. It was the beautiful and terrible fate, Tomas lamented, that they had all chosen. Delivery was just a matter of time.

10

To Erae's eyes, the battle had been nothing more than brief flashes of light in the midday sky. The first frigate exploding—that had been unmissable, and now its remains seared a rainbow of heat and flame into the air, arcing towards a sole, inevitable ending. If the Liberator-class ship had achieved its orbit before being destroyed, the pieces might have stayed aloft for centuries. Then again, collision with a starfighter at point-one was bound to ruin any object's inertia.

Those watching from the camp had cheered and whooped when the explosion bloomed in the sky like a second sun. There had been no harder choice than to put forward the idea of ballistic pilots; Erae's stomach still flipped at the memory of it. But death had been a sure outcome without them, and the decision had been unanimous. Still, she couldn't help but feel like there might have been a better plan, a way to beat the odds without a single pilot dying. Epieta would have thought of something.

Erae looked at the three SpaceJet-400s coming down to land, one trailing smoke across the pale sky; three survivors, despite outnumbering their foe two-to-one. They had lost, which meant Erae's plan had been in vain. Now, the Defiant were pulling out before the CSF's infantry wiped them off the surface of Rahga.

The *Silver Comet* was visible in the distance, following the vector of the other three starfighters. It was the only Defiant fighter to score a kill in the battle. Erae should have known Amarie would sneak off the first chance she had, and now the young woman would claim her kill justified her disobedience. Erae could imagine her smiling from behind the yoke.

If Amarie had been with the other fighters from the start, they might have taken out more of the enemy. The notion was not lost on Erae. *Another consequence of my leadership,* she thought sourly.

The three closer craft continued out of sight towards the far end of camp. The trail of the smoking SpaceJet widened and faded, softening until it was an indistinguishable strip of haze. It had vanished in, all things considered, no time at all. There, then not, just like the lives lost today. Erae felt her eyes become hot against the cold desert air.

"Captain?"

Erae looked down at Ruth, who had come up beside her. Erae forced a smile.

"How did it go, ma'am?"

Ruth sighed, clapping her beak as she did so. "I gave my people your offer, but there is anger in the ground. Many of them feel that you are leaving when our need is greatest, and they sully your name for it. It is bad for them to take these thoughts to their graves."

"I'm sorry," Erae said truthfully. "It's harder for us than you know." Every single Defiant soldier would have chosen to stay and fight if it would have done any good, as certain as Eladdiyr was kind. But they couldn't win, and killing a few CSF troops wouldn't solve that. It wouldn't bring their friends back to them, nor save those still alive. At least, that was the justification Erae kept telling herself.

"I wonder if … if we hadn't come here, the Core might have left your rebellion alone. To leave you with our mess …"

"Nonsense," Ruth shook her head, wattle swaying. "This fate was with us from the beginning, under our feet. We could weather oppression no longer. Live or die, this had to happen."

"Have *any* taken the offer?" Erae asked.

Ruth managed a grim smile. "We may be angry, but some of us are still wise. As many as you can take with you, they will go. Mostly women and children, at the behest of our warriors. Promise me your ruler will care for them as I do and teach them that good powers are still at work in this universe."

The joy at knowing the Rahgese would be joining them sobered as Erae realised what Ruth had meant. "You're not coming with us?"

"No, dear," Ruth said. "This rock has been my home all my life, and I've lived longer than you might think." She uttered a soft laugh. "No, the desert will take my bones. Tonight or tomorrow, in battle or a soft bed. I will join the ground."

Erae bent down and embraced the old Kilya. "I wish you all the strength in the universe," she said.

"And I you," Ruth looked up as the wind increased. The *Comet* was coming in for a landing a few dozen metres away, dust and sand billowing in the wake of its engines. Grains scurried away as Amarie cut to attitude thrusters, and her landing struts touched down.

Erae sighed and straightened. "You'd best go," she said. "We'll be in the Stone District Square tonight for the evacuation. Make sure your people pack light."

Ruth nodded, leaving Erae to face the next battle alone. She sighed again, a long, trying exhale, then made her way over. One hand went to her chest, gripping her pendant through the material of her jacket.

She stopped just shy of the ship, her boots crunching the gravel. Air hissed as the starfighter's canopy seal popped, and Amarie climbed out and down. She removed her helmet, staring hard at Erae with her piercing green eyes. She knew she was in trouble.

She's nineteen, Erae reminded herself yet again. *Be firm, but gentle.*

"Captain." Amarie broke the silence first, her tone daring.

"You disobeyed my order," Erae stated in reply.

"I've brought us one death closer to victory."

That was it, right out of the gate. For all the friendship Erae had shared with this woman, there yet remained one major philosophical rift: the path to victory. Addressing it now wouldn't get her anywhere.

"This is a war, Amarie," she said. "We are given orders, and we … we follow them. Otherwise everything falls apart."

A strand of wind cut through the space between them, blowing Amarie's hair forward and Erae's back: one attacking, one defending.

The attacker laughed. "Our war *is* disobedience, Captain. We're Defiant. It's in the name." More wind punctuated her remark, framing her face with curls of candescent, plasmatic fury. "How does Remiel put it? *If you, in due consideration, find any law of the Cluster to be unlawful by the law of your heart, it is then your duty to change that law.*"

"*Or change your heart,*" Erae finished the quote, restoring its intended meaning. "My orders kept you safe."

"My actions," Amarie's voice rose in parallel with the surrounding gale, "brought all of us closer to victory!"

"That's beside the point!" Erae's voice began to match the tumult of her foe, but she forced it back down. "Please, Am, we've been through this! Why you do something is just as important as how. The pilots who gave their lives today gave them to protect this world and its freedom. If you had been shot down, what would it have been for?"

Amarie's hands balled into fists. "I would have died for the honour of a friend!" The younger woman's anger waned enough to let her true sorrow seep in. "Every step we take to victory makes her life matter." Her green eyes blinked back tears. "It makes her death matter."

Each word was like a corrosive force against the resolve around Erae's heart. She wanted nothing more than to run to her hurting friend, but she stood her ground. "Epieta's legacy isn't honoured by the lives we destroy," she pleaded. "It's honoured by the lives we save. Your breath makes her matter. The hope you give others makes her matter.

"This is the example set before all of us, the reason for the Defiant's existence: when our king's son died, he took no enemy down with him, but instead gave *life* to those who might follow." The corrosion bored through her core, forming acid tears under her own eyes. "You would throw your life away for the sake of the enemy, but I'm asking you to keep it for the sake of a friend."

Amarie's glare softened, but she had one more barb to throw. The wind calmed as the dart left her lips, sailing unswervingly into the chest of its target.

"Is that what you told the pilots you sent to ram the frigate?"

Before the missile had even struck, Amarie realised what she had said. Her eyes widened. "Oh no, Rae. I didn't mean—"

"*They protected the people!*" The walls of resolve burst, flooding the desert street in hot, guilty tears. Erae buried her face in her hands, but it was too late; the dam had already broken. The last bricks smashed through her ribcage as they fell. One by one they landed in the pit of her stomach, next to the faces of the good men and woman she had sent off to die.

It didn't matter that the ballistic pilots had all volunteered for the mission. It didn't matter that they'd known what was required of them, and powered up their starfighters anyway. Their deaths were on her hands, and she knew it.

A new thought entered her mind. What would she have done if Amarie had volunteered? She might well have, just to get back at those who had murdered Epieta. Another thought: what in time and space could she say to the friends and families of the pilots who *had* volunteered?

Erae realised she had dropped to her knees, the cold sand sucking the heat from her fatigues. Strong arms were wrapped around her, pulling her in as Amarie's voice repeated, "I'm sorry, I'm sorry, I'm sorry …"

"So many have died," Erae said into her friend's chest. "If … you … I don't …"

Amarie squeezed tighter, a warm embrace against the frigid winds. "I'm not going anywhere, Rae. I'm staying right here." The two sat there for a while, in the dust. Erae continued to weep, each drop scolding her for weeping. She was stronger than this, she knew.

They pulled apart after a time neither of them knew to count, and Amarie gave Erae a cautious smile. "You know, we're making a habit of crying," she said.

Erae cracked a hollow laugh, discovered her throat was incredibly dry, and smiled back. "Well, you've been gone a while, and hugging Marpe isn't quite the same." There was no being in a million star systems she cared about more than the woman right next to her. Other friends, mentors and family she might have, but this bond was stronger.

She sniffed and wiped a collection of mucus from under her nose. "I'm sorry," she said. "I know you did what you thought was right. But not every order is about what goes on out there."

She tapped Amarie lightly on the head. "Sometimes it's about what goes on in here, too."

Amarie's smile dipped, but she nodded, dyed locks swaying. "I know, and I'll try." She pulled herself up with a grunt, then offered a hand to Erae. "Those Wasp pilots were far tougher than the fringe-system rookies the Core usually sends our way. I think we're starting to turn some big heads back at the Capital."

Erae nodded, letting her friend help her to her feet. She took a moment to bat at her clothes, shaking off the clinging sand. "Two frigates is too much firepower to spend on an operation like this. They're here for us, not the Rahgese."

"So we're pulling out? I caught the call as I came in."

It was good to be talking business again. Amarie led the way to the *Empress* as the discussion continued. How ridiculous, Erae thought, that they could discuss war and strategy until the stars grew cold, but a conversation of the heart ended with blasters drawn.

But that was the two of them, if they were anything. Amarie looked sideways at her in between sentences, and she smiled.

They were both still mad, of course—at each other, at the Core, at themselves. The deaths of their comrades orbited overhead, waiting for another moment to come crashing in.

But they were together, and their king was with them. That alone would see them past any failure, and every fear.

She looked up at the arc of smoke and ash that scarred the sky.

She was very much afraid.

Tomas stood tall as he looked out over the ranks of soldiers gathered before him and Captain Forn, but inside he felt bent, as though his soul had wilted from the poison of grief. Both men stood on an observation balcony in *Boundless'* port hangar. The deck was expansive for a ship this size, nearly filling the frigate's entire portside block. It went from the control balcony where Tomas stood to the magnetic airlock that sat just before the engines.

There had been no time to talk to his squad, to console them. There had been no time to console himself, for that matter. Dragged straight from his cockpit to a debriefing conference, and from there to this assembly, the inability to see his friends ate at him more than the exhaustion that came after a fight. He had spied their faces in the crowd, all six in a row somewhere in the middle. Their heads were bowed along with everyone else in a minute's silence.

The port hangar was usually occupied by six of the twelve L-715 dropships *Boundless* had at its disposal. Nicknamed 'Tombstones' by the common soldier, the wingless craft would dive cone-first into the atmosphere before braking with their four rotatable engine blocks. Other than the conical cockpit and the engines, the dropships were literal steel boxes. Up to fifty soldiers could cram into each hold, fully kitted out and ready to hit the ground running when the back ramp lowered.

They'd moved the craft out onto the dunes an hour ago, and now *Boundless'* full complement of crew and soldiers stood with stiff formality on the kuwrium deck along with Dirk Squadron, whose Wasps were also bathing in the pale sunlight outside.

"Brothers and sisters of the fleet …" Captain Forn's deep bellow broke the minute's silence, the metre-tall Yiishi expelling surprising volume for his size. Though the sentient used no microphone or amplification, Tomas had no doubt the speech was heard even at the back of the room.

"… we today acknowledge an unprecedented loss of life at the hands of our enemy." From his station behind the Captain, Tomas couldn't hear any noise from the floor below. The inevitable shuffling of feet or untimely coughs never made it to his ears, so he chose to believe they weren't happening. From his perspective, time itself had paused to allow this salute to the fallen.

Forn went on. "Herald Liuwayu, and his men and women of valour came from backgrounds innumerable. They lived lives and had dreams each unique and different, but one service united them: the destruction of all who stand in the way of the peace of the Cluster!

"To this service they pledged their lives, and braved the cost of doing what was right. Their example alone makes worthy their sacrifice, but we can make it worth more still." Forn paused, moisture glistening on his dark, flat nose and small fangs. "The rot-woven kech that have slain our comrades lay siege to this planet. They have bullied its helpless, both rich and poor, into submission and slavery."

Tomas could see determination setting into the faces that looked up at their captain. He felt his fists tightening, his voice itching to let out a war cry and hop back in his starfighter, sights set on his foe. Some tacticians would have launched their ground offensive as soon as their landing struts touched down, but that would have left the men dispirited and desperate. A moment for the dead was not only an act of honour but also refocused the common man to his three truest purposes: the brother by his side, the civilian under his shield, and the enemy before his gun.

Forn puffed out his chest as he amplified his voice, his orange fur leaking over the collar of his white captain's uniform. "Will you avenge the fallen?" he shouted, and the hangar shook with the responding "*Yes sir!*" of half a thousand soldiers. A foot stomp accompanied each syllable, and Tomas felt the vibrations climb through his boots and into his chest cavity.

"Will you defend those who still stand?"

"Yes sir!"

"Then ready yourselves! We mourn now." The captain eased his volume down. "And mourn we should, to give our brethren the honour due them. But when night falls, we strike!" Tomas joined in the following cacophony of applause, though his heart wasn't fully in it. The CSF had just, numerically if not proportionally, lost a battle. Yet it seemed every soldier's mind already clutched at victory as if it were assured.

As if the victory would somehow bring back the dead.

Forn turned towards Tomas, fixing him with four beady eyes shining with the vigour of the moment. He gestured out across the masses, inviting Tomas to give a speech. Tomas curtly shook his head, feeling his stomach twist at the notion. Giving a squadron of eight a pep talk was one thing, but rallying two companies of infantry? He'd sooner choke on his words. Quil, if she could invade Tomas' thoughts, would point out that he'd choke either way.

The assembly complete, the soldiers broke rank, dissolving into knots of chatting friends or heading for the tubes that would speed them to other portions of the ship. Tomas' gaze defaulted to where his pilots had stood, but he couldn't spot them in the dispersing throng.

He began to turn back but stopped as a distraction of colour caught his eye. Right at the back of the hangar stood two golden warriors, staring blankly through their masked visages. Tomas blinked. What were the Sun Guards doing *here*?

"Commander!" Startled, Tomas jerked around towards Forn. The gruff captain's head only came up to his sternum, but the power of his four-eyed stare made it feel like Tomas was looking up at *him*, not the other way around.

"Uh … sir," Tomas said.

"What are you doing: running a pre-flight? The sun settles quickly, and we must yet plan how to smother the Scourge-spawn occupying this worthless sand-sphere." The captain turned to lead Tomas from the balcony, furry paws clasped behind his back, his booted paws pattering along the deck.

The thought of another long meeting made Tomas want to throw himself over the railing to the hangar floor. What he needed was to see his squadron, to help them through their recent loss. *Or at least,* he added to his thoughts, *I need them to help me.*

"With respect, sir," Tomas toed his words, knowing full well that Forn was already having a bad day. *But aren't we all?* "I wish to convene with my squadron to, uh, prepare them for the coming battle."

"Prepare them for what? We need to plan, you dollop of coilslug slime, while we've fuel for victory!" The Yiishi swivelled back to face Tomas, his large ears seeming to lag a half-second behind his squat wedge-head. "I see through you, Commander, and you need to straighten your priorities. Your priorities, Commander! This planet, our men, my reputation cannot come second to your pining over one dead pilot."

He fixed Tomas with a narrow glare. "Or do you want to be the second fool to fail me today?"

"Pardon, sir?"

Forn prodded him in the stomach. "You heard me, Commander," he snarled. "Liuwayu was a washed-up relic, and he just cost me half my attack force. *And* he didn't even have the decency to live and face me for it, what's more! What, did he forget the code to the lifeboat? Get lost in the corridor?"

Tomas was stunned. How could Forn be so callous? "Sir, he didn't have time."

"Bah! Save your excuses for your own career, Amets. Is your squadron cast from a weaker mould than my brave and valiant soldiers? Than my crew?"

Tomas straightened, indignant. "Of course not!"

Forn grinned fiendishly. "Good. Then they'll survive without you to mother them. Come on." He turned and resumed his patter-march.

"I … yes, sir," Tomas had no choice but to fall in step behind the captain. He supposed he should consider himself lucky that he was included in the planning at all, though he expected he would be listening more than talking. Whatever it took to get the meeting over with as quickly as possible.

His friends were waiting for him, as was his enemy. Tomas didn't want to keep any of them.

11

Seven Wasps screamed across the desert sand, kicking billows of grit into the night as their low path took them over dunes blurred by speed into a dark, featureless mass. Tomas led the triangular charge: a spearhead to clear the way for the dropships not a minute behind them. No longer in the void of space, he could feel the vibrations as crosswinds struck his wings, and heard the glorious roar of the engines as they chewed through distance measurements like a ravenous Kalgorian deathbeast.

He nearly removed his padded helmet so he could take in the sound unimpeded, but decided to keep his hands on the yoke. He could only relish the moment so much when a job had to be done.

"Forty seconds till visual," he said over the squadron frequency. "Readying missiles now." He reached a hand to the three yellow switches and toggled the first one. His missile stock had been replenished from stores aboard *Boundless*, so his pilots could afford to start the engagement with a bang.

"Five; primed."

"Three; primed."

"Six; primed." The reports overlapped each other for the next few moments, each voice as hard as iron. There would be no quips or taunts in this fight.

Tomas had caught his team just before deployment, on the sands beside their parked starfighters. He'd called them to him, yelling over the ion blasts of launching dropships and the orders of haste booming from the mouth of every officer in sight. Helmets in hand, the Dirks had formed a circle and leant in close.

"Listen up," he'd shouted, seven heads nearly touching as they looked at the ground, ears strained to hear one another. "This fight isn't for Rahga. It isn't for Forn, and it's not for you or me."

"We fly for Ernn," Tomas had looked up, locked eyes with each of his friends in turn. "This is your memorial, your funeral song. Let's make it one worth singing." He'd flashed them a wicked grin. "Aim true. And if you see that cloaked fighter … blow it straight to the Four Pits."

"Ten seconds till visual."

The light pollution from Madhebah City bled over the tops of the desert hills as they drew near. Tomas sucked in a breath, preparing his mind to adapt to whatever situation they found when they crossed the last rise. What awareness did the enemy have? What strategies would they implement? The tactic of the ballistic fighters still ate at his conscience, but for different reasons than it had initially. Those starfighters hadn't shown on scanners, which meant they'd engaged their point drives in deep space, locked onto the station's signal, then deactivated to avoid detection. That kind of preparation meant the terrorists had known roughly when the CSF would arrive at the planet.

Had Tomas failed to detect a scout ship waiting at the shift gate? It was unlikely, and such a craft would have had to wait there for days lest it miss their arrival. But the alternative was a spy within the CSF. He wasn't sure which was less believable.

Stop it. You were supposed to be preparing your mind, not distracting it. Tomas tightened his grip on the yoke, pulling it towards his chest as the squadron crested the final rise. His Wasp led the wave of fighters as they rode the curve of the last dune like a ramp, announcing their presence in certainty as they shot over the crest and into the moonless sky.

"Madhebah in visual contact." He barked into the comm, looking down at the soon-to-be battlefield.

Below them was a vast sandy flat, the far end of which erupted with the craggy formations of the gorge. Most of the low-standing buildings were cupped by the safety of the rocks, while a sparse spattering of houses and factories made it out almost halfway across the plateau. These were the first points of possible danger.

Tomas levelled off his climb a few hundred metres above the twinkling settlement. The whistling of wind against the hull died down as he cut power to the engines—a manoeuvre made possible now that he could be slowed by the atmosphere. For a moment, it was as if he was back in space, with just the humming idles of his ship greeting his ears.

With a flare of sizzling light, a plasma bolt punctured the night air, then another, and another. Large packets of azure energy rose towards the Wasps like an inverted rainstorm, showering the patch of sky they were headed into.

"Split and dive, Dirks. Call 'em as you see 'em." Tomas leant calmly into his yoke, dropping just shy of the deadly plasma salvo. These would be the anti-air emplacements Forn had mentioned back on Gerduk, the ones he'd planned to raze from orbit. There were eight of them, forming a rough arc some distance from the Madheb ravine. The buildings surrounding the emplacements lit up with each release of energy.

The plans had changed.

The concentrated fire from the anti-air turrets split up as the gunners tracked individual starfighters. Tomas rolled and juked his fighter around the streams of fire, the wind howling around him. He narrowed his eyes as the details of the ground grew against his front viewport, blinking at each plasma flash that scraped by his shields.

These energy blasts were much stronger than what the average star-fighter spat out, and it wouldn't take many to turn any one of the Dirks into a living fireball. The upside was that the rate of fire was slow, and the closer Tomas got to the turrets, the harder it would be for them to track him.

"Any sign of the fighters yet?" Quil asked the team, her concentration evident in her tone as the seven starfighters fell like dead birds towards the desert floor.

There was a staggered chorus of negatives from the comm.

"I am getting heat and radio signatures from a few locations," Klord said. "I will mark them on the grid shortly." Tomas risked focusing on the scanner for a few seconds. Eight of Dirk Five's markers referred to the gun emplacements, but there was a host of other signals that varied in strength. At least one would be a radio tower, but the others could be ships or defence mechanisms waiting to spring upon the rescue force. Most were much closer to the ravine than the perimeter of anti-air batteries.

"Keep your eye on those sigs, Dirks." Tomas was bearing down upon the turret emplacement nearest him and could see the intimidating weapon kicking back its barrel with each blast. The plated machine was attached to a swivelling base atop an old stone control bunker. "Our primary targets are these guns. Silence them before our troops get here."

There were a few houses clustered under the shadow of the plasma turret. As Tomas pulled out of his dive level with the emplacement, iner-tia slamming his body forward against his restraints, he wondered if they were occupied. Considering the terrorists had taken the gun station, it was doubtful. That doubt would have to do.

Conjuring up a cloud of dust as he bottomed out in a wide street, Tomas angled straight towards his target. The AA gun fell silent as it tracked him, possibly out of fear of destroying the surrounding buildings. That hesitation would be the last thing the gunner knew to regret. The solid tone of a missile lock sang out from Tomas' console.

He pressed the trigger on his yoke and felt the push of his payload jetting forward from behind his head. He looped his starfighter away as his missiles hit the bunker dead-on, detonating in an atmosphere-fuelled explosion that splashed against and up the armoured wall.

Sound, heat and pressure pushed through the air and against Tomas' Wasp, taking him by surprise and canting his fighter towards the looming walls of an ore refinery. After a dangerous second he managed to correct his trajectory, mouthing a curse against the minutiae of atmospheric combat. The aspect you forgot was always the one that killed you.

The smoke cleared, granting Tomas vision of the destruction he had caused. Metal armour plates had buckled and melted, some falling away from the near side of the stone walls and striking against the nearby buildings. The stone itself showed some cracking, but no breaches.

He bit back a second curse and reprimanded himself for not aiming at the turret itself. It had been a while, he admitted, since he'd taken on something more durable than a starfighter. One pair of missiles wouldn't get through every hull in the universe.

"Lead, these guns are some fat Raan Jey." Dan had drawn the same conclusion. "We can take them out eventually, but you can kiss our bombs goodbye."

"Acknowledged, Three," Tomas responded, then thought for a moment. They couldn't afford to waste time.

"Alright, team," he said, keeping his starfighter low to the streets as he circled away from his target. "I want everyone to concentrate on my marks." He highlighted the outermost turret and the next turret over.

"Work out from there, creating a channel for our dropships. Six, transmit this path to Captain Forn and tell him to keep his ships flying low." He waited for Memiele's affirmative before continuing.

"Two, you're my wing. We'll fly past the outer ring and buzz the centre of town; see what else they might have in store for us."

"With pleasure, Lead." Quil's blue marker abandoned its attack run on one of the emplacements and banked towards an intercept course with the street Tomas was barrelling through. He varied his speed and altitude frequently, aware of how predictable his current flight path was, yet disinclined to forsake the cover of the intermittent buildings.

Dirk Two fell into position behind him, her Wasp's engines adding to Tomas' in a noisome crescendo that bounced along the ground. They held their speed back, making them more enticing bait but allowing them time to react if the bait was taken. It was better to spring an ambush now than when the dropships arrived, but neither pilot was ready to give their lives to such a strategy.

The closer they got to the ravine at Madhebah's heart, the higher and thicker the stonework grew, until the two pilots were barely scraping by the multi-floored factories and refineries. Down this trench they sped, eyes darting from their sensor boards to each rooftop and alleyway that blinked by.

"Sharp turn ahead," Quil cautioned. Tomas saw a rise of market buildings running along a cobbled promenade at the head of the main road. A marble archway decorated with golden script split the row at its centre. There was no way the Wasps would fit through the gap.

As the wingpair approached, Tomas caught a faint, wide heat signature on his radar. The arch appeared to lead into a town centre or square, guarded on all sides by commercial establishments. Perhaps the Defiant had set up a base of operations inside.

The road's end was upon them, and Tomas was forced to make a decision. "Up and over, Two." He commanded. "Mark any targets on the first pass, then we'll swing around if necessary."

"Copy that."

There was just enough time to sneak a look at the rest of the battle playing out on his monitor. Three of the distant AA guns had been razed, and the dropships were passing between their smoking remains. Even as he watched, the first of these ships began its eager descent, a belly full of soldiers waiting to be released.

Then it was time. Tomas' attitude thrusters flared to life as he hugged the flight stick to his chest, tipping his nose skyward. He killed his main engines, tightening the pivot, and slapped on the reignition as they came underneath him. Dust exploded out from under his jets, splashing against the buildings on either side as he rocketed into the air above the street.

When he had cleared the rooftops, Tomas snapped a half roll and pulled his Wasp's belly to the sky. Then he was speeding over the square, with only a brief window to tip his head back and study what occupied the ground below.

When he did, his heart plummeted to the sand.

The square was full of natives, huddled in terrified groups as they ducked and pointed at the two starfighters screaming over their heads. Forming a loose perimeter around these natives were armoured soldiers wielding plasma blasters. A few of these opened fire on Tomas and Quil, but the weapons did little more than dazzle Tomas as they grazed against his Wasp's shields.

"Lead?" the trembling anger in Quil's voice was distinct in Tomas' earpiece. "Are those—"

"Hostages," Tomas finished for her, and felt his anger—and fear—build. The situation had just gotten infinitely more terrible. As the far edge of the square swept underneath them, he rolled upright and patched into the command frequency.

"Captain, this is Dirk Leader," his mouth was dry as he spoke. "The terrorists have hostages in one of the district squares. Repeat, this is now a hostage situation. I recommend we break off and—"

"Break off?" Forn interrupted with a yell. "Nonsense! All civilians are hiding in the ravine. We knew the mercenaries were hired by a local insurgency, and now I see you've found them. They are traitors; kill them all."

The last three words were uttered so simply. Tomas blinked, bile rising in his throat. The natives had appeared unarmed.

Quil pulled away from Tomas' wing, banking her Wasp back towards the populated square. She'd patched into the conversation without him knowing again. Tomas quickly leant into his yoke, feeling the weight of inertia as he willed his craft to follow hers.

"Wait, Two!" he cried, then said to the Captain, "Sir, let them be. It's not worth the risk."

"Risk?" Forn snapped. "Each kech-brained terrorist you spare could kill one of my men, men that I will not *risk* on the whim of your scorch-souled cowardice!"

"He's right, Tomas." Falaquil levelled out of her curve and slowed, climbing in preparation to dive into the square. "These people killed Ernn. We need to stop them from hurting anyone else." He could hear the anger in her voice, and the resolve.

Tomas was incredulous. How could everyone be so far from reason? "This is insane, Quil, and you know it. These people might need saving. Break off, Quil!"

"By the sixth sun, where does your insolence end?" Forn screamed across the comm, his deep voice jumping an octave. "Dirk Two I order you to open fire *immediately*."

Dirk Two dove, still some distance ahead of Tomas' Wasp and any chance he had of interfering. She dove, but she didn't open fire yet. Perhaps she was listening to him. Tomas begged every mote of speed from his engines, trying to catch up. What would he do once he caught her? What was Tomas willing to risk for the people below?

"Quil?"

Pitiful lances of light reached out to her Wasp from the ground, like insects trying to dissuade an avalanche. Quil's guns still hadn't responded. Tomas searched the square, looking for anything that would prove Captain Forn right. Willing it.

Two transports sat to one side of the clearing. Lines of people were being ushered up the ramps, obscured in the darkness. The foremost figures were much smaller than the nearby guards. His eyes widened.

Children. They're saving the children.

"Quil!"

"Tomas, we have a job to do!"

"Amets, if you don't join her, I will personally see to it that both your careers are vaporised!"

There was no more time. There was no more room for words or thought. Tomas' blood sang in his ears, and his heart drummed like a pulsar in his chest.

Like lightning without rain, Dirk Two's plasma cannons fired upon the square.

A guttural scream ruptured Tomas' throat as he pulled up into the path of Quil's dive.

Every bone in his body was wrenched as Quil's belly shields and his forward shields scraped and wrestled. Sparks and screams of energy forked out from the impact, and his viewport nearly tinted itself black trying to block out the sheets of molten light. Her plasma salvo raked first across the tops of buildings, then empty sky.

"*What are you doing?*" Falaquil's fear was as much his as her own.

The collision flattened Dirk Two's dive until she rode on top of her wingmate, resting on the dual strain of two particle shields that couldn't hold.

And they didn't hold. With a shuddering bloom of blue light, both shields collapsed, and Quil's Wasp slammed into Tomas' canopy. Speed was ripped off the Wasps like plates of metal, and though Tomas couldn't see outside, he could feel them begin to plummet. He pulled on his yoke, desperately attempting to push his partner into a climb.

Falaquil's attitude thrusters poured their plasma across his vision as she did the same, and her hull scraped forward over his. Every alarm that could ring was ringing, yet Tomas could still hear the buckling pressure of one death machine on top of the other.

"Tomas!"

"I'm sorry." It was all Tomas could manage from between his clenched teeth.

Then her Wasp was past his, and the full blast of her engines detonated across Tomas' fighter as she shot into the sky, throwing him into a violent rolling dive. His viewport shattered, raining shards of weave-glass onto Tomas' helmet, arms and chest as he tried to wrest the ship from its turbulent flailing. Glass knives ripped gashes through fabric and flesh alike, but the wind sucked any cries from Tomas' lungs.

The roll of the craft pinned Tomas against his crash-webbing and greyed his vision. He reached for the ejection lever under his seat, but his bleeding arms remained fastened to the buckled hull. There was a blur of red sand and fleeing people, then of Quil's starfighter climbing into a star-lined night.

With a soundless roar, a large freighter swallowed his view of the stars, accompanied by a grey starfighter. Smoke and flames erupted on Quil's Wasp as the freighter opened fire, and it canted out of sight.

Tomas found the breath to scream, and then Rahga rose up and crashed into his Wasp, engulfing him in darkness.

12

As soon as the *Silent Empress'* boarding ramp hit the ochre rust of the square, Erae was halfway down it and sprinting towards the crashed starfighter. The cowering locals moved aside like darkness in the path of light. Fear was plastered to their expressions, and they flinched and paled at every distant explosion. Children were wailing, as were some of the adults. The main battle was too far away for them to know how well it was going, but every face asked her the same knowing question as she passed by:

"How long do we have left?"

She cleared the crowds and took in the sight before her. The QW-12 Wasp starfighter had slid on impact, churning up cobblestones and shearing off the starboard wing. Two of her Defiant had ventured in for a closer look while three more warded the crowds away.

Erae sought out the closest of those three. "Is everyone alright?" she asked. "Did anyone get hit?"

"Our troops were clear, ma'am, but ..." The private trailed off, letting the cries of the square finish the thought. His gaze strayed to where the wails were loudest, and then he looked away. The nearby flames were a grim flicker in his eyes.

Slowly, the crowd started moving towards the *Empress*. The other two freighters the Defiant had brought with them had already taken as many locals as they could squeeze in. They would wait for the *Empress* on the far side of the Madheb ravine, and together her team would launch off towards the shift gate and freedom.

I thought we had more time. Erae looked at the size of the shuffling mass. Some of these people, she knew, would get left behind. *Eladdiyr, give us more time.*

"He's alive!" The exclamation came from one of the men atop the wreckage. "The pilot's still alive!"

"Get him out!" Erae gave the command even though both men were already hard at work doing just that. She jogged over, flinching against the wall of heat that emanated from the craft's smouldering engines. The cool night sizzled and battled against the hot plume of ash and smoke climbing from the starfighter's stern.

That plume was sent dancing and curling as Amarie blew by in the *Silver Comet.* After the *Empress* had blasted that other Wasp out of the sky, Amarie had insisted on circling around as a guard against reinforcements. Now she landed her ship next to the *Empress,* hidden behind haphazard lines of sentients making their way to Marpe at the cargo-hold doors.

Erae turned back to watch as, giving a collective grunt of effort, the soldiers hefted a limp body out of the Wasp's buckled front end. She and the private joined them by the port mandible and reached out to help take the unconscious man's weight. Together, the four of them carried the pilot a safe distance from the crash and lowered him down.

"What do we do with him?" one asked.

Erae watched the weak rise and fall of the pilot's chest. Over his heart lay the CSF crest: two white wings shadowed by two more in orange. The symbol of her enemy.

A large shard of weave-glass had skewered his right arm, and the wound was bleeding heavily. One of her soldiers began to dress it, and she knelt to unfasten the pilot's helmet.

What had caused this man to crash? Erae had seen the last moments of the Wasp's descent from her cockpit, but nothing more. The defence turrets weren't close enough to have shot him down.

She studied the pilot's bruised face. His dark brown hair was cut in the severe fashion loved—though not enforced—by the CSF, and he was clean-shaven for probably the same reason. A rivulet of dry blood ran from his tall nose to his lips.

Erae wondered what colour his eyes were.

"We leave him," she finally answered and stood up. There were about a hundred natives left in the square. Erae could see Amarie jogging towards them through the thinned crowd.

"He'll live until his friends arrive. Let's make sure he's the only one of us here to greet them." She pivoted around to leave and flashed a smile as Amarie arrived.

"The sky is clear," the younger woman reported, "but it won't be for long. We should launch while we can." She peeked over Erae's shoulder at the pilot.

Her body went still.

Erae looked back at the pilot, then at her friend's horrified expression. A cold breeze battered against her and settled in her stomach.

"He killed her, Rae," Amarie whispered against the wind. "It was him."

"What?" Erae whirled back to the Wasp pilot as if expecting him to wake at the accusation. "*What?* Are you sure?"

Amarie nodded her head, paused, then shook it slightly. Tears filled her eyes. "There were so many people ... I was on the other side of the gate. But *he had her*, Rae. She ... I saw her die in his arms."

"I thought a Jerassh security guard killed her."

"*I don't know!*" Amarie shouted as an explosion rocked the buildings at the edge of the square, followed by the scream of starfighter engines. Erae looked up, but the sky was curtained in firelit smoke. How had it gotten so close?

Amarie stepped forward, pulling her pistol off her hip. Erae caught her arm.

"What are you doing?" she demanded.

Amarie's eyes were hard. "It was him, Erae! You have to believe me!" She pulled against the grip on her arm, but Erae held on.

"You can't do this."

"I'm not letting him live!"

Erae stepped around and planted herself between the pilot and the weapon. "We have to, Am. If he followed us here, we need him alive."

"Why?" Amarie demanded. "Why does he get to live when she had to die?"

Erae opened her mouth to answer when two Wasp fighters tore over the rooftops, dove, and rained streams of plasma into the square. Pockets of earth exploded into the air as the blue fire struck again and again, carving through flesh and stone. A bright flash came from the lead starfighter's shoulder mounts, and the world turned white.

Then it turned black, then red.

Erae coughed, forcing herself to stand up. Amarie was struggling to her feet, her flight suit caked with dust. She opened her mouth, but no words made it over the ringing in Erae's ears. The square's eastern edge was gone, transformed into a pile of stones and a wall of fire. The only other people she saw were shadows in smoke.

Eladdiyr, please. The ground trembled beneath her feet. *Please.*

Erae turned to the Wasp pilot, still unconscious on the ground. She began to pick him up.

"Erae!" Amarie's scream sounded distant, mute. The young woman pulled at Erae's hand.

"Erae, we have to go!"

Erae ignored her, setting the pilot on her shoulders with some difficulty. He was heavy. She took a step towards where she had last seen the *Empress*, but her knee buckled, and she fell.

"*Erae!*"

She couldn't leave him. Not until they knew what he knew, and if any of them were still safe. She got a new grip on the body, pushing with her legs—

The weight left her as two Defiant soldiers came alongside, raising the pilot off her shoulder. One pushed her forward and pointed, not at where she had been going but to the right. Together, they ran.

It wasn't long before her freighter was in view. The lines of people had vanished; rescued or killed, she couldn't know. The gangway was still extended, though, and the two women sprinted up it, ash in their lungs. Erae turned at the top to check on the soldiers behind her.

Her gaze got caught halfway as she saw the first wave of warriors pour into the square from the east. Eight figures marched at the head. They were clad in radiant gold, their armour backlit by the scorching flames. The light caught every line of their horribly beautiful masks, but their eyes were as dark as death. CSF troops rushed in behind them, blue plasma lancing from their rifles into the smoke.

"Get clear!" Amarie pulled her through the airlock to allow the others in. Before the door finished closing, Erae felt the bone-jarring shove as Driz launched the *Empress* from the surface of Rahga. The deck shuddered as something struck the shields, and Erae felt the ship turn, then turn back again. She started up the ladder to the cockpit.

"Erae—"

"Get him to the medbay, Amarie," she called down. "That's an order."

As she climbed, the ship continued to jerk and pivot, each turn briefly felt before the inertial sink shunted the force away. The shuddering strike of a plasma bolt could not be dispersed in such a way, and Erae was nearly knocked off the ladder twice before she fell through the final hatch and scrambled into her seat.

[Two fighters behind,] Driz called to her, his full attention on flying the ship. He yanked his controls to starboard as far as he could reach, nearly taking himself out of the chair in the process. [Shields holding at sixty per cent.]

"Missiles?" she asked him.

He shook his head, uncertain. He wasn't going to stay still long enough to find out.

"And our ships?"

He swung back around, then down, effectively throwing himself on top of the yoke. [They point-jumped before we left the ground,] he squeaked. [I need a clear moment to match the heading.]

Erae keyed her yoke to sync, and it began bucking in tandem with Driz's movements. Outside the viewport, the starscape whirled and spun, blue bolts shooting past above them—left—above again. The *Empress* rocked with another hit; the pursuing fighters were out for blood.

"Ready to seize controls." Erae gripped the yoke, letting the motors take her hands as they pleased. She relaxed into the movements, predicting where Driz was taking the ship next. If they could get a second to breathe, the *Empress'* larger engines would accelerate them faster than the Wasps could keep up, and they would be free to engage their point drive.

"Now!" Driz keyed the control over to her, and the fate of many was once again hers. But unlike battlefield command, this was something she could handle.

"Get the chin gun ready," she told him, snapping a turn to port before diving hard. The desert rose into view as she looped back towards the planet, and she goosed the attitude thrusters to tighten the arc.

The pursuing Wasps shot past but were back on her tail a second later. The *Empress* was fast, and the thrusters on her fins could handle the toughest turns, but her bulk betrayed her whilst in the atmosphere. She clenched her jaw as the desert rushed towards her, rolling dark waves waiting to swallow her whole.

"Light it up, Driz!" The waves exploded as the chin gun released its salvo, sand billowing high into the air. Erae rushed into it, rolling and kicking to the side. Dust choked her vision as the engines came around, launching more sand into the night. The *Empress* skidded on momentum, shaking as its own wake slammed into the side of the hull. Driz cut the gun as the cloud overtook them completely, hiding them from their pursuers.

"Ready on the point drive," she barked.

[Captain wait! We'll be torn apart!]

She threw the engines to maximum, launching from the cloud. The Wasps were on her instantly, their shots glancing off the shields. They broke to the side as Driz opened up with the gun for a second time, and the *Empress* shot past.

"Keep firing. The hot air should reduce drag." Erae reinforced the forward shields as much as she could without drawing power from the engines and keyed for the shift gate's coordinates.

Pit-scum. It was behind her, past Rahga's sunward side. She'd forgotten about that. She glanced at her altitude, then at the radar, and the two Wasps coming around for their final run. A random heading would have to do.

"Engage the drive."

[Captain, I don't …]

The *Empress* continued to climb, as did the enemy. It would be moments before they fired.

"*Do it!*"

[Captain!]

"*Now!*"

For five seconds, nothing seemed to happen, then the ship launched forward, fire spilling across the canopy as the *Empress* tore through the atmosphere and collided with the bolts Driz had fired moments before. An alarm began ringing, warning of imminent shield failure, but Erae held on, cranking the drive up to point-two.

The sky darkened as the ship rose, and the flames thinned and died. Stars glittered beyond the weave-glass, visible once more.

[Holding at … nine per cent.] Driz panted. His nose whistled softly as he took a deep breath. [Please, don't do that again.]

Erae nodded dumbly, slowly peeling her fingers off the yoke. If the shields had been any weaker …

But they had held, and her team was safe. They were *safe*. Finally, there would be no more death on account of Erae's poor decisions. Until the next mission, anyway.

Thank you, Eladdiyr. She smiled despite herself.

"Controls are yours, Driz." She closed her eyes, falling back into her chair. No more death.

"It's time to go home."

13

When Tomas came to, his first sensation was pain. Sharp fire drifted up and down his body, needling into his flesh. His head ached terribly, each throb pumping through his nervous system, and his right arm…

He couldn't feel his right arm.

He opened his eyes slowly, blinking against the light. He was in a small room, boxed in on three sides by stacks of vacuum-locked crates of varying size. Some of the stacks towered all the way from the greasy steel-grate-on-steel floor to the ceiling, also steel. Garish yellow magnet strips, their paint scratched and faded, ran along the centre of both surfaces, and dropped a pebble of despair in the pit of Tomas' gut. Those strips were used on space stations and ships in case the artificial gravity failed.

Tomas wasn't on Rahga anymore.

The walls, as much as he could see them through the kingdom of storage crates, were padded in grey synthetic hide. Where the walls and ceiling met, illumination tubes seeped a pale light across the space, thick as soup.

Tomas shivered. His flight suit had been taken, replaced by a threadbare medical gown. The sleeping mat he had woken up on was in marginally better condition, but was at least keeping his skin off the bare metal. How long had he slept? A few days, at least.

He reached a hand up to check for stubble, but a weight pulled at it. His wrists—two of them, he realised with no small degree of relief—were cuffed and bound by an iron chain. His ankles were also bound, and the chain that connected them ran under a section of the grated floor, tethering him to the centre of the room.

Sensation slowly returned to his right arm, heavy and stiff. An anaesthetic patch had been applied to his forearm, just above an ugly line of white scar tissue.

I'm a prisoner. The Defiant have captured me.

The conclusion was obvious, but Tomas' brain was still catching up. How had he gotten here? He tried to remember the square, and the collision, and—

Quil.

His last sight had been the trail of smoke her Wasp left as it careened below the building level. He had tried to stop her, tried to do the right thing.

Had he killed her?

The possibility made him want to throw up.

Why was he here? Why was he alive? Why him and not her? The questions ricocheted through his consciousness. A thin groan escaped his cracked lips.

I need to focus, a small part of him cautioned. *I don't have time for grief; I need to escape.*

He forced himself to draw a long, shaking breath and hold it for a few seconds. When it did nothing to calm his fears, he tried again. He had been trained for such situations; he just had to remember what that training was, and quickly.

If the Defiant had locked him in a storage room, it meant they weren't used to keeping prisoners for extended periods of time. Either this installation was a transit point to his captors' final destination, or he was only a few interrogation sessions away from *his* final destination. No matter the truth, he had to get moving.

He started by testing his cuffs. They were quite solid, as were the chains and grating panel. With the proper leverage, he might be able to snap a link, but the chain on his feet was short, too short for him to reach any of the surrounding crates.

But he was thinking again, and the mindset let him pretend he had more control than he did.

Tomas looked at the piles of vac-crates, then at his mat. If he could use it to reach one of the smaller crates and slide it over …

The floor began to rattle to the rhythm of multiple pairs of feet. Hurriedly, he laid himself back down on the mat, fighting a wave of nausea as he did so. His eyes fixed on the rounded, windowless door that was the storage room's only exit. The footsteps came to a halt on the other side. He held a breath and listened.

The door hissed and slid back on its guide. Tomas closed his eyes, his heart beating against his ribcage. He didn't know what he might gain by pretending to be unconscious, but he was willing to try anything to get an edge over his kidnappers.

The floor vibrated as the footsteps drew closer. Most of the noise stalled early into the room, but one pair of feet came all the way up to Tomas' face before stopping. A shadow fell across his eyelids.

"He's awake." The voice was male, and not unkind. The speaker sounded amused, if anything. "Up with you, master pilot."

Tomas remained silent, keeping his breathing level. The sooner he responded, the sooner the interrogation would begin, and the torture.

For all his service, he had never been a captive before. Would he manage to hold out against the pain and agony that was sure to come, or would he spill every last CSF secret before the first blow? Did he even know any secrets? Would the Defiant believe him if he didn't?

"Master pilot? I would not test our kindness to you. Saving your life has spent most of it."

Saved for information or ransom, true as core, Tomas thought sourly. *And I'll be finished if I can't escape before you realise I'm good for neither.*

The grating rumbled, and before he could brace, a kick caught him straight in his stomach. He gasped in pain, then shouted as he was hauled up by his cuffs and onto his knees. He opened his eyes just in time to catch a gloved fist between them, snapping his head back.

"Amarie!" a female voice barked.

Tomas blinked through the pain, finding himself staring down the barrel of a plasma pistol. Behind it stood a young, dark-skinned Human woman with hair like candied fire. Tears glistened in the corners of her eyes, and hatred coloured her face.

"Stand down," the second voice said. "Or you can watch from outside."

Amarie hesitated, then slowly holstered her weapon. She stepped to the side, and a large, cloaked man took her place, a bulb of water cradled in one hand. He pressed the nozzle to Tomas' lips.

"Drink," he said gently, and Tomas was too busy staring to question the order. The man's face was pale and transparent, his head crowned with dusty sunbeams, or so it appeared. His eyes were candescent rays, but they were dimmer than Tomas expected. The being's face seemed haunted by a shadow of grief.

"You've seen my kind before," the man said. It was not a question.

Tomas kept drinking from the nozzle, relishing as the cool liquid washed down his throat. He hadn't realised how thirsty he was.

"How did you ..." the being shut his eyes briefly, darkening the room. "No, we shall come to that. I will start with that which pains me least, for both our sakes." He withdrew the bulb from Tomas' reach.

"My name is Raphael," he continued. "I won't waste breath asking your name, but I do want something to address you by. What is your rank?"

Despite the fear, confusion and danger, Tomas couldn't resist smiling. Did these pirates not know how to read rank slides? Every computer in the Cluster could access public information like that.

"Silence will only harm you," Raphael warned, his tone hardening. "If you will not cooperate with me, there are others who are far more convincing. Tell me your rank."

Tomas found the strength to shrug. "I'm a Squadron Commander," he said.

"We want the truth, worm!" Amarie spat from the side. "Not your rot-woven cover."

Raphael frowned, ignoring the outburst. "Commander." He said the word slowly, as if tasting it. "That is your only role?"

"Of course." Tomas returned the expression. Cover? What would he be covering for?

Raphael's frown deepened, and he straightened, leaving Tomas on his knees. "His words are true," he said.

"Scorch sear me they are! He's a spy! He followed us from Jerassh!"

"Please, Miss Gayyam," Raphael held up a hand. "His actions are the same, regardless of title."

"Actions? She's *dead*, Raph. Why is everyone acting like it doesn't matter!"

"I share your pain, my Lady. But we must lay it down, or it will cloud our sight."

Tomas tracked between the two figures. The fear he had settled was stirring again, and the scraps of information he was getting only added to the swell. The air felt coiled, or loud, or *something*. He was still addled by anaesthetic and pain. He squinted as Raphael turned his luminous gaze back onto him.

"Tell me, Commander," he said, "why you were at Jerassh not long ago."

They think I've hunted them, Tomas realised. *But I haven't. I've just stumbled into where I don't belong.*

"The security staff had fallen ill," he answered. "My taskforce was in the area, and my team was one of many ordered to fill in."

"Security."

"Yes, for one week."

Raphael's eyes flashed. He glanced at Amarie, then back down at Tomas. "You met my sister there."

"Yes." Another piece, though Tomas had guessed as much. "She and her Ebon buddies attacked my friends."

Pain exploded on the side of his head, knocking him onto his hands.

"How *dare* you!" Amarie shouted. "You attacked *her.* I was there."

"Miss Gayyam, please," Raphael had stepped back. "He only saw her distraction—"

"No," she cut the man off. "I've had enough of this soft-stepping." She launched a boot into Tomas' side, forcing the breath out of him. She struck again, and he scrambled away, only for his feet to snag on their chain. A hard shove rolled him onto his back.

"Amarie," a female admonished. Tomas had forgotten there was a third person in the room. He didn't dare look for her now. His life was balanced on a wingtip, and his pulse was racing, but not from fear. Surprisingly, his fear had vanished, replaced by a taut-wire anticipation. He watched her boots, waiting.

"No, Erae," Amarie pulled her pistol off her hip and stalked towards him. "The disc can wait. The method can wait. I want to hear him say it." She lowered the barrel in line with his head.

"One time, Spy. Did you kill her?"

She'd stopped too soon. But Tomas could fix that. He forced a smile. "The adults ask the questions, sweetheart. Go play someplace else."

Amarie's face contorted, and she took another step. Tomas quickly held his hands up to guard his face. "Okay, okay," he said. "I'll confess."

He lowered his hands to the floor, shifting his weight slightly. He had one shot at this.

"I ... did not kill your friend."

"*Liar!*" Amarie screamed, stepping forward again. As soon as her boot left the floor, Tomas pulled hard, yanking the sleeping mat from under her remaining foot. The whine of a plasma discharge filled the air, and a shining bolt sizzled over his head. Amarie hit the floor on her back, gasping in pain, her pistol clattering to the deck beside her.

Then he was up, pushing off the floor just enough to launch himself on top of Amarie. She bucked her knees into his ribs as he scrambled forward, but she was much smaller than him, and badly winded. He planted an elbow into her chest as he reached for her weapon, snatching it up just before Raphael got to it. Twisting back, he jammed the barrel hard against Amarie's throat, his finger on the trigger.

"*Stop!*" he screamed. The room froze.

Amarie went still underneath him, her breath coming in half-choked gasps. Her eyes were wide with a child's terror, her wrath forgotten. "Erae," she pleaded.

"Let her go." Erae's voice came from somewhere close above him, hard as ice. Tomas felt a gun press against his head, and pushed down on his stolen weapon in response. Amarie cried out.

"They say every dead man gets one shot," Tomas said, his senses straining for any movement. "Don't make me use it."

"Alright." The pressure left his head, though Erae was certainly still aiming at him. "Let's everyone stay calm. You aren't going to pull that trigger."

"Aren't I?" Tomas bit out. "Apparently I'm a cold-blooded assassin. Right, Raphael?"

Raphael didn't respond.

"*Right?*" Tomas shouted, and Amarie whimpered beneath him. Tears filled her eyes.

"You did not kill her," Raphael said softly. "I am sorry."

"And you won't kill Amarie now," Erae added, her voice gentler than before. "I heard about how your ship crashed, Commander. You were protecting them, the people."

"They were innocent, helpless," Tomas retorted. "You aren't."

But she was right. Tomas couldn't kill someone in cold blood, not even with his own life on the scales.

"Let the girl go."

Tomas shook his head. "I'm getting some answers, and I'm getting out of here," he said. "You can start with my chains."

"She's a child, Commander," Erae said. "If you want a hostage, take me instead."

Tomas thought about it. It was better than torturing a teenage girl, but this Erae woman was too calm, too prepared.

"I'll take Raphael," he said, and lifted himself off Amarie's stomach. His gun never left its mark.

"Captain?"

"Get his chains, Raphael," Erae's tone held relief.

Tomas stood while the ghostly being knelt and tended his ankles. As soon as he felt the cuffs release, he shifted his aim from Amarie to the top of Raphael's head. He leant into his hand slightly, so he would feel if the man moved, then risked a look around.

Erae stood across the room from him, two gloved hands firmly on her pistol. She was a near-Human—a mongrel breed—with skin of dappled arctic hues and hair like the deepest void tied in a flowing tail down her back. Her pants were dark brown, as was her sleeveless shirt, which fit close to her slender frame and left her cerulean midriff bare. Over her shirt hung a loose pewter coat with the shoulders cut out of the sleeves. These cut-outs exposed her upper arms, which were marred by cobalt patches of some sort—perhaps bone—looking for all the Cluster like embedded sapphires.

But none of this compared to the eyes that stared at him from behind the trained pistol. Erae's irises were a depth of the darkest ultramarine and indigo, radiating from her pupil in marbled streaks. Countless white flecks glittered within them, like constellations of diamond light, or a reflection of the galaxy entire, pulling him in.

It was an intricate beauty, and Tomas might have stared longer but he could not withstand the baleful glare she sent his way. He averted his gaze.

"Go," she said to Amarie.

"Erae …"

"We'll be fine," she assured the girl. "The Commander wants to talk, so we'll talk."

Amarie scurried to the door and pressed a card against the lock. It slid open, and she was gone.

A key card, Tomas frowned. *Shouldn't she have used her palm-chip? That's the system for every other door and lock in the Cluster.* He didn't have time to dwell on it now.

"Your first question?" Raphael asked calmly.

The frown became a smile. It seemed *he* was the interrogator now, and it suited Tomas fine.

"First, what are you? He raised an eyebrow. "And how do you know I've been telling the truth? Are you psychic?"

Raphael smiled politely without moving his head to look at Tomas. "Not quite, I'm afraid," he said. "I have the ability to detect truth and lie, but I cannot read thoughts. Hence our need to ask you ourselves."

"How does this detection work? By reading my pulse?"

"The colour of your spirit, actually." Raphael did look at Tomas this time, his eyes bright. "Not the answer you were expecting? There may be a few of those."

Tomas shook his head, protesting the truth of the idea. These traitors still had every capacity to lie to him, even if he couldn't lie back.

"What are you?" he asked again.

"I am a Neiru, a guardian of a race of guardians, protecting the Cluster from unseen evils. The sixteenth pure race, though it might be more accurate to call us the first."

"Neiru …" Tomas' eyes widened as he remembered. "Celah Neiru?"

A look of puzzlement passed briefly over Raphael's face. "Only to those who know the difference. Was that on the disc you stole?"

"What disc?"

"The one Epieta had with her," Erae said. She had opted for sitting on one of the larger vac-crates, her pistol still squarely aimed at Tomas. "One of our … *threats* … was tracked to a gang network based in Jerassh. A plant of ours set up an idle recorder, but his transmissions ceased. We sent Epieta and Amarie to get the information out."

Her eyes shimmered. "We'd sure like to know what happened next."

Tomas felt a lump stick in his throat. "They were hunted, but your foe was too late. One of my … " he halted, aware that he was still a prisoner with very little fuel for escape. "A CSF operative got to her first."

He recalled how the light had faded from that woman's eyes as he'd held her, ivory blood seeping through her cloak. If he'd been quicker she would have been stunned, not murdered, but there had been so much going on. The stampede, his team in danger, the raging Ebon …

Tomas stiffened, his expression hardening. "But we're just another one of your threats, I suppose. Another one of your *evils*."

"A ship is known by its energy signature," Erae returned without batting an eyelid.

"Is that so? Last I checked, guardians didn't run around conquering small worlds."

"*We were—*"

"*If you please*," Raphael interrupted. Erae stopped herself with a glower. "I would like to know how she died."

"I told you," Tomas snapped down at him. "It was an intelligence operative."

"But how?" Raphael pressed. "What method did they use?"

"A sword, a red one, through her heart," he said.

"Thank you, Commander," Raphael said, and Tomas knew it was sincere. He had endured the loss of friends too many times to wish that pain on anyone, even criminals.

Scourge seal it. He sighed, dropping his aim a fraction.

"Tomas," he said. "My name is Tomas."

He looked up as Erae choked back a gasp. Her blue face had paled, and she stared at him with wide eyes.

"Captain?" Raphael ventured.

"I …" She shook her head, twisting the barrel of her pistol with her free hand. It locked in place with a click. "I'm sorry. This conversation is over." She rose to her feet.

Tomas brought his aim back to Raphael's head. "I'm not staying here," he warned.

"I ... can't," her voice wavered as she brought her weapon to bear. "I have to leave."

Raphael raised his hands to stop her, but it was too late. Erae pulled the trigger, and white lightning leapt from the barrel. Without thinking, Tomas fired his own weapon.

The stun ray slammed into his chest, shooting hot pain through every nerve. He collapsed in a spasm, his jaw locking against his shout of anger, his body numb before he hit the floor.

He saw the tail of Erae's pewter coat disappear around the side of the sliding door, and then Raphael stood over him, confusion and apology on his face. There was no mark or burn on him.

That was my one chance. Tomas pushed with his mind, but his body didn't budge; it was more of a prison than the walls or chains had ever been. The Neiru's eyes became dazzling beacons as his vision greyed. *My one chance to escape, and I blew it.*

Raphael reached down and shut his eyelids with a hand. He was dimly aware of his body being moved and chains being fastened, but the sensations came and went, and time had no meaning. Eventually, though, he knew he was alone, sleep far from him, anger and shame looping in his mind.

How would he ever get home?

14

When the Ebon Horde invaded the Cluster, they didn't approach the various governments with overtures of peace, nor demands for surrender. Their first and last communication came from the cannons of their dreadnaughts and the screaming engines of their clawcraft fighters.

And once a world was conquered, they didn't establish a new authority, nor did they imprison, conscript or enslave. There was no argument to their wrath, only the destruction of all who were too bold, or too slow, to flee.

Their conquest burned and stripped, the Ebon would move to the next system, leaving corpses instead of planets and frozen cores instead of suns. What the stellar energy was used for—to fuel their ships or some other cruel purpose—Erae had never discovered. The Horde had been a scythe of darkness, cleaving the light from thousands of star systems.

But this Barren Zone, as it was called, was not dark. Overhead, Erae could still see all those dead stars, distant rhinestones of fury and light embossing the gossamer fabric of space-time. The Hagion System, where the Defiant had established their base, was light-years away from the closest living star, but she could still see them shining.

Time hadn't caught up to them. The light reaching her eyes was years old, ignorant of its peril as it blazed through the void. The ghosts of a thousand systems lit her view, life persisting amidst the scars of death, and the perfect place for her people to hide.

The Shard was an artificial superstation, meandering in a lazy orbit barely fifty kilometres above the iron-silicon core of Hagos, the Hagion System's fallen sun. Underneath, the station was a warren of tubes, walkways and docks. Above this spread a twinkling garden city, three kilometres wide, its atmosphere protected by a thick, shielded dome.

It was a fragment of the life the Defiant worked towards, taking broken people and inviting them to share in the hope of a new kingdom. The Shard was a far cry from the open seas and skies of Nava, where she had grown up, but it was still her home.

"There you are, child. I've finally found you."

As if you didn't know where I'd be, Erae thought bitterly. She was sitting on the edge of a granite outcropping overlooking the West Park. Whenever she was stressed, she would retreat here, under the dome's eternal night sky, able to imagine that her troubles were far below her.

Even though it was a measly ten-metre drop to the lower field.

She didn't acknowledge Remiel as he sat down, the cloudlike wisps of his long beard spilling over the simple cloak that all Celah Neiru favoured. She felt the glow of his spectacular gaze on her as he waited, but he said nothing. He knew she would speak first.

Tomas.

The name slid around in her mind, its sharp edges digging into the space behind her eyes.

Tomas. Commander Amets. Dirk Leader.

"I dreamt I was him," Erae began, and Remiel listened. "I ... I couldn't remember the name at the time. He was in a starfighter at the Battle of Tachillah."

She loosed a shaky breath, feeling her eyes dampen. "I ... he was chasing Ben-Eloah's ship."

The words lingered on the breeze, whistling through the golden leaves of the dewbark trees that populated the park around them. There was so much in those simple words, and Erae didn't know where to start the process of unravelling it all.

The man I saved from death is the one who killed our prince. The follow-up sentence stuck on the roof of her mouth, too vile to swallow, yet she couldn't spit it out.

Remiel's voice, old and measured, rose from beside her. "When did you have this dream, child?"

Erae closed her eyes and felt a tear escape them. "The day Epieta died."

"Ahh," Remiel breathed out long and slow. "Even in grief, Eladdiyr shows us his wisdom, his assurance. Do you see it?"

"No," Erae sniffed. "What don't I see?"

"A pattern," Remiel said. "Two Humans flying into the path of those they love, to save those who don't love them."

Erae screwed up her nose. "That commander is nothing like Ben-Eloah."

"No?"

Erae looked at him in disbelief. "Of course not! Ben-Eloah sacrificed himself to save us from the Ebon. He gave up everything, and the Cluster didn't even know. They called him a traitor."

"And the pilot?"

"The pilot ..." Erae hesitated, caught in her words. In her mind, she pictured a desperate crowd parted in two, a burning starfighter driven into the earth between the halves.

But he was one of them. He had shot her friends out of the sky, had held Amarie at gunpoint the first chance he'd gotten. He'd even shot Raphael in the head, unaware of the Neiru's immortality.

Her tone hardened. "The pilot isn't forgiven for a lifetime of ignorance by one act of mercy," she said. "He's fighting on the wrong side, whether he knows it or not."

Remiel nodded. "That is why you must teach him."

"What—*me?*"

"Who else?"`

Erae turned towards him. "*Anyone else.* Remiel, I can't!"

The old Neiru looked pointedly at her, and she ducked away. *I can't,* she repeated to herself. *Even if I wanted to, there's no way Tomas will listen to me. I mean, I shot him less than an hour ago!*

Streaks of light began to flicker across the sky as the Shard's shields vaporised a cloud of dust, possibly a remnant from the planets that scattered from orbit when Hagos went cold. Yellow-orange ribbons fell around the dome, looking much like the fuses, Erae thought, of a bomb.

"How did Epieta die?" she asked softly, changing the subject. "I mean, I didn't think anyone could kill a Neiru."

Emotion passed across Remiel's face. He took a moment to master himself.

"The sword Commander Tomas spoke of," he said, "it must have been a Neiru weapon. You have seen my brothers and sisters carry similar tools."

She nodded. She had seen Michael's battle spear a few times. Its shaft was an ivory white, inlaid with jade script, elegant and beautiful. She had assumed it was for ceremony more than actual fighting.

"There were many such weapons before the Second Formation, though only two beings had the skill to forge them. Our king is one, and the other was dealt with long, long ago."

Remiel tugged at his beard. "Only these artefacts have the strength to take a Neiru's life. I never imagined a Human would find and use one. More likely it was given to him."

Erae's eyes widened. "You mean the Core and the Peret Neiru are working together?"

Remiel flinched at the mention of the Celah's sworn adversaries. His gaze dimmed.

"An official alliance is far from certain," he answered her. "Though both parties have well enough reason to do us harm. It may be the Peret have shared their knowledge, hoping the Core will distract us from the true war that waits beneath the veil."

War. To Erae, it felt like she had been at war all her life, but when Remiel uttered the word it carried a different weight. It deadened the breeze, coercing the leaves into a viscous silence.

"Are the Peret … stronger than us?"

"Ah, that depends on how you measure strength. The Peret love power, yes. They hoard it, build it, ever seeking to gain, always dreading to lose that which they have. Unaided, none of us would be a match for even their weakest member.

"But do not fear," he added hastily as he saw Erae's falling expression, "for we are not unaided. We have each other, and we have our King. Eladdiyr's strength to theirs is as light to the darkness, And the Peret are fewer than we, for their might does not like to be shared."

He placed a hand on her shoulder, and she leant into it, drawing warmth from the contact.

"I …" Erae's thought left her, and she closed her eyes. Her worries could wait. She had everything she needed for the moment, and that was enough.

She and Remiel said nothing for a while, each busy tracking their own thoughts, or the movement of the trees, or the feel of the rock underneath their hands. Eventually, Remiel excused himself and left, leaving Erae much the same as she had been before he'd arrived.

Only she wasn't the same. She'd remembered her peace, and it rested upon her questions like a warm blanket, or a cloudless sky. She rose and dusted herself off.

Tomas wouldn't fully recover from the stun bolt for another few hours, which gave Erae time to distract her mind with anything else. Then she would see him, because that's what the Defiant needed her to do.

She prayed her peace would last that long.

The door slid open, and Tomas scowled.

"Go away," he told his visitor. "I'm not answering your questions. You, or anyone else."

"Naturally," Erae sauntered in anyway, a tray of food balanced in her hands and some clothes tucked under one arm. They were his clothes, he realised: his flight suit and underclothes. She placed both loads on the ground, out of his reach. A bowl of beige soup sat on the tray, accompanied by a roll of sprout bread.

Tomas smirked. "Is that the best bribe you have? My own suit and a stale meal?"

Erae matched his smile, shifting her weight to one side. "This meal is fresh from the troop mess and no different from what I had, but this isn't a bribe. For now, I just want you to listen."

"And if I don't listen?" Tomas asked, pulling himself up straighter.

"You don't exactly have many options."

He slammed his cuffs into the floor with a crash, the sound pealing around the room. He'd hoped Erae would flinch, but she only compressed her lips, her eyes boring into him.

"If you seriously think—" He slammed his wrists again, harder.

"*Stop it!*" She kept her voice just shy of a yell. She stepped forward. "Is this your grand escape plan, Commander? Acting like a *child*? Clinging to petty victories while you sit there shivering in your gown?"

"It beats listening to you!" Tomas snapped back, but inside he knew she'd hit the mark. He didn't have much of a plan, not yet. He needed information, and she was offering it, so why was he angering her?

But that didn't mean he could just apologise and play nice, either. The two glared at each other, testing wills.

"Fine," he ground out. "I'll endure your propaganda after I'm fed."

"*While* you're fed," she corrected. "But I need you to do something first."

Oh really? "And what's that?"

"I need you to accept that you're stuck here, at least for now. I can't have you jumping on people's throats every chance you get." She smiled slyly. "It's not like it helped you last time."

He despised her, by the sixth sun he did. He would get out, and he would see her in chains for her crimes. Then, once their positions were reversed, they would have a just discussion, true as core.

"Have it your way," he said.

"And how good is the word of a CSF commander?"

"Better than the word of a degenerate captain."

"We'll see." Erae approached, pulling a key from her pocket and crouching down. He watched as she freed first his feet, then his hands, but he resisted making any move against her. Chains in hand, she retreated past his flight suit and, with a pointed look, slowly turned her back to him.

The nerve of this woman. Tomas considered his options. Erae's holster, he had noticed immediately, was empty. Even if he overpowered her, a quick scream would be all it took to bring the guards rushing in, stun bolts flying. There was a chance he could kill her before then, but what good would that do him?

He huffed loudly, stood, and began to dress. The suit was burnt and ripped in places, but it was clean. His wardrobe change complete, he planted himself on a vac-crate with the tray in his lap. The soup was still warm and actually tasted quite nice. He made sure not to show it on his face when Erae turned back to him.

Relief lined her eyes. Perhaps she hadn't been as confident as he'd thought. She took a seat of her own, pulling it directly in front of the door.

"For millennia," she began. Tomas groaned long.

"Stow it! I promise this is the short version."

I bet it is. Tomas chewed on his bread and let her continue.

"For millennia, the Neiru have shared the story of Eladdiyr with the Cluster. He is an ancient being, wise, good and powerful, and he loves his people dearly. The Neiru serve him and teach us how to live better, fuller lives. The Core didn't interfere with him, and that was that.

"But then the Ebon arrived. They were birthed from darkness, created to destroy, and their masters won't settle for just part of the Cluster. We faced annihilation, but Eladdiyr had a plan to save us. He sent us Ben-Eloah, his Human son. Ben sacrificed himself at the battle of Tachillah, by his death imparting a new strength: Eladdiyr's strength, within our very hearts. And now …"

She paused. "Well, now they're coming back. The Ebon, I mean. And we need to stop them by using the power we've been given. And the Core oppresses its people more and more every day. So when a planet or a colony has had enough, we help them take their lives back.

"That's the simple version, at least. Not that any of it's simple. It, well …" Erae trailed off, gauging Tomas for a response.

Tomas swallowed his latest mouthful. "An immortal king?" he asked.

Erae nodded gently.

"Served by your magic, mind-reading Neiru?"

Another nod. "I wouldn't quite call it magic, and they can do far more than detect lies, but—"

"And his son, his *Human son* Ben-Eloah, saved us from the Ebon Horde. By *dying*."

The Captain hesitated. "Tomas, I—"

"*How, dare, you.*" He stared at her, caught halfway between rage and disbelief. "How dare you take credit for the Ebon's defeat? For the victory my brothers and sisters paid for with their blood? Tell me, Captain, where was your oh-so-powerful king on the day of the final battle?"

"Tomas, it's not like that. It's—"

"Then what is it like?" Tomas had just enough restraint to lay the tray aside before standing up. "Because if your Eladdiyr is as powerful as you claim, why didn't he help? You can't count the number of unmarked graves that orbit Tachillah like sand, but we did!"

He beat his chest. "I counted each one of them right here. But I didn't count your king. And I watched his son fly into the open arms of the enemy. They didn't so much as fire a single bolt at him."

"I know." Erae kept her voice calm, which just made him angrier. "I know what you saw, and I know what you felt."

"You could never know."

"Well I do," she locked eyes with him, looking like she had more to say. But whatever she was thinking remained unvoiced.

"None of this ... insanity explains why you are fighting the CSF," he pointed out. "If you want to believe the Ebon are coming back, then have your fantasy. But leave the Core alone."

"The Rahgese asked us to help them, Tomas. The work bosses were driving them into the ground."

"Then they should have raised an enquiry. There are channels for that sort of thing."

"You don't think they tried?" Erae countered. "Your government claims that peace is here for all the Cluster, yet the same infliction repeats on a thousand worlds. Those who cry out are silenced, those who wish to leave are hunted, and the very being that grows the food is the first to starve. The Core completely ignored Rahga's plight until the fighting started. And when you came, forgive me if I didn't see any of your negotiators or diplomats. I was too busy saving women and children from your golden death troopers."

She backed down, and some of the fire left her eyes. "There were more to save because of you. Thank you."

"Yeah, well don't count on it happening again," Tomas bit out, but the words felt false. Maybe he and Erae weren't so different after all. They were both officers of war, each doing their best to protect people, but one of them had been misled by their leaders, tricked into doing more harm than good.

How would he begin to help her see it? These Neiru were clearly masters at inciting devotion, and the Defiant were eager to comply. He stared at the captain in front of him. She seemed so sure of her path, but that only added to the tragedy.

"When I was ... saving them," he began softly, "my wingman got shot down. Do you know if she ...?"

Erae shook her head. "I didn't see. Your troops were right on top of us. If she was alive, I'm sure they got to her in time."

"Your people shot her," he spoke the words without venom.

"And you shot our pilots. And we destroyed your frigate, and the nobles were starving the locals," she said. "Two thieves in a feud will steal the whole world if you let them."

"*Right.*"

"But it only takes one to give it back." Erae studied him for a moment. He returned the stare, caught again by her beautiful eyes. They reminded him of midnight snow beneath an aurora sky, and of sun-beads during a solar eclipse.

"Tomas," she said at last, "we need to know what was on that disc. We believe it has information about the Ebon and the approaching war. I know you can't retrieve it, but anything you can remember—times, locations, names—could save untold lives."

One of her arms made half a movement, as if she had debated reaching out. "I've talked with the others. We're prepared to let you leave if you tell us what you know."

Tomas' brow furrowed. "Just like that?" It didn't escape him that he had no way to enforce Erae's promise. Once he had fulfilled his half of the bargain, she could easily keep him here to rot.

But he didn't have much choice, and he knew it. Erae knew it too. He closed his eyes, recalling if anything he'd seen could somehow give the Defiant an advantage against the CSF. Nothing.

"Fine," he said. "This is what I know."

15

The roaring engines cut off, reducing the deck's movement to the subtlest vibrations, and Tomas breathed a sigh of overwhelming relief.

He was going home.

Erae had left him in his cell for two days after their conversation. Two days with only her word as assurance that the Defiant would set him free. The guards who had fed him would not speak, ignoring all his questions and demands. He had nearly given up hope when Erae arrived with a quiet smile on her face and a blindfold in her hands.

When he'd been allowed to see again, he was in a dingy cargo hold with rusting walls and sallow lights. They were going on a supply run to the Dragon Scale Nebula, she'd said, and once they docked at the colony station he was free to find passage as he pleased. When the engines had ignited, the whole freighter had felt like it was tearing apart, but now they were silent. Presumably, the freighter had entered the Shift and was cruising at the idle mercy of impossibility, leaving Tomas with silence and thought once again.

And his thoughts unsettled him. *Immortal sorcerers, Ebon schemes, fanatic rebels and an ancient king. All with only a few motes of evidence to prove it.* Yet those motes were there, eating away at Tomas' understanding of the universe. The strange powers of the Neiru were the first, including the vanishing act Tomas had seen in the stolen recording. When Tomas had described the dark beings, Erae had called them Peret Neiru and had been visibly frightened at their mention. They, she said, were the architects of the coming Ebon war.

The CSF would uncover this plot, Tomas decided. If there was any truth to these claims, then the Core would be swift to seek them out and punish any force that came against the peace they had worked so hard to build. And that included the Defiant.

For they were criminals, true as core, and would stand trial for their various crimes. They weren't wholly rot-woven—their actions on Rahga, not the least of which was saving Tomas' life, were proof of that. But those mercies didn't forgive them for their years of rebellion, and he would see that they received the justice due them.

It was his duty, after all.

There wasn't much to entertain him in the hold. On one side, two cargo skiffs were strapped tight to the deck. Three loading bots sat in a rack next to them, all looking in need of a good clean. A wheelbase and telescopic torso comprised the lower half of each robot. Atop this sat the bot's core unit, which included a large wrapping claw made from many joined segments. This claw had its own thruster ring, allowing the bot to detach from the torso as work required.

One of the units had been left on standby, the lights beneath its receptor strip winking on and off in staggered rhythm. Tomas cleared his throat.

"Oi, Bot."

The lights blinked rapidly. "Unit Cee-Zero-Ar-One-Five-Five-Eight activated," it buzzed in a sawtooth monotone. "Awaiting command."

"What sort of places has this freighter been to?"

C0-R1-558 paused. "Unclear inquiry," it droned.

"Uh, access navigation log."

"Missing module: navigation log."

"Access starport records."

"Missing module: starport records."

"Access past cargo manifests"

"Missing module—"

"Alright, disregard." Tomas scratched his head. Was there anything he could ask that would be helpful?

He flinched as a clunk sounded somewhere above him, followed by a rattle of gears and chains. A rail guide had started moving on the far bulkhead, lowering a platform from one of the upper levels.

"Bot, enter standby," Tomas said quickly, hoping the command would be masked by the sound of the lift. The platform was descending fast, and as it approached, he heard singing.

"*There is upon the ocean swell, a music soft and sweet. It laps against the golden soils and welcomes us to sleep.*" The voice had an odd quality to it, the syllables rolling and sloshing down to him as if the cargo hold were filled with water.

"*Dear close your eyes, the night has come. The sun drifts o'er the sea. But don't you cry, don't shed a tear. You're held now by your king.*"

The lift platform descended into view, and on it stood a large grey humanoid, plated from head to foot in what looked like solid rock. Bright red and orange tubes sprouted from the creature's chin like a beard, and larger growths wove together to form two arms and hands. The face was a stone mask with two dark cavities for eyes, and they fixed on Tomas as the lift wheezed to a stop.

"Master Amets," the being gurgled. The voice seemed to ride up from his stomach and out the beard tubes. "I would like to invite you up to the ship proper, now that we are engaged, en route, embarked."

"You're …" Tomas stared up at the thing. It was two heads taller than him, at least. "You're a Qua'seth."

"A pleasure to meet you," it replied. "My name is Marpe."

"An entire community of corals, acting as one realised individual. Amazing."

Marpe tilted its head back and forth—laughter or pleasure, perhaps? With only holes for eyes and no other facial features, expression was impossible to discern. "We aren't so different from your organs, your cells, yourself," he bubbled.

"No," Tomas said, "I suppose not."

"Onto the lift then, Tomas. Unless you wish to sit here for the journey entire, and without food or drink, at that."

There was no reason to disobey. Taking a last look at the loading robot—which had returned to its passive, blinking state—Tomas joined the Qua'seth on the platform. With a press of the controls, the lift began to rise through the levels, and Marpe presently resumed his quiet singing.

"His feet are clad in scales that shine, his crown is set with pearls. And when he speaks it quiets the gales, so trust in him my girl."

"A song of your people?" Tomas ventured.

"What?" Marpe turned with a jolt, as if surprised Tomas was still there. "No, not mine, no. This is a Navan lullaby, taught to me by the captain. Though it does remind me of my own home. Thus, I sing."

The lift eased to a halt beneath a large, open hatch. Marpe climbed up, bowing the edges of the deck with his weight. His legs were covered with the same hard, dead coral as his chest and head, and could only bend along thin seams. It was nearly a full minute before Tomas had the space to squeeze up after him.

"You're kidding," he said when he had picked himself up. Marpe had made his way over a ladder rising from the centre of the room and was pulling himself slowly, rigidly onto the first rung. His head canted towards Tomas.

"Forgive my discourtesy, dishonour, disrespect, Commander; I should let you go first." He began lowering himself back down, the descent taking just as long. "Two decks up, then through the door over your right shoulder."

Tomas raised an eyebrow. "Why do you do that?"

"Sorry?"

"Repeat yourself with different words."

"Ah," Marpe gurgled as he retreated from the ladder, allowing Tomas ahead of him. "Words are puzzling things, beautiful things. Sometimes I disagree on which one to choose. Other times, we choose all of them."

Tomas nodded. It made a sort of sense for a being like Marpe. "You know, one word would save you time."

"Yes, but time—hmm?" Marpe paused as if listening. "Yes, saved like one saves sand with a sieve. Still it runs away." He stood like a statue as he talked. "But he sees it differently, I suppose. Faster or slower for vapour, I wonder?"

"Uh …" Tomas stared into Marpe's eye sockets, feeling oddly excluded from the conversation.

"What? Oh!" The stone head jerked back to life, tilting back and forth as it had before. "Up the ladder, Tomas, Deck Three. You'd better climb, stop wasting time."

"I—sure, whatever." Tomas took the rungs two at a time, if only to assure himself that speed was still possible. He reached his target deck and looked around at the four unmarked doors.

With Marpe as slow as he was, Tomas could easily make trouble for himself. Find the armoury, steal a knife from the galley, stow away, storm the cockpit—he almost felt guilty for *not* trying to leverage an escape. Enemies surrounded him, and the moment he forgot that fact, he would fail both the Cluster and himself.

But Erae had promised to set him free, and Tomas could not jeopardise the knowledge he had gained on trying to add to his fortunes. This ship wasn't one worth the effort of commandeering, anyway.

He approached the door Marpe had mentioned and held his palm to the scanner. When nothing happened, he tried again, then huffed. Of course it wouldn't unlock for him, which meant he'd have to sit here until Marpe lumbered his way up. What else had he expected?

But … no, this wasn't a scanner at all, just a button to release the door. What were these Defiant up to? Every door he'd ever opened had used his I.D. chip, whether it was restricted or not. Tomas hovered his fingers over the release, then pressed down.

The door slid to the side, rattling slightly. Beyond was a short, dim passage and a second door. Tomas walked through and opened it. The room that followed was a misshapen semicircle with two large weave-glass viewports set in the bending outer hull. A long sitting divan rode this wall, covered in red reptile skin, and before it sat a low table of mist-stained wood. A painted cloth hung down one of the internal bulkheads, depicting a wild ocean vista below a blue sky. A faded planet took up most of this sky, kissed by the spray from the tallest waves.

From his right, he heard the sound of a door releasing its seal. He turned towards the noise to see the girl Amarie step into the room, a ration bar poking halfway out of her mouth. She froze when she saw him, her eyes wide, then she rushed forward and snatched an ornament from the table.

"Wait!" Tomas ducked as she hurled the object at his head, stepping to keep the table between them. "Marpe told me to come here!"

Amarie tore the ration from her mouth. "Can you do anything but lie?"

"I swear it!"

"Why?"

"I don't know!" Tomas raised his hands, palms open. "Maybe because he's *nice*?"

Amarie sized him up, probably calculating how quickly he could react if she launched across the table at him. She wanted revenge for her humiliation in the prison cell, he could see. Tomas wasn't about to let her, but if they fought now, what would happen to his chances of getting home?

Slowly, fighting every instinct in his body, he lowered himself to his knees and put his hands behind his head. Amarie scowled at him, emerald eyes flaring.

"Stay there," she ordered, backing towards the door Tomas had come in. It opened as she reached it, and she bumped into a wall of grey coralstone.

"Wonderful," Marpe leaned into the room. "You two are already getting acquainted."

She looked up at him. "Marpe, what were you thinking? He's a prisoner, not a tourist."

"Commander Amets is our guest. I thought—" He held out a hand as she tried to squeeze past him. "I thought …" She tried the other side, with the same result.

"Get out of my way!"

"I thought," Marpe said, "that you could keep him company. I'm afraid my mind moves to quite a different current, tide, stride."

"You're joking." Tomas and Amarie said in unison. Marpe's head swayed in delight, but Amarie swivelled to him with a glare.

"I am *not* babysitting this CSF pit-scraper."

Said the bratty child to the decorated soldier, Tomas thought, but held his tongue. She caught enough of it by his expression, anyway.

Marpe wasn't moving. "Isolation withers the soul," he said. "I should know, for mine is shared. What? Yes, the planets. What good are they unbound from their sun? They sequester, wander in void; cold and death their path, peril, doom. But gravity draws us ever in, and as the stars … "

"Enough! I get it!" Amarie threw up her hands in defeat. Tomas edged to the side as she rounded the table and planted herself on the divan. Tomas hesitated, then rose from his knees and sat on the far end. Marpe closed the door but remained standing.

The seat was softer than he anticipated. Short hairs grew from the gaps in the reptilian scales. Was this the hide of a natural or an engineered creature? He'd have to research it when he got back to base.

And that can't happen fast enough. I'd rather be anywhere than on this ship. He and Amarie could agree on that much. He wasn't here to make friends, and the sooner they dropped him off at whatever fringe-side station they were going to, the better.

Tomas glanced over at her, her hair a blazing silhouette against the darkness of the Shift out the viewport behind her. She was too young to be getting wrapped up in all this mystical nonsense. Or maybe he was too old. Most fighter pilots died in their first two years, and he'd been flying for over a decade. But there was something in the taste of it he couldn't walk away from. When he flew, he felt as young as Gerad and Quil, true as core.

"Finished staring?" Amarie spat at him.

"Sorry," Tomas looked down at the table. "I was just thinking that girls your age shouldn't be gallivanting around on the whim of an ancient, magical king."

She rolled her eyes. "I saw a cute advert on my tome-tile. Rebellion's the flavour of the month, you know."

"I was being serious."

"I don't give a fifth limb if you're serious. I—" A damp rumble inside Marpe's chest cut her off. She sighed.

"What I *meant* to say is, not everything about Eladdiyr makes sense to me. The Neiru don't exactly speak in plain sentences. But he's powerful and kind, and offering us all a better, freer life. That's more than Councillor Duidain's ever done for me. Him, or anyone else."

"You trust these Neiru beings?" Tomas asked.

"I trusted *her*," Amarie said, faltering slightly. Tomas reddened. He had forgotten why she was so angry with him.

"Commander Amets," Marpe offered, "Amarie is a starfighter pilot just like you, did you know?"

"Really?" Tomas said. "You can fly?"

"Better than you," Amarie quipped, raising her chin. Whatever pain she'd shown was once again hidden behind a mask. "If I'd been in the sky a minute sooner at Rahga, I could have taken on your whole squad. As it was, I got one and you didn't even penetrate my shields."

Tomas blinked. "You were the pilot of the cloaked starfighter?"

"The *Silver Comet*. Thanks to you I had to leave it on Rahga. Your CSF buddies probably had it for scrap."

Tomas couldn't believe it. Here he was, sitting beside Ernn's killer, trying to play nice and make friends. A red whirlpool began to twist inside his stomach. How had he been deceived, for even a moment, that the Defiant were good people? Justice would come for every one of them, at his hand, if he could help it. They may have saved him, but one act of mercy did not outweigh a lifetime of treachery.

"You killed my friend," he said at last.

"And you killed more of mine," Amarie shot back. "Or did you forget that part?"

"Nothing more than you all deserve," Tomas said. "You can run around the Cluster, breaking laws and waging wars, but justice will always prevail."

"Commander, please," Marpe said. "Amarie … "

"Justice?" Amarie laughed. "Give me a break. You don't know the first thing about justice."

She levelled a gloved finger at him. He'd seen Erae wearing a similar pair. "How many people have you killed? Not Ebon—*people*: pirates, criminals, Partisans. Peace costs many lives, doesn't it, Commander? Only you aren't the ones paying. We are. The Rahgese are."

"That was misinformation," Tomas defended himself. "I tried to tell them." Yes, he killed people as a pilot, but only as a last resort, after every other measure had been spent. Sometimes evil had to be solved directly. He was proud to be part of that solution.

I'm not above making mistakes. I'm also not above doing whatever it takes.

Amarie stood. "You think justice comes out the barrel of a CP-10? Fine, 'cause I've got rounds to spare. Erae talks of the king's mercy and forgiveness. Well he's got vengeance too, and I'll give you a taste if you ever come after us again.

"Forgiveness ..." she shook her head in dismissal. "Erae told me to apologise for accusing you of killing Epieta. But you *would* have killed her if you'd known who she was. You'd have killed me too."

Tomas thought about it. "I'd have captured you."

"And when I fought back?"

She wasn't going to scare him with the truth. She certainly wasn't going to condemn him. "Yes," he answered. "I would have killed you."

Amarie's stance changed—relaxed, almost. "Well then I am sorry," she said, walking past Marpe to the door. She keyed the release. "I'm sorry you'll never get the chance."

The door closed behind her, leaving Tomas without the satisfaction of the final word. He wasn't sure what he'd have said. He stared at the bulkhead for a while, trying to decide how he should feel.

In a way, Amarie had surprised him, but only because she was exactly what he had expected the Defiant to be: idealist fanatics raging against the established order and setting the Cluster on fire.

But Erae, Raphael and Marpe were a different breed of rebel, one he didn't yet know how to define. That made them more dangerous in his eyes, despite the kindness with which they'd treated him.

And amongst all of this, they're taking me home, just in exchange for what I knew about the Peret Neiru. Tomas sighed and turned to Marpe.

The Qua'seth's head was swaying softly back and forth.

"Waste of time," Tomas told him.

16

Erae watched from her console as Tomas walked out the airlock and down the ramp. The Commander looked over his shoulder with every second step, and once he was on the ground he stood and stared back at the *Empress*.

[You should have blindfolded him again.] Driz tutted from his chair beside her. [He'll make a report of the ship.]

Erae kept her eyes on the monitor. The image was too small to see any expression. After a moment more, the miniature Tomas turned and walked away.

[Captain?]

"We couldn't," Erae said, shutting off the feed. She stretched. "People would wonder. The CSF presence here is pretty lax, but a kidnapping is difficult to ignore."

Driz gave a contracted snuffle. [Won't he turn us in?]

"Not yet. He has some sense of honour." She set about shutting down most of the ship's functions. It would raise suspicion if they launched this soon after docking. "He'll make his report back at the capital; from then on, it's fair game. I just pray we opened his eyes a little."

[Only Eladdiyr knows.]

Erae nodded absentmindedly. She still wasn't sure what to feel about Tomas, but he wasn't her problem anymore, and she needed to focus on the next one. And this … this was a monster. She finished the shutdown and keyed the intercom.

"Crew to the lounge. Repeat, crew to the lounge. Crisp, you free?"

Driz hopped off his chair and pattered to the ladder while she waited. Eventually, a sharp voice broke across the comm.

"I can detach, but if my readings are correct, that waterlogged luddite of ours shut the hatch on me. If you care for efficiency, you will descend and operate it."

Erae smiled knowingly. That was about the closest Crisp ever came to asking for help. "No, it's all right," she replied. "Just stay on the comm. This won't take too long."

"*On the comm*? I see my value is revealed once again. One with the furniture, out with the refuse dump."

"Oh, do stop, you'll hurt my feelings," Erae chided. "Besides, you might just be the most important part of this mission."

That shut Crisp up, at least long enough for Erae to swing herself onto the ladder. The speakers crackled again as she climbed down.

"I require more certain terminology, Captain," Crisp said. "Am I the most important or not?"

"You might just might be," Amarie answered for her from the lounge's comm panel. Erae passed through the doors and grinned at her. They left the panel active and sat next to each other on the divan. The viewport shutters were closed, blocking out any passing eyes from the station hangar. This meeting wasn't for public consumption.

They waited as Marpe arrived and stood on the table's far side. Driz could be heard ferreting around in the galley, and he eventually waddled out with a bulb of jolt in each hand. He hoisted himself onto the divan, and Erae could begin. She sent a silent prayer to Eladdiyr.

Aloud, she said, "I trust everyone reviewed the information Tomas gave us?"

Everyone nodded. "Good. Are there any questions?"

"Is it reliable?" Crisp asked through the comm.

"Remiel believes so. Tomas doesn't think the Peret have anything to do with the Core, so he had no reason to deceive us."

"Does that mean the Peret *do* have a deal with the Core?" Amarie asked.

"Depends who you ask in High Command," Erae said. "The debate hasn't changed since the Ebon lost the Great Invasion. It doesn't matter much anyway; we still have two evils to face."

"I guess." Amarie reached for the bulb Driz hadn't drunk from, but he squeaked and snatched it from the table just in time. He glared at her and cradled the beverage to his chest, still sucking on the other bulb. "So how do we fit in?"

Erae leaned forward, her stomach bubbling. "Tomas said the Peret are going to Shbiy IX. We're going to meet them there."

The room stared at her.

"We're *what?*" Amarie cried. She gripped Erae's arm. "Meeting with the Peret Neiru?"

"Sorry, bad choice of words," Erae corrected rapidly. "They're meeting. We're watching the meeting. Spying. We're spying, sorry."

[That's not much better.] Driz said.

"They'll kill us!" Amarie said.

"The night that lurks beneath the waves; they shall consume and snare both mind and soul," Marpe added helpfully.

"Just … hold on," Erae prised Amarie off her arm. "They won't even know we're there. If we want to know what their plan is, this is what we must do."

"I need details," Amarie demanded. She was scared to the point of anger. "Now."

Erae nodded. "Gabriel meditated towards Shbiy," she began. "He has foreseen a convergence of evil on one of the packing houses, so the guess is that's where they're meeting. Tomas couldn't recall the date of the recording, so we don't know when they're going to arrive. Our plan is to set up cameras and observe from the ship."

"In and out?"

"In and out," she promised. "We'll be resupplying while we're there, so the port authorities have no reason to suspect us. I've also asked Captain Ira and the *Avail* to stand by if the unexpected happens. As for the packing house, we have a friend they wouldn't suspect even if they wanted to."

"Joy beyond calculation," Crisp buzzed sarcastically over the speaker. "My true worth is shown at last."

Erae laughed. "You wanted to be valued. This is your big chance."

But Amarie didn't look assured. Her last infiltration had ended in disaster, and now the stakes were even higher. The CSF she could handle, but the lords of the Ebon? The reality of this war was dawning on them all.

"Is this really happening?" she asked.

"Yes, Am, it is."

"Aren't you scared?"

Erae was terrified.

"Eladdiyr is our strength," she told the girl. "And I'll be right beside you the whole time." What good it would do if the Peret somehow caught them, she didn't say. Amarie had heard all the same stories she had. The Ebon were a light wind in comparison with their masters.

And Amarie wasn't the only one who had failed her last mission. Amarie wasn't the only one who had stood by as the people they loved died.

It took Tomas all of four minutes to locate the nearest CSF guard post. Convincing the officer on duty that the bedraggled, unshaven Human before her was actually a ranking Commander of the Fleet took much longer. Dragon Scale Station, it turned out, rarely bothered with I.D. scanners, and his flight suit looked like he had stolen it off a corpse. A second guard had to go ferreting through storage while Tomas argued.

Eventually the scanner was found, and the guards appropriately chastised. Tomas made a note to request a full audit of the regiment once he was home. In the meantime, he had much more important things to report. He sent a brief but detailed packet through the guard's encrypted Fal-Comm booth—not that he trusted any encryption sent from this floating junk jumble—and settled in to wait.

Live calls were impossible on Fal-Comm, as it took hours for a message to travel through the Shift. Tomas was trying his best to sleep on a couch in the guard's lounge when the reply came through.

"Eeeee!" Sigsby's bright yellow lens filled the screen as he opened the message. "You are alive! I knew you had not lost function yet. Keep a hand on your yoke Commander, I will have a shuttle embarked for the nebula in one hour, true as the Core. Your squadron will be elated. Sigsby out."

Relief poured into Tomas, and he felt tears in his eyes. Until now he hadn't realised how doubtful he'd been that he'd ever see his friends again. He had survived the crash, but in a way it had stuck with him like a delayed sentence. At any moment, the Defiant could have settled the debt, but now he was free, true as core, and nothing could dampen the moment.

There were a few hours left until the shuttle arrived, so Tomas set about cleaning himself up. After a shower and a shave, he headed to the plaza for a meal. He thought about changing from his ripped and charred flight suit, but it was a survivor of the journey as much as he was. He pressed a thumb against the pin on his collar.

It wasn't until the shuttle had collected him and he was almost back at Gerduk that he considered what he might be coming home *to*. His General, whom he had failed. Captain Forn, whom he had disobeyed …

And Quil. Would she be there at all?

She has to be. If I made it through all this, then so did she. It was more a demand than a logical reason, but it was all Tomas could summon. He left his seat as the shuttle entered one of the launch tubes. Guide lights blurred past the viewports as they descended, pulsing along the cabin bulkheads. He stood by the rear exit ramp, one hand bracing for when the landing gear touched down.

With a hiss of hydraulics, the ramp lowered to the ground, revealing a familiar hangar half-full of grey and orange Wasps that sat in eerie shadow under the hangar's emergency lights. It was the middle of the night, apparently.

Tomas' heart fell. He hadn't expected to be welcomed like the Chief of Council with all his pomp, but he'd at least hoped someone would have been around to gasp and stare. Even a mechanic on his lunch break would have sufficed.

The rings didn't stop turning while I was away. He spurred his feet down the ramp, his boots ringing on the metal. When he reached the deck, in comparison, the sound was barely heard. *You're home,* it seemed to say, *get on with it.*

As he passed the last row of starfighters, he caught sight of two figures lurking inside one of the corridors. They were leaning close together against the wall but straightened when they saw him. One turned and bolted down the corridor and around the corner, but the other stepped forward into the light.

Memiele smiled.

"Commander—" was all she managed before Tomas sprinted into her, wrapping her in a fierce hug. He quickly remembered his place and broke off, but she wouldn't let him go, something between a sob and a laugh catching in her throat. Eventually, they separated and she wiped her huge, Dabanian eyes.

"Welcome home, Commander."

"Thanks, Mem. What were you doing waiting here?"

"We didn't know when you'd arrive." Memiele blushed and glanced downwards. "Klord and I were on scout duty."

The deck shuddered. Someone was coming. Tomas looked down the corridor to the corner. *Many* someones. The sound of running feet was joined by a long, rising yell in a very familiar voice.

"*Coooo-mmaaaann-ddeeeerr!* Dan shot around the corner, his momentum nearly crashing him into the far wall. Then he was heading straight for Tomas, arms open. Memiele hurriedly backed away, but Tomas planted his feet ready for impact, grinning broadly.

Dan still nearly bowled him over, and when the rest of the squadron rounded the corner, Tomas had no chance. Gerad was next, then Klord, then Teliac and his four crushing arms. Tomas quickly surrendered the right to breathe, and then to stand. Down they went to the sound of Memiele's tumbling laughter. Somehow they disentangled themselves without loss of life or limb, then someone grabbed his hand and pulled him to his feet. His eyes found her face and the world stopped.

"You're alive."

Quil responded by pulling him in, which caused a second round of hugs from everyone. Tomas held them all tight, in his mind vowing never to let go again. The Defiant could go to the pits for all he cared, and Erae and Eladdiyr and the Ebon with them. None of that mattered now.

"I don't think I've ever seen Teliac hug someone before," Gerad joked as they separated.

"And you shall not again if you—tch—value your eyes," Teliac replied, but his tone lacked menace.

"Take 'em. I'll still fly better than Dan."

"Kech-dung you will! Back of the line, rookie!"

Tomas shook his head, smiling. "Nothing's changed, has it?"

"Of course not!" Dan said. "And you're stuck with us until Marduk stops shining, so get used to it."

"Actually," Klord said, "there have been a change of significance." He gestured towards Quil.

"That's dangerous territory, Five," she said.

Tomas raised an eyebrow.

"How is it d—oh!" Klord broke off as Memiele elbowed him in the ribs. Her face was red. The rest of the squadron was waiting intently.

Quil sighed, flashed Tomas a sheepish smile, then belted in a sharp voice:

"Squadron, ay-ten-shun!"

The team snapped straight, their arms at their sides and huge grins on their faces. Gerad was snickering.

"Commander Amets needs his rest, and we have a flight drill in the morning. You are dismissed."

"*Ma'am, yes ma'am!*" the Dirks shouted in unison and, with a series of sloppy turns, began marching back down the corridor. Tomas felt a flutter inside as he suddenly caught on.

"Did you …" He looked at her rank slides. Each had two thick red stripes below a black star.

"Commander Quil."

"Commander *Caron*," she corrected with a wink. "I do have a last name."

"Congratulations."

"I'm not sure I deserve it."

"I'm sure you do," Tomas said. He'd seen Quil come so far, and he couldn't be prouder, both as her commander and friend. That was why he'd recommended the promotion to General Niyott. To see her receive it, safe and alive against all hope, was …

It was awful. Tomas' joy evaporated as the instant of his betrayal—not of the CSF but of *her*—filled his mind once again.

I could have killed her. I chose to risk her life and mine. What can she think of me for that? How can she forgive me?

Quil must have seen the change in his expression. She gently took his wrist, searching his eyes. He dropped them, not wanting to let her see.

"Quil …" he began.

"You need sleep," she said. "And food. Come on. I'll tell the General she can debrief you tomorrow."

"But …"

"Later, Commander." Her tone sharpened slightly, and he stopped. She led him along the corridor, a soft grip on his arm the whole time. He didn't fight her, though he felt that putting the meeting off would only make things worse.

He was finally home, but the joy he had hinged his hopes upon these past days was eclipsed by shame. Quil was right: he *was* tired, and his mind was exaggerating the problem. He needed to sleep in his own cot, in an oblivion his confusion and fear couldn't enter. Then, in the morning, he would make sense of it all.

And he would find the words to apologise, even though words would undoubtedly fall short.

"I'll have something sent from the mess," Quil said as they arrived at his room. She reached for the palm scanner, but he got there first. He could do this much on his own. The door slid open.

"Thanks, Quil."

"Always." The grip lingered on his wrist, then disappeared. "It's good to have you back, Tomas."

He smiled. "I couldn't abandon you to Dan and Gerad, could I?"

The joke felt flat, but Quil laughed and shook her head.

"Until tomorrow, Commander."

"Until tomorrow." Tomas watched as she walked away, her braid swaying behind her. She was too good to him, he knew. It would have crushed her had she shot the Rahgese, only to learn of their innocence. Tomas had saved her from that.

Yes, tomorrow would be better. He would make sure of it.

17

Erae had known the mission to Shbiy IX would have its risks, but she'd still hoped she could get both feet out of the airlock before encountering them. As it was, she'd only placed one boot on the ramp when she tripped and nearly tumbled off the side. She caught herself in time, biting off a yell as her left leg slammed into the *Empress'* hull. She scrambled back onto the ramp and lay for a moment, cursing her blunder. A passing pilot stopped to look at her, but a challenging stare sent him on his way.

"Rae?" Amarie stepped onto the ramp, a kit bag slung around one shoulder. "What happened?"

"Nothing." Erae checked herself. Her leg throbbed where she'd hit it, but otherwise she was okay. "The gravity threw me off, that's all."

Shbiy IX was the largest satellite orbiting the swollen gas giant called Shbiy. Its gravity was eight-tenths of a standard world's—quite bearable, so long as you watched your footing. The moon was wreathed in spindly, wind-bent forests and grassy plains, and the sharp smell of sap was almost enough to overpower the nauseating fumes of the gas refineries.

Gas was the system's primary concern, but it wasn't harvested directly from the planet like one might expect. Rather, gas farmers herded and bred swarms of bloated, membranous creatures called groons. These groons rode the winds within Shbiy by converting the atmosphere into a propellent, which the farmers refined and sold as fuel. The forests seemed to thrive on the repugnant by-product that belched from the chimney stacks, but it set Erae's eyes watering.

The midday sun didn't help, for wherever Erae looked, a hull or building was ready to reflect the light into her face. Fortunately, it wouldn't last. Shbiy IX was tidally locked with its parent planet, one side forever facing the glowing orange sphere. At their current longitude, the sight took up most of the western horizon, and the sun—Shb—was only a few hours from disappearing behind it. Then planet and moon would go dark, and Erae's mission would begin.

"Next!" A Human port inspector had approached the bottom of the ramp, his eyes glued to his tome-tile, an I.D. scanner in his other hand. His gut spilt out the front of his untucked shirt, and he wiped his mouth on his sleeve before squinting up at them. He peered closer when he saw Erae was sitting.

"Need th' … medic?" He said the last word as if it was foreign to him.

"I'm fine, thanks," Erae said sharply, refusing Amarie's hand as she got to her feet. Her leg protested as she put her weight on it, but she managed to keep her face straight as she limped down the ramp. She'd take a stim later.

The inspector looked her up and down, then did the same with Amarie, who kept a hand just shy of her holster. His skin was blotched and oily, and even when he wasn't speaking his mouth never fully closed.

"Th' Port Vilspire welcomes you and yours," he drawled. "Are th' sweetins here for pleasure or work?"

Erae crossed her arms pointedly. The inspector's face split in an ugly grin.

"Work it is. Manifest?"

"We're empty. Looking to collect." As Erae said this, a low hum caught her attention. Driz had piloted one of the skiffs out of the cargo hold and was bringing it around. He had the loading bots with him. Dust skittered out from the skiff's thruster ring.

The inspector wiped his mouth and nodded. "Right it is. Three for th' scanning, and three for th' toll. That's … ninety Draik." He tucked his tile under one arm and held the scanner out.

"Actually," Erae checked no other inspectors were nearby before reaching into her coat. If she had read this man incorrectly, they would have to move fast.

She pulled out two gold coins edged in red. "I think we'll skip the scan."

The inspector's eyes lit up as soon as he saw the coins, each of which had one hundred Draik downloaded into it. He chuckled darkly.

"I shoulda known, I should." He made his own, much more obvious check of the surroundings. "Pleasure *and* work. Colour of spoil, you are."

Erae frowned. "Excuse me?"

"Ya blue, sweetin'!" He jabbed the scanner towards her stomach, forcing her back. "A mutt, and living up to th' name. An-i-mal." He licked his lips. "Not that I'd turn down a good thing."

"Watch your mouth!" Amarie took a step, but Erae shook her head.

"Don't worry about me," she said. "You're the one who shares a species with him."

"Oof, a mortal blow, that," he replied. "Four hundred Draik and I'll forget it."

"Three." Erae forced a frown, but inside she felt her anxiety lift.

"Three-half."

"Done." Erae pulled out two more coins—one red and one blue—and he snatched them up with surprising speed.

"Pleasure, sweetin'. Like I said." He entered a command into his tile. "Looks like this bay is closed for maint'nance. No ship, no scans." With a final wipe of the mouth, he lumbered away to the next waiting ship.

Amarie pulled a face at his back. "Do you think he was part Gitorian or part Raan Jey?" she asked.

[Rann Jey] Driz chittered from the skiff. [His skin was wet like a slug.]

"I think he's revolting all on his own," Erae said, "but he kept us off the record. That's what we wanted." She tried to ignore that he had been right. She was living up to the mongrel stereotype, and bribing spaceport security was only the beginning. She prayed it would be worth it.

Erae took a stim for her pain, then the women loaded onto the skiff, and Driz drove them towards the commercial district. By the time they arrived, the sun had kissed the edge of Shbiy's banded atmosphere, and what had been a bright day was now swamped in orange gloom. It would have been beautiful anywhere but in the city, where the smog thickened the light and the factories cast huge shadows. But the Peret Neiru hadn't picked their meeting place for beauty.

"Alright, Driz," she said. "Try to be quick with supplies. And nothing umbral; we can get weapons on a different trip."

[Aye, Captain. I've got the list.] He halted the skiff and let them off. [Quick now, Crisp.]

One of the loading robots wheeled off the skiff's bed. "This terrain is hardly suitable for—"

"Shush!" Erae held a hand over Crisp's grill. "Not a word more, or we'll really be in it." She looked around, but those passing by were too busy with the market to hear anything.

Amarie tugged her shoulder and pointed. "Surplus store. Should have the uniforms we need."

"Right, good." Erae tapped Crisp's head. "Just … stay here a minute more. And keep quiet."

Crisp didn't respond, but its lights flashed in a way she took to mean irritation. Having a Shell in the crew was a wonderful asset, and one who delighted in breaking the Automaton Laws even more so. Crisp had dwelt in all manner of constructs since she'd known it, and none of them had been humanoid.

But Crisp was also the team's biggest grumbler, and nothing heated its coils like the slow inefficiencies of sentient lifeforms. When Erae and Amarie returned fifteen minutes later—now dressed in brown packers' uniforms with boots and hardhats—Crisp's lights were strobing at record speeds. It might have wheeled around or snapped its claw, if only those actions weren't a waste of charge.

"I know, I know." Erae skirted past it and popped a service panel off one of the other loading bots. "I said one minute." Digging her hand in, she scraped up some grime and smeared it on her coverall. Amarie did the same, even adding some to her face and hair. Infiltration was Amarie's world, and she had both feet in.

[Eladdiyr guide us,] Driz said when they were done. [You two look destined for trouble.]

Amarie smiled sweetly. "We *are* the trouble," she said.

Until the Peret arrive, at least. Erae kept the thought to herself, and with a confident nod the trio headed out. The crowds and lantern-lit shop awnings swiftly gave way to industrial warehouses and floodlit depots. For every ship that rose from its pad, another took its place, welcomed by a small army of workers and robots. It was a kingdom built of vac-crates and sun-steel, and Erae was a glaring intruder.

A dozen facilities were passed before they reached their destination. Workers were moving in and out of the warehouse lot at leisure, heads down, uniforms dirty, minds busy with the next job card, or thoughts of lunch, or why they were docked an hour's pay for being two minutes late to the scanners. With a few nods and glances, Erae and Amarie were in.

"That'll be the offices there," Amarie murmured, angling a finger while keeping her hand by her side. Her head barely moved as she took in her surroundings. "Not too many cameras. Warehouse ... hmm, there should be an accessway to service those conveyors from the refinery, but are they on the inside or ..."

She led them to the shadowed side of the office building, keeping her gait casual. Most of the workers were either unloading the trucks parked under the conveyor belts or loading the ships docked on the far side. The Defiant had scrounged the People's Archive and found some promotional stills of the warehouse interior, but that was the extent of their information.

For now, at least. Amarie studied the wall for a moment, then took out her flick knife and cut a small hole in the polyplex. She pulled a cable from one of Crisp's secret compartments and connected it to the wires she had exposed. The Shell swivelled around to block the hole with its body.

"Schematics, cameras, lights, guards," Amarie whispered, dropping her kit bag and pulling out some tools. "Control if you can, information if you can't. And don't trip any alarms, or we're all scorched."

The faintest voice came from Crisp's grill. "I am not *Human*," he buzzed. "Failure is not in my parameters."

"Just hurry up." Using her tools, Amarie started unsheathing the servo-motors on Crisp's claw. Erae watched them with one eye while the other tried not to stare at the distant workers.

"Talk to me, Rae." Amarie didn't look up from her task.

"About what?"

"Anything. Husband, kids, your upcoming vacation on Shbiy VII."

"*Oh.*" Erae forced herself to relax. "Uh ... family's good. I've been hanging out with my sister recently. She's as stubborn as a sleeping kech, but I love her."

Amarie smiled and rolled her eyes. "I hate *my* sister," she said, pretending to tighten one of Crisp's gears.

"Really? What about her?"

"Lousy pilot. Lousy cook. But worst of all is her snoring."

Erae swivelled in shock. "I don't snore!" she exclaimed.

"Rae..." Amarie inclined her head.

"Sorry." Erae lowered her voice. If Amarie wanted to play games, that was fine.

"If you hate your sister so much," Erae said wryly, "will she be invited to the wedding?"

"What wedding?"

"Why, yours and Michael's, of course."

Amarie jumped back as the gears pinched her finger, swearing aggressively. Her face was flushed, and Erae had no trouble guessing why.

Michael was the greatest warrior of the Celah Neiru, and if he didn't have ethereal skin and coruscating eyes, he could have been ripped straight from an army recruitment poster. He wasn't often on the Shard, but Amarie always knew when the Neiru arrived, as did a great many other of the female Defiant members.

The Celah was tall and handsome, with a chiselled face and a voice so sweet it might have been foxvine nectar. His wispy white hair—which Amarie just adored and had gushed to Erae about on more than one occasion—was usually tied in a short ponytail behind his head.

Erae admitted her own heart had skipped a beat upon first meeting the legend. But if she was honest, she'd rather admire that ivory spear he carried around.

"Like I said," Amarie growled when she had stopped swearing, "I *despise* my older sister."

Erae ignored the jab. "When did you last see him?" she asked.

"I didn't *see* him, okay? I *saw* him. There's a difference. It's not like I even talked to him."

"When?"

"Right before he went into the meeting with the others."

Erae thought back, but she hadn't been in any meetings with Michael recently. "Which others?"

"Remiel, Raphael and Gabriel, of course." Amarie freed herself again and counted fingers. "Uriel, Techinnah, Saraqael, Raguel, Hadaria ..."

"*All of them?*" Erae couldn't believe it. She'd never heard of all twelve Neiru— eleven, she corrected with a pang of grief—meeting in the same place. They were usually spread across the entire Cluster.

Amarie's expression repeated the question she'd asked back on the ship. *Is this really happening?* Erae's answer, unfortunately, was the same.

"If you are finished," Crisp said, its voice low, "there is an external stairwell at the rear of the warehouse that leads to the catwalks and conveyors. I can copy the signal frequency to disable the lights."

"Cameras?" Erae asked. Amarie pulled the cable out of the wall, then started reattaching the plating on Crisp's claw.

"Yes, but also no. The monitoring network has been entirely shut down. I cannot deduce the —"

"*You! There!*"

Erae jumped around as someone half shouted, half roared across the lot at them. A Gitorian was lumbering their way, a foreman's sash across his scaly green chest.

Erae's hand reached for her gun, then remembered it was in the kit bag with her other clothes. Amarie kept putting Crisp together.

"Why aren't you lugs lugging crate with the rest?" The foreman stopped just short of Erae and towered over her. Gitorians were a bulky reptilian race with ridged foreheads and protruding jaws. A wing was folded up behind each shoulder blade, and while their brains weren't as developed as other sentient species, their claws and tempers more than compensated.

"Just fixin' this bot, boss." Amarie flicked her gaze up for only a moment. Erae nodded her agreement.

The foreman growled. "Repairs in the repair hut."

"Yeah, that's where we came from. I wanted to test it with a proper load, but the claw seized before we got there. It'll be right in a few."

His eyes narrowed, and Erae held her breath. They said Gitorians had trouble recognising one Human from the other, and it was quite dark, but Erae wasn't exactly Human. His nostrils flared, blowing hot air across her forehead.

Eventually he leaned back. "One minute," he said. "Not few. Then back on the crates."

"Yes sir," Erae said. The foreman grunted once, then walked away.

"Am?"

"I'm nearly done," Amarie replied. "We'll make our move when the shift changes over."

"Sound's good. Until then, I suppose we have to do our jobs." Erae paused.

"Well … sort of."

18

"Watch it!" Tomas shoved his yoke forward, diving under the stream of plasma fire. He ducked as the Wasp responsible roared in from behind, far too close for comfort.

"Scourge-spawn!" he exclaimed. "We're not here to simulate collisions, Seven." He finished his forward loop to come out on what would have been Gerad's tail, but the younger pilot had already banked to the left. Tomas followed suit.

"I'm careful, I'm careful," was the response that crackled over the comm. It was a private channel, as the other Dirks were all paired up in skirmishes of their own. Each Wasp's plasma cannons had been tuned to their lowest power—no more impactful than a dart of light. But you couldn't fine-tune a starfighter collision.

Attitude thrusters blasting on full, Tomas cut speed and rotated towards his target, keenly aware of the space around him and any additional foes that might be within scanning range. There were none of course, but it was a matter of habit to check. It was also habit that added little pivots and speed fluctuations to Tomas' manoeuvre to keep from presenting an easy target. More often than not, it was the unseen enemy that killed you.

Gerad was ahead in his curve but needed to execute a complete turn-around to bring his guns to bear. Tomas only had to track Gerad's turn, and it wasn't long before his crosshairs were trailing just behind Dirk Seven's distant silhouette.

He swore as his quarry suddenly threw all acceleration into reverse. He slammed his fingers on their triggers, but the shining blue bolts went wide as his rotation took him past Gerad's Wasp much quicker than expected.

Knowing he couldn't reverse his spin before his rival shot him down, Tomas slammed an open palm into his acceleration lever, sticking him to the back of his chair as his inertial sink struggled to shunt the force away.

An alert flashed across his visor, indicating a simulated drop in aft shield strength. Gerad had scored a few glancing hits on Tomas' tail, and now his blip on the radar banked to starboard as he prepared to finish the job.

He wouldn't find the win that easily. Hoping Seven was out of range and would remain so for the next few seconds, Tomas pulled back on his yoke and began to climb. By the time Tomas approached the apex, Gerad was already rising to meet him—or diving, depending on the view.

The void lit up with azure rain as Dirk Seven hammered his opponent's forward shields. Tomas grimaced as his simulated shield rapidly lost power, as told by the numbers on his dash.

Alright Gerad, watch and learn. Tomas fired his Wasp into reverse, waited half a second, then stopped reversing and put all power into his ventral-stern and dorsal-bow thrusters.

Gerad, as Tomas hoped, had seen the initial deceleration and thought Tomas was slowing to catch Gerad in front of him. He corrected course, only to find himself passing behind as Tomas kept his original momentum and rapidly flipped head-over-tail. Tomas lit up his cannons, raking energy along Dirk Seven's canopy. Gerad dipped away, but Tomas reignited his main engines and gave chase. Two seconds later, his computer beeped with the cheerful tone of a confirmed kill.

"How close?" Gerad did not sound pleased as both pilots brought their ships around and matched velocity.

Tomas released his breath and lifted his visor to wipe away the sweat on his forehead. "Eighteen per cent left on my forward shields, Seven," he said, "And twelve on my dorsals. You made me work for it."

"Not hard enough, apparently." Gerad was despondent.

"Hey now, the rings weren't built before dinner," Tomas assured him. "You're improving every day."

"That doesn't mean much if I can't win."

"We don't fight to win. We fight because we'd rather lose our lives to death than to fear."

"… it's a training match, Lead."

"I know." Tomas looked at his screen, which still showed the words "Kill Confirmed" in bright red. He also saw his fuel was getting low.

He broadened his frequency. "Finish this round, Dirks, then head back to base. I'll see you there." He dropped to Gerad's wing and let the younger man guide the pair of them home.

Military exercises were conducted a short distance from Kaldea Prime, keeping the planet between them and the shift gate. Civilians had no reason to be out that way, and it was only a ten-minute flight by point drive back to the military moon.

It was a relief to be flying again, and a greater relief to fly with a clear head. There was a lot on Tomas' mind, and while some of it would be laid down once he was debriefed, he wouldn't truly be able to put the past weeks behind him until Erae and the Defiant were behind bars. But combat practice demanded too much attention to allow silly thoughts about Eladdiyr or anyone else invade. Mind, body and ship were bent to one simple purpose, and Tomas would find refuge in it when he could.

As he approached Gerduk, the small disc of Marduk peeked over the cratered surface, painting the heights in blinding white and throwing the valleys into darkness. Kaldea Prime hung off to one side, wearing its double ring with pride. The glittering lights were a beautiful contrast to the unadorned blue sphere below them.

No better life. Tomas executed a spin for fun, then followed Gerad through the launch tube. Steam fizzed along his engine cowling as he lowered to the floor and began to ease the power of his thrusters. The sound of artificial wind around his hull lessened …

The Wasp fell two metres onto the landing bay floor as the thrusters cut out completely. Tomas smacked his helmet against the top of his canopy and let loose a string of curses.

"Commander?" Gerad came through. "What happened?"

"I'm all right," Tomas said, "I'm more shocked than hurt. The control sensitivities on my new Wasp are all over the place. These kech-brained technicians may know how to build a starfighter, but they should try flying one for a change."

He doffed his helmet and ran a tentative hand over his sore spot. It came away clean, but Tomas suspected there would be a lump, and he'd probably develop a headache over the next couple of hours. He popped the canopy seal and climbed out.

The mechanics were already busy with the fuel line, but Tomas managed to pull one aside and ask that his thruster controls be recalibrated.

"Of course, Commander," was the response. "I'll see to it once you're back."

"Back?" Tomas frowned. "I've just gotten back."

The mechanic shrugged. "Your Wasp has a priority refuel notice. We only get that when you have somewhere to be."

"The whole squadron?"

"No sir. Just you."

It can't be another mission, then. But what does that leave? Tomas thanked him and began to head through the rows of fighters. There was probably a notice waiting for him on his tome-tile, which was in his quarters.

He pulled up short as something caught his eye. One of the fighter profiles hadn't been quite right. He took a few steps to the left.

There, towards the far corner of the hangar, was a sleek two-man fighter dressed in grey. It wasn't unlike in shape to the SpaceJet-400s the Defiant had used at Rahga, though it was longer by half, and there was an elegance to the curves in its hull.

An ion cannon was mounted underneath the fighter's stern. Tomas smiled and shook his head.

"The *Silver Comet*, I presume," he said to himself. He hadn't noticed her last night. "What would Amarie do to get you back, I wonder?"

He considered what would happen to the ship now. It would be too good a thing to fly it into battle against the Defiant, maybe even shoot Amarie down with it. Quil would be his co-pilot, of course, though she'd bristle at having to sit while he did all the flying.

Tomas continued, but as he passed the last row he was immediately hailed.

"Commander!" The voice was Sigsby's. He spied the Shell coming from the hangar entry, its lens a polite but unfriendly blue.

"Hello, Sigsby." He greeted his friend cautiously. "What can I do for you?"

"You can change into your parade dress," it responded, "and have a shower. I may not have an olfactory sensor, but I know pilots always smell after combat."

"Nice try," Tomas laughed. Pilots, like most militia, hated their formal uniforms. "Seriously though, what's up?"

"I have not executed any wit, Commander. You must wash and change immediately. You will be late otherwise."

"Into parade dress? But I thought I was getting debriefed soon."

Sigsby's lens flashed orange in brief irritation. "That is correct, and the reason you must be in proper uniform."

Tomas didn't understand. "The General doesn't care about parade uniform!" he protested.

Sigsby's lens cycled through several colours in quick succession, eventually settling on a pale green he had never seen used before. "You poor, uneducated lifeform," it said. "General Niyott is not conducting your interrogation."

"Then who ..." Tomas began, but Sigsby flashed bright red.

"Do not interrupt, Commander. It is bad manners. You are going to the surface.

"You are going to see Chief of Council Duidain."

Three hours later, washed, dressed and only a few minutes from his destination, Tomas still didn't know what to think. He'd never been down to Kaldea Prime's surface before, and he'd certainly never been to the Hall of Council.

He'd also never been shot down and taken prisoner by misguided terrorists, so there was likely a connection. But that didn't explain why the Chief of Council was personally debriefing *him*. For the tenth time, Tomas tugged at his collar, hoping everything was straight.

The time was twelve hundred—an hour from midday—and though Marduk was far away, it was still bright enough to set Kaldea's frozen surface alight in a dazzling display that pained the eyes. There was no snow on

Kaldea Prime, for there wasn't enough atmosphere or moisture to produce it. Life and warmth might have been possible beneath the ice, but not so above.

The hall itself was a resplendent citadel of hewn obsidian blocks, hidden in the broad shade of the equatorial rings. Only at sunset and sunrise did Marduk deviate far enough to the north or south to suspend the eclipse, and then the Hall brought forth its glory. Crystals of all colours ran in artificial veins up the towers and domes and glistened like starlight rivers as the fleeting rays preyed upon them. Of this phenomenon, Tomas had seen only images on his tome-tile, but even they had been enough to slacken his jaw.

There were three domes, one for each federation that had joined forces against the Ebon and remained under a treaty of common peace. The Central Systems controlled the largest portion of the Cluster and thus had the largest dome, followed by the Chammuah Crescent and the North Wilds. Not that anyone could want for space in a building this large. As Tomas brought his Wasp to land on a reserved pad attached to the Core's dome, he saw just how big it was.

The landing pad used the same atmosphere projection technology as the Rings orbiting above him, so Tomas was able to breathe freely as he opened his canopy. The temperature was a different matter. It was *freezing*. He marched to the waiting doors as quick as he could without breaking form.

Beside the doors stood two Sun Guards, their masks fixed upon him in wordless assessment. How they weren't frozen solid was beyond Tomas, but he couldn't imagine that their armour had heating units. It didn't seem right for a perfect soldier to rely on comforts such as those.

They made no move against him as he passed, but their heads and rifles tracked him without fail. He reached the I.D. scanner beside the door, but as soon as he pressed his hand down, he jerked it back. The metal was so cold it burned him. The guards said nothing, but Tomas imagined their judgement. He gingerly hovered his palm near the scanner, and the doors slid apart.

He entered a large antechamber walled in gold and decorated with rich, vivid tapestries. On the far side, past a row of lift tubes, more guards stood aside two ornate doors that arched to the ceiling. Between the guards was an Ebon servant—a doorman—his blinking collar the least colourful object in the room.

Tomas swallowed and approached. "I … is this the Chief of Council's office?"

None of the sentients moved at first, and Tomas mentally kicked himself.

Great job! You just asked a question to a room of mutes, he thought, but as he did the doorman bowed his head, turned, and pushed in the doors. Without any better instruction, Tomas straightened his collar and followed him in.

The office he entered was as large as the antechamber, but the back wall was entirely glass and looked out upon the endless ice. Shelves lined the remaining walls, but instead of books or discs, they were filled with statues and artefacts from every culture and craft. Ceremonial weapons hung on plaques, and jewelled chains and diadems gleamed from within glass cases; the gracious honours paid by every star system in the Cluster. Yet all this came no further than the edge of the room, not daring to intrude upon the grand obsidian desk at the centre. Behind it, reclining in an opulent, high-backed chair, was Chief of Council Duidain. When he saw Tomas, he smiled wide and jumped to his feet.

"There he is, there he *is*! Haha!" He was around the desk and pinning Tomas in a firm embrace before he had time to react.

"Sir …"

"Please, please, 'Councillor' will do fine. But at least you remembered not to salute me this time, eh?" Duidain stepped back, grinning to his ears. "Now come, sit down, sit down." He ushered Tomas into one of the seats before his desk, which were just as luxurious as his own, if not as large. The desk was a single piece, smoothed and lacquered on all sides. A single vein ran across the top of the table, following the stone as it curved around the Councillor's seat, and within it gleamed a river of large, uncut diamonds.

Duidain returned to his chair, but it would have been generous to say he *sat* in it. The man hardly kept still.

"Commander," he said, each word stencilled by his bright, geometric smile. "you don't know how *comforting* it is to have you back with us. What a story you must have!"

"Yes ... I suppose I do." Tomas felt caught with his shields down. He still didn't understand why he was here, and not in Niyott's office, giving a detailed report that Duidain could read and reread a hundred times if he wanted. He glanced around the room, noticing at least four more Sun Guards. "Thank you for your concern."

"Ah, but Tomas—I can call you that, can't I?—what head of government would I be if I didn't care about the wonderful, wonderful men and women who hold it all together?" Duidain leant forward. "I want to hear it all, every detail you were going to tell Layla. She can have the recording later."

Tomas blinked. "Well the first—"

"Oh my, no, how could I?" Duidain cut him off, looking beyond him and clapping his hands twice. "Refreshments! Refreshments please."

To Tomas, he said, "Forgive my terrible rudeness, not offering you food. It doesn't become me at all."

Tomas jumped as an Ebon waiter brushed past his chair and placed a tray of pastries on the desk. A second came around the other side with a decanter of fire spirits and two glasses. Neither servant had made a sound, and vanished as quickly as they had arrived.

"Much better," Duidain poured a glass for Tomas and handed it over with a grin. "Now, what were you saying?"

"I'm sorry, Councillor, I'm completely lost." Tomas decided to shoot with the truth. "Why take an interest in my situation? How do you even know I was missing? Rahga and the Defiant wouldn't make more than a footnote in your daily report!"

For a moment Duidain's expression reflected his true age, and he sighed. "Every time a son or daughter of the CSF passes away, I sign the condolence that we send the family. There were quite a few to sign after Rahga, you know.

"But *one* of the letters had not been released to me. I asked why, and they said the primary witness was refusing to sign for the death! I imagine you can guess who?"

Tomas couldn't help but smile. "Falaquil."

"Precisely! Commander Caron was adamant. She saw the Defiant shoot you down, but if she could survive, then so could you." Duidain shook his head in wonder. "Your unit serves as a paragon of the loyalty we so pride in the CSF, and the Core entire. If only my fellow councillors could cooperate like that, haha! You've trained them well, Tomas."

"No better than I was taught myself," Tomas said, but he wondered. *Shot down* was not what had happened at all. He had risked Quil's life, yet she had lied for him, protecting him from charges of insubordination. How could he ever repay that? How could she ever forgive him?

He needed to talk to her more than ever, yet he was trapped here. Tomas drained half of his glass and forced himself to relax as the heat of the drink washed through him. At least Duidain's interest finally made sense.

"I suppose I should start from when I regained consciousness." Tomas took a deep breath, then proceeded to tell of all that had happened from his crash to his release. Duidain was enthralled at once, paying close attention despite interrupting frequently to ask questions. When Tomas began describing the Celah Neiru, he became so rapt he even forgot to smile.

"Imagine that ..." he muttered around a mouthful of sweet-tart, "to face such a people ..."

The mirth only returned when Tomas began expounding on the Defiant's warped devotion to their king and the impending war the Ebon were devising. He obviously thought no threat would ever come from his silent servants, and Tomas had to admit that the more he explained Erae's views, the more ridiculous they sounded.

It was only when he got to his release that Tomas hesitated. As far as Niyott knew, Tomas had destroyed the disc without looking at it. Duidain might laugh, but what would his General do to him once she found out he had not only viewed it, but shared its information with the enemy?

Besides, Niyott said that CSF Intelligence already knew everything about the disc, Tomas defended himself. In the end, he told Duidain that Erae let him go once she realised he would never be recruited into the Defiant cause.

"As well you wouldn't!" Duidain remarked, leaning over to refill Tomas' empty glass. "Breaking the law and warring against imaginary armies! I must congratulate you, Commander, for it takes a certain quality of man to rob his enemy while shackled and starved!"

Tomas blinked. "Rob, sir?"

"Of course, haha!" Duidain slammed the decanter down, rattling the tray. "You've given us names, descriptions, even the rundown of that scrap-and-polish ship of theirs! And let's not forget motives. Yes, Tomas, each of these is a weapon we can use to eradicate the renegades."

He paused, adopting a cautious expression. For the second time in the conversation, his smile vanished. "You do understand, don't you, that these people must be dealt with?"

Tomas swallowed, and the office seemed to grow a little colder. If given the choice, many Defiant would choose to die rather than face trial for their crimes. Tomas didn't wish that on any of them—even Amarie, whose zeal was more a product of youth than anything else—but that wasn't up to him. The CSF would offer justice, even if it wasn't taken.

"I understand, Councillor," he answered. "The Defiant mean well, but they have broken the law and hurt people."

"And *that's core*," Duidain smiled again, and the coldness went away. "They are misguided, Tomas. They use violence to make themselves heard, and I can never respond to that. If I did, I would be eroding the democracy my citizens place their trust in, abandoning it even.

"That being said, I will have my people look into the situation on Rahga and make sure the workers are being treated fairly."

"That's good to hear, Councillor," Tomas said truthfully. "Is there anything more you want to ask me?"

"If only they had let slip their plans or the location of their base, we could deal with them at once! Alas, it cannot be helped." Duidain considered for a moment. "I do have one question, and then I'm sure you have places you'd rather be, eh?"

"You obviously haven't tried the wine on Gerduk," Tomas said. He'd actually enjoyed himself far more than he'd thought possible for a mission debriefing. General Niyott had certainly never offered him pastries.

"I can't say I have, no, no! But to my question." Duidain held up a finger. "Now I'm no soldier, but I wager it is far easier to shoot at a stranger than it is a person you know.

"But you've met these people now, heard their wayward stories, remembered their names. If your unit encounters the Defiant in the field, can I trust you to do all you can to bring them to justice? Even if—and against all reasonable attempts otherwise, of course—it means their death?"

It was the same question Amarie had asked him, and his answer was the same now as back then. But as Tomas went to speak, Erae's face appeared in his mind. There was kindness in it, and yet also a fierce and admirable determination. The constellations in her eyes stared straight through him.

"I'll see it done, sir," he said and shooed the face away. "True as core."

19

Tomas had barely landed and popped his canopy when Dan pulled him out of his Wasp and across the hangar.

"Come on, Lead! The shuttle's waiting!"

"For what? Dan, slow down!" Tomas broke free of his friend's eager grip. What had come over this moon? Every time he landed he was being ushered somewhere else, with barely enough time to make a squeak. He could see the shuttle Dan had meant sitting not too far away, its engines already lit with pre-flight.

Tomas planted his feet, jerking them both to a halt. "Words, Dan. Now. What's happened?"

"Can't you trust me?" Dan tried to frown but quickly dismissed the idea. "Forget I said that. But I'm still getting you on that shuttle."

"*Dirk Three!*" a stern voice barked across the hangar. Dan released Tomas and snapped upright, then swore when he saw who it was.

"I told you to *ask* Tomas, not kidnap him." Quil was walking towards the shuttle from a different angle, the rest of the squadron behind her. She glared hard at Dan.

"Scorch sear me, Two, I thought you were Niyott!" Dan recovered from his shock enough to twirl his moustache. "Been working on your disciplinary tone, have you, Commander?"

Quil placed a hand on her hip. "No. I just don't usually waste my breath on an unsolvable kech like yourself."

"That's awful harsh." Dan held out a hand. "I was only joking."

Behind Quil, Teliac clicked his mandibles. "Tch-tch—we know, Three. You're *always* joking."

Dan began some eloquent admission of guilt, but Tomas lost focus when he finally registered what everyone was wearing.

Gerad was in a suit and tie, Klord and Memiele had donned their smartest tunics, and Teliac's jet exoskeleton was so polished that Tomas could almost see his reflection in it. Falaquil outdid all of them in a red and gold dress that fell just below her stockinged knees. The thread of her sleeves was so sheer that it looked like red flowers were flowing down her arms by their own attraction. A gold finger loop held the end of each sleeve.

"Took you long enough, Lead," Quil smirked. "Although Dan didn't make it easy."

Tomas turned back to Dan, who appeared to be in his flight suit, only the cut was all wrong. Dan winked and spun with a flourish. When he came back around, he was wearing an electric-blue blazer that shimmered as he moved.

Tomas blew out an impressed breath. Programmable clothing—known as dot-thread—cost a fortune, and well more than Dan's military salary could afford. Either the rogue had won big at cards while Tomas was away, or he had placed himself in debt for the next decade.

"What's the occasion?"

"You, pal!" Dan slapped him on the back. "Well, if you'll let us. We wanted a night on the town before Niyott shoved another mission our way."

"It's not night-time yet, Dan," Gerad said.

Dan glowered. "How many times do I have to tell you? It's a planet, Seven. It's always night-time somewhere." He turned back to Tomas. "The shuttle pilot is ready to take us wherever you want to go. Restaurants, casinos, clubs; anything."

"With a two-drink limit and a respectable curfew, yes, anything," Memiele chuckled. "But only if you're up for it, Tomas. We know you've had a lot to process."

"I'd love to come," Tomas said. He still felt a bit drained, but his friends were a certain cure for any illness. He elbowed Dan. "Thank you for *asking*."

"My pleasure," Dan slapped him again and let out a whoop of excitement. "Let's go Dirks! First round is on Gerad."

The group started towards the shuttle, but as Tomas turned to follow, Falaquil caught his arm. She pointed him to a caddy bot hovering near the entrance corridor. "Your sult's in the top compartment," she said. "Dan never thinks of everything."

"Thanks, Quil," Tomas said. It was the bare minimum of all he needed to thank her for, but it was a start. He resisted the guilt that constricted his insides. Perhaps he would thank her tonight.

Dan shouted at them from the boarding ramp. "Come on you two, the revelry awaits!"

"Grab your things," Quil squeezed his arm. "I'll remind him how to address ranking officers." She strode towards the shuttle, and Tomas hurried to the robot, a welcome smile on his face.

There was no way they were leaving him behind.

"Erae?"

"Yeah?"

"Do you ever have doubts?"

Erae halted her crawl along the catwalk and turned to squint at Amarie. The warehouse's light fixtures were below them, beating incessant heat onto a fresh shift of packing workers. She didn't dare shine a light of her own. Even whispering felt risky, despite the conveyors and chutes that rumbled below their hands and knees.

Amarie wasn't moving. Erae cupped a hand over her earpiece. "What's happened?" she asked.

She caught a glint of Amarie rolling her eyes. "Nothing's *happened*; it's just a question."

"I am learning so much from you both about the excellence of stealth," Crisp buzzed into her ear. He was hiding by the stairwell outside, waiting to patch into the cameras Erae and Amarie were setting up.

Amarie scowled. "Forget I asked."

"Am—"

"I said stow it," Amarie nudged Erae's feet. "Keep going."

Erae complied, taking each movement slowly. She alternated between watching her hands and staring through the grating at the workers below. There were three dozen or so sentients, and many more robots besides. It would only take one of them to look up, and their whole plan would collapse.

"This'll do," she said, indicating a section of railing. "We can see most of the factory from here, and a second cam past the junction should cover the blind spots." She eased herself up and reached for the kit bag as Amarie handed it to her.

"I still don't get why the Peret would meet here," Amarie said. "I don't think the work ever stops."

"There is a reprieve in the schedule at O-four-hundred local time," Crisp said. "It lasts until dawn."

"And we'll be gone long before then," Erae said, taking out a camera mount and a tube of holding clay. "If the Peret even arrive today. It could be days still. But Gabriel has never earned doubts from us before."

"By the suns, that's not … whatever." Amarie shook her head and focused on the camera. Erae tapped her on the shoulder, motioning for them both to take out their earpieces.

"What?" Amarie said crossly. The nearby machinery nearly drowned her out.

"Tell me what's wrong, Am." Erae tried to look her friend in the eye, but Amarie shrugged away. She had been fine earlier, but something must have happened during their packing shift. She fidgeted with the camera while Erae waited.

"It's not the mission," she said at last, putting the device down. "It's everything."

"What do you mean?" Erae was patient.

"I don't know. I've seen so much crazy stuff with the Defiant, but there's so much more I haven't seen. Things I *need* to see. Did you ever meet the king's son?"

"Well, no. But my parents did." Erae thought about it. The closest she'd ever gotten to Ben-Eloah was in Tomas' dream. "But I've felt the peace of Eladdiyr inside me. That means more than anything the Neiru teach us."

"I know, I have too," Amarie hesitated. This was really worrying her. "Sometimes I just feel like, maybe I'm making that feeling up. Just sort of wishing it so that I have a reason to kill the CSF."

Erae flinched at the wording, but at least now she understood. "I doubt sometimes too," she said gently. "There's so much I don't know, and sometimes it feels like I can't trust myself any more than a stranger."

"Then why go on?"

"Well, belief is partly a feeling, and partly a choice," Erae explained. "Even when the night is darkest, and we can't *feel* the sun, we trust it will come around again."

Amarie shifted. "Whenever I go undercover, I get a glimpse of a normal life," she said.

Erae nodded. Packing wasn't glamorous, but it was a safe, honest job. "What do you think?"

"Today was pits!" Amarie snorted. "But other days, on different planets … I remember my parents. They both worked so hard. They just wanted me to have a normal life, and what did I do? I put a gun to his head."

Erae took her hand. "Am, you know that's not—"

An alarm began to wail.

Erae had her earpiece on in an instant. "Crisp, what did you do?"

"What did I do?" Crisp shrieked. "What did *you* do? Your communications went silent, and now organics are running left and right! It is a gas leak, or a furnace leak, or both!"

"We're coming down."

"No, Rae look!" Amarie pointed through the grating. On the floor below, the workers who had been scrambling towards the exits were now pushing back against their fellows, crying out in alarm. Erae put her nose to the grate but still couldn't see why. For all the light in the building, the doors remained hidden in shadow.

She gasped as the shadow grew suddenly, creeping up the walls in shards of black crystal. A silent terror fell on the packers, and they huddled in the centre of the room, turning this way and that as every exit was sealed off by the darkling ice. The loading robots continued their work, unfazed by the chaos.

"Patch me in, patch me in!" Crisp demanded in her ear.

Wind began to whistle past her ears, and she could see papers and litter flying around as the air was pulled into a single point some distance from the workers. The point resolved into a man of boiling darkness, stricken with crimson scars, his head crowned with ten horns.

"Rae, we need to go *now*," Amarie hissed.

Erae stared at the figure. It was the very articulation of terror she'd imagined, but one could only be so afraid of a nightmare whilst it remained within dreams. The Peret Neiru was very real, from the flash of his fangs to the glowing white eyes she found so horribly familiar.

"*Erae!*"

The Peret raised a hand in an almost languid fashion, stretched a finger towards his trembling captives, and shot a white-blue arc of lightning at them.

It struck the closest worker, who screamed and contorted as the energy raked across his body. The lightning branched out, dropping two more victims to the ground, where they writhed in agony. The tang of ozone and seared flesh filled Erae's nostrils, but she still couldn't move. Her eyes didn't stray until the last of the three workers stopped moving. The Peret lowered his hand, rolled his shoulders back, and spoke.

"As trivial sport as you are," he growled, "I would still rather that you run."

At the last word, the spell on the crowd was broken, and yelling they scattered across the floor. The Peret snarled and leapt amongst them, arms wreathed in flame. Never had Erae seen such furious rage. He was a storm of death, swifter and more powerful than any mortal, hurling crates in the wake of his charge, or warping directly before his quarry and searing them with fire.

He leapt over a fleeing Kilya, cratering the ground with his impact and summoning a shockwave of earth and ice. The Kilya's body was lifted and bludgeoned by the wave, lifeless in moments, and as she fell the Peret's hand darted to snatch her head. Her flesh blackened beneath his grasp, her feathers engulfed like kindling. He tossed the corpse aside, then raced towards his next target.

Erae's gut retched, and the reaction dispelled her paralysis at last. "The camera," she gasped to Amarie. "We have to."

Amarie's face was pure terror as she handed the device over. Erae heaved again, and she would have lost all function had her brain not shunted from conscious decision to a circuit of pure instinct and training. Her hands were steady as she attached the camera to the mount. "Crisp, are you receiving?"

Crisp's reply was irate. "It took you long en—by all predicted dooms! Captain, remove yourself immediately!"

The women were already sprinting across the catwalk, sped by the horrible screams below them, screams that every second surged louder and yet grew closer to final silence. Amarie led the way, but as they reached the door to the exterior she skidded to a halt. It was too dark to see anything, but that told Erae enough.

The ice had covered this exit as well. Was the entire building frozen over? It didn't matter—this was the only exit in reach. Erae yearned for a weapon, though she knew nothing could harm the creature below her. They were defenceless.

Well, not quite. *Eladdiyr,* Erae began in her head, then felt she needed to say the name aloud, despite the onrushing silence. There were very few screams below them now.

"Eladdiyr, we are found in your shadow, held by your reaching arm. See us in our darkness, and by the gift of your son, let this darkness not take our hearts."

"Erae, get us out of here!" Amarie was frantic, reaching towards the ice yet recoiling the next moment, as if touching the dark crystal would reveal their location. "He's going to kill us! Erae!"

Erae pulled her close and covered her mouth with a hand. They locked eyes, bodies trembling, as the last sounds from below faded away. There was only one hope for them now, and beyond that, the silent pleading that if they were fated to die in this warehouse, it would be swift, and it would be together.

From the floor came a new voice. It rang with a beautiful, haunting melody. "Such mess, brother, and such smell! Must we suffer for your indulgence?"

"No more than I suffer it myself," came the snarling reply. "Where is my challenge, my promised foe? This is no herald to war!"

"Which is why you are no herald, Charon dear. A blade rusted by use."

"Which makes you what? Charon shot back. "Rusted by slumber?"

All this time, Erae and Amarie held each other, drawing strength from each other's eyes. Now they slowly separated and, driven by one horror against another, knew it would be better to see their death approach than wait for it in cowering blindness. They flattened against the catwalk and crawled back to the centre of the warehouse.

Carnage devastated the floor. Vac-crates were flung everywhere, dented and split open, or charred and warped by heat. The bodies were worse. It seemed Charon had taken pleasure in the precision of some of his kills, and in the absolute ruin of the others.

He stood facing a second Peret, a female. Her hair fell in long, slender wisps, and a single black horn adorned her head. This was Remiyyah, if Tomas had described her correctly.

"Is it by slumber," Remiyyah crooned with a jagged smile, "that I have snared us servants and spies without end, hmm? Even now they search for the blue captain and the Celah's hidden base. If I desired it, they would die to queen me, and not even then perceive the source of their want."

"Save your lies, hag! Your life is spent as a prelude to my legacy! I will paint the stars with the blood of these vermin!"

A small, chipper voice piped up. "Could you paint inside the lines? This floor is all *sticky*." Erae angled slightly and saw a third Peret, much smaller than the first two. A pair of blood-red horns, sharp and slight, poked out from a bob of misting hair. She was bouncing from crate to crate, at times suspending herself in the air and floating gently down.

The other two turned towards her. "Orexis, dear?" Remiyyah said.

Orexis lighted atop a loading bot—still dutifully trundling towards the conveyors—and bent over to peer at it. "Yes, sis?"

"Do mind you don't get it on you. It does reek so. Almost as nauseating as a Celah."

"Not on me, never!" Orexis shook her hands as if she'd touched the ichor, and Erae shuddered. Something about a Peret in child form was more disturbing than anything else she had yet seen.

Charon spat in her direction. "Mewling rat."

"Club-faced, um, oaf!"

"Silence, both!" Remiyyah hissed. Her poisoned smile had vanished. Charon snarled.

"You dare command …" he trailed off. Orexis stopped bouncing. All three turned towards a fixed point, their eyes shining upon the far wall like spotlights.

A breath of ice filled the air, chilling Erae's bones. She tightened her grip on Amarie's hand, which she'd forgotten she'd grabbed. A fourth Peret had suddenly appeared in the room, without the prelude of smoke or sound.

He stood tall, and even the shadows seemed to lean away from him, and yet were drawn upon him as with chains. Five black horns formed a circlet upon his brow, and while Charon had numerous scars, this Peret had only one.

A single strike of red ran from ear to ear, cutting through where his eyes should have been. His nostrils flared, and his head swivelled to take in the room, through what senses Erae could only guess. Finally, he fixed on his siblings, who kneeled before him. They greeted him in unison, and Erae heard fear in their voices as they spoke.

"Hail Krateo, Lord of our Kin. Hail the night of our Master."

20

Most people who visited Kaldea found themselves on the outermost ring, which despite its larger size was at least twice as crowded as its sister. Unbroken streams of shuttles ferried the working class from Port K to the high-rises and spires that shaped Ring Two, while private spacers whizzed their smaller freighters and yachts directly from the shift gate into the air-car-filled skylanes.

The deeper you delved into the heart of the superstation, the less civilised the company became. The particulate detritus of millions of lifeforms sifted through the levels, past walkways and bridges, collecting like plastic sand on a seashore against the solid foundations of the ring. Cleaning bots kept up as best they could, but it was never enough.

Below this rotting soil ran a labyrinth of maintenance warrens, dark and dangerous. Here dwelt the most decrepit and hopeless of lifeforms: the sunlight-starved descendants of what used to be people before they'd gambled, squandered or otherwise lost their way off-ring.

Ring One, the inner ring, still had its tiers of society, but the rungs of the proverbial ladder climbed much higher. From barons and mob bosses to system governors and megacorporation CEOs, anyone who was *someone* owned a spire on Ring One, even if they never visited it.

It was on Ring One that the Dirks found themselves, in a vibrant entertainment district some two hundred metres above the kuwrium-plated ground. Though the restaurants and clubs were as diverse as the species they catered to, each square managed to tie itself to a particular culture or theme, which meant that as the Dirks meandered through the streets, they were met with one enticing set of sounds and smells at a time, instead of the muddled bombardment some lesser worlds might have presented.

"I'm telling you, this Taphuun place is the genuine article," Gerad was saying to the group with some insistence. "The head chef is related to one of my kitchen staff back home. If their woodroach duster is anything like his …"

"I don't think I have the appetite for insects tonight, Seven," Quil protested from beside Tomas. "The Dented Horizon is just around the corner, and it's right next to C-square. The Chamisi clubs always have the best music."

"They'll have other dishes!"

"Maybe we should split up," Memiele suggested. "Grab food to go and meet in C-square in thirty minutes."

Gerad considered it, then shrugged. "It's Tomas' choice, I guess. It's his night."

They all looked to Tomas, who crossed his arms. "This is *our* night, guys, come on. The stripes are off," he tugged at the shoulders of his grey dinner jacket, void of his military rank slides.

"I appreciate the gesture, but I don't want to fly in your brackets for the rest of my life. Let's celebrate *us*, not *me*, and just have some fun. Copy?"

He got a chorus of nods. "All right," he said. "I think splitting up is a fine plan."

In the end, Gerad was the only one who wanted to order from the Taphuun Typhoon, despite his continued assurance they were missing out on the best meals of their lives. He headed south along the skywalk while the six remaining Dirks headed north.

The air was crisp and refreshing, a result of the temperature-controlled air underneath Ring One's atmospheric shields. A lot of money went into making the outside parts of Ring One feel as genuine as possible; no one wanted to feel like they were cooped up on a giant space station. Ring Two had similar systems, but as with everything else, they were of a lower calibre.

There was only one thing the outer ring held over the inner, which was quite literally the ring itself. The intricate texture of Ring Two's underside was an inexorable obstruction across the night sky, undoubtedly impressive to behold. But Tomas would be lying if he said he preferred it over a view of the stars.

"Hey, Lead," Dan nudged Tomas as they followed the others along the street. "Have you noticed yet?"

Tomas looked down. "What—your blazer? How did you get your hands on one?"

Dan grinned and tugged on his cuffs. "It looks great, doesn't it?" he said with a high giggle. Some passing women looked his way, and he switched to a cough.

"It involved multiple—*multiple*—high-speed chases and the demolition of several buildings, but I'll tell you later. What I *meant* was, have you noticed Five and Six?"

Tomas looked. Klord and Memiele were at the front of the group, and their casual chatter was barely audible over the background clamour of the skywalk. Tomas angled his head around Teliac and Quil to see them better.

"Are they …" he caught sight of it, and his heart warmed. "They're holding hands." Walking close together, with their wide tunics blocking much of the view, it had been difficult to spot.

"She made her move two days after we got back from Rahga. About time, I think." Dan's smile was like a beacon of joy and mischief shining out into the frigid night. "Between her shyness and his, uh, logic-ness?—they're taking things adorably slow. I haven't seen them hold hands before today."

Dan was right; that was adorable. Tomas was glad the two had found each other; there had been so much pain and grief lately that any good thing was a welcome change. He'd have to congratulate them some other time.

Romantic relationships were allowed, if not encouraged, within the Core Star Fleet, but some safety rules accompanied them. Most important was that the relationship could only begin between soldiers of identical ranking. Love was not a tool for currying favour or sneaking your way through the ranks. Relationships were dangerous enough without adding more slugs to the barrel.

Dirk Three was still smiling deviously, but his attention was more on Tomas than the happy couple. Tomas arched an eyebrow at him.

"What is it, Dan?"

"Oh, don't play innocent, Lead. This is your big chance!" Dan gave his ribs a knowing elbow; only Tomas didn't know what his bald friend meant at all.

When Dan saw he wasn't getting through, he gave Tomas an overdramatic sigh. "Two, Lead." He grabbed Tomas' head and angled it towards Falaquil, who was minding her thoughts beside Teliac. She'd donned a coat over her dress to keep out the cold.

Tomas freed himself from Dan's grasp, his pulse hot with disbelief. "Do you think about anything else?"

"I mean it, pal," Dan said. "Surely you notice how she acts around you, or how she's *always* around you. I've noticed plain, the others have noticed, scorch sear my ears I even heard Sigsby comment once."

Tomas was shocked. Had he been that oblivious? "She's my wingmate. It's good practice to get to know one another," he said as justification.

"*Ex-act-ly*," Dan drew out the word. "You two have a bond forged through battle, a passion fuelled by the daily dance with death, a solace against the uncertainty of tomorrow."

"You're insane. Eloquent, I'll admit, but insane." Tomas had never thought about Quil as a romantic possibility. She was a great pilot and a better friend, but his thoughts had never progressed beyond that. Besides, she was so young.

"But she's so young!" Tomas reinforced himself aloud.

"How is that a bad thing?" Daniel Pandyne, master wooer of women and breaker of hearts, was not giving Tomas an inch of argument to stand upon.

The conversation had been gaining zeal and volume, but halted as Quil turned to look at them, a brow raised. When she turned back, Tomas felt a breath of disappointment inside.

No … not disappointment. Loss. The burning skies of Rahga flashed through his mind, tumbling and spinning around a single starfighter, a trail of smoke, and a terrible *almost*.

He would apologise to her. Tonight.

"Still with me, Lead?" Dan whispered.

"No," Tomas whispered back. "Even if she feels as you say, which I doubt, and even if I mirrored those feelings, which I don't, pilots of different ranks can't … oh."

Dirk Three's eyes sparkled in their sockets. "Lead, I'd like to consider myself your best friend. Your wiser, better-looking, best friend." He gave an emphatic twirl of his moustache. "So trust me when I say it won't get better than this. Commanders don't stay wingmates for long. She'll move to her own squadron, or you'll get promoted, or who knows?"

He winked. "But not tonight. Tonight is *perfect*."

Tomas, to his amazement and despair, felt colour rushing to his cheeks. *But why?* He asked his misbehaving body. *I wasn't enamoured before her promotion, so there should be no difference now.* But there was a difference: a possibility. And despite Tomas' internal protest, his mind started to think about that possibility.

The Dirks, sans Gerad, of course, had reached the neon-lit presence of the Dented Horizon. Memiele, Klord and Teliac took their leave and headed across the nearest bridge in search of their cuisine of choice.

It was just as Tomas followed Quil into the diner that he realised he was doomed.

"Wait up guys," Dan half-jogged towards the bridge, but not before tossing another wink to the wind. "I've changed my mind."

Tomas had conceived twelve different yet equally horrific endings for Dirk Three by the time he'd turned around. Quil stood inside the doorway, shaking her head at Dan's spontaneity. "Shall we?" she said, gesturing ahead of her.

Tomas mimicked her headshake, but for a much more complicated reason.

"We shall," he replied.

After looking at the menu far longer than was necessary, Tomas and Quil left the diner with a box of batter boulders to share, plus two dipping sauces. Quil also insisted they each get a sweet-smelt for dessert, and Tomas was too distracted to argue. If the grease and sugar resurfaced after ten minutes of dancing in the club, that was on her, he'd said. Possibly in a literal sense.

Back in the cool night, they had plenty of time to wait while the others ordered their food. Tomas wouldn't have minded if not for Dan, but thanks to Dirk Three, his brain was working overtime, and each second was filled with ever-wilder questions.

Had she always looked this pretty with her hair down? It was usually braided on Gerduk. Was there something in that smile she just flashed him, or wasn't there? Was it normal to smile back? And scorch sear the beating of his heart, he hadn't felt this much adrenaline in a decade of military service.

The duo entered C-square, and as they passed an open club, Tomas' heartbeat was lost in a storm of synthetic noise. Skull-drum dance battles and synclet fusions surrounded him for a moment, and then the doors closed, and the calmer ambience of the square resumed.

Ribbons of light—magenta, violet and lavender—were strung from stone columns to the storefront awnings. A wind machine sent the ribbons curling and swaying, drawing Tomas' eyes, and the soft scales of a sliding harp orchestra riffled along the marble cobblestones.

This was the native music of the Chamisi, and they had mastered it long before the tides of galactic commerce pulled them into broader, more percussive genres. Not to say that the dance clubs were bad; the Dirks planned to be inside one within the hour. But Tomas thought the Chamisi displayed great tenacity by not letting the wants of others drown out their culture.

The centre of the square was crafted to replicate an old ruin. Columns slanted at odd angles as if built on uneven ground, and some had been knocked off their bases, acting as benches and tables for the few lifeforms walking around. Most of these were the wormlike Chamisi, as the other species were either entering or leaving the clubs.

Quil approached one of the pillars and ran her hand along the curving, serpentine glyphs adorning it. "Bal-Lachash is amazing, don't you think?

The clink of the chisel speaks the word as it cuts the stone. The stone remains, but its voice is gone; A language you can only hear once."

Tomas sat on one of the pillar-benches and set the batter boulders on a table. "I thought their hand signs were called Bal-Lachash," he said.

"That's right," she replied. "But if the Chamisi are telepathic mutes, where did the word come from? Not from hands or chisels."

Tomas shifted so that Dirk Two had room as she sat beside him. A puff of mist formed as she breathed out, curling not unlike the glyphs on the stone, or the winding ribbons above. Her red dress was a beacon of colour compared to the greyscale scenery, warm against the cold of the night. Seated as she was amidst the ruins, under soft pink lights, Tomas wouldn't have been surprised if an artist had crafted the scene.

The others still hadn't arrived. *Dan's probably stalling them*, Tomas wagered. Why had his words taken such a hold upon the evening? Tomas had known nothing but kindness from Quil, and up until now he'd assumed it had no further purpose. But now every past action was called into doubt, seeking rapidly for answers.

Did she care for him, and did he care for her? Tomas wasn't sure he had the skill to tell. He'd never been in a committed relationship before. While other young men and women had been hastened into love by the yoke of the invasion and the doom it placed upon everyone, Tomas had focused on his studies, the academy and finally his career. It had been a defence against loss, or risk of loss, and the pains he had known it would bring him.

Becoming a Commander had changed all that. It was his duty to encourage his team, comfort them, and most importantly, to see them through death and out the other side. Getting to know his squadron had caused him a lot of pain over the years, but it was the pain of a life worth living. Tomas knew that now.

With great effort, he shoved the subject to the side. If the other Dirks wanted to take their time arriving, he could at least address the other weight on his shoulders. The one that had haunted him since he woke up in that cell. He put down the batter boulder he'd been pretending to eat.

"Quil, I need to talk to you about Rahga."

"Ah." Falaquil put down her own meal. "I wondered what was bothering you. What's on your mind?"

"Thanks, Two. I …" He'd thought about what he would say, but his mouth had seized now that it was time to say it. He'd nearly killed her, killed them both. How did he begin to apologise?

"I'm so sorry," he said in a heavy out-breath that couldn't begin to reveal his true remorse. "I'm so, so sorry Quil."

"I know," Quil looked down at her hands, which were fidgeting in her lap. "It's all right, Tomas."

"But it's not! A commander always puts the lives of his pilots above his own. I gambled yours on a hunch and nearly lost everything. You crashed because of me, and I can never forgive myself for it."

Quil tried to reassure him by smiling. "It's not your place to forgive. I know you meant the best."

"I rammed you with my Wasp!" he exclaimed.

"I forgive you."

"You shouldn't."

The wind stirred the square's soft lights into a gentle sway, the slide harps slipped long, rising notes in harmony from the speakers, and Falaquil Caron placed a hand in Tomas Amets' own.

"I *forgive you*, Tomas."

He could feel his heart pumping an electric heat along every vein in his body. It ran up to his fingers, where a second heartbeat matched his. Her storm-coloured eyes were large and brilliant as they looked upon his own.

"You lied for me," he remembered aloud. "You told everyone that I had been shot down."

Quil nodded.

"What did Captain Forn say? He heard our audio."

She smiled. "It was all circumstantial. He knows you abstained from firing upon the terrorists, but that's it. When you crashed, he decided you'd learnt your lesson, and I daresay you have."

Tomas still couldn't believe it. Even when he had hurt her the most, Quil had stood up for Tomas and protected him.

A strange thing happened then, and it was like the lifting of a fog or the settling of a pond. When it was over, Tomas knew he cared for Quil. It wasn't love, so far as he knew, but it could be someday. He wanted it to be.

His remorse deepened as this truth came upon him, but so too his relief that they were both unharmed. "I wish Forn had never given that order," he said.

Quil blinked, withdrawing slightly. Tomas hadn't noticed that they'd both been leaning in. "You mean you wish you hadn't disobeyed?"

Tomas shook his head. "They were innocent factory workers, Quil. Families and women and children. The rebels told me."

"Those rebels," Quil said in a darkened tone, "are liars and criminals. Are you forgetting that they captured you?"

"Well yes, but—"

"*Are you forgetting that they shot me down?*" Quil took her hand back, leaving a phantom of its touch on Tomas' skin. "You did the wrong thing, Tomas, and we very nearly paid the price. Please, please tell me you see that."

"You're right, I'm sorry," Tomas relented, but he saw the uncertainty on her face. He *knew* the duplicity in his heart, and it burrowed a hole in him deep and dreadful.

He'd told Duidain he'd capture the Defiant, and that was true as core. He'd told him he'd kill them, and he was prepared to follow through. And he could be no happier than to have Quil at his side when the time for justice came.

But the Rahgese peasants had been innocent and unarmed. Nothing they had done deserved slaughter. He wasn't going to repent of his protecting them. Not even for her.

Quil stood, her face closed and cold. "I'll see you inside," she said.

He watched her go, watched as the wind tugged the hem of her red dress and the light shimmered like an aurora on her invisible sleeves. It felt like a gravity well had opened in his stomach, and his soul was rapidly falling in. Not because he'd found and lost a love—that was too recent and wondrous to have taken hold.

Tomas lowered his head into his hands. It was the same mix of confusion and despair that had rushed to meet him with the ochre surface of Rahga. The truth was as far from him now as it had been then, and any time he tried to pierce that dark cloud, he found himself shooting at his own friends.

"Lead! Lead?" Tomas looked up. Dan was coming towards him with the others in tow. He raised an eyebrow. "What'd you do with Quil?"

Tomas smiled, or he tried to. "She's already inside. I thought I'd wait for you lot."

Dan frowned for a moment, then pasted on his own smile. "Ever the kech's mother, aren't you pal? We're all here, safe and sound. We even picked Gerad up from childcare!"

"Very funny," Gerad knocked Three on the side of the head. "Can we move?"

"Hold on, boys." Memiele squinted. "Lead, you don't look so good."

"Just getting some air," Tomas lied. He put a hand on his stomach. "Dented Horizon caught me off guard."

Dan laughed and shook his head. "Sure it did. Alright, I'll help you in, you coilslug. The rest of you get inside. Seven, hold my dinner."

"Look who's the kech's mother n— hey!" Gerad's sneer cut off as Dan shoved a food parcel at him. The rest of the Dirks headed for the club as Dan bent towards Tomas.

"So," he said under his breath, "how did it go?"

"Please, not now."

"Still fighting nerves? Don't worry about it! The night's long enough, right? A drink for you both and the dancing will do the rest."

"You're a Scourge upon me, Dan, you really are."

"Save it for the wedding speech. Now up we go!" Dan pulled Tomas to his feet with a grunt. Somewhere between the merciless wit and moronic resolve, Tomas knew Dirk Three was only trying to help. He wanted Tomas and Quil to be happy, and was far more attuned to their feelings than Tomas had known.

"Do you hear that?" Gerad had started towards the club, still juggling the food parcels, but now he turned back towards the main skywalk. He stopped after a moment, but Tomas could only hear the soft music of the square.

"What is it?" he asked.

"It sounded like a firefight," Gerad walked a few steps, then jogged a few more. "People are shouting. Come on!"

Dan and Tomas looked at each other.

Tomas shrugged. "At this point, I'll take any distraction." They went over to Gerad, who was pointing a parcel vaguely across the bridge.

"It sounds like it's over … woah, look at that!" A covered figure sprinted along the far walk, scattering the thin string of pedestrians before them.

A moment later, a pair of golden warriors charged through the resulting wake, one stopping to fire his weapon.

The criminal dodged, and the bolt slagged a section of railing. Pedestrians began screaming, but that only drew Dirks Leader, Three and Seven closer to the action.

"Sun Guards on the hunt, can you believe it! Look, there's another one!" Dan pointed, and sure enough, a third armoured soldier was approaching from the opposite end of the walk. What sort of crime, thought Tomas, would draw such vicious attention? There weren't any police or CSF in sight.

Trapped, the criminal backed against the skywalk railing. The Sun Guards slowed as they closed the net, their guns silent for now. Dan ran up to the railing on the near side of the lane, leaning over it to see better.

There was a moment or two when no one moved, then suddenly the criminal was over the edge, arms and legs splayed. Tomas ran to the railing and looked down.

"It's a Daban!" Dan cheered. "Look at him go!" The Sun Guards fired, but their target swooped and dipped behind an aircar. Tomas lost focus in the stream of vehicles, and only picked the fugitive up again when Gerad pointed.

"He's aiming for the lower walk. What in—check that landing!" The criminal, shrinking against the metallic abyss, had become a ball as they landed on a bridge further down. After rolling a few metres, they popped back up, pushing the startled crowd aside.

"It's a mongrel Taphuun, on my moustache and my life!" Dan spun around and clapped his hands twice. "Which way to the tube? This—no— follow me!" He sprinted along the walk.

"Wait! Dan!" Tomas tore after him before understanding why. The fervour of the scene was contagious; each crisp breath spiked with the thrill of the chase. Gerad came up behind them, arms and legs pumping, the food parcels nowhere in sight.

"We don't … have … weapons," he panted. "What … are we even … doing?"

"Watching!" Dan shouted from in front, running like the skywalk was the Scorching Land itself. "Sun Guard … never … awesome!" he spat out.

"Are you … insane?"

Tomas patted Gerad on the back without stopping, urging him onward. A huge grin split his face, warming his cheeks despite the cold. This *was* crazy, but it was also simple; far simpler than returning to the club and being with Quil.

And if Dan had traded his mission of romance for one of adventure, that suited Tomas fine. He would keep his friend from getting shot or arrested, and he had his commlink if things got out of hand.

The trio caught sight of the tube-shaft and banked towards it, earning odd stares from everyone they passed. The lift was just lowering into position, which gave Tomas enough time to ask Dan between breaths, "How will we … find the … the …" Tomas couldn't think of the word and made a circulating gesture with his hand. "We've lost sight of him."

"We have," Dan panted, "but they haven't." He pointed over Tomas' shoulder. There, past the chasm and the speeders and aircars, the Sun Guards were getting into a lift tube of their own. If there was any action to be found, it would be by following them.

Gerad coughed. The young rookie was leaning against a building, sweat glistening on his forehead. He still looked worried, but his eyes gleamed with that same energy they all shared. He caught Tomas' eye and shook his head.

"What gives, Lead?" he rasped. "I thought you were feeling sick."

21

"Can you feel it?" Krateo said. His voice was a silver whisper that permeated the room, an echo flickering just behind it like a serpent's tongue. Erae shuddered and glanced at the camera on the rail above her. She didn't dare check the angle. She didn't speak, didn't move. She dreaded discovery with each breath, but swallowing them would have done her no good. And she couldn't do anything against the drum of her heart.

The rational part of her brain reminded her that she was surrounded by loud machinery, swaddled in darkness, and masked by the stench of death that filled the whole warehouse. The rest of her didn't care.

"The approach of destiny. The arrival of fate prolonged," Krateo continued in his deep, sliding cadence. "Have any of you guessed the form that invades this plane?"

The other Peret nodded humbly. "There is an evil on the aether wind," Remiyyah said. "It cannot be our Master, for its taste is new to me. But it is powerful, more than I."

"Yes, Sister Shroud, more than even I. For it was by our Master made, and it enters now from its cradle beyond time and space. This moon will be its first witness."

He hissed, his sightless gaze drifting from one sibling to the next. "We are bound by time, and though our wait has been long, our suffering has been mere. Not so this devastation. It has not known to wait, and so each second will summon the unquenchable hunger of the ancient voids."

"Then it is for us?" Charon asked.

"For us, Brother Commander? Nothing is for *us*. The sword is just as sharp to the wielder as to the foe."

"B-but it feels so strong!" Orexis stammered. After the formalities, the young Peret had sat on a large vac-crate, and now she rocked back and forth, hugging her knees. "Won't it kill us too?"

Charon snorted.

"It could," Krateo answered, "if so wielded. It is a fierce beast, this coming sword, but it has no will. Will is the curse we were born with, and not a tool of our Master."

He ran his tongue across his gleaming fangs. "Imagine it. We must strive for destruction, but for this ruin, destruction is merely a symptom of being. How blessed it is!"

What can they mean? Erae wondered. Krateo and Charon seemed to be intoxicated by a ghoulish ecstasy. And who was this Master? Remiel had only told her of the Peret, but even then the topic caused him so much grief that she could understand why the rest remained unspoken.

Krateo's words had frightened Orexis further. "How do we control this weapon if it is without mind?" she cried.

The Kin Lord laughed darkly. "Calm, Sister Siren, calm. Your obsession blinds you." He held up a hand to stay her next protest. "Brother Charon, enlighten her."

Charon was happy to oblige. "You and Remiyyah think nothing beyond your mental enchantments," he snarled contemptuously. "But sometimes the best injury one can inflict upon the brain is a cold blade between its parts."

Remiyyah rolled her eyes, and Orexis paused her fear long enough to stick her nose up at him. "You are equally blind," she scoffed, "and crude. Not all of our problems are solved with your shiny stick."

"Spineless snake," Charon spat, stepping towards her.

"Witless mule," she retorted.

"Enough!" Krateo shouted, and a tremble fled across the walls. "I'll not have my time wasted by your inferiorities. "Orexis cowered, and even Charon withdrew. Krateo fixed upon him.

"What is the report from our Master's armada?" he asked.

"We stand ready to deploy, my Lord," Charon said with pride. "Six thousand Plague-class dreadnaughts crewed and armed, Starfighters and infantry beyond count. At your word a hundred worlds could fall in unison, Kaldea first among them."

"Yet it will not be among them," Remiyyah tutted. "Forget not the deals we have struck, Charon dear. We have let that fool pretend to valour and strength, for seven years no less, and in return he will not lift a finger against us."

"A worthless bargain," Charon growled and spat. "No mortal offers us true contest! Why continue the charade? A promise has no bind on us!"

He fell silent as Krateo held up a hand.

"Indeed not, Brother Commander," he said, the room again washed in his susurrate echo. "Yet the bargain will hold, for it suits us still. Mortals can be tenaciously hopeful when left to it. United in danger, the poisons we have sown are repelled. Even one victory conjures a storm of that sickening courage, that tempered anchor to life.

"And to any life at that. The heathen no longer crawl towards the utopian vision we dangle before them. Their existence can be utterly entrenched in pain, each thought and breath, yet they will defend it as a treasure most precious." Krateo grinned, fangs flashing.

"I know how you long to wrest it from them, brother. I share this desire, but we have been given a different delicacy. By one of their own, the lives of many are given to us. To us! How deliciously novel. Yes, we have waited, but fear would have no flavour without the torture of time to ferment it. We shall wish it lasted longer, once there is nothing left."

So, there had been a bargain after all. Erae was less shocked by the confirmation than she'd expected. Someone, likely Duidain, had bought immunity from the Peret in exchange for mortal lives. Now she had seen their power, she could almost understand.

Amarie shifted beside her, her face red with simmering rage. Some emotions were apparently still stronger than fear.

"But rejoice, brother." Krateo sighed long, regaining her attention. "It is time for war."

He closed one hand, and from it a polluting darkness began to spill out, creeping across the floor in tenebrous claws. When he opened it, Erae saw he held a jet ring set with a white gemstone.

"Whoever wields this band has dominion over Kithmakh, the first of the ruins our Master has devised before the end. A vessel of war, now in the hands of our fiercest warrior."

The first ruin? She watched as Krateo held the ring to Charon, and the younger brother swayed in response. With forced restraint, he reached out, lifting the ring from his elder's hand. As his sisters watched with envy, he raised it and slipped it on his finger.

He screamed.

Light and darkness burst from the ring, shaking the columns and tearing the ice-covered doors from their frames. The catwalk and conveyors lifted from their housing and slammed down again, Erae and Amarie with them. Erae yelped as her injured leg struck the grating, but the sound was lost in the unearthly shriek from below. Remiyyah and Orexis shrank back, but Krateo held his hands wide, basking in the pain of his sibling.

"The ice, Erae!" Amarie whispered frantically over the comm. She clambered to her feet and pulled Erae with her. Sure enough, the ice that had barred their way was gone, as if all Charon's energy was consumed with the fight below. His shriek transformed into a roar of defiance, and a second roar met with it, but not from the other Peret.

"*Hunger.*" The voice growled and cracked, like the very moon was splitting beneath them. Erae took a step towards the stairwell, but her leg protested, and she hissed through her teeth. Foreboding pricked the back of her neck, and she looked down.

Krateo's head was turned up towards her, his smile gone. Could he see her? Sense her pain? Her chest seized, gripped with ice.

Look away. Please, Eladdiyr, take him away.

Krateo looked down, and Erae staggered to the stairwell. The alarms were still ringing outside, red lights flashing, wind howling. And still the growl of the ring followed her, caught in the back of her mind.

Her leg burned, and her lungs felt coated in glass. Amarie caught her as she tumbled down the last few steps.

"Hurry up," Crisp buzzed coolly. He trundled ahead of them through the deserted lot, the way lit by flashing hazard lights. "That shockwave destroyed the camera. I will not join it."

Erae didn't respond. She grabbed another stim from Amarie's kit bag and jammed it into her leg. Then she ran.

Tomas couldn't run much further. As pilots went, he was as fit as the next candidate. But Gerad was younger than him by a few years, and Dan could outrun the Shift itself if he had the right focus. Usually that focus was slender and bashful, or metal and golden.

The Sun Guards might not have been a stack of Draik chips swept from the card table, but Dirk Three kept after them all the same. Tomas had worried that Dan would draw too close and the guards would mistake him for an accomplice to the mongrel fugitive, but he needn't have bothered himself. The golden warriors were Dan's match in zeal and vigour, scattering the crowds before them. It was all Tomas could do to keep up.

He'd never been this low on Ring One before. The aircars were fewer, and the chasms narrow. Tomas glanced up through the layers of walkways and bridges, trying in vain to see the light of the stars. The air felt pressed-down and charged-up, buzzing from the tube lights and steaming from the vents.

And yet they couldn't be more than halfway down. There were still plenty of people ambling around, at once freer and more exultant than the tucked-in society above them. It was louder yet quieter, as though each sound carried a secret. Or it was all in Tomas' head. He lost sight of Dan briefly as he skirted one of the enormous pillars that pushed through the street to support some unnamed monolith far above.

There he was, still on the right path, but getting further ahead. He seemed to ride on the shoulders of those beside him, dodging between parties of sentients, his strides sure. Tomas wiped his brow, spared a look at Gerad, and kept going.

Ahead, the three guards cut across an auto-walk, vaulted over a low wall and dropped from sight. Dan followed less than a minute later but stopped at the wall. The nearby lights reflected off his scalp and kept Tomas from losing him a second time. He excused his way forward and found a moment to breathe at last.

"There they are," Dan pointed down. On the platform below was a vast market packed with stalls of all kinds. Colourful tents and awnings shouldered against the foundations of hulking spires, and banners hung from every bridge and beam within reach. The air was a haze of delicious smells and delightful sounds, A trove of life, Tomas thought, hiding beneath the larger world.

"They jumped that?" Gerad exclaimed. "It's got to be ten metres down!"

"Sun Guards," Dan said by way of explanation. He was still pointing to the three they'd followed, who were sifting through the field of lifeforms with measured care. Whenever one passed a stall, the vendors would hush and the patrons ask to be excused. Silence would hold for a moment, then the guard moved on, and the seller would again shout the quality of his wares.

"He must be down there somewhere," Dan muttered. "But I wonder how they know it. There's got to be a thousand people in that square!"

Tomas looked around but couldn't spot anything in the mass of beings. Skin, scales, fur and feathers all blended together: a microcosm of the Cluster, with new faces joining every second. But the Sun Guards seemed sure of their search, guns sweeping back and forth. The criminal couldn't stay hidden forever.

He studied the edges, expecting to see a hooded villain jumping into a ravine and gliding away, but rising walls cut off almost every avenue. A few ramps led up to the surrounding walks, and thin alleys were carved between the spires. Some paths were so thicketed by pipes and boards that they formed tunnels, and it was anyone's guess where they might lead.

It's a bowl, thought Tomas. *This is the last place I would hide if I were a Daban.* He climbed the walls with his eyes, searching for hidden ledges. A Daban-Taphuun would have strong claws.

If not the walls … he looked at the bridges spanning the marketplace. Banners and flags curtained the metal, riffling in concert whenever a breeze swept through. But over to the right, the movement was disturbed, the fabric catching on something beneath the walkway. Tomas nudged Dan.

It took him a moment, but then his lips curled past his moustache. "Underneath, eh? Good eyes, Lead."

Gerad pushed him out of the way, trying to follow his line of sight. "What's the plan?"

"Uh," Tomas considered. Until this moment, they had been observers of justice. Any action now—even calling to the guards below—would change that. But wasn't this what CSF officers were supposed to do? Did duty draw a line, or clock out when the shift had ended?

The answer was clear. Tomas reached into his pocket for his earpiece.

"You both have comm?" he asked.

"Always," Dan said and tapped his ear.

"No." Gerad grew flustered. "Should I have?"

Tomas shook his head. "It's a wartime habit. Never know when you'll get called to the defence. It's fine. Just stick with me." He turned to Dan. "Can you shake him loose?"

Dan frowned and looked at the bridge. "Yeah. I'll find a brick or something."

"Or something. Just be careful."

"Careful as a cruiser." Dan winked and headed along the walk. Tomas and Gerad made for one of the ramps into the square.

"What do I do?" Gerad asked.

"Keep a bead on the target and run in when he falls." The crowd pressed against them, but Tomas ploughed through, one arm outheld. The banners being disturbed were more towards the centre now, underneath the bridge's apex.

"I'm in position." Dan cracked in his ear. "Where's the target?"

"Under a green Imortech flag," Tomas answered. "See it?"

"Hang on." They were amongst the stalls now, and the current of the crowd forced them beneath a stretch of canvas. The bridge disappeared. Sellers flattered and cajoled in every known language, waving their wares in front of him.

Tomas paused at a knife vendor, but quickly dismissed the idea. Adding a weapon would only endanger the crowd.

"Got it," Dan said. "Green Imortech. I can make the jump, Lead, but I'll need a three-second count …"

"Make the jump?" Tomas forgot the knives and followed Gerad back into the open. Dan had climbed over the railing of a neighbouring bridge and edged cautiously along it. His legs were bent and his eyes wild. "Three, that's not a brick! Three!"

"Two, one …" Dan leapt, caught the banner and swung underneath the bridge. He kicked out at something once, twice, then lurched as a weight fell onto the other side of the material.

"Look out!"

The swing reversed, and as it did the banner tore from the spar that held it. The Daban leapt from the cascading folds, arms spread to glide away, but Dan caught onto his leg. They tumbled down together, crashing through the roof of a stall.

"Dan!" Tomas and Gerad fought their way against the current, even pushing people out of the way. The stall had been some kind of garden-shop, now reduced to spilt soil and smashed ceramic. Dan and the fugitive were missing.

"Dan!" Gerad called again. Tomas' comm popped.

"-right through! He's torn right through my jacket!"

Tomas keyed to respond. "Dan! Where are you?"

"East, into the alley." Dan's voice was pained and angry. "The guards are on him again, but I can't keep up. Follow the blood."

Red splatters formed a line between the feet of the crowd, fresh and shining. Tomas' hand went to his hip, but he was still unarmed. They'd pushed their adventure too far.

He started running. "Are you hurt? Three?"

Dirk Three didn't respond. Tomas ran faster. He and Gerad followed the trail to the edge of the square, in the shadow of the towering walls. There was the alley, as narrow as a mining fissure and nearly as dark, but progress here was quicker than amongst the masses. Dim amber lights kept them from stumbling as they sidled past hissing pipes and under rattling fans.

Gunfire! Tomas ducked instinctively as plasma bolts squealed through the darkness ahead, too quick to see anything by. He guessed a hundred metres between him and the action, but it could easily have been twice that much. He kept going.

The passage was wider now, split by side passages, and if not for the flashes of battle ahead, he and Gerad might have taken the wrong path. He could see better now, which meant the tunnel was near its end. Urging more energy to his limbs, Tomas pushed through and into the open.

They were in a low, paved street that wound tightly between the station's spires. Slate-roofed apartments stacked against each other, fenced by hedges of softly glowing fungi. A small wooden bridge arched over a ravine as if it were no more than a neighbourhood brook.

Beyond the bridge was a firefight. Bolts ricocheted from the bulkheads, charring stone and shattering windows. The Sun Guards were pinned on one side, taking fire from multiple directions. They'd been led into a trap.

One guard peeked up—down again to avoid fire—then snapped a burst towards one of the hedges. A man screamed, and the fire from that corner grew quiet.

"Three?"

Dan's voice crackled in his ear. "I'm on the skywalks, but I've lost them. Where are you?"

"The thick of it!" Tomas replied. He watched in awe as a Sun Guard broke from cover and darted forward with a dancing step that defied the aim of the enemy weapons. The few shots that landed were dispersed by his armour, and the other two Sun Guards were quick to target the source of the salvos, one after the other.

Gerad—what was he thinking! The young pilot had crept over the bridge towards the ambush, his head low. Tomas scurried over, his heart racing, and saw what Dirk Seven had already discovered: a door hinging open, and two more assailants angling to take the guards from behind.

They struck before Gerad could, pulling wicked knives from their sheathes and leaping onto the crouching guards. One guard was felled in an instant, his dropped weapon skidding along the cobblestones. The second twisted and sunk his barrel into the gut of his ambusher. One muffled blast and the cloaked figure went limp in his arms. The smell of burnt flesh filled the air.

Tomas ran forward, scooping up the fallen rifle. The trigger unlocked with a pulse of his palm, and he brought the barrel into line.

The remaining assailant had engaged the second guard, who pulled a knife of his own to block the furious swings of the attacker. After a rapid flurry the attacker inverted his grip and snapped his hilt into the guard's jaw, cracking his mask and sending him spinning to the ground. It gave Tomas the space he needed, and he placed two bolts into the assailant's chest. The figure dropped dead.

"CSF! We're CSF!" Tomas held the rifle out with one hand, desperate not to be confused with the enemy. The skirmish was over, the last weapons silent. Gerad straightened behind Tomas, his hands high in surrender.

The third guard returned from the far end of the street, unspeaking, his gun pointed down. Tomas stepped forward, but his boots struck something soft. He looked down.

The Daban half-blood, the one who had started it all, was face down on the pavement. A symbol was stitched on the back of his tunic: one circle inside another, crossed by three lines. Tomas knew that symbol. Behind him, Geard inhaled sharply.

"*Lead!*"

Tomas snapped up. The second guard was getting to his feet, his cracked mask abandoned by his feet. His face, as he looked towards them ...

Darkness. Nothing. Ebon.

The guard—Ebon—raised his knife and began to howl, the sound of it piercing through Tomas' skull. The other guard added his own death whistle and raised his rifle.

Tomas fired. The guard's weapon was too far to the right to respond. He put three rounds into the face of the closest guard, ducking as he heard the whine of a discharge and saw a flash out the corner of his eyes. He scrambled left and fired again, tracking the source of the shots before he knew where to look. The first bolt weakened the guard's chest, and the second penetrated, lifting him off his feet and into the wall. Tomas' heaving lungs became the only sound.

He turned suddenly, as the path of the battle replayed itself in his mind. The flash of gunfire. The angle of the enemy weapon.

No ...

Gerad was on his back, eyes open to the sky. Smoke curled from the black hole in his chest. His hands grasped the air.

"*No!*" Tomas ran and dropped to his knees, cradling Gerad's head in his hands. "Seven! Gerad, talk to me! Gerad!"

Gerad gasped, and his eyes locked with Tomas'. His lips moved slowly.

Dan cut into his ear. "Tomas, what happened? Did I hear—"

"Call the evac, Dan! Medical, now!"

"Evac? Tomas, where are you?"

"*Call it!*" Tears ran down Tomas' face, and Gerad blinked as they splashed onto him. He gasped again, and the blinking stopped.

There was no void of space to swallow Tomas' scream this time. It bounced between the spires, scraping him raw. He shuddered, then lowered Gerad's head to the ground and passed his hand gently over his eyes.

He fumbled with his comm. "Pick up," he whispered. "Pick up, Quil. Please pick up."

22

Tomas hurried into the carpeted lobby as fast as he could manage without running. A few seconds wouldn't bring back what he'd lost, but they might save what he still had.

Quil was powering down the private skimmer she'd commandeered. Dan was with Gerad on the medical bus. The other Dirks were waiting at one of Ring One's military hospitals.

The hospital is a formality. Tomas thought. *Gerad is dead.*

The lobby lights had been dimmed for the evening shift. Sigsby looked up as Tomas headed directly for Niyott's door. "Commander! My, you look dapper this—"

Tomas cut her off. "Is she in?"

"Yes, but ..."

Tomas keyed the door and stepped through. "General, this is an emergency. The Ebon ..."

General Niyott was sitting behind her desk, an expression of shock swiftly morphing into outrage. Beside her, wearing a broad smile and not the least startled, was Rekkuul Duidain.

Tomas felt an arresting gauntlet land on each shoulder. He turned to see the golden stares of the Sun Guards who had been waiting just inside the door.

"Stand down, stand down," Duidain said. The gauntlets lifted.

"*Commander Amets!*" Niyott roared. "How dare you cross my door uncalled! There is no offence, no injury ..."

"Layla," Duidain cautioned. The General rounded on him, ready to unleash a second barrage, but then she realised her target. With visible restraint, she turned back.

"Salute, Commander Amets."

Tomas did so, shamed by his explosive entrance. His emotions had been a tightly-wound cord since Quil had picked him up. He couldn't allow himself to think back to the scene, or he'd come undone. Gerad's drained face lurked behind Tomas' eyelids, waiting for his thoughts to calm. His mind replayed the expressions of confusion, of failure, of fear, that had crossed his friend's face as he'd died.

"Speak, Commander. Speak and pray that this intrusion is worth your pending unemployment."

"Come now, none of that," Duidain said. "He's clearly distraught. Give him time."

Tomas nodded numbly. What could he say? He'd constructed an entire speech on the journey up, but his audience had rapidly changed. The Sun Guards were here, as was Duidain.

Does he know what those masks hide? He picked them—he has to. A private Ebon army, right at the CSF's heart.

He looked over his shoulder at the beautiful golden visages. Inhibitor collars were nowhere to be seen.

"I ... came to speak to the General," he said slowly. "This is a sensitive matter."

Duidain chuckled. "My, this is exciting indeed. Guards, you may wait outside."

The warriors hesitated, then keyed the door and left. Tomas felt his shoulders drop several centimetres. Duidain, however, remained seated.

"Pardon Councillor, but …"

"Speak, Amets," Niyott ordered.

Tomas' heart crawled into his throat. He swallowed it back.

"Officer Belte … Gerad … is dead."

Tomas didn't see the effect his words had on the room. He'd closed his eyes tight as he fought to keep himself talking.

"We were caught in an engagement between a detachment of Sun Guards and some … others. It was a guard that killed Gerad. They turned on us when we saw what they truly were …"

He opened his eyes and stared at the Chief of Council.

"They were Ebon."

General Niyott was frowning, her hands clasped on the desk before her. Duidain had leaned back in his chair, a smile still beaming from his perfect teeth.

Tomas' right hand was shaking. He balled it into a fist.

"The Defiant call us their enemy," Tomas said. "The Defiant also say the Ebon are not truly beaten. They are not vanquished nor enslaved but are amassing new troops. We call the Defiant pirates and lunatics, but they're preparing for a war they believe is just one Shift-jump away.

"So tell me, Councillor, what exactly is going on."

Duidain shook his head. "Remarkable." He turned to Niyott. "Is he not remarkable?"

"When he's not insubordinate," the General ground out, "or accusing a council member of being in league with pure evil."

"Layla! I never knew you to care about me so. Haha!" Duidain's mirth seemed uglier by the second: a garish and grating light in a room that should have been grey. Did he see all of this—see Tomas—as one quaint joke?

"Remarkable to the end. My boy, did—ah!" He looked past Tomas as the door opened. "Come in, Agent. You're late."

Tomas found himself standing to the side as the figure passed, but whether he moved or was pushed, he couldn't say. The newcomer was tall, dressed in the silver-whites of a CSF officer, and a narrow visor of black hid his eyes. He was breathing heavily, and sweat beaded on his forehead.

"I have come very far, very quickly," he said, his voice dark. "*You* were not supposed to send for the pilot until I arrived."

Duidain spread his hands. "But I didn't! He arrived quite on his own, and for the same purpose, no less!"

"Did he?" The agent's gaze snapped to Tomas. The visor looked to be solid metal, letting nothing in or out. Without a doubt, this was the intelligence operative Tomas had seen on the Jerassh shift station.

Minutes seemed to pass as the agent's breath settled. Tomas kept his own breaths shallow, feeling as though they were an affront. Sound and thought were not permitted, caught in an iron vice.

Abruptly, the agent turned to Niyott. "You have an assault to plan," he said.

Niyott glowered but stood. She nodded once to Duidain, glanced at Tomas, rounded the desk and left. Tomas' jaw slackened. He watched with frozen blood as the agent seated himself in Niyott's vacant chair. The visor continued to stare Tomas down.

"He has seen them, then?"

Duidain grinned wide. "Oh yes! Just now on one of the rings, I gather."

"And he survived?"

"So, quite so! Though another pilot was killed. I was just—"

"You are an extraordinary being, Commander Amets." The agent smiled unkindly, cutting Duidain off. "Tenacious beyond the call of service. Beyond obedience even, it seems."

Tomas dared to speak, though his voice came smaller than he intended. "I want to know what's going on, sir."

"Curiosity is a trouble, Commander," the agent tutted. His voice had a hissing edge, like a smothered flame lashing towards fresh fuel. "Puzzles are safest when left to those who know all the pieces. Otherwise you might end up speared on a friend's blade.

"Or," he tilted his head, "the blade might be your own. Who chose to follow the Sun Guards tonight?"

Dan. It was Dan. Tomas swallowed. "One of my pilots had the idea."

"The one that died? It matters not. Ideas are for the soldiery, but *decisions* are made by people of responsibility, aren't they *Commander?*"

Tomas felt a claw of ice rake across his heart. "I didn't ask to be told what I already know," he bit out.

Duidain reached a hand across the desk. "Come now, Tomas. Don't guilt yourself. If it's a puzzle, then you'd better get a few more pieces, eh? Guards! In here, if you please."

The door slid open again, a sound Tomas was quickly associating with his pain. The guards stepped in, ignorant of how their presence made his anger boil in tandem with his grief and fear.

"Remove your helmets" Duidan ordered. Tomas flinched, but forced himself to watch as the guards each raised their hands to their mask and lifted it up.

Blue eyes. Pink skin. A mole, even, on one left cheek.

They were Human.

"I must apologise, Tomas," Duidain said. "I did not think the Defiant were this powerful. Or *bold*, indeed! Running around our very homes. Supplanting my retinue with their dark warriors—to think of it!"

"The Ebon ... and the Defiant?"

The agent nodded. "You were at Jerassh. You saw the commotion they caused. Surely you trust your eyes more than the sympathetic recruitment pitch they fed you?"

Tomas began to nod, then stopped. "But tonight. The guards—I mean the Ebon—chased the Defiant. Slaughtered them."

"A tamed deathbeast is still a deathbeast, Commander. The Defiant overestimated their control."

It should have made sense, but it didn't. Something churned within Tomas, unwilling to be settled, loudest whenever the agent's words might have drowned it out. He pictured Raphael's eyes, pained with the loss of his sister.

"I don't know," he said at length. "I don't think the Defiant would go that far."

Duidain laughed. "But of course they would! Have you forgotten the prince you slew? The Ebon welcomed Ben-Eloah with—"

"*Enough!*" The agent jumped up suddenly, his voice a growl. An arm shot towards Duidain, just shy of grabbing his throat. "That name has no place here! That scoundrel died, and the Defiant eagerly follow him to the same fate."

Duidain's mouth was wide in fear, his face pale. He suddenly looked very small and very old.

The agent turned back to Tomas. "Their lies poisoned you too easily, I think," he snarled. "No small feat, seeing how they've murdered two of your friends. Did you not love them, Commander?"

"No!" The reply was feeble. Tomas shrank back, wilting beneath the callous gaze of the agent's visor. Why couldn't he say it louder? He knew his life had been bought by the blood of his friends. They followed him, flew with him, died for him. That was why he couldn't stop fighting for what they believed in.

"Well? Do you not want justice? Revenge?"

"Yes."

"Do you?"

"I do!" Tomas shouted. "Of course I do!"

From beneath the visor came a wicked smile. "Good."

The agent sat down again, his fury diffused as quickly as it had been summoned. Duidain's shaking breaths became the loudest sound in the room. The Sun Guards shifted their feet, their helmets held beneath one arm.

The moment was brief. Directing a smirk at Tomas, the agent reached into his suit, pulled out a data disc, and tossed it onto the desk. It looked like any other, but Tomas knew what it contained.

"You should never have kept this, Commander," the agent mocked, "but you can yet bring salvation out of your evil. You sought for adventures and secret councils? Well, here we are! We hold back the dark things of this world, and now you get to help us.

"In fact ..." He glanced at Duidain, who hesitated before offering a polite smile. "You have already provided the very means of your redemption."

"I'm sorry?" Tomas asked. "What are you talking about?"

"The disc, Commander. I found it in your quarters, and it tells me the Defiant have enemies in the Shb System. Without question, they will have gone there to face them. You will capture them there, and avenge all those they have aggrieved. We shall hold every piece, and no truth will be hidden. Surely this is the justice you seek?"

It was. The storm in Tomas subsided, leaving a sombre but unshakable decision. Tomas pictured Amarie in chains, her self-assured scowl broken by the weight of her defeat. Next would come Marpe, Raphael, and Erae. She belonged there, no matter the mercy she had shown him.

But the CSF still had its issues, and Tomas was no longer blind to that. He almost wanted to be, but the option for ignorance had been taken away from him. Captain Forn was one example: proud beyond recourse, dutiful beyond kindness. This agent was another. When he smiled, Tomas felt gored by a jagged blade. The thought of Erae under his hands ...

"I'm in," Tomas said, ignoring that he probably didn't have a choice. "But only if you let me keep my promise."

The visor stared. "Go on."

"I made a promise to myself," Tomas continued. "Captain Tamah and her crew were my captors, and I vowed that I would see them in chains. I would like to handle their interrogations personally."

The agent grinned, his smile twice as wide as Duidain's had ever been, and no less joyful. "That," he said, "is a truer justice than any I could deal. You've surprised me again, Commander Amets, and I'm sure you will make your fallen squad mates—and the CSF—very proud."

Tomas shook his head. "I only do my duty."

"As do we all."

The question of the Ebon was still unanswered, but capturing the Defiant would change that. Only then could Tomas sort the lies, deliberate or otherwise, from the truth. And for Gerad's sake, he would.

The agent rose and held out a hand, his visor flashing white as it caught the light of the sun lamp. His hand caught the light too—or rather, a ring on the agent's index finger, fixed with a white jewel.

Light. The CSF had called themselves a light against the darkness of the Ebon. Hope, when hope was all they had. But while light could illuminate, it could also blind.

Which is it this time? Tomas wondered grimly as he grasped the agent's hand in his own.

It had only taken ten minutes to send a message to the Shard. Considering the size of the report and the numb shock Erae was in, it was remarkably quick.

But that did nothing to reduce the fourteen-hour wait that was to follow. Shb and Hagos were not neighbouring stars, and Fal-Comm transmission speeds had no pity for those who had just stumbled into the end of the Cluster.

That's what it felt like—the end of the Cluster. Only Erae didn't know when it would begin, or if it had already found her. She could have left, shooting off with the boarding ramp extended, imagining hordes of Ebon rushing after her, desperate for home.

But what if they followed her? What if she was needed here to prevent what might otherwise be? No, it was far better to wait, repeating to herself the vain hope that their presence had gone undetected. For every minute they were still alive, the notion was more likely, yet her anxiety only grew.

Sleep was torture, and it took Erae three hours of restless wriggling to catch even a wink of it. When she did, it was infected with horrid, whorling darkness that seeped under the door and leered over her cocoon with bright, piercing eyes.

She lurched awake to the sound of distant explosions.

"Erae!" Amarie was screaming from the catwalk, urging her towards the stairwell. But cold talons of ice barred their way, reaching forward to snare them. Hideous snarls filled her ears and raked across her skull and spine. The grating heaved beneath her as—

"Erae!" Amarie shoved the side of her cocoon, waking her properly. "The packing house, it's on fire!"

"What?" she dragged herself out of her haze.

"Just now! You can see the smoke over the spaceport wall." Amarie stepped back to peer through the viewport. "It was them. They're going to find us!"

She was speaking Erae's own fears aloud, but at least that gave Erae a chance to combat them. She climbed out of her cocoon and squeezed next to Amarie.

The sky was still dark where she could see it past the glaring lights of the spaceport. Shbiy Prime's orange glow stained the rooftops, making it seem as though all of Vilspire was ablaze.

And it might yet be. She could see the cloud of smoke rising from the direction of the warehouse. Was this the start of the Peret's war, or just a way of destroying evidence?

"We were never seen," she reasoned. "The cameras were disabled, and are now probably destroyed. It's in our head, Am, that's all."

Amarie kept her eyes on the smoke, her shoulders low. "It won't matter," she muttered.

Give me something to work with, Am. I can't keep having hope for the both of us. "I get it, Am. I'm scared too. Terrified. But they would have come by now if they knew we were here. Why wait? You saw what he did to them!"

The deck shook with another distant explosion, and a great belch of red smoke joined the first. Both women jumped back, Erae's hand grasping for her pendant, Amarie's for her holster. They'd slept in their clothes last night—a healthy precaution.

"Look." Erae forced calm. "We just have to make it till morning. We'll think better in the light. Remiel will send us new instructions, and we'll be in the Shift before lunch."

Amarie shook her head. "They know who we are."

"They never saw us, I promise!"

"You don't get it, do you?" Amarie clenched her fists, then gestured out the window. "They *know who we are*, Erae! He told them, just like I said he would!"

"Who?"

"Tomas!" Amarie glanced back and forth as if she might spot him lurking in the corner. For a student of stealth and shadows, exposure was the greatest fear. "I sat with him. I even dared to pity him!" Her hand went back to the holster.

"I hate him!"

Erae retreated a step. "It wasn't his fault. He didn't know anything about the Neiru."

"You believe him?" Amarie glared at her with wild eyes. "He's one of them, Rae! You heard it right from the mouth of the enemy. The CSF are working with the Ebon. Every one of them! I should have killed him.

"In cold blood, Am?" Erae countered. "He was saving people—"

"He was deceiving you! Why are you always against me? Why is he worth protecting?"

"I'm protecting you!" Erae yelled. "You don't walk away from murder, Am. It marks you, chains you, turns you into one of them. We have to be better!"

"No, we have to be stronger." Amarie drew her pistol, flipped it, and pressed the sight against Erae's chest. "We could have killed him, but we didn't. Now he's told his admirals, and they've told their generals, and the whole Ebon army knows who we are. And those *things*," she threw a hand towards the viewport, "cannot be killed. I can't stop them, Rae. Can you?"

"Stopping the Peret has never been our job."

"You're right—stopping the CSF was." Amarie's voice became deadly even. "So next time I get the chance, you'd better not get in my way."

Erae didn't need the accusation to be spelt out for her. Tomas had been captured on her orders. He'd been healed, fed and freed by her. She had always known what might come of it.

She still believed it was right.

"If you keep charging in, bolts flying, you know …" Erae breathed deep as she tried not to say it. "You know what will happen."

Amarie didn't blink. "Not before I've killed scores of them. My death is worth that."

"And what about your life?" Exasperation wore at her. How long would this argument replay? "You think the CSF are nothing, yet you've weighed yourself against them. What is the cost?"

Amarie's lip quivered, but she forced a shrug. She'd closed herself off. "Nothing. It will cost you nothing."

"You know …" a black hole formed in the pit of Erae's stomach. "That's not true."

"I know."

They stared at each other, unwilling to attack, unable to retreat. The lights from the spaceport cut across the deck between them, across the pistol in Amarie's hand.

She brought her arm down. "I'm taking a walk."

Erae watched as she keyed the door to leave. It seized halfway, resisting even when Amarie shoved against it. Muttering a curse, she slammed her weapon into the hull, squeezed through, then struck the hull again from the other side. The fading sound of her boots could be heard as she climbed down the central ladder.

When all was silent, Erae took a small step forward, closed her eyes, and leant her head into the water pipe on the wall. Her thumb and forefinger pinched the bridge of her nose, one word on her mind.

Failure. Failure to be a captain. Failure to be a sister. Failure to be a friend.

Eladdiyr save her.

The wall speaker crackled to life. [Captain? Do you have a moment?]

She sighed and stretched an arm to the panel. "Driz, this had better be important."

[It's a message from Gabriel, Captain. We're expecting one, I know, but—]

"It's too soon," Erae finished for him, a shiver pulsing through her. "They can't have gotten my report yet, let alone sent a reply." Her head left the water pipe.

"On my way."

Driz had the message queued to her monitor by the time she arrived. He was sitting on the back of his chair, a sleeping blanket wrapped around him, an empty bulb in his lap.

[Everything all right?] He asked as she clambered through the portal.

"That obvious, huh?"

[It's a face you seem to wear more and more,] he chittered. He scratched an ear. [Also, it's a small ship.]

"I'll put makeup on next time," she said sarcastically. She hoisted herself into her seat, reached above her head and activated the recording.

Gabriel flickered onto the screen, white eyes flashing at her. Of all the Celah Neiru, he was always the most serious, the most grave. Warning was evident on his thin, ghostly face.

"Do not fear, Captain," he began. His voice was like wind blowing through hollow ice. At times it had refreshed her, but now it stood her hair on end.

"I believe this message will reach you too late."

23

"Time and attention are crucial if you are to survive the next moments," Gabriel continued. "A CSF task force is headed to Shbiy. If you leave now, there is a chance you may escape it."

"Start the pre-flight," Erae ordered Driz. She punched the comm, and a ready alarm sounded throughout the ship. She strapped herself in as she listened.

"If you do not escape, you must choose your course wisely and swiftly. Great pain is headed towards you, and the CSF ride the crest. I cannot say who may survive."

Erae ran her hands over the switches, warming the engines. Lights turned on, and with a sickening lurch, the gravity activated around her, shifting her weight to her feet. "How far away is Captain Ira and the *Avail*?"

[Three minutes by point drive.] Driz chittered. [I'll put out the yellow alert. Wait, we're receiving comm.] He keyed it through.

"I've told you, we've already paid! I'm not going to double it because you can't keep a record!"

"Amarie!" Erae's pulse raced. "She's outside, Driz. External cameras."

Gabriel vanished from her screen, his final words mixed with the ready alarm and Amarie's strained voice. She was at the end of the boarding ramp, her body poised for combat.

"But you scanned us yesterday! Scorching kech, do you know what time it is?"

Not far in front of her was the oily port inspector, his scanner in one hand, tome-tile in the other. A port guard flanked him on each side, holding their weapons casually.

Not now. Erae pleaded. *Eladdiyr why now?*

She could only hear Amarie's side of the conversation. She was edging back towards the *Empress*, her hands ready by her side.

"Of course I have nothing to hide! It's the principle! Who's to say you won't attach some random crime to my record and blackmail me with it?"

"I'm going down." Erae released her webbing and stood up.

"Alright, don't warp yourself! I'll take the scorching scan. If I'd known what sorta place this was, I'd—"

Amarie drew her pistol and fired, catching the inspector in his open mouth. He flew back into the guards, and Amarie dove for the cover of the boarding ramp. The two guards opened fire.

"No!" Erae cursed, lunged towards the ladder, then doubled back. "Driz, open the bottom cargo doors."

She punched her console, and the engines roared to life. Amarie snapped off a few more shots, but they went wide of their target. She was pinned, with no freedom to aim.

Erae keyed her mic. "Amarie, can you hear me?"

"Tell me you're bringing the gun around."

Erae placed a hand on the acceleration lever. "No time. Get as close as you can and mind the ion wash. Shields in three."

Amarie jumped towards the hull, her clothes and hair battered by the dust the engines were stirring up. The guards fired after her, but the bolts dispersed with a blue crackle before they could land.

"Don't fry me!"

"Into the cargo bay, now!" Erae twitched the lever, and the *Empress* lifted off the ground and began to hover. Ionic discharge blasted out from under the engines, clipping Amarie's shins as she hurried around, disappearing from the monitor. The guards kept tracking her from outside the shields.

Erae twisted the yoke, sending the ship spinning. The boarding ramp struck both guards from behind, flooring them. They didn't get up.

"Hold still!" Amarie cried. Erae flicked between the cameras but couldn't see where she had gone.

[Local fighters are scrambling.] Driz warned. [The port authority is sending a hail.]

"Am?"

"Doors closed," Amarie said. Erae shoved her palm against the acceleration lever. The *Empress* shot into the sky with a deafening crack, blackening the ground beneath it. In seconds, the spaceport diminished to a single point on the radar. Vilspire soon followed.

"How many fighters?"

[Two, and not very fast.]

"Make sure Captain Ira's pilots are suiting up. Amarie, get in the gun."

"If the lift ever makes it down, sure!"

The ready alarm was still wailing. Erae flicked it off. Where was the shift gate at this hour? She found the heading and adjusted her angle.

Driz squeaked in alarm. [Some fighters just point-jumped in! They're bearing towards the moon.] He swatted his console. [I'm reading six drive signatures, starfighter size.]

And we've barely left the ground. Looks like you were right, Gabriel. Erae checked the status of the point drive, then the chin gun. Her options were running out.

"Call *Avail* in," she told Driz as she angled towards the incoming fighters. "Don't shoot until I say. Let them think we're trapped."

[And if they don't want to talk?]

"They'll talk." Erae tightened her grip on the yoke. "They have to."

The *Empress* cleared the last threads of atmosphere, vaulting into open space. The radar showed six CSF Wasps rapidly closing in front of her and two more closing behind. Erae slowed the engines and focused on breathing slowly.

Anxiety had left her, despite the absolute mess they were in. Waiting for her doom, it seemed, was much more harrowing than doom itself. She couldn't fight her nightmares, but she could fight this.

She zeroed her acceleration, letting inertia dictate her course, resting her hand lightly on the lever. Her other hand was fused to the yoke as she watched the distance between ships scroll down.

[We're receiving a new hail, Captain.] Driz said. [It's coming from the lead Wasp.]

"Put them through." Her eyes ran over the status board again, checking everything was ready.

A soft static hiss trickled out of the cockpit's speakers, followed by a voice. "*Silent Empress*," it said, "By the order of General Niyott of the Core Star Fleet, your ship and crew are under arrest. You will break from your course and enter a high orbit of Shbiy IX. Then you will power down all active systems and await instruction. If you fail to comply with these commands, you will be deemed hostile and we will forcibly detain you."

The voice was distorted somewhat by the refractive effects of the *Empress'* shields, but Erae thought it was familiar. She looked at her co-pilot.

"How long till the *Avail* arrives?"

[Eighty seconds.]

Too long to stay silent. Erae keyed the mic. "Negative on course change, Wasp. Our thrusters seized on lift-off. I'm trying to organise a repair vessel from the ground."

"It's nice to know your so-called kingdom isn't above deceit and lies, Captain Tamah."

"I …" Erae's comeback stalled as she realised to whom she was speaking. "*Tomas?*"

"You can't run this time, Captain," Tomas said gravely. "If you surrender now, you will receive a fair trial for your crimes."

"*Lying Scourge-ridden rat!*" Amarie's voice cut in through the internal system. She'd made it to the dorsal gun. "Erae, tell him I wish I'd shot him as he lay bleeding in the sand! Tell him I'm not going to miss a second time, and it'll be more than he deserves to die at my gun!"

If it buys us more time. "Amarie says she regrets saving you," Erae summarised.

"She shouldn't. My pilots have a score to settle with Miss Amarie, and I may be the only thing restraining them. In fact, they—excuse me." Tomas paused as if listening. "They vow to drink her blood-mist while it's still warm, using her vacuum-frozen finger bones as straws."

Erae smiled despite herself. "You wouldn't happen to have a Gazam amongst you, perchance?"

"The sooner you power down, the less likely he'll be the one conducting your interrogation," Tomas responded coolly. "This is your last chance, *Empress.*"

Erae glanced at Driz, who held up four fingers, then three, two …

Guide me now, my king, with your hand on mine. Don't let my friends die.

… one. With a protracted flash of metal and light, *Avail* disengaged its point drive and burst into sight before them.

"Enemies marked, all squadrons deploy and engage. Fly without fear, and hear the horns calling!" Captain Ira's exuberant cry set a warmth in Erae's heart. "*Avail* to *Empress*. *Avail* to *Empress*. Everything alright, Captain?"

Amarie cheered through her headset, and Driz drummed his paws on the dash. The *Empress* shook as Erae punched the acceleration, fire stirring in her spirit.

"*Empress* here. We've encountered some lane traffic, but something tells me it'll clear soon."

"Copy that *Empress*. Tekoa! Ahoh! Sweep that squadron of living debris aside!"

The *Avail* was an AAR12 Spine-class carrier. Its bow was tall and wide, a heavily armoured 'skull' that narrowed up and backwards into a long squadron hangar roofed with cannons. As Erae watched, twelve starfighters launched from each side simultaneously, forming into flights and banking towards Tomas' location on the radar.

"Erae," Tomas warned, his voice tense. "No one has to die. Call them off."

On the radar, the CSF Wasps were drawing together: six red blips ensnared in a net of blue. The two starfighters from Vilspire had broken off their pursuit and were running for home. Erae shook her head.

I guess Remiel was wrong about you, Commander.

"You're in my exit vector," she said aloud. "This call isn't mine to make anymore."

"You'll kill them!"

Erae faltered. Tomas sounded genuinely panicked, but for her life, not his. She pulled back on the lever.

"Avail …"

"Contact!" Ira and Driz cried out at the same time. "Four points headed our way. Level the shields, auxiliaries up!"

Both ships had generous scanning ranges, but that meant nothing to the speed of light. Erae watched in rising horror as a bright streak split the space between *Avail* and her starfighters, slowing into the shape of a

Liberator-class frigate. Another Liberator appeared, then two Syphon-class frigates, Wasps pouring from their sides. The Defiant fighters curled away from their target to face the new threat.

And Erae was too far away to help. There was a moment of revelation on each side, a collective breath from each lifeform and waiting star.

Then plasma scarred the night.

"All guns fire!" Ira barked out his commands. "Target the Syphons. Culverins, fire! Helm, send us down and get the spine guns in range. Tekoa Squadron, draw them over our head."

Erae launched the *Empress* forward, aiming towards the roiling cloud of starfighters. The radar was a hive of blips, banking, spinning, winking out. There was no point counting them. Against four CSF frigates, the Defiant could only pray.

Save them, Eladdiyr. Don't tell me I've killed them again.

The Liberators manoeuvred to *Avail*'s stern, concentrating their fire towards the gun emplacements on top of the carrier's spine. Shields flashed and failed under the joint assault, and the hull began to char and peel.

It was a timid scene compared to the firefight at the ship's bow. The two Syphons had drawn alongside the carrier's head and were pummelling it mercilessly. They were ugly, brutish ships, choked with guns at the front and sides, clustered with engines at the rear.

"Hold tight, Ira, we're nearly there." Erae glanced at Driz, who had both paws on the weapon controls.

"Keep firing! Focus on the port side. Shields—*what?* What are you doing, *Empress?* Break off!"

"Leave?" Erae shook her head. "All of us or none of us, Captain."

An explosion rippled along a portion of *Avail*'s spine, and the comm was swallowed in static for a moment.

"—all that's good and peace, run!" Ira cried. "You're the only ones with a chance. We came here to get you *out,* Tamah! You're the reason—" Static broke across the rest.

Don't say it like that. Please don't.

Erae felt sick. She couldn't live with her guilt if she fled, but she might not live at all if she stayed. And if she did die, it would be in fear of the duty she didn't have the strength to face. Everything was driven by fear.

But it doesn't have to be. Please, Eladdiyr, tell me the choice to make.

On the radar, blips began winking out. Blue, red, more blue. Faint, soundless explosions dotted the sky, each an airless marker of a starfighter pilot's last breath. Another soul joined the canopy of stars.

"Surrender."

The voice wasn't so much heard as felt within her, and it stamped onto Erae's brain like a firebrand. She blinked, ignorant to the approaching battle, all sense turned inward.

Surrender had never been an option. It hadn't crossed her mind. More importantly, it didn't make sense. Yet the thought had invaded, and as she tried to recall the sound, it came only in her own voice, calm and at peace.

Was this … *him?* Truly? She had yearned to hear the King's voice all her life, but now everything was risked upon her belief. Suddenly, she was afraid, not because she didn't know what to do, but because she did.

"Surrender."

Her hands shook as she pulled back on the lever and began to zero her velocity. She hovered over the power controls momentarily, then shunted energy away from the guns. Driz barked in alarm.

"My gun's cold!" Amarie panicked over the comm. "Something's wrong. Erae, we'd better—Erae! Was this you? What are you doing? We have to help!"

Erae's whole body was trembling now. Her finger struggled to key the mic.

"Captain … Captain Ira …"

But the Captain wasn't listening. Between bursts of static, she heard him frantically giving orders to his crew, and she heard the answering reports as hull integrity was breached and thrusters began to fail. The Syphons were targeting the main rotary engines, and the shields were broken through.

On the portside hull, blue fire struck sun-steel. The engine casing resisted at first, then began to warp, red-hot metal peeling up like a beautiful flower, then swelling as if returning to a bud.

"Erae *do something!*"

The *Avail*'s portside plasma culverin kicked its barrel back and forth, bombarding the attacker with shuddering orbs of energy. The whittle cannon mounted on the top of the skull also turned to fire, and a blizzard of electrons, invisible but full of deadly power, tore through the short void between the ships, accompanied by a guiding beam of plasma.

The Syphon's shields flared and crackled where the electrons impacted it, evaporating with a coruscating burst. The next payload to leave the culverin carved a molten trench across the frigate's vulnerable topside, exposing several deck layers and the vertical drop hangars on either side. The ship was destroyed.

But it was too late. *Avail*'s port engine exploded, and as its blossoming fire engulfed the main engine, a second set of explosions occurred. The comm was filled with pain and exclamation as two-thirds of the skull was swallowed in pressure and heat.

Then the fireball retreated into itself, and those two-thirds were gone. The speakers hissed and popped, then fell silent as the channel was lost.

"No!" Amarie screamed and slammed against the bulkhead. Driz just stared.

Her mind numb, Erae muted the output from the gun-well's microphone, then set her own to broadcast on all frequencies.

"Captain Tamah to Defiant forces, Captain Tamah to Defiant forces. Cease fire. I repeat, cease fire and reform into your squadrons." She swallowed, then continued. "CSF forces, this is Captain Tamah of the *Silent Empress*. As the highest-ranking surviving officer … I officially declare our surrender."

"Acknowledged, Captain." The replying voice was female, cold and broadcasting on the same inclusive spectrum as Erae. "*Intrepid* to all CSF forces: withhold fire. The fight is ours. *Empress,* prepare your vessel for boarding."

The thrusters finished decelerating and shut off, dropping the cockpit into near silence. The flashes of combat stalled, then ceased. The glow of drive emissions winked out as starships found the survivors of their squadron and shut down their engines. Soon the space was nothing but dark, floating hulls, the dreaded living indistinguishable from the tortured dead. Erae switched off her monitor, not daring to count the blips that remained.

"Please, *Intrepid*, the *Avail* might have launched their lifeboat," she said. "Please search for survivors."

"Of course, Captain. We'll have the port send a rescue shuttle," the woman answered. "You and yours have an appointment with justice, and I'd hate to see any of you take the easy way out."

24

Two hours later, they were back on Shbiy IX, in one of the moon's vast, grassy fields. The motley Defiant starfighters—Spacejets, Wasps, War-Moths, and even an old Lunar-56—were arrayed in misshapen flights fifty metres away. There should have been more of them, Erae chastised herself. There should have been twenty-four. But Erae had called, and *Avail* had come to save her. They had sacrificed themselves for her freedom, yet here she was, knees in the dirt, hands behind her back.

Midnight was long past, but the field was not dark. The western sky was aflame with the intense oranges of Shbiy, which reflected its star's light with cosmic diligence. It stared Erae down, searing a brand of treachery across her heart. The whole field was stained in colours of fire, summoning the souls of the slain in wicked shadows upon the long grass. They reached for her with slender, accusing fingers.

She had chosen this for them, based on a single word. The only consolation was that they were still alive, but as she watched the Defiant fighters patrol slowly overhead, she had to wonder for how long.

The rest of the CSF ships were on the far side of the field, hidden behind a low rise. Pilots and infantry troops continued to trickle over the hill to join those already guarding the prisoners until Erae was sure all three surviving frigates had been emptied. It reminded her once again how badly they had been outnumbered. How badly she had failed.

The *Empress* was resting tall and silent beside the starfighters and the rescued lifeboat—a second consolation, though she had seen no sign of Ira. He'd died fighting for his cause, a captain worthy of the title.

Erae was kneeling in the front row of prisoners, her hands bound behind her with a synthetic cord that dug into her flesh; there had been too few handcuffs to go around. Her blood was sticky and warm between her fingers, but it wasn't *her* blood that filled her thoughts.

The reaching shadows drew closer.

She ducked away from them. *We are still alive*, she forced herself to repeat. *We are alive, and with life comes hope.*

Surrender had saved some of her friends, but if Erae didn't do something, those lives would be spent wasting away in some dark, forgotten cell. Charges of treason and murder were not easily shaken—not when the evidence would shortly cause a meteor shower in Shbiy IX's upper atmosphere. That alone would have them mining asteroids for life.

It would only be by Erae's cooperation and willingness to talk that some of them might walk free. The rest would just have to wait and hope—hope that Eladdiyr saved them before they withered away.

She needed them to hope.

The soldiers guarding the field fell silent, and Erae looked up to see a group of approaching officers. The woman who led them wore the lavender-on-white attire of the CSF's senior ranks, her white hair kindled red by the planet's light. Her steps were as sure and precise as a drill sergeant's despite the awkwardness of the low gravity.

Eight others joined her as she marched towards the captives, some wearing fleet uniforms, the rest in flight suits. As they stopped, Erae studied their rank bars. The stern Human female was, it seemed, a general. Those with her were a mix of captains and commanders. Erae's eyes met with one of them.

Tomas looked away before she did.

The general stopped walking and turned to confer with the officer on her right. He was a tall Human, wearing a black visor over his eyes. He grinned ferociously as the general turned back to address the prisoners.

"Which one of you is the so-called Captain Erae Tamah?" she called in a clear voice that rang across the field.

Erae couldn't raise her hands while they were bound behind her, but she wasn't about to break her silence. She struggled to bring her feet beneath her, gasping as panic took over. She knew what came next, and she wasn't ready.

She was terrified, drowning in the anticipation of what might be days, weeks, years of pain. Guilt and fear were a dual torrent upon her shoulders, far stronger in pulling her down than the moon's weak gravity was.

But it was time to be brave, if not for herself, then for her friends. Her whole body trembled beneath the skin as she stood.

The General's head snapped towards Erae with a robotic rigidity, and she marched forward, her hands clasped behind her back in a mocking parallel to Erae's own.

The Defiant prisoners to either side shrunk back as the woman stopped in front of Erae. Her burnt-copper gaze trapped her in its sights.

The General turned to Tomas. "This is her?"

A nod. "Yes, General Niyott."

"Good." The General lashed out with a backhanded slap, swivelling Erae's jaw and sending her careening to the ground. Fire exploded on her cheek.

The light gravity carried her as she fell and rolled, but only slightly. She took the impact on her side, and her head smacked into the grass with enough force to blur her vision.

Blood filled Erae's mouth. She tried to spit it out but only succeeded in a partial expulsion that dribbled over her cheek. Her wrists burned as she fought against her bonds, instinct driving her to use her hands, desperate to right herself and get the weight of her body off her lungs.

Pain first, and diplomacy second. Is it any wonder we don't like the CSF?

Her assailant spat, and Erae felt the saliva strike her back. "Pathetic." She grabbed Erae's shirt and hauled her to her knees, leaning in close enough for Erae's nose to catch traces of jolt on her warm breath.

"So, this is the half-breed mutt that thinks she can command a rebellion. Your reputation speaks far greater than the sorry excuse you've turned out to be. A rim-world bully too scared to face her foe head-on!

"Too scared to kill a prisoner, too scared to die with honour, too scared to speak," she mocked. "Was it your mother or father that was a spineless alien worm?"

Erae replied with a fresh collection of saliva and blood that sprayed all over the General's face.

Niyott didn't flinch and launched a fist straight into Erae's nose. Only the hand holding her shirt stopped her from falling a second time. A groan of pain escaped her lips, feeble and broken.

"Suited slime!" Erae heard Amarie's yell through ears that pounded with blood. "Leave her alone, you Scourge-bitten slug sack!"

"Bite your tongue, rebel!" A guard stepped forwards and slammed the butt of his rifle into the back of Amarie's head. She went down with a whimper, falling below the shoulders of the other prisoners.

Erae squirmed against the General's grip, twisting to see over the heads between her and Amarie. *Don't speak,* she willed. *Stay silent, and they'll forget you.* Erae needed to be the target here. The surrender was hers, and so was the sacrifice. No one else needed to get tortured or interrogated or hurt.

The General wrenched her back around. "What's this? I do believe the dog is capable of feelings. Maybe there's some Human left in you after all."

"More than in you, witch," Erae ground out.

The General raised her fist again, and Erae closed her eyes, bracing for the impact.

"Look how scared you are!" Niyott laughed and threw Erae into the dirt. "Why did I come all this way for such a worthless lifeform!" She wiped the blood from her face. "You're going to crack like a jar-lizard egg in a light breeze."

I need to be stronger than this. Shame flooded Erae, colouring her cheeks darker than her bruises did. Her head pounded.

"Don't worry about your precious little pet over there," Niyott continued. "Commander Amets told me which of your friends will help me appear the most … *persuasive.* I'll keep them nice and safe for a long, long time.

"The rest, though …" the General sneered and sidestepped to the pilot kneeling next to Erae. In one swift motion, she drew her pistol and jammed it against the Daban's skull-tight forehead. He looked up at the weapon with wide, terrified eyes.

"The rest have a more immediate use to me." Before Erae could do or say anything, Niyott pulled the trigger.

"*No!*" the sound of the weapon's discharge was inaudible against Erae's scream. She watched, horrified, as the pilot fell back. The top half of his head was a bloody, smoking hole, and the smell of ozone and burning flesh was instant and putrid in the air.

How could she? How could *she? We were promised a trial.* The thoughts collapsed in on themselves as Erae knelt with her mouth open, her soul still screaming even though her breath had run out.

What have I done? We're all going to die! Amarie and Marpe and Driz and Crisp are all going to die!

A primitive, animal sense of mortality overcame her, and she began to shudder.

I'm going to tell these people everything I know… and then I'm going to die.

"Stop!" Tomas stepped up to General Niyott but faltered one action short of grabbing for her gun arm. "General, we promised these people a just hearing for their crimes."

Niyott drew the smoking barrel of her weapon towards her face, inspecting it. "Know your place, Commander," she said without looking at him. "I won't spoil the prizes we promised you. You handle your orders, and I'll handle the justice."

Tomas shook his head and swallowed, aware that every ear in the field was turned towards this conversation. "We can't kill prisoners, ma'am. They've surrendered."

Niyott faced him, eyes narrowed to slits, and waggled the barrel of her gun under his chin. "I can't kill them until they've had a fair trial? Is that core?" Her tone was measured and cunning, but it was also a question from a superior officer and demanded an answer.

"Yes, General."

"Fine," she twirled her handgun once before setting it back in its holster. Turning away, she raised her voice to address the soldiers, both captive and free.

"Commander Amets desires fair trial for our guests, and a fair trial they shall receive," she announced, looking down at the sullen, kneeling rows. "Captain Forn, read out the charges."

Tomas realised too late what the General intended, and how foolish he had been. Niyott caught sight of his expression and rolled her eyes.

Captain Forn stepped out from the group of officers and bared his fangs at Tomas. "The first charge," he grumbled, "is resisting arrest."

"Do we have witnesses?" Niyott asked the night. Three dozen hands shot into the air.

"Second charge: destruction of Fleet property. Third charge: unprovoked assault." Forn stamped his boot with each proclamation. He didn't pause as Niyott barked out her rhetorical question for witnesses, nor as she received increasingly inflamed responses.

"Failure to present identification, obstructing peace, unlawful protest." Forn kept going. Out of the soldiers present, those crewing the *Boundless* cried the loudest.

"*Treason!*" Forn drew his voice above the others, leading them into a crescendo of hateful noise. "*Treason and murder uncounted!*"

"Guilty!" cried a guard.

"Make them pay!" sang another.

What were you expecting? Tomas admonished himself. *This is a war. What outcome could you have hoped for?*

"I was hoping for justice," he said to himself. He looked at the prisoners, who were shrinking away from the torrent of abuse and malice, curling into the smallest possible targets. Only a few were unflinching, but their stoic expressions were cracked with pain and hopelessness.

This is justice. This is what's right. These people are murderers.

Niyott held her hand up, and the cacophony quieted. Once the last soldier had fallen silent, she redrew her CP-10 and pointed it at the sky. "The verdict is guilty!" She again held a hand against the howling cheers.

"What is the sentence for these now condemned? Who will declare it?"

"I will."

Tomas watched in horror as Quil distanced herself from the enraged company and stood beside Forn.

"Commander Caron, what is the sentence for a person guilty of treason?" Niyott aimed at the nearest prisoner.

This isn't justice. It can't be. Tomas looked at Quil but couldn't manage to catch her eye. His wingmate was too focused on the action in front of her.

This *was* justice, the very same that Tomas had always believed in and upheld. Justice meant life for life, but it also meant death for death. In paying back one act of hatred with its kind, the cycle would never end, and oblivion would find them all.

Then I don't want justice, Tomas thought, and a determination set itself within his heart. *I want mercy.*

His hand strayed to his pistol, but someone caught his wrist and pinned it behind him.

"Careful, Amets," Duidain's intelligence agent hissed in his ear. "You'll spoil the best part of the show." Tomas struggled, but the grip was firm. He felt his pistol slide from its holster, then the agent shoved him away.

General Niyott was still waiting. "Commander Caron?"

Quil didn't smile like the others. Her face was a mask of grim purpose, of exacted finality.

"The sentence is death."

Niyott squeezed the trigger, and a bolt of electric plasma tore through the flesh between the prisoner's shoulder blades.

No!

She moved to her next target. "For murder?"

"Death." The whine of the blaster hit Tomas at the same time the acclamation of the crowd did, and a second being fell down as a corpse. The agent chuckled.

Tomas needed to do something. He looked around, seeing no remorse or uncertainty on the faces around him. He looked to the prisoners.

Amarie had crawled over to Erae, and both women had their backs to each other. Their heads were bowed, and their cuffed hands held each other feebly.

Marpe was farther back, but the Qua'seth's imposing frame was difficult to miss. Tomas could read no expression on the alien's stone face.

A third shot pierced the night. "What do you think of your trial, Amets?" Forn jeered, but Tomas ignored him. He was too busy looking at the Yiishi male that had crawled into the protection of Marpe's lap. His eyes were closed, and his lips were moving.

He's praying. Tomas could see now that many of the rebels were muttering under their breaths, their voices swallowed by the louder exclamations of their oppressors.

General Niyott sighed dispassionately. "This theatre wastes time." She stepped around her latest kill. "Keep the captain and her crew members alive. Dispose of the rest."

The guards raised their weapons.

Tomas closed his eyes. "Eladdiyr," he whispered. "I don't care who or what you are. These people are dying for you. If you exist, you need to help them."

"Ready?" Captain Forn shouted. His pistol was drawn along with the rest. "On my command …"

A sound like the crack of a leather whip split the night, loud enough to be painful, and it echoed across the plain. The company of soldiers ducked and looked around.

"By the sixth … what is that?" All heads turned to the soldier who had cried, then tilted up as they followed his outstretched arm.

A colossal ship had appeared far above the sky, and it was the very picture of death.

The hull was bone white, its front edges stained orange by the glow of the planet it bore menacingly towards. The main body was comprised of many curving ribs that reached up from where they connected at the base, creating a skeletal cage around a central sphere of violet energy. Tomas thought it looked like a shift gate.

The base ran under the sphere and connected to the huge engine block in the stern. Tomas could see no weapon emplacements from this distance, but it looked like there was plenty of room for them, and even more at the bow.

The front of the ship was arced first forwards and then backwards in the shape of two enormous, sinister horns, not unlike the limbs of an archaic hunting bow. They each spread out as wide again as the ship's fuselage, the greatest section of the bow tripling the width of the vessel's stern. In the centre of these horns, the hull was shaped into the design of a gruesome maw, lined top and bottom with gleaming Shbiy-stained teeth.

Utter despair filled Tomas, though he didn't know why. His whole body felt simultaneously weak and strong, as if gravity had fled at the sight. The vessel was idling slowly across the sky and would pass overhead in a few minutes. Tomas was still searching for the weapon emplacements when several streams of dark particles began to emit from the central orb, passing between the ribs and into space.

"What is it doing?" one of the prisoners said. The streams grew and fragmented, becoming difficult to spot as they left the bright silhouette of the ship. The spreading fume was intermittently illuminated by the sun, the planet and the orchid light from the glittering orb.

"It must have been hiding on the far side of the moon!"

"What are you talking about? That thing is too big to survive in the atmosphere!"

"How big is it?"

Tomas was only half-hearing the frantic chatter until that last comment. His eyes widened. How big *was* it? The ship's bow was above them now, and its ribbed fuselage blocked a generous portion of the sky. The glowing orb lighted the spaces next to it, dimming the stars.

"Beautiful beyond pain." The agent was chuckling deeply, shaking his head. Noticing Tomas' gaze, he spread his arms and bowed.

"Enjoy." Smoke rushed up from beneath his feet, and he was gone.

By the sixth sun …

"All of you, over here!" Niyott alternated between barking orders and shouting into her comm. Tomas hurried over, dread on his tongue.

"General …"

"Our scanners aren't picking anything up," she addressed the officers before he could finish. "The vessel must have some sort of cloaking."

"Why would a ship that bright have a cloaking device?" someone asked.

"Maybe it isn't cloaking," Quil answered, her face pale. She hadn't taken her eyes off the ship. "Maybe it's out of our range."

But that would mean …

Tomas hadn't thought his soul could sink lower in his chest. The central orb didn't look like a shift gate. It *was* one. The real thing, captured and engineered into the superstructure of the gargantuan ship that now revealed its true scale.

From bow to stern, the ship was as long as a terrestrial planet. and just as wide at the horns. What looked like idling motion was really tremendous speed, and what looked like black glittering dust …

One of the streams had grown very close, fanning out above them.

"Contact!" General Niyott declared triumphantly, then frowned. "Say that again?"

Tomas was close enough to pick up the tinny voice panicking into her earpiece. "Over a thousand individual contacts, ma'am," it said, "and more by the second. Starfighter-sized."

Tomas felt true despair now. He looked again at the approaching black cloud.

"Clawcraft," he said. He looked at Quil, then at Forn, and then at the General. All malice that had been in their faces was replaced with fear.

"Run."

25

"*Run!*" Tomas shouted a second time, and it was like the detonation of a bomb. Every soldier that heard it took off, the majority sprinting for the rise that led back to the CSF's landed fighters and frigates. Their actions were ungainly and lopsided in the gravity, and many stumbled into each other, confusing the escape.

Those who didn't hear Tomas' order saw the effect of it, and like a rippling shockwave, the rest soon followed, breaking from their frozen stances and joining the uphill landslide. The prisoners also struggled to their feet, their hands still bound. Tomas turned towards them.

"Tomas!" Quil took hold of his left shoulder and swung him around. "What are you doing?" she said. "We need to get in the air!"

Someone must have called ahead, for he could hear the warming engines of the three frigates build in contest to the sound of trampling feet. Quil ran her grip down to his elbow and pulled him after the retreating throng.

Tomas slipped his arm out from under hers, then in a move that surprised both of them, he pulled in and embraced her tightly. "Go," he said into her ear. "I have to free them."

Quil did not try to hide her exasperation. "Why?" she asked as they separated.

"Because they can't fly with bound hands," he answered. The last few soldiers were brushing past him now. Glancing up, Tomas saw that the cloud had resolved into individual fighter formations, each diving towards a different part of the moon.

"They're criminals!"

"They're people, Quil. I won't let them die."

"You'll never make it!"

"I've got fuel left yet."

"Tomas …" Quil saw there was no stopping him. She released her grip.

"You'd better be right behind me," she said.

Tomas nodded, turning and sprinting away before Quil could catch the lie in his eyes. As he drew near to the huddled captives, he looked down at his hands. One held Quil's CP-10, the other her flick knife. He was sure she would have felt him take them off her belt.

Maybe she had. Tomas shook his head and holstered the pistol. He continued to run.

He aimed towards the closest prisoner: a sour-faced man who yelped as he saw the CSF pilot charging his way. He tried to flee, but Tomas yanked him back by his cuffs.

"Get off me, Scourge!" he yelled, kicking out with his foot, barely missing Tomas' shins.

Tomas didn't bother with persuasion. He held his right palm on the man's shock cuffs. "Release, confirm release." He shouted at the restraint.

There was a slight tingle as the device read his I.D. chip and confirmed his authority. The cuffs loosened, then dropped as the rebel struggled free. He turned around as he realised what Tomas had done.

"Don't just stand there!" Tomas said. "Start untying your friends. Get everyone with shock cuffs to come to me."

The Human blinked a few times. "… yes sir," he managed to say, bowing his head before running off. Tomas risked another look at the sky before doing the same. The upper atmosphere sparkled with a hundred red-white flares as the first starfighters plunged into the atmosphere.

Erae opened her eyes when she felt someone push her away from Amarie. She saw the flight suit.

She saw his face.

Tomas managed a rueful smile as he cut Erae's bonds.

She smiled back, though it hurt her face to do so. "I guess this makes us even," she said.

He stopped smiling, and even looked stung by her words.

"Hey!" Amarie whacked her tied hands into Tomas' shin. "Sometime before we die would be good!"

Tomas crouched down to cut her free, leaving Erae to wonder at everything that was going on in his mind.

It was the least pressing matter by far. The night was punctured by dozens and dozens of clawcraft growing bigger and brighter with every passing second. A carnivorous roar sliced along the fuselages diving into the atmosphere, joined at the tail by the whine of engines. As she watched, the closest formation resolved from amorphous meteors into the unforgettable shape of pentagonal cockpits gripped from the back by five black talons, the tips of which pointed ever towards the pilot's next kill.

Two formations had targeted the near section of the moon. The first flew towards the few starfighters already in the air. The CSF pilots rose to meet their quarry, and dogfights soon ducked, wove and spiralled across the higher sky.

The second Ebon squadron had no such opposition. They levelled out fifty metres above the grassy plain and charged, spitting plasma from their quin cannons. Ploughs of storm-fire raked across the earth, boring down on the prisoners fleeing for their starfighters. They came closer, closer.

Tomas grabbed Erae from behind, throwing both of them into the dirt and shielding her as the formation tore past in a violent wash of wind and sound. Explosions rumbled along the surface, and screams and heat followed in the wake of the destruction.

The field was on fire.

"Wait! Stop! My knife!" Tomas leapt off Erae as Amarie ran past, sprinting in the opposite direction to the other Defiant pilots. He patted his side. "And my gun. She took my gun!"

Erae felt the fresh pain being knocked over had induced, and with it new energy. She had been about to watch her friends get gunned down on the consequences of her orders, but they were still alive. *She* was still alive, and might stay that way if she focused. This was her scene, and her king was still with her. She could do this.

"She's going after your general," she explained to Tomas, rising to her feet. The clawcraft were curling around to make another pass on the rebels. She ushered urgency into her voice. "You need to stop her, Tomas. She'll get herself killed."

He looked at her. "What will you be doing?"

"I'll pick you both up in the *Empress*," she pointed to her ship, which had survived the initial pass and was now powering up its engines. When Tomas looked at her quizzically, she explained. "You left Crisp aboard. It must have gotten the shields up in time."

"Who?"

"Later. Go now. Hurry!" She gave him a shove in the direction of the rise. "None of us are dying here tonight."

He nodded and started after Amarie.

There was so much Erae could have questioned. Why was Tomas help-
ing her, let alone obeying her orders without dissent? But she didn't have
the luxury of time to think it over. Turning back to her ship, Erae drew in
a breath and ran.

Tomas ducked as the Ebon clawcraft swept past him from behind, cannons blazing. He flattened himself onto the grass and covered his ears as
the banshee wails of their engines shook the air overhead. He could see
Amarie doing the same, the firelight silhouetting her as the starfighters
angled down on the CSF ships. One of the Liberators was already in the air,
and the enemy formation broke in half as the frigate returned fire, splitting
like a river against a rock. The frigate's cannons tracked the movement,
and as the fighters jetted past one of them was clipped by a plasma bolt, its
engine detonating in a white-hot explosion.

Tomas was on his feet as soon as the clawcraft passed him, trying to
make up as much ground as possible. He knew General Niyott would be
the last person to board the last ship. Her captains could handle themselves
in the air without her, and she would ensure no soldier was left behind.

She valued the lives of her soldiers, if not her enemies.

The field had become a maze of burnt ash, unburnt grass, and the
crackling flames that divided the two, forcing Tomas to navigate between
walls of consuming inferno. Tomas spared a single thought to the hundreds
of clawcraft that had flown towards this moon, and to the knowledge that
this scene was playing out on every inch of the satellite.

Possibly on every satellite, now that he saw the true scale of the world-
ship. The clawcraft had seemed like sand in his eyes. He couldn't begin to
imagine their full number.

Amarie was light on her feet and had mastered the gravity better than he had. She was nearly at the rise, drawing alongside the last of the fleeing troops. She ducked as one brought his weapon to bear, and the knife leapt from her hand.

The trooper screamed as it struck his wrist, and his shot went wide. Amarie leapt upon him, twisting the blade from his wrist and into his stomach. She pivoted to the side as a second trooper rushed in from behind, and she brought the gun down onto the back of her neck. The knife arm lashed out twice more in quick succession, and both soldiers fell away. Without looking back, Amarie crested the hill and disappeared down the other side.

Tomas pushed against the ache in his legs and climbed up shortly after her. The first thing he saw was the starfighters lifting from the ground, the collective blast of their thrusters stirring up a micro-storm of dust and debris that battered at his eyes. He caught sight of General Niyott in front of *Intrepid's* starboard boarding ramp. She was beckoning to the last of the soldiers, encouraging them aboard.

"Amarie!"

The girl had lowered herself to a crouch halfway down the hill, still a good thirty metres from the General. She took her commandeered handgun in both hands and aimed along its length.

It was all the time Tomas needed to reach her, but he restrained from tackling her to the ground. Part of him, he realised, wanted Amarie to take the shot. The General deserved it for what she'd done to the Defiant. The corpses she had let fall by her feet—the empty husks of men and women who had surrendered to her—were an inconsolable image in his mind.

It seemed everyone deserved punishment and death. The Defiant, for their treason. The CSF, for its tyranny. Tomas, for his failure to see all of this in time.

He looked up as a familiar whine greeted his ears. The Ebon were coming around for another pass. Niyott looked up, then down at the hill. She drew her weapon.

"Amarie!"

Amarie squeezed the trigger, but no bolt of blue lightning shot out the other end. Tomas had forgotten about the weapon's chip-lock. Below them, Niyott took aim and fired.

A single shot, perfectly centred on its target. Amarie held the pistol up on instinct, and it detonated as Niyott's plasma bolt ruptured the gas chamber in the magazine.

Tomas staggered back from the light and shrapnel. When he lowered his arms, Amarie was lying against the hillside, blood across her face. She wasn't moving.

Tomas slid towards her, a bolt spearing through the space he'd just occupied. Niyott was still firing. A clod of earth disintegrated by his left ear as he bent and lifted Amarie into his arms. A second plasma bolt hit just below it, spraying dirt into the air. The whine of the clawcraft grew louder.

There was no time to check for a pulse, nor the mindset to find out if he had just let another person die. The clawcraft swept down, and Tomas hurled himself back up the hill. He heard cannons and impacts behind him, and the General's attack stopped. Seconds later, he had to duck as a flame-wreathed clawcraft somersaulted over his head, the frigate cannons that made the kill still loosing rounds after it. It hit the ground and exploded as Tomas reached the top of the hill.

He risked one look behind him, but the *Intrepid* had already lifted off. The only CSF craft still on the ground were a pair of Wasp fighters; one cold, one lit with pre-flight. Tomas stopped atop the crest, staring at the active Wasp's tinted canopy. He knew she was staring back.

The roar of engines came from his other side, but they were a different pitch to the clawcraft's piercing squall. The *Silent Empress* was racing up the plain towards them, held aloft by the attitude thrusters on its bottom fins. The grass was blown flat beneath it, and spot fires were extinguished in its wake. A clawcraft took some passing shots at the freighter, but the *Empress'* shields harmlessly absorbed the salvo.

Tomas looked one way, then the other. Then with lead in his heart, he turned and ran towards the *Empress*.

The freighter slowed down and began to pitch skyward, bringing its main engines underneath it. Tomas kept running. The airlock ramp began to extend.

Amarie stirred in his arms. "You're saving me?" she asked blearily before coughing hard. "Why?"

"It's called mercy," he told her, "and it's overdue."

She went to say something else, but a second coughing fit got in the way.

Marpe was waiting on the deck above as Tomas cleared the airlock. His crusted legs rattled against the floor as Erae sped them through the atmosphere and away from the burning moon.

"Pass her to me," he rumbled, lowering his sinewy arms through the portal. Tomas lifted Amarie up, then followed himself. Three others were also on the landing, their expressions ranging between anger, pain and fear.

"What was the injury?" Marpe asked.

"Blaster detonation," Tomas breathed, still catching his breath. "I don't think the bolt penetrated."

Amarie's had lost consciousness again, her expression pained. Her face and neck were peppered with burns and small shrapnel. Most of the blood on her face had crusted over, but fresh blood coated her right arm, reflecting the pale tube light. It dripped from the rags of her sleeve and stained the deck.

She looked incredibly frail cradled against Marpe's stony chest. The Qua'seth studied for a moment, then turned to the others.

"Into the medical bay. I might have need of your delicate, dextrous, small digits." He began to lead the way, moving quicker than Tomas had seen before.

"What about me?"

"Crisp will collect you."

"What?"

"He means me, you incongruous fleet-stiff!"

Tomas looked up in shock. A large claw descended from the next deck up, hovering by the power of its thruster ring. It was the top half of a loading bot.

"Crisp?"

"In silicon and steel. The captain wants you in the gunwell. None of these crewers know what they're doing."

Tomas stared.

The robot's lights blinked furiously. "Are you waiting to rust? We have multiple clawcraft in pursuit, and I am not about to terminate because of your torpidity!"

"But … you're a Shell," he said dumbly, "in a robot body. That's illegal."

"Then shoot me! Or better yet, grab my claw and *help us get out of here*!"

As if I haven't broken enough laws today. Tomas ducked between Crisp's pincers and brought his arms over the top. The wind from the thruster ring intensified, and his feet left the ground.

"Before we die," Crisp buzzed, "I want you to know I lied."

Tomas looked sideward at the Shell's control box. "Sorry?"

"I do, in truth, have a navigational module." The thruster ring fired, and they rocketed through the decks.

Erae wrestled with the yoke, pushing the attitude thrusters to their limit as the *Empress* rolled beneath the approaching clawcraft's line of fire. Five bolts converged on empty space, and Erae pitched around to bring the chin gun to bear.

She wasn't fast enough. The hull shuddered as ballistic plasma struck her shields, and the Ebon was once again above her, keeping out of the chin gun's limited arc.

"Erae?" A tinny voice popped through the comm. "Erae, do you copy?"

"I copy, Tomas." She threw the acceleration lever back and the clawcraft shot past. She pitched up and tried to match the fighter's turns so Driz could bracket it in his fire.

"I'm in the gunwell. How do I help?"

"I need a few seconds of clean flying to engage the point drive," she said. "But these Ebon won't let up. Can you keep them off our tail?"

"Which heading?"

"Any scorching heading!" She jerked to port as the clawcraft twisted around, catching it in the stream of plasma. The shields fell, and it burst into white flame. "Just start shooting!"

The manoeuvre had brought the ship directly in line with the skeletal world-ship. It was hard to understand how far away the thing was because she still couldn't grasp its size. New shapes emerged from the central shift gate: dreadnaughts with long, cylindrical hulls and jagged central decks. Even they were only specs against a single rib of the mechanical goliath.

But dreadnaughts weren't the current concern. She pitched again as a CSF starfighter screamed past, swiftly pursued by a trio of Ebon fighters, projectiles spewing from their talons. The Wasp exploded, its four wings spinning in different directions. The clawcraft split and began to come around for their next target.

She just needed to reach the edge of the swarm.

"Anytime now, Tomas!"

26

Anytime, sure. Tomas finished strapping himself into the gunwell's control chair and pulled the arms down either side of him. He was in a weave-glass dome that projected out the top of the *Silent Empress'* hull, giving him a terrifying view of open space. The chaos of battle was all around him, whirling and rolling as Erae fought to keep the freighter in one piece.

Amongst the turns, Tomas saw the world-ship. Deep in its jagged maw, a violet light was beginning to build, much stronger than the glow of the shift gate. The construction of such a beast was unthinkable.

"Tomas!"

A control stick was on each arm of the chair. Tomas studied them and looked around. "Where's the gun?"

"On a pivot ring outside the glass," Erae explained. "Left stick hinges the gun and rotates both you and the ring. Right stick splits the barrels— *aargh!*" She broke off, and the world spun on Tomas' head as the *Empress* began a tight loop. Under his boots, Tomas felt the localised thunder he'd come to associate with a direct hit.

"Sorry, these Scourge-spawn are fast. Just … figure it out!"

"Yes ma'am." Tomas gripped the controls, and the weave-glass lit up with a spattered assortment of red and blue lights. It seemed the whole bubble was overlaid with the current positions of all nearby ships.

Alright then, time to see what we can do. Tomas pulled back on his left stick, and a metal arch sporting two hefty cannons lifted from the surface of the freighter. He twitched to the side, and the ring the arch was attached to swivelled in its housing. A twitch of the right stick set the cannons diverging along the arch, headed equidistantly to the edge.

"This has got to be the most unconventional rig I've ever seen," Tomas complained. "And the arch blocks most of my view."

"What do you think the overlay is for?" Erae retorted. "Amarie can shoot it just fine, so shut your mouth and start thinning this crowd."

A trio of Ebon clawcraft angled in from the side uncontested, each of their fifteen guns blasting eager plasma. Tomas pivoted himself around and depressed the stud on the left stick. Wicked azure bolts spat out from the cannons in tandem, powerful and fast.

Tomas tracked his fire up as the craft streaked overhead, their salvo scattering across the shields. Tomas nicked the back of the lead fighter, but then the metal arch jerked to a halt. It had reached its apex.

Ridiculous. Tomas swivelled the rig around, but the clawcraft had already sped below his arc. *What I wouldn't give to be in my Wasp. Or in any fighter.*

"Coming in from the front!" Erae sang out. Tomas turned and saw the growing red blot on his bubble. The *Empress'* forward guns loosed their streams, but the Ebon fighter was too swift.

Tomas lined up and fired, but as he did, Erae dropped the ship from under him. The Ebon's bolts flew over the ship and into space, but Tomas' shots also missed.

"Stay still, would you!" he barked into the comm.

"I'm keeping us alive, which is more than what you're doing!" was the snapped reply.

The ship shook as another shot penetrated the shields.

Tomas forced himself to relax his grip, pushing his fears to the corner of his mind. He knew how to do this, but at the same time he couldn't over-think it. Sometimes it was best to let instinct take over.

The trio of enemy starfighters was approached from starboard, intent on a second overhead pass. Tomas swung the gun into line and started firing. Brilliant light lanced out at the incoming party.

The clawcraft split apart but kept their vector. Tomas tried to stay ahead of the lead starfighter with his movements, keeping the pilot focused on something other than hitting the *Empress*. Free from harassment, the other two fighters dived in on their prey.

With a hard jab on the stick, Tomas pivoted his aim onto them and angled up as fast as he could. The starfighters drew closer and larger, large enough that Tomas caught sight of their slit-screen canopies as they rocketed past.

This time, Tomas was ready and had entered the start of a swift about-face. As both fighters jetted past, he leant into his right stick, splitting the guns. In a burst of light, the left cannon struck against the first clawcraft's shields. Tomas ducked involuntarily as his target flew into the second cannon's line of fire, exploding in a brief and blinding display.

Not finished yet, Tomas completed his pivot and tracked towards the second fighter. His cannons continued to release their energy, beating out their bolts with the sound of an accelerated heartbeat. Tomas angled until his target was hemmed in on either side by his diverging beams. The enemy pilot could choose to go up or down, and nowhere else.

Before he could make that choice, Tomas pulled back on his right yoke and scissored his fire straight into the fighter, penetrating its shields and detonating its engines. The clawcraft dispersed into a thousand glittering black fragments.

"Ha!" Tomas whooped. "That's two!" he yelled into the comm.

"About time," Erae cut back, but he could hear she was grateful. "More incoming."

"Where?" Tomas asked, but it was a pointless question. Red dots littered the overlay. Drawing a quick breath, he lined up and hit the studs.

Time quickly became a lost perception buried beneath the race for survival. Tomas never stopped firing, striking distant foes even with his missed shots, his guns finishing one target while his eyes blinked away sweat and looked for another. Every impact from the enemy forced a duck and a wince.

It might have been a week or a minute when Erae spoke again. "Just a little longer," she said. "We're nearly through, and they can't match our acceleration."

With the *Empress* having engines the size she did, Tomas had to agree. The majority of the engagement had already fallen away.

"What about your pilots? They'll get left behind too."

"Have you seen the numbers, Tomas? If we stick around here any longer, we'll all die. We just have to—hang on, rolling." The stars whirled around Tomas, giving his stomach the illusion of falling backwards, and he caught sight of one final clawcraft barrelling down above him.

He started to raise the arch, but it wasn't going to be fast enough. The cannons were too low from Tomas' previous kill.

Plasma drilled down on the shields above him, sending skittering waves of energy across his view, and still the cannons weren't high enough. The clawcraft didn't let up either and seemed ready to hurl itself straight into the *Empress'* hull.

Tomas thumbed his studs all the same. "Continue the roll!" he ordered.

Erae obliged, and the extra movement brought Tomas' guns into line. The clawcraft vanished in a cloud of brief and violent flame.

"Yes! Not bad for a Core-stiff," Erae cheered.

Tomas let go of the control sticks and sunk back into his chair, a sweaty grin plastered to his face. They were going to live after all. He panted in the relative silence, feeling the heavy thrum of the freighter's engines as they sped them all to freedom.

His smile faded as the inertia of the last roll brought his bubble around, and Tomas saw the enormous Ebon world-ship bearing down on Shbiy. It was much smaller than he had last seen it, but that it was even visible at this distance was gut-wrenching. Its white ribs were washed in the hue of its shift gate core.

The light in the mouth had grown, bleeding out past the painted teeth, dazzling his eyes. When it didn't seem like it could get brighter, the surge vanished, then shot forth in a beam of blinding strength. Tomas watched helplessly as it lanced out, severing the dark void to spear into the waiting gas giant.

"Erae, are you seeing this?" Tomas' heart was in his mouth.

As the beam struck the planet's banded clouds, they darkened, and a riotous stain spread from the impact. Then, after five seconds during which Tomas didn't dare to breathe, he saw the planet swell. At first, he thought it was a trick of his mind, and he stared harder at the darkening disc that was, at this distance, no larger than the palm of his hand.

Shbiy Prime swelled again.

"They're … pumping it full of energy," Erae said over the comm, her tone awed. "It's going to ignite."

As he beheld it, the planet exploded in a shockwave of light. It reached the *Empress* within seconds, frying the shields and tripping every alarm. If it wasn't for the auto-tinting of the weave-glass, Tomas' eyes would have been reduced to charred sockets.

It took a few moments for the tinting to reduce. When it did, Tomas' jaw dropped.

"They induced fusion," he whispered, though he couldn't believe the words even as he said them. But he was right. Deep in Shbiy's heavy atmosphere, the energy had enveloped and overwhelmed the gas giant's liquid hydrogen core. At an excess of fifteen million degrees, the first hydrogen atoms fused, compounding the present energy in a rapid and unstoppable chain reaction. Shbiy had become a star.

Within minutes, there would be no life on the moons of Shbiy, perhaps now considered planets. Within minutes more, those planets would be themselves consumed.

The light faded from the mouth of the grinning, skeletal beast. Then Erae engaged the point drive, and it was gone.

Erae had watched everything on the external cameras until the shockwave overloaded her shields and burst the camera lenses. She spent the next two minutes switching between trying to silence the myriad alarms and simply cursing at them, shouting as if the contest of her will might get them to shut up. The silence that followed—when it followed—was more upsetting to her than the noise.

A whole world—no, a system of worlds—had been wiped from existence, and no sound of it would ever reach her ears. Not a scream or a shout or a drum-splitting crack. In a morbid sense, her ship's alarms had been that cry, and she'd silenced them as a matter of habit.

She fell back against her seat. It was all happening again. Why was it all happening again? This was the start of the war she'd always expected but never truly thought would arrive. She'd trained for this, helped raise an army for this.

She doubted the Defiant's full strength could land a scratch against that giant warship.

There was a sound from behind her, and Erae jumped. Looking over her shoulder, she saw Tomas had climbed the last rung of the central ladder and, at the unexpected onset of a different gravity zone, struck himself against the bulkhead.

Tomas, the hero who had killed Ben-Eloah.

Tomas, the enemy who had saved her life.

"Sorry," he mumbled as he climbed the rest of the way through.

"No, it's alright," she said, her mind yet to sort itself. "We … uh, we'll be at the shift gate in just under three hours."

There wasn't a third chair in the cockpit, so Tomas didn't take one, crouching instead between her and Driz. "What speed are we doing?" he asked.

"Point-two-four. I'll slow us down before … before we hit the gate. We won't be home for another thirty hours or so."

Tomas stared straight out the viewport, his mood sullen. "Yes," he murmured. "Home."

Erae realised what she had done but couldn't find the words to apologise. They both fell silent, and even Driz had the tact not to tread on the moment.

Eventually, she spoke. "Thank you—for saving us, that is."

Tomas looked at her from the corner of his eye. "You saved me first."

Mentally thrown, it took a moment for Erae to react. In the end, she nodded, and the exchange ended. She realised she couldn't empathise with the sacrifice Tomas had just made. He'd turned from everything he'd ever known to help them … her. She'd never made such a decision. She'd never been faced with the challenge.

And now he was here with them, and she could see the fear in his eyes, at the corners of his mouth. What had he leapt into? He was all alone.

She edged out of her seat. "Come on," she said, touching him lightly on the shoulder. "We should see how Amarie is doing."

"Right," Tomas rose and looked at her. "You should get yourself checked out too, you know."

"What?" Erae put a hand to her face, feeling the crusted blood under her tender, swollen nose. "Oh ..."

"Doesn't it hurt?"

"I guess I've still got too much adrenaline in me." Erae stepped towards the ladder, swayed a bit.

"Whoah," Tomas reached behind her and steadied her by the elbows.

"I got it," Erae shook her head. "I got it."

[Go to medical, Captain,] Driz chittered softly. [I can handle the embarkation.]

"What did he say?" Tomas inquired, but Erae just nodded and started down the ladder, steadying herself at each new rung.

By the time she reached the med-bay, a Shell-smith was pounding an incessant rhythm into her head with its hammer. Each pulse of dull pain lined up with the beats of her heart.

She could survive it, though, and Erae was much more concerned with how Amarie was doing. With Tomas not far behind her, she keyed the door open.

The medical bay wasn't quite deserving of its name. The room was as run-down and rusting as the rest of the *Empress*. Erae loved her freighter like little else, down to the last rivet, but even she could admit when upgrades were in order.

The room was dominated by two large cylinders—the oxygen and water reclaimers. Smaller tanks bracketed the reclaimers, storing the valuable resources. Aside from the life support, there was only room for one medical cot and its care station, which was a glorified bandage dispenser and vitals monitor. There simply wasn't the space or the budget for anything better. On lighter occasions, Erae joked that it was motivation to avoid getting injured.

She didn't appreciate the joke now, as she came around Amarie's side. Her friend was unconscious on her back, looking peaceful despite everything. It didn't stop Erae's heart from melting with worry. Marpe was busy on the far side, readying a bandage wrap. On the bench beside him was a dish holding tiny metal fragments.

Her friend's shirt and pants had been cut off her body, exposing her wounds. Her right arm and shoulder were covered in small cuts and burns, along with her face and both wrists. It was an ugly sight, but Erae preferred it to a plasma bolt through the heart.

Most of the damage was superficial, but a few of the wounds were deeper and wider. These had already been glued into thin, snaking lines.

"Oh Am," she murmured, and her hand stroked Amarie's mop of dyed curls. "This is the cost, and it's dearer to me than a thousand foes. Yet you risked everything for just one."

Did Amarie know that whenever she charged into the night, it wasn't just her life in jeopardy? They were sisters, bonded in fire, and death would take them both, if it took either of them.

Tomas stepped forward, and for the briefest moment Erae thought he was trying to get a better look at Amarie in her undergarments. She was two steps into her intercept course when she realised what he was staring at.

Amarie's combat gloves, like the rest of her outer clothes, had been removed to give access to her treatment. Her left hand was already clean and shrapnel-free. Marpe had slathered the worst parts in burn cream, and it would get a bandage or two once the more critical wounds were dealt with.

The right hand was just as naked as the left, and its silver surface glinted in the med-bay's artificial light. A jagged hole was blown through the anog-ite-aluminium casing below her thumb, exposing the servomotors and wiring within. The fingers twitched as Marpe pressed a bandage to her upper arm, kuwrium bones sliding against one another.

"When did she get that?" Tomas asked. He hadn't had any idea of the prosthesis' existence, which was just as well. Erae felt an empathetic pain in her own right wrist just looking at the replacement, and massaged it reflexively.

"You can ask her when she wakes up," Erae told him, then lowered her hands and smiled. "She won't thank you for saving her, you know. In fact, she'll hate owing you a debt."

He smiled back, though his eyes remained on the hand. "Nothing new, then."

Erae beheld the peaceful, if battered, face of her life-long friend once more. "No," she said, "nothing new at all." It was, she thought sadly, the greatest lie she'd ever heard.

27

"Lights."

"Lights!"

Waking from a nightmare was never as bad as waking into one.

Tomas blinked up at a dark ceiling. Just a ceiling. Not *the* ceiling. The ceiling was far away, three corridors down from the hangar, first room past the junction, approximately two kilometres below the surface of Gerduk.

His room was first because he was the commander. His pilots followed him, his enemies feared him, and when someone needed saving, he never refused the call.

He wasn't a commander anymore. What was he?

"*Lights!*" And to top it all off, the apartment didn't have automated lights.

Tomas stood and made his way across the room with his hands out. The light switch was by the bedroom door. He flicked it on, then reached through the doorway to turn on the lights for the rest of his polyplex prison.

The apartment consisted of the bedroom, a main room, and a bathroom, and it was both the smallest apartment Tomas had ever seen, and the largest accommodation he had ever owned. It hadn't been furnished yet, save for the bed, but what was that to him? The only thing he had left were his clothes and his knife.

No, not his knife. He looked back to the bedroom, where the weapon lay on the ground beside the bed. He walked over and picked it up. A doubled pair of wings had been scratched into one side of the handle—the CSF crest.

"What have I done, Quil?" He whispered the question. "In all the universe, how did I find myself here?"

The knife didn't answer, and Tomas doubted he would have liked the words if it had. He was conjuring enough of them himself.

I'm here because I'm a fugitive. A traitor. A coward. And for what? A people he hardly knew, a king he wasn't sure even existed, and a cause that was as good as lost. The Defiant didn't have the means to withstand the Ebon. The swarms of clawcraft alone would be enough to decimate every last rebel, not to count the many dreadnaughts Tomas had seen disembarking at Shbiy.

And not to count the thing they had disembarked from. He closed his eyes and saw its grinning maw, large enough to swallow a fleet. A ship as big as a planet that could warp anywhere, destroy anything…

And Tomas, with his stolen knife, was going to stand up to it?

Tomas sank to a crouch, one hand pressing the folded blade against his forehead. The pressure provided a point of reference for his pain, his grief, his fear. He remained that way for a while, pressing harder and harder until he drew one thought out from the tangled knot within his brain.

What was the point of him throwing away his life and everyone he loved if they were all going to die in the end? Why make all the hard choices if none of it helped them win?

We don't fight to win, Tomas had said to Gerad not very long ago. *We fight because we'd rather lose our lives to death than to fear.* Gerad had fought, and he'd died afraid.

But … Tomas lowered the knife. Gerad had died afraid, but fear wasn't what killed him. The Ebon were the killers. From before his birth, to the victory at Tachillah, and now again at Shbiy, they had slaughtered and destroyed without remorse. They would never stop killing, and so Tomas would never stop fighting them. Not as long as he had someone to fight for.

And if he was afraid, then that meant he was still fighting.

"Forgive me, Gerad." Tomas straightened and threw the knife gently onto the mattress. "I can't beat them on my own. I can't make your death count, but I can make them work real hard for the next one, true as core."

He left the bedroom, heading through the main room onto the balcony. Cool air kissed his face. The city spread out below him like a jungle ruin, enmeshed in an unordered covering of trees, vines and flowers. Above him, the stars glittered beyond the glass of the protective dome. Not all of those stars still existed. If he stood there and waited a while, he wondered, would he see one of the lights wink out forever?

True as core... the phrase was like scripture to him, but what did it really mean? Was truth the justice that Niyott had executed upon the Defiant, or was it the words of an intelligence agent who vanished like a Peret Neiru before his very eyes? Or was it Duidain, who knew all these things and hid them behind a perfect smile?

Tomas kept looking up. Those stars weren't truly there, yet they found the strength to keep shining. Maybe he didn't need truth to shine. He looked back to the city below.

Or maybe he was finding a new truth, one that would never stop shining.

Erae awoke in her cocoon on the *Empress*, and it took her a few moments to piece everything together in her mind. When she did, she disentangled herself from her hammock as quickly as possible.

Amarie's cocoon was empty. She expected it to be empty, but that expectation did nothing to set her at ease. Blinking away sleep, she threw on her shoulderless overcoat, boots and hip holster. It felt light and uncomfortable without a pistol in it, but Erae wasn't about to go back to Shbiy to reclaim hers. She'd have to settle that score later.

Keying the door proved successful for once, and Erae was down the ladder and through the airlock in less than a minute. Her haste shook the lingering effects of sleep from her as she hurried along the docking tube as fast as she could manage without running. A few seconds wouldn't help Amarie any, but they would console Erae's heart a great deal.

Upon reaching the war hospital, she followed the faded mag-strips towards the admittance counter only to find it vacant. It was normal to find the station unoccupied, as there was always a steady supply of wounded soldiers—from covert spies to legitimised thieves to pilots—who needed tending. Erae let herself around the counter and called up the list of patients on the nurse's terminal. When she'd found Amarie's bed, she headed off.

The first thing she saw when she slipped through the privacy curtain was Marpe's hulking form. He was standing by the bedside, his whole body stone-still in an unresponsive state—the Qua'seth's equivalent to sleep. As Erae understood it, standing was just as restful as sitting or lying down.

She felt a pang of guilt for not being the one to spend the night with Amarie. She'd intended to, but most of the trip back had been sleepless, and every attempt to close her eyes had swiftly conjured the drifting hull of the *Avail,* or the firey plain of Shbiy, or the Ebon world-ship shattering the sky above her. Erae had fitfully nodded off at the end of the journey, but apparently Driz hadn't woken her up for the landing.

She placed a hand on Marpe's damp forearm, and the gentle giant stirred.

"Go get something to drink," she told him. "I'll watch her."

He turned towards his ward, inspecting her sleeping form, then nodded and excused himself from the cubicle. Erae pulled a chair close to the bed and sat down.

A pained groan escaped from further down the corridor, causing Erae to wonder how many of the pilots and crewmen from Shbiy had ended up here, and how many patients were from other deployments. The Defiant rarely went a time without sticking its nose in one disempowered lifeform's business or another.

Any patients from Shbiy were here because of her.

Her thoughts were interrupted when Amarie shifted in her cot. Her eyes flickered open.

"Hey there," Erae whispered. "You're looking better."

The young infiltrator yawned and felt at the plaster on her chin and left cheek. "That might be because there's less of me to see." She eased herself up on her arms and looked around. She looked at Erae.

"You're looking worse," she said with a wry smile.

It was true. Erae's jaw had purpled nicely: a noticeable dark stain on her blue skin. It was certainly noticeable to Erae, who could feel the slight ache in every word she spoke.

"That's not what I meant," Amarie said, reading her friend's thoughts. "Where are the others?"

"Driz and Crisp are on the ship, resting. I've sent Marpe to get some nutrient water. He stayed all night with you, you know."

Amarie nodded and brushed a curling scarlet lock away from her face. "And Tomas?"

"We've put him in one of the new apartments for now. After thirty hours on the *Empress* I thought he could use the time alone."

"*Thirty hours*?" Amarie slumped against her headboard. "That stinks." The comment trailed into silence, during which she glanced furtively at Erae with her piercing eyes, then averted them to her bedsheet.

"I ... I need to apologise to him."

Erae nodded her understanding. Her mind had wrestled with the conflict of blaming Tomas and forgiving him since they'd met. He had killed Ben-Eloah, after all, and done plenty else to aid a corrupt system.

But he had just been doing what he thought was right; doing what he could to protect those he loved. She couldn't fault him for that. And Ben hadn't been unwittingly killed; he had sacrificed himself.

That sacrifice extended to everyone, including Tomas.

She rested her hand on the cot, and Amarie's gloveless prosthesis quickly found it. "I can have him called for if you'd like."

"No, I'll be out of here soon enough," Amarie said, still looking down. "I have to apologise to you as well. I think I finally understand what I've been putting you through."

The grip on Erae's hand tightened. "When she hit you ... I was going to make that general choke on her teeth. All I could hear was her laugh, mocking us. I nearly had my chance to make her pay, and I screwed it up.

"I don't know what happened next; half of it passed like a fog and the rest like a dream. I was in so much pain, but I was never afraid. I knew you were coming for me, that the instant I took off across that field you would come for me."

Tears began to run down Amarie's face. "And I thought, if you'd been the one in trouble, if a clawcraft had hit you, you would have been alone. I wasn't coming for you. I could have killed the lot of them, but you would have still died.

"It's just like you said. I've been throwing my life away for my enemies. Not like you." She again looked Erae in the eyes. "When you die, we won't remember the people you've killed. We'll remember the ones you saved."

She sniffed and wiped at her eyes with her plastered hand. "Can you forgive me?"

Erae raised herself from her seat and pulled Amarie into a fierce hug. "You don't even have to ask," she said. "You are a burning star, Amarie Gayyam, and I'm sure your death will be a nova as glorious and powerful as your life. But I'm in no rush to see it."

Amarie gave a cathartic laugh, and the two women rested in each other's arms. Erae leant into the embrace, but eventually the energy changed, and Amarie pulled away to look Erae in the eyes.

"Are you okay?" she asked.

Erae cocked her head. "Me? It was only a few punches, Am. I'm fine."

"I don't mean your face. I know how you think, Rae."

"I don't know what you're trying to say," Erae said, though she knew full well. This wasn't a conversation she wanted to have now. These weren't thoughts she was prepared to address.

The younger woman's face softened in genuine concern. "Erae …"

"I know," Erae lied, evading both the next sentence and her own heart.

"It wasn't your fault," Amarie said it anyway. "You aren't to blame for their deaths. No one—"

"I know," Erae cut her off, and let her arms drop. *I know what you're trying to do, and you might even be telling the truth. But healing this wound means opening it first, and I can't do that right now.*

"I need to take a shower," she said, standing. "I'll be back later. We can talk then."

Amarie opened her mouth to protest, then closed it again and nodded. Her head returned to the pillow, and she closed her eyes. She was clearly still exhausted.

But she was alive. Erae kept that thought close as she left the room without another word. After everything that had happened these past days, that was no small miracle.

Tomas was seeing a young Kilya male out his door when Erae arrived, and she stepped aside to allow the boy to pass. He mumbled a quick pardon as he exited, but turned around once out in the hall, his eyes the size of planetoids and his beak agape. Once the door was closed, there were several seconds before Tomas heard the patter of retreating boots on the carpeted floor.

Erae had left her hair down, and the dark locks made her beryl-blue skin appear to glow by comparison. He caught the faint scent of soap as she passed him into the main room.

"It seems you're quite the celebrity around here," he said, referencing the boy.

Erae passed a dismissive hand before her face, and Tomas saw she was still wearing her black combat gloves. "I'm easier to recognise than most. If it had been Michael coming through your door, the kid would have outright fainted. What was he here for, anyway?"

"Breakfast," Tomas answered, and gestured to the covered tray he'd set on the kitchen bench. "I must say I had expected it to come from an adult, not a youth whose wattle has yet to be cut." He raised an eyebrow at the Defiant Captain. "He can't be older than ten."

She nodded. "Eight, I'd have guessed. There's always something to be done here, and we don't let them train to fly or fight until they're fourteen. Sixteen, for Humans and Dabans."

"Because of the Ebon."

"Yes, because of them." Seeing no chairs were present, Erae perched herself on the bench. She removed the tray cover over Tomas' cooked meal and peered at the assembled egg, meats and salad. "None of us really enlisted in this battle. It's just our way of life. We trained first to save ourselves from death, then to save others."

She chuckled. "Not that any amount of training could save us without Ben-Eloah's sacrifice. And we didn't understand what that was about until it happened."

Tomas didn't follow. Erae jumped so quickly from premises that seemed natural to ideas he knew nothing about. "Remind me again, what happened?"

Erae looked apologetic. "Sorry. I forget how new all this must be. I … I shouldn't be the one to try and explain it …"

"Why not? You seem to understand it well enough yourself."

"It's one thing to know a subject and another thing entirely to teach it," she sighed, and pinched the bridge of her nose, contemplating her next words. In the end, she shook her head. "I'm sorry but I can't. I'd hate for you to get the wrong idea about all of this. You can ask Remiel later.

"He's called a meeting; a war briefing, if you will. He's asked that you attend with the rest of us." Erae paused. "This was the reason I came here: to formally ask you to join our cause. We're going to need all the help we can get."

Tomas had known the offer would be coming. It was his chance to keep fighting, to press through his fear. But now that the time had come to voice it he found the words catching on his tongue.

"I don't know," was all he ended up giving her.

The more he thought about it, the more Tomas believed Eladdiyr was real. Someone had been directing him these past days, had landed him here on this station in the middle of nowhere.

But that didn't mean he belonged with these people. If Eladdiyr existed, then what had really happened at the Battle of Tachillah seven years ago? Tomas had thought himself a hero; shooting down a traitor and then help-ing vanquish a deadly horde. Ben-Eloah's blood was on his hands, and the Defiant could never know.

So where did that leave him? Tomas couldn't go back to the CSF. Niyott might forgive him for his actions, but he couldn't forgive her. He couldn't go back to orders he knew were wrong. And he didn't think he could ever face his friends, knowing he had left them to fight their way from Shbiy without him.

What did they think of him, if they even thought he was alive? What did Quil think of him? His thoughts were a siege inside him, and if his defences opened to let anything in, they would overcome him.

"I have nowhere to go."

Voicing even that small worry was like the falling of a single snowflake that starts an avalanche, and it cascaded into a destructive force inside him. The image of the Ebon world-ship was seared into his mind, its ray of energy boring into the gas giant below. It echoed in his ears like a soundless bell.

Erae lowered herself from the bench and crossed over to Tomas. Her expression held understanding, but how could she know? He found himself staring into her depthless, glittering eyes.

"You don't have to go anywhere, if you don't want to. You could be here, with us." She looked down for a moment, checking her thoughts. "I'm sorry I ... you won't believe me when I say you've gained far more than you've lost. I wish I knew a different way to say it, and I'm not devaluing your friends ... I ..."

Tomas cut off her tumble of words. "What have I gained, Erae?"

Erae slowed, took a breath. "Him. If you want him, that is." She tugged off her left glove, exposing her arctic skin.

"What are you doing?"

"Hold still," she said, "and close your eyes."

Tomas didn't move. "Explain."

"Please? I'll explain after. I can't promise anything, so I don't want to … disappoint you."

Tomas relented, closing his eyes. He felt her touch her palm to his forehead. The hand felt cool.

And then it was suddenly hot, and the heat poured down his head like molten liquid under his skin. Wind roared around him, and Tomas swayed under the sensation, but a stiff grip on his shoulder stayed him.

The heat swept the siege of thoughts surrounding him—Niyott, Quil, the Ebon, his helplessness and fear—each was itself surrounded, washed up against his battlements and melted away. It was peace as he hadn't felt before, light and warm. He willed himself to be lost in it, even as he could still feel Erae's hands upon him, the pressure of his feet upon the ground, an itch on his nose.

Then the hand was gone from his head, and the sensation faded, but not completely. Tomas opened his eyes to find Erae wearing a weightless, perfect smile. There were tears in the corner of her eyes.

"How did you do that?" Tomas breathed.

"I didn't," she said, and a three-beat of musical laughter fell from her. "Thank you, Eladdiyr. I can't believe that worked."

"What?"

"This is what he gave us, Tomas. Our king. A limitless love and an immeasurable power. It isn't ours, and he doesn't always use it how we want him to, but it's as much proof as I'll ever need that he cares for us. Why is beyond me; I'm just so grateful he does."

"It's …" Tomas placed a hand on his forehead, expecting to feel some mark or locus of energy. "I've felt it before."

"Do you remember when?"

Tomas closed his eyes. "Yes. The explosion at Tachillah."

She nodded, and her grin sobered. "The lure of his kingdom isn't in the strength of arms, but in repairing a broken heart and a hurting universe. The Ebon and their generals want us to be afraid, and to fight out of a selfish, self-preserving fear. But we fight to protect others, and for now, that's all I'm asking you to do. Help us save the Cluster."

Tomas turned and walked to the door, each step a protest to the tears threatening to run down his face. That feeling …

He couldn't understand it. He didn't *deserve* it. Why would Eladdiyr give him this, after Tomas had mocked and doubted and fought. When he had murdered Eladdiyr's son? He turned back to Erae, who was tugging her glove on.

"It's okay," she told him.

"It really isn't. You don't know what I've done. If Eladdiyr is creating a better universe, he's not going to want me in it. Not after that."

"Tomas, I … " Erae hesitated and took a small step towards him. "Eladdiyr showed me the battle in a dream. He showed me *your* battle. I saw how it ended."

"Then you know why I could never be one of you." Tomas shut his eyes against the truth of his words, overwhelmed by the shame that burned his skin. "He died because of me."

"He died *for* you." Erae's voice grew softer even as it drew closer. "It's okay, Tomas."

He could feel the air shift as she stopped in front of him, but he didn't have the strength to look at her. How, then, would he have the strength to fight the Ebon? Or to set right the hurt he and the CSF had caused? He couldn't.

I can't beat them on my own.

Yet he didn't feel alone anymore. The feeling of peace persisted.

"I need some time," he said softly.

"Of course," Erae replied. "A lot's already happened, and I've only added more. I'll be back when it's time for the meeting."

Tomas didn't respond. The air shifted before him, and he heard the door open and close.

What now, Eladdiyr? He thought, projecting the words in a random direction as if to be heard. *I feel this. I feel you. But your son's blood is on my hands. Can you forgive that?*

If he was expecting a response, he didn't get one.

A truce, then. Stop the Ebon, save my friends, then we'll talk. Tomas stopped himself, wondering for a moment if he had lost his mind entirely. At this point, what difference did it make?

28

Tomas was ready when Erae returned to collect him. Ready didn't mean settled, though, and she could almost see each thought as it piled in his mind, threatening to sink the entire vessel. Even good thoughts could drown a person if they came too fast and too wonderful.

She hoped at least one of his thoughts was wonderful.

They didn't speak as they walked between the Shard's climbing towers. Hedges lined the sidewalk, and trees bowed to form shadowed arches. The eternally starlit twilight didn't welcome much talk. It was a peaceful place, but considering all that had happened, Erae would have felt safer seeing daylight from a sun. Now that the war had restarted, even sunlight might become a rare luxury.

The war room was still bright, however—a comfort once Erae had blinked a few times to let her eyes adjust. Three tiers of seats circled around a large central table with an interactive screen embedded in its surface. The light panels allowed few shadows to touch the cream carpet and padded grey walls.

Four Celah Neiru were present in the room, along with three other command staff. Erae was surprised she and Tomas were invited to a meeting as small and prestigious as this. But maybe everyone else was busy. There was certainly enough to do.

Erae and Tomas joined the others, sitting in the inner ring beside the table. As they did, Remiel stood up, both in greeting and to begin the meeting. His wrinkled face distracted the translucency of his skin, making him seem more solid, more Human, than the other Neiru.

"Captain Tamah," he began, his voice rustling like forest leaves in a gentle wind, "thank you for coming. And to you as well, Master Amets." He nodded to them both, then focused his half-lidded gaze on Tomas.

"I am called Remiel, though maybe Erae already made me known to you. Brother Raphael you know, of course."

Raphael beamed from his seat next to Remiel.

"Allow me to make known to you Michael, our chief warrior, and Gabriel, our chief seer." The two brothers smiled and nodded in turn. Michael's grin was as proud and handsome as Erae had ever seen it, but Gabriel's looked strained, and faded quickly.

Remiel continued. "Also with us are Master Boaz Surestar, Lady Feybb Hil and Master Saan-Seon Traed, our stationmaster, squadron-master and troop-master. And of course, I mention and honour our king, whose words we speak and whose path we tread. Eladdiyr, let your will be known through this council."

Erae nodded her affirmation, as did the others, whom she knew well. Everyone except Tomas, who looked around with mild confusion. He must have felt like an intruder, a prisoner even, sitting next to her. And Erae couldn't do anything to help.

"Now, the matter at hand, and the cause for such urgency: the Ebon resurgence and the plight of all free peoples. Gabriel, please relay what we know." Remiel sat down, as the stern Neiru replaced him. Unlike the others, Gabriel didn't have any wisps of hair. His face was hard, his voice cold.

"We've been aware of the Ebon's growing forces for some time, as you know," he said. "War was expected, but it will be different this time, and not only because they have grown in strength. Their total force numbers several thousand capital ships, but these have been split into groups of two or three dreadnaughts, appearing all over the Cluster. A task force disembarks, razes any colonies or installations it finds, then drains the star and leaves. A joint assault on Kaldea would be more strategic, but this widespread annihilation is meant as a weapon of fear. And it is working.

"Our sources tell us the CSF has retreated all its forces to defend the Core's most populous and treasured worlds. They are leaving the Cluster to die."

"As if we'd expected any different," Surestar, a bulky near-Daban with coarse grey fur, interrupted angrily. "Duidain is as dark on the inside as the Ebon are on the out."

Erae glanced at Tomas, who looked both hurt and resigned.

Traed, a dark-brown Gazam with a pale chest, chipped in. "Surely this—tch—cowardice, along with Captain Tamah's report from Shbiy, leaves no doubt as to the nature of our foes. The Core made a deal with the Horde to protect their elite, and every day since has—tch—been a ruse to blind us."

The insectoid fixed its compound eye on Tomas. "They are all of them dishonourable."

Erae rose. "They are all of them *lost*, she said, staring Traed down. "Lost, and in as much need of Eladdiyr's help as the rest of the Cluster. Whatever deal the Core struck is quickly reaching its end, or have you not heard that Ebon slaves have been breaking their collars like straw and slaughtering their owners?"

Traed clicked his mandibles derisively. "Then they have received the end their bargain deserves."

"Yes," Tomas said, his voice calm but not timid. "And you claim your prince died to give all people a life they *didn't* deserve. Or did I abandon my friends for no reason?"

"Well said, Tomas!" Raphael grinned. "Well said indeed! For both those who are aware they do evil and those who do it blindly, we cannot have hatred but pity! They are a victim to themselves more than they are a threat to others, and we must save both if we can."

"Agreed," Gabriel said, regaining command of the floor. Erae sat down. "More pressing than the dreadnaughts is the planet-sized ship Captain Tamah reported to us. I have asked, and Eladdiyr has shown it to me. It is called Kithmakh, and our fallen brother Charon commands it as his own. He sends it like the rest of his fleet: to destroy the weak and unarmed, avoiding the defended worlds. The shift gate it carries can swiftly summon any dreadnaughts that Charon keeps in reserve, though the occasion might be rare. I ... do not know how we can destroy it."

The already sober atmosphere became dismal. Hil, a freckled Human woman with red cheeks, spoke up. "You mean Eladdiyr hasn't ...?"

Gabriel shook his head. "He has not shown me this. Not yet." Disquiet crossed his face, but he quickly mastered it. "So, what do you intend to do?"

"You mean," Hil asked, "you don't have a plan?"

"The plan, child," Remiel said, "is not ours to make. Not when it is your lives that hang in the balance. No, Eladdiyr has not revealed the next end to us. Why would he, when it will be revealed through you five now? The doors are yours, not ours."

No pressure, Erae thought sourly. *All my plans have gone perfectly up to this point.*

Tomas stirred beside her. "If I may, why am I here?" He looked around the room. "I just arrived yesterday. You can't trust the fate of your people to me. I'm not even sure I'm on your side!"

Surestar snorted, but any comment was forestalled as Remiel lifted a hand.

"You are tied to this, Tomas Amets," he said. "Since the day you met Epieta, your path has been woven through our enemy's and our own, perhaps closer than we know. In addition, you and Captain Tamah are the ranking survivors of Shbiy, and have seen Kithmakh with your own eyes. You may hold truths others do not."

Tomas didn't look convinced. "I didn't see anything good. That thing—Kithmakh—we can't fight it."

Erae nodded. "But we can avoid it," she said. "At least until we know more. I suggest we ambush the smaller task forces, one at a time. We can evacuate those we save and bring them back here. The Ebon already ravaged this system, so I doubt they'll return to it."

"We may have enough room for over a hundred thousand refugees," Surestar warned her, "but we've only the resources to sustain a portion of that number."

"Then we'll work it out. The alternative is letting everyone fend for themselves, just like the CSF are doing."

"So, we stop one attack," Hil said, "but what then? We have two dreadnaughts, one cruiser and perhaps forty frigates of war. We might achieve two victories, or even three, but the Cluster will perish just the same."

"What other choice do we have?" Despair was edging closer. It built in waves, here in a raised voice, there in the sharpness of a gesture. Erae tried to make herself louder than her fear. "What other path could we possibly take?"

"Beriah," Surestar offered. "We collect our forces and make for the hidden system. Without a shift gate to mark it, the Ebon may never find us. Why spend ten thousand of our brothers' lives to save ten thousand strangers? Or none at all, as chance may have it."

"We'd be leaving the Cluster to die!" Traed planted four fists on the tabletop. "My squadrons will not run. Not without a fight!"

"If we fight we lose!" Boaz cried. "What don't you understand? We thought we could win. We trained and we built and we schemed. But it wasn't enough. Captain …" he turned to Erae, pleading.

"Captain, you saw it. Fighting will only delay death. We've saved so many people already. Will you send them to die? *We can't win.*"

"I ..." Erae faltered, feeling her throat constrict. "All I ever do is send people to die." The confession was too much. She turned away from Surestar's expression of triumph, Hil's expression of sympathy. The sympathy was worse.

She glanced at Tomas, and his eyes met hers. They were brown eyes, pools of deep earth rimmed in thin, burning gold. *Why?* they seemed to say. *My friends died, and I thought it was for something. Did your friends die for a reason? Tell me why.*

"They died to give us a chance," she told him, then straightened to tell the rest of the room. "They died because they trusted me when I told them that their reasons meant just as much as their actions. They died because they had hope."

Tomas asked. "Who did they have hope in, Erae?"

Erae breathed out. "Eladdiyr."

Tomas stood. "And is Eladdiyr strong enough to defeat the Ebon? Even Kithmakh?" After he was met with silence, he added. "You'll have to tell me, because I genuinely don't know."

"He is," Traed answered.

"Of course he is," Lady Hil said.

Tomas spread his hands. "Then fight like he is. Let's strike the Ebon right at the helm. There's nothing we have to lose that they won't take from us eventually."

Traed clicked his mandibles approvingly, but Boaz was taken aback. "Eladdiyr's favour I do not doubt," he said, "but we can't know how he will help us. Do you propose to just cruise up to that colossus and *pray?*"

"I'm not talking about Kithmakh," Tomas said. "I'm talking about its master."

"Charon?" It was Raphael's turn to look shocked. "Tomas, you would have a better chance of scratching Kithmakh than you would a Peret Neiru. He can't be killed by mortal devices. Only a Neiru artefact can mark his flesh."

"Which we have," Michael spoke up for the first time. His voice was the growl of a noble predator on the hunt. He leant forward. "But I do not think the lord will leave his ship without reason."

"We can give him one," Erae said. "Charon craves contest—I saw as much on Shbiy. As powerful as Kithmakh is, nothing can challenge him. It must drive him mad."

Tomas thought, then nodded. He looked at Michael. "He also really wants to kill the Celah Neiru."

"More than you know." Michael fixed his eyes on the two of them, and they kindled in chromatic fire. "I like this plan."

"And what of saving the people?" Boaz demanded.

Remiel smiled. "This is but the start of a plan. Stick around, and who knows what might complete it?"

He looked at them all. "And with a little faith in our king, we may even pull it off."

The Warden-1318-class dreadnaught known as *Sunbird* was every bit as impressive as it was elegant. It was the star of the fleet the Defiant had amassed over the years and, in Tomas' opinion, quite worthy of the position.

The top hull was thick, broad and long, sweeping down and back in an organic curve that left its port and starboard engines a vast eight hundred metres apart. Cradled beneath the centre of this crescent was a central structure, a multitude of decks, including the bridge at the bow, hangars to either side and more engines at the stern.

The bulk of *Sunbird's* armament was mounted on the top of the crescent wing, the design intending a most noble strategy. The dreadnaught would dive under its opponent like a Shaqan depth-glider, inflicting ferocious damage with its complement of plasma batteries and ion cannons. At the same time, its wide hull sheltered any ships leaving the hangars or fleeing an engagement. From port to starboard, it was a vessel designed to stand in the gap and take the hits for those who could not, and that was exactly what they needed right now.

Tomas paused his walk along the corridor of one of *Sunbird's* central levels and admired the sight through the viewport. The protective wing swept out from overhead, a blazing strip of yellow-gold melting into deep crimson at the ends, where the engines were housed. The central body was painted white, like a puff of smoke riding beneath a wave of fire.

If wars were won with flare, the Defiant would knock the CSF all the way to the Eye of Urim, true as c—

He sighed. This would take some getting used to.

A number of other starships were nestled under *Sunbird's* grand wing, all preparing for imminent departure. Just beyond, Tomas could see the other dreadnaught the Defiant owned: a conical Cyclone-class dreadnaught. It was a Dabanian design, as was the Tempest-class cruiser beside it and the Squall-class frigates scattered amongst the rest of the craft. The Dabans took the winds of their homeworld with them wherever they went, it seemed, and the roiling clouds and streaks of yellow lightning that decorated these ships were a testament to that idea.

Tomas resumed his walk, shortly entering the mess hall. Erae, Amarie, N'drizo, Crisp and Marpe were already seated at one of the long tables, though no meal was being served. There were few idle rooms on a dreadnaught, so once the *Empress* had been secured in a hanger, the group had retreated here, out of the way of the many rushing crewmen trying to get *Sunbird* ready for the fight.

Tomas had only left them to be introduced to his new squadron, the Slates. Thankfully, they were a squadron of Wasps, not SpaceJets or some other model. Tomas had already surpassed his limit for change these last few days. He should have stayed with them, he supposed. But the crew of the *Empress* made him feel the least out of place.

"What did you think of Wing-captain Eleazar?" Erae asked by way of greeting.

"Nice enough. Firm, respectable." Tomas took his seat. "I don't think the rest of the squadron care to have a CSF pilot amongst them though."

"That'll change once they see you fly. Many of our soldiers used to be CSF in one form or another.

"Right." Tomas shrugged. It wouldn't faze him either way. "Any update on this end?"

Marpe nodded. "We will be embarking in just over two hours. Then it will be a forty-nine-hour journey to the Kaluma system, and a further six to the planet Kaluma itself."

It was a long time, and all Tomas could do was wait and worry about what would happen when they arrived.

"So Kaluma is Charon's next target?" he asked.

"It is the next target we will reach in time," Marpe answered. "Not an hour after we land, our enemy will appear. Gabriel has been told."

"Does he know if our plan will work?"

Marpe paused. "I do not know," he gurgled. "I have not spoken with him myself."

"Surely he would have told us," Erae put in. "Especially if he'd been warned of our failure."

"Warned?" Crisp buzzed. Its claw barely cleared the top of the table. "Is common sense not warning enough? I ran the numbers once, twice, a thousand times, changing all the variables I could and assuming the best possible performance from our team. I say now what I said when you informed me of this ridiculous scheme: we cannot win!"

"We know, Sour-Circuit. You remind us every ten minutes," Amarie sighed, her fingers drumming idly on the plastic tabletop. "But we don't have all the information."

Crisp blew an electronic raspberry out of its mouth speaker. "Ten minutes? It has been seven hundred and three seconds since I last broached the issue. Perhaps if you were not a bot-brain, Infiltrator, I would have concluded a possible success!"

"How's about I conclude my knife into your brain?"

"Quiet, the both of you," Erae admonished. "Pointless bickering will only get us killed faster. Crisp, it's okay to be scared. I am too."

"I am not scared," Crisp said indignantly. "Just because we Shells are aware, you think we have all the weaknesses you do. Scared? I am accurate is what I am!"

The table fell silent. Every moment of Tomas' life was sifting through his mind. He kept coming back to his night on Ring One. To Gerad's death, and how he might have prevented it. To Quil and what he might have done, or said, that could have been different. He knew he didn't have the chance to change the past, but what of the future? Would he ever see them again? Would he leave Kaluma alive? He didn't want to die.

The expressions around the table all told the same story. When the plan had first been formed, blooming off the back of Tomas and Erae's precarious ideas, everyone had been enthusiastic. That feeling had tired by the time they'd boarded the dreadnaught, and a grim determination had taken its place. Then a despondent resolve and finally, now, trepid anxiety.

"I'm ... scared too," he said softly, looking at no one in particular.

"As am I." Marpe laid a hand on Tomas' shoulder, warm and damp.

Driz chittered an admission of his own.

Amarie rolled her eyes, but they got stuck halfway. "Yeah," she said with a breath. "I'm terrified."

"Oh, of all the ..." Crisp emitted a static-like snort. "Sure, whatever. I am scared too. We are all scared. Are you happy now?"

The crew of the *Empress* looked at each other, and Tomas found himself on one side of a glass wall, peering in at a bond he had not had the opportunity to share. Not with these people, anyway. They knew each other's strengths and weaknesses, their triumphs and failures, their traumas and joys.

Once again, he thought of the Dirks. He remembered their smiles, their love. He remembered their crushing embrace when he returned from capture. What reception would he get if he returned now?

Tomas could only endure the thoughts so long and pushed them away from his mind. When he did, he found that Erae was studying him.

"Our king is with us," she said to the group, mistaking the source of his pain. "He guided us together for this moment, and he will never let us be alone. "

Tomas smiled for her sake.

"Yes," Marpe said. "Yes, we all breathe, live, labour. We rest, release, die. There is no better place for all such things than the firm hands of Eladdiyr. Be assured now, my family, that he knows what is to pass. And if he knows, then what room is there for fear?"

He rumbled as he spoke. "Do you think it was our skill, strength or valour that kept us to this point? It was not, nor will they keep us now. My life has been long, children, and my future longer. I tremble to know I might lose it, but I will not flee and be left to wonder what might have been."

"You see, we have a cosmic ..." He stopped. "I'm sorry. I am as incessant as the sea."

"No, it's fine," Amarie said, offering a small but brave smile. "Thank you, Marpe."

"Yes. Thank you." Erae added.

Marpe's head tilted towards Tomas. "I believe in Eladdiyr like I believe stars shine, worlds turn and water flows. I know, Master Amets, that you do not."

Tomas felt caught by the accusation, but it was only the truth. He dodged Erae's piercing gaze and forced a laugh. "You've locked me, Marpe. I guess my world turns the wrong way."

Marpe's head didn't sway in laughter like Tomas hoped. "You, Tomas, have the opportunity for something far better."

"What would that be?"

Marpe creaked forward. "You get to *choose* to believe," he said.

29

If Kaluma was to be the last system she ever saw, Erae decided she would not be disappointed.

The ancient, swollen primary and its solitary planet clung to the lineless edge of the Cluster, well and truly in the region known as the North Wilds. Even if the CSF had been standing up to the Ebon resurgence, they would not have braved their ships to suffer the lawlessness that reigned here.

But as Erae guided the *Silent Empress* from one of *Sunbird's* portside hangars, that lawlessness was far from her mind.

She had stepped off the edge of the universe.

The Cluster fell away beneath her; a tumbling pool glittering and radiant, and above her there was a darkness as ceaseless as the Shift. Only in the Shift it was just a visual impediment; a trick snared in the laws of speed and light. Out here, in the ether not just between stars and systems but between entire galaxies, there was true nothingness.

Michael leaned over her shoulder. "Pull up a smidge," he instructed warmly. Erae complied, and the diamond curve of the Cluster fell out of sight.

"Oh my ..." Erae gasped as a new light poured across the weave-glass. For the void was not empty. There above her, not quite opposite the Cluster below, was the Eye of Urim. Currents of resplendent gemstones whirled and stretched in a spiral ceiling that faded at the far limit of Erae's vision.

Stars innumerable gifted their myriad colours into her eyes and drew her gaze ever inward along four elegant arms towards the galaxy's liquid iris.

This was no edge, but a ravine between marvels, a rift between the small and disorganised world she knew, and a world wild and unfathomable, yet shaped and formed.

"I thought it was a lot smaller," she breathed. "Or a lot further away."

Michael grinned from beside her. "I've been to the Cluster's zenith a thousand times over a million years," he told her. "It never fails to amaze me."

Erae glanced at Driz. The Yiishi had starlight caught in all four of his beady eyes. She flicked on the comm.

"Are you seeing this Am?"

"All of it," Amarie confirmed, emotion coating each word. "Rae …"

"Hold on," Erae pulled on the controls, sending the *Empress* into a slow spin. Beautiful and serene, the universe rolled around her head, and her heart swelled. A hand went to her chest.

"You should see it from where I'm sitting," Wing-Captain Eleazar commed in from Slate One. "I had to stop myself from popping the canopy." The squadron of twelve sat behind Erae on the radar.

Erae cut the signal, lest a true conversation start up and take her away from this moment. *If I survive*, she vowed, *I'm not leaving until I grab a vacuum suit and go for a spacewalk.* She didn't turn her attention to the approaching planet for a full minute more.

Kaluma hung before her bow, bleak and brutal. While other planets' surfaces could bear the scars of great pain and destruction, Kaluma's surface was itself pain.

It began when the planet's third moon—an unstable boulder of water-ice—fell from the sky. The planet had embraced its dying child in a fiery grief that covered the whole of the planet. What formations or life there might have been before were washed away by molten tears. Kaluma wept.

It would have been an age before the planet's surface had begun to cool, an age prolonged by the tidal engine of Kaluma's two remaining moons. When at last the lava stilled, those same tidal forces pressed and wearied the granitic crust, folding the rock like clay.

The moons were relentless, ever imposing their dominion over the world below them. The hills cooled and cracked, spewing sulphurous gasses into the air. Volcanoes drilled the landscape, and fresh lavas formed basalt maria over much of the world. What water there was had more compounds suited for death than life, and slid upon the shallow shelves of the broken land in herds dictated by the tyrannical satellites above.

"Why would anyone settle here?" Erae asked the Neiru beside her.

Michael shrugged. "For some, because they can, and because no one else will," he answered. "For most though, I believe there are huge crystals hidden within the granite rock: products of the time it took for the crust to cool. "

Erae nodded. Her eyes roamed the darkness of the highlands, the soft glinting shallows of the sea. "Ten thousand colonists, was it?" Such a small number to save, though it also meant there would be less death if the Defiant couldn't pull this off.

"That's what the last census said. But this is a pirate world, Captain. There is little in word or deed that you can trust."

"Why do you think we're bringing all these ships and troopers with us?" Erae said wryly. "Come on, it's time to say hello."

When the *Empress* drew within sight of Kaluma's only settlement, Erae was perplexed to see there was a crowd. By her reckoning, any hint of an invasive force would have sent the town of rogues scurrying to their various hideaways, or at least the rings of stilted stups that bordered the colony's mines. Carts and balloons dotted the grey maria with colour.

Trying to look as unaggressive as possible, Erae brought the ship in to land a good hundred metres from the edge of the gathering. Water fled from the wake of her engines as she worked the controls, then rushed back in once the landing struts touched down.

"Right then," Erae summoned her nerve as she unstrapped from her chair. With a tone-heralded click, the artificial gravity shut down, and Erae's stomach complained as the weight at her legs shifted to her back. She looked to the side at Michael, who was already standing on the cockpit's back wall.

"Are you ready?" she asked him.

"Yes."

She turned to Driz. "Are *you* ready?"

The Yiishi laughed and casually put his paws back behind his head. His little legs kicked in the air.

[I'm always ready, Captain,] he chortled. [I get to stay on the ship.]

"Lucky you," Erae twisted out of her seat. At least the gravity felt standard here. That was something. "Just don't fall asleep."

Driz stretched out and patted the drinks processor he'd recently installed in the cockpit. [Not a chance.]

Once she reached the airlock, Erae made sure to check her rifle's charge twice. Then, with a breath, she keyed the release.

Pressure equalised with a hiss, and the door slid open. The sickly smell of sulphur rushed inside Erae's mouth and nostrils. Holding a hand against the glare of noonday, she stepped onto the ramp.

The water sloshed and hissed against the heat of the *Empress'* engines, climbing and retreating against the ramp as it tried to rid itself of the motions caused by the landing. It was deeper than she'd thought and would come well past her knees once she was on the ground. Driz would have been in trouble, had he wanted or needed to join them.

"Captain."

Erae turned as Michael called to her from the bottom of the ladder, Amarie and Marpe descending behind him. "Yes?"

The Neiru looked at her, his eyes soft. "Some of us will die here," he said. "Know we are not dying for you, nor by your hand, but for our king."

For our king. "Thank you, Michael," Erae said, and meant it. She took a breath, eyeing the water.

She flicked a glance back over her shoulder to the Neiru. "Is it safe?" she asked him.

The pale figure nodded. "Just don't drink it."

Erae spared a second glance, this time upwards. She couldn't see any stars against the wilting blue of the sky. Amazing, the difference a sun and an atmosphere could make. Suppressing a grimace, she led her crew into the filmy aqua. She lost a small breath of air as the cold liquid seeped into her pants, and a second as the water suddenly rocked and bucked, climbing much higher than Erae had prepared for.

With a series of splashes, four Tombstone dropships touched down beside the *Empress*, courtesy of the Liberator Frigate that was lowering itself to the surface some seconds behind. Kuwrium ramps fell, and waves of armoured Defiant soldiers spilt into the sea. Sunlight reflected in whatever unscratched patches of helmet, pauldron or breastplate it could find. Rifles and blasters waved like reeds.

Erae unslung her own weapon to check it hadn't been soaked by the tumult, sucked in a fresh breath of pungent air, then continued to wade.

The hundred-and-something metres felt much longer while trudging through water, and even though the ocean steadily shallowed, Erae was drained by the time she passed the first of the stup clusters. These rings were more permanent than she'd first perceived. Concrete pillars held a circular road some three metres above the water, and the cheap white buildings were packed onto the inside edge.

The crowd she had spied before was still there, now arrayed less like a gathering and more like a blockade. The first two lines of people were all large and mostly male. The ocean pooled around the ankles of their knee-high water-boots.

Erae tried to smile warmly, but she doubted it could counter the sight of a few hundred infantry marshalled behind her. She stopped a stone's throw away, Michael and Amarie just behind her.

"Git gone, half-blood!" A jeer catapulted towards her from the crowd. "We got nuthin' for you to take and you wouldn't git it if we did." Unlike the group of soldiers on Rahga, the remark failed to get a cheer. Rather, a chilling silence stirred into the sweaty air.

The settlers, Erae saw, had little in the way of mended clothing, nor healthy faces. What was in abundance was a wild glint in the eyes, and a weapon on the hip or in the hands.

Erae swallowed. "Is anyone in charge here?" she called out.

A gnarled root of a man, all stubble and bark, stepped forward from the front line. His thick moustache and beard licked the bottom of a metal plate that covered one eye. *A stereotype. How wonderful.*

He stared Erae down, his hand heavy on the butt of his modified pistol. "I'm the sheriff," he drawled. "And I reckon I wanna shoot you."

Amarie took a step forward, but Erae waved her back. "You got a name, sheriff?"

"You gonna pay for it, bluebird?" The sheriff spat into the water. "You'd a noticed that thar's a few thousand of us here. We like bein' left to ourselves, so you'd be doin' yourselves a mighty favour by gettin' the scorch off our turf."

I'm sure you've noticed the two dreadnaughts in high orbit, but you're lucky I'm not here for a bluster contest. Erae batted the impulse away. "The Ebon Horde has returned," she announced, loud enough for the crowd to hear her.

"A black fleet is on its way, and it intends to kill you all. We have come to help you evacuate, and to protect you."

The sheriff didn't reply.

"Please, we only want to help."

"Thin what's ya foot-army for?" a shrill voice cried out of the gathering.

"Exactly what I said," Erae responded, trying to find a tone that suggested obedience and haste without being threatening. "To protect you and to help with the evacuation."

"What's him then?" The sheriff stuck a finger past Erae's shoulder, and she turned to see that Michael was the target. The Neiru stepped forward, and a murmur accompanied him as he came into full view.

"Do not be afraid," he said calmly. "I am here to help you."

"I seen you in a dream last night just gone," the sheriff said.

Syllebeth, Erae smiled in quiet wonder. *Remiel must have asked her to give us a helping hand.*

"Why are you all gathered, friends?" Michael asked.

"It's a fest!" someone shouted, and a small chorus of whoops followed from a section of the crowd.

"That's right," the sheriff agreed. "Pops, our alpha moon, is gon' clipse the sun in nor an hour. Thin at midnight this planet goes an' clipses Gran, the beta. It's not happened since we bin here, and it won't happen again before we go. I ain't missin' it for no ghost-man and his pet."

Erae looked to the sky and found that one of the moons was indeed already edging in front of the sun. That explained the tide.

"And your dream?"

The sheriff took his hand off his holster long enough to run it thoughtfully through his beard. "Maybe I dreamt ya," he said, "or maybe I di'nt. But I don't believe no Ebon are comin' here."

"I know you don't," Michael said, "but we will remain here just the same. For ten minutes, at the least."

"Ten minutes?"

"Yes," Michael said, his smile falling. "That's all the time we have left."

"Twelve, you there?"

It took Tomas a moment to realise the speaker was talking to him. He pulled his eyes away from the majesty of the stars and keyed his mic. "Sorry Eleven, still not used to my designation. What's the word?"

He could see Slate Eleven's Wasp drifting in formation not far ahead. The rest of the fleet was scattered around them, once again tortured with the task of waiting, as if the journey here wasn't sufficient. There were no frigates to escort, no enemies to shoot. Not yet. They would all come soon enough.

Slate Eleven pinged back. "I've got no word, Twelve. Though I can sing a song or two if —"

"Don't let him sing," Slate Three cut in. "For the love of all good ears, don't let him."

"Retracted. I wanted to ask Twelve what got him shoved into a sorry squad like ours."

Tomas forced a sigh. "I'm just a man who got very good at following the wrong orders, Eleven. Thought I'd try my hand at disobedience."

"Must have been some rot-woven orders if they landed you on my wing. But don't worry about that. We *love* disobeying orders here. Ain't that right, One?"

"Stow it, Flak." Wing-Captain Eleazar was curt with his reply. "We're forty seconds from T-zero."

Tomas looked at his monitor, and the timer that ticked down. T-zero was the rough time Gabriel had assured them Kithmakh would arrive. Each Neiru was unique, Erae had explained to him. Each had a special role in the kingdom, and Gabriel was the messenger. He asked Eladdiyr questions, and he got answers—most of the time.

It was yet another part of the plan that relied on trust, and Tomas' supply was running short. But the whole fleet was waiting with him. That had to count for something. He rested his hands on the yoke.

The timer hit twenty, then ten. Then zero.

Nothing. White knuckles and empty space. Tomas watched and waited. *A thousand Draik says that as soon as Flak speaks, it's over.*

But the comms remained silent as the seconds ticked by. Plus thirty-one … plus fifty-eight, plus ninety-five —

A skull-splitting crack tore through space. In the distance—though far too near when considering flight speeds—the fabric of reality folded, then tore open. A grinning white maw charged through the rift, followed by two reaching horns. The rest of the beast followed, and the rift knitted closed.

Kithmakh had arrived.

The comm lit with an equal mix of curses and appeals to Eladdiyr. Tomas at least had been prepared for what he would see, but that in no way lessened the dread, the despair that rose inside him. He closed his eyes, willing it away and failing miserably.

How could they hope to defeat it? The world-ship's horns stretched larger than the planet that spun helplessly behind him. The fleet had placed itself like a shield along the equator of Kaluma, but a better description would have been an *appetiser*. One beam, one bite, and they would all be nothing but crumbs.

Not if it goes to plan. The plan says Kithmakh will never fire. The plan says we don't die. It was yet another thing to trust, but Tomas was staring at a very convincing counter-argument.

"Ground control reports that the evacuation has begun." Eleazar broke the squadron's silence. "The local ships will be launching first, and they'll need shepherds so they don't kill each other in the scramble to *Sunbird*. Topaz has the first batch; we have the second. Tighten your wits and say your prayers."

Prayer. Right. Tomas nudged his acceleration lever as the Slates built up speed, readying themselves for the task ahead. All his life, Tomas had relied on his wit, skills and nothing more. They wouldn't keep him alive now.

Actually, that wasn't quite true. In the past, when Tomas had found himself facing an obstacle he couldn't conquer, he'd had his squadron, his friends. Maybe praying to Eladdiyr wasn't too different from trusting that his wingmate had his back.

Well, I trusted you enough to fly into this death trap, Tomas thought. *Now it's up to you to get us out.* As far as prayers went, that would have to do.

A glow caught his eyes to the right, and he turned to look. His breath halted.

Within Kithmakh's mouth, a brilliant light was building. Violet-white streamed out from between the monster's teeth, the excess energy of a barely contained destruction.

No. Charon don't do it. You know he's here. Can't you feel him?

"One?" Flak commed the squad. "This looks a lot like plan B."

"Give it a moment," Eleazar replied, but Tomas could hear the anxiety. After a moment, Eleazar added, "Slates, match my heading and prep for a point jump."

Tomas complied, tearing his gaze away from the mounting glow. Kaluma was on his left now, oblivious to its fate. *And Erae won't launch in time.*

From the grey surface, a beam of sun-yellow shot out, spearing into space. It didn't strike Kithmakh—it wasn't aimed anywhere close. It was a signal, an announcement to the heavens that lasted only a moment.

It was a taunt.

Time seemed to pause, and then, with a sputter, Kithmakh's glow withdrew. Tomas rediscovered his breath, but if anything his heartbeat rose. He tried not to wish too hard, fearing the weight of it would have the opposite effect.

From the writhing shift gate within Kithmakh's ribbed fuselage, something emerged.

"Contact! Plague-class dreadnaughts are inbound." The voice was not Eleazar but Admiral Five, the Shell commanding the task force from *Sunbird*'s bridge.

"Three signals are vectoring towards the system's shift gate, intending to block our escape. The other three are vectoring towards our position. Four minutes to engage."

The plan was working.

"Stay sharp, Slates. Prepare for our first escort run," Eleazar barked. "This is it."

The plan was working, and it did *not* feel good.

30

"Transports inbound. Slates on me; keep your arms tucked in."

Tomas felt the engine surge behind him as he pushed forward on his yoke, rolling his Wasp towards the incoming transport. He pitched down, Flak's Wasp just ahead of him, the rest of the Slates a wedge of blips on his radar.

"One, it's Nine. Shouldn't we break off? Those Plagues just point-jumped. They'll be here in no time."

"Negative, Nine. The whole reason we're running escort is because of the enemy. Get them aboard, then get out, that's the plan." Eleazar's voice no longer held worry. Whatever scare he'd had at Kithmakh powering up had vanished now that a job needed to be done. Or perhaps fear was irrelevant when it didn't increase one's odds of survival.

Tomas glanced at the distant monstrosity. It waited motionless, basking in the diffuse glow of its gate. It was watching, savouring. There was no point chasing already caught prey.

Get them aboard, then get out. A sound plan, but with three dreadnaughts blocking their escape and three more coming towards them, its execution was far from certain.

Various local starships and one Defiant transport rose towards them from the cloudless sky of Kaluma, emerging from the shadow cast by the nearest moon. It was drifting in front of the distant sun, swallowing the fleet in its umbra. Tomas tried not to think of it as an omen.

"Break in pairs," Eleazar ordered. "*Sunbird* and *Security* will designate open hangars as you approach. Lead them in, then form up for the defence."

With a chorus of affirmatives, the Slates split off, and Tomas followed Eleven towards their designated charge, a small, battered shuttle. It couldn't have held more than twenty lives.

But this is the hope, the bonus. The real plan is killing Charon. That task fell to Erae's team, more specifically to Michael. Tomas was just getting people out of the way.

"Guns to mark!" Admiral Five barked across his thoughts. "Drop dorsal auxiliaries on my command. Enemy vessels arriving in three, two, one."

Three dark, slow streaks of light sped past the hulking moon and contracted into being. Plague-class dreadnaughts were formed of two smooth hemicylinders wrapped around a jagged lamination of decks, sensors and hangar bays. A ring of engines stoppered the design at the rear, and cannons bristled along the outer surface. From the front, the oblong profile of the dreadnaughts looked not unlike the barrel of a gun, stapled top and bottom by the twin crescent hulls.

Colour burst across Tomas' radar as clawcraft and troop dropships launched from their hangars, racing towards the Defiant dreadnaughts. Plasma lit the night from both sides, and the battle had begun.

Tomas and Flak were halfway to *Sunbird,* the shuttle guarded between them. Flame and fury blazed on the top of *Sunbird's* wings, but the underside was safe for now.

Slate Nine was on the comm again. "One, we've got to help!"

"Negative, Nine. Not yet."

"But the Ebon!"

"They'll keep a little longer. We have orders."

Tomas felt every beat of his heart as he dove into the sanctuary of *Sunbird's* protective hull. Beads of sweat ran down his forehead beneath his visor. The radar was quickly dissolving from three red singularities to a swirling storm, and soon even this space would be full of swarming fighters.

He eased his acceleration back as they reached the hangar. The shuttle headed through the mag-screen—a fleeting victory. Tomas and Flak banked away.

"Form up, Slates, and prepare for combat."

It's too soon. So many hours of waiting, and now the battle rushes towards me. Tomas felt a wave of nausea and lifted a hand to his head. They were trapped like rodents, like insects under a glass screen. This was a small fraction of the enemy force that ravaged the Cluster. A summer hunting party, and the Defiant were the witless prey.

Why? Why am I so afraid? I faced a force a thousand times larger than this. I survived. Only at Tachillah he'd been part of a fleet equally large, and he hadn't known anything about immortal warriors or monstrous world-ships.

Tomas' hands shook, threatening to yank him from formation and hurtling towards open space. His eyes skipped down to the planet below, trying in vain to spot the glint of the last rising transport; the signal that the planet had finally been evacuated, and they could all run away.

Scorch that, he just wanted to see the *Silent Empress* rising towards him, whether the task was complete or not. Then …

Tomas stopped himself, and his hands fell away from both his head and his yoke. It wasn't the Ebon army that scared him, he realised.

Seven years ago, he had fought side by side with his squadron, and they had flown toward life's black hole together, skirting the unknowable line between emerging victorious or slipping past the inescapable event horizon. He would have died for them, had *expected* to die for them, and in his last thoughts would have known no fear.

Looking out the viewport at Kithmakh, at the Ebon fleet, he had that same expectation, yet he could not accept it. Not when he thought of *her*.

Because Erae Tamah had something he didn't, some inward-kept thing he had glimpsed lighting the depths of her eyes, had felt when she touched her hand to his head. This spirited, blue-skinned captain whom he hardly knew had invited him into a world he hadn't even begun to understand, but *he wanted to*, and he wanted to know her as well.

But Erae was down on Kaluma, and Tomas was up in space. The future he sought hinged on every action while death waited patiently behind a white-toothed grin.

In that moment, it terrified him. It screamed at him to flee. To fight on only brought death.

Eladdiyr! he despaired into the void. *Eladdiyr what do I do?*

There was no answer.

What do I do?

There was only silence.

Or … nearly. In the silence was something. Something between a voice, a thought and a feeling. And what resulted wasn't really said, or even felt. It just was.

Tomas knew why there was no booming voice to answer his question. It was because he already had an answer inside him. It had been whispered to him every day of his life.

Images of people flashed through his mind. Erae, Marpe and the Neiru. Quil, Dan, the Dirks, even his sister and parents.

Eleazar buzzed his ear. "Clawcraft incoming. Keep them away from the hangars and evac ships. Stick to your wings, and I'll see you on the other side!"

The radar bled. Crimson indicators crawled over the screen as they devoured the kilometres between them and Tomas. He brought a hand back to the yoke. Settling a final shaking breath, he flicked the switch on his first pair of missiles.

He had his answer.

The Slates sped towards their enemy, both formations preceded by hails of blue fire. They split and dove, metal roaring past in blurs, backs pressed to seats and vision greyed by force. Tomas launched through the centre like lightning through the eye of a storm. Plasma ripped from his cannons into the darkness of the eclipse.

He would fight on.

Erae held her rifle steady, tracking the Ebon dropships through her scope. Her heart had been stuck in her mouth for fifteen minutes, ever since the space battle had begun. She could feel each pulse of blood in her fingers.

She didn't dare look upwards, at the sky turned black as night and the violence that lit it. The violet glow of Kithmakh's core was by far the brightest and biggest of the stars.

The waves around her shins picked up as the Ebon dropships touched down. The three vessels were circular discs: slightly conical, thinning to a Human's height at the edge. As they descended, a dozen needle-like struts split from their undersides, rotating until they stabbed like knives into the dark liquid below.

The eclipse was complete, but there was no festival. The last few locals scurried and ran from their homes, precious belongings or children bundled in their arms. Some were overburdened as they struggled through the water that had risen with the moon; some fled with just their skin and clothes. Normal conversation was absent, and any sentient noise came as either a whisper or a scream.

There were more screams now, as rank upon rank of black shadow fell from the belly hatches of the dropships, their legs joining seamlessly with the murk that sloshed around them. Erae's thermal scope was blind to them. She and her comrades could see only fog and fear.

Time to change that.

"Now!" Erae shouted, and light flooded the area. Some of the lights the Defiant had brought with them, but others were strung up along the pillars of settlement rings, bright and brilliant. The Ebon soldiers were visible now, though the water looked blacker than ever.

The lights also brought Michael into crisp focus. He stood between the dropships and the waiting Defiant soldiers, who had spread themselves out as a line between the enemy and the last evacuation transport. Portable barricades had been scattered around to provide cover, and small groups of riflemen were keeping watch from the concrete rings above.

Michael's hair was like snow in the new light, and he held his ivory spear towards the dropships in a commanding statement of impasse.

A final figure leapt from the lead dropship, and the lights that hit him passed somewhat through, catching on ribbons of crimson within his flesh. The same red crowned his head in ten horns, and his eyes flashed.

He spoke, and his voice echoed off the pillars and bounced inside Erae's skull.

"I saw a star fallen from the sky unto the earth," he boomed. "The star had unlocked the darkness, and it opened upon the worlds. From the darkness came fire and smoke, and the furnace of his wrath was greater than any sun. From the smoke walked his swarm, and in power they covered the land."

Every voice and heart paused in wait, leaving only the noise of the fleeing settlers as they sloshed towards the transports. Only the two Neiru dared speak.

"You pervert words not your own, Charon!" Michael called and pointed his spear at his Peret foe. "How shallow your strength must be, that you bolster it with lies!"

Charon snarled. "My powers are higher than yours could ever be, *Guardian of the Righteous Heart.* My arsenal is death, and my army legion." He held his hand aloft, drawing a crimson sword from the air as if from a sheath. Erae's eyes widened.

Michael took a step forward. "My power *is* weak, but I am found in a strength not my own. Brother, dear brother, why have you hardened your heart? I wish a different end for you."

"I choose my own end!" Charon roared, and faster than sight, he struck.

Suddenly appearing before Michael, the Peret brought his sword down in an overhead slash. Michael caught it on the shaft of his spear, and the sound of the impact travelled along the water. He backstepped the stab that followed, twisting away.

Charon's speed was outdone only by his ferocity. He warped with each step, attacking first from the right, then low on the left. Erae could only watch in fear, vividly recalling her encounter on Shbiy. This was a fight she couldn't possibly help with. It was out of her hands.

Michael's hands, though, were up to the challenge. The Celah used the length of his weapon to his advantage, keeping the two combatants apart, pivoting away when Charon warped in close.

The exchange stalled, then Michael was on the attack, driving Charon back towards a nearby pillar. Charon blinked to the other side, but the spear was already on the way, barely diverted by the edge of his blade. The Peret roared.

"You cannot best me, brother!" He dashed to the side, throwing a flurry of quick jabs at Michael's tranquil face. Each found only air or ivory. Then Michael executed a dash of his own, skirting by the last of Charon's thrusts and pushing hard against him with the flat of one hand. Charon rolled backwards and slashed with his free hand, catching Michael's cheek with his claws. He came up a few paces away his eyes bright with rage. The water that pooled around his legs hissed and bubbled. His fangs flashed in the floodlights as he brought his hand to his mouth and licked the white blood from it.

"I have waited millennia to taste your blood again, brother." He smiled. "It does not disappoint."

Michael held his spear to the side and bowed. "I am honoured to have brought you one small happiness before you die."

"Such a gift deserves one in kind." Charon laughed darkly. "I offer you the dying screams of your friends." He raised his sword.

Behind him, the Ebon surged forward, and Erae felt her heart race. This was it. She glanced to the side and found the stalwart faces of her friends beside her. Amarie had two pistols at the ready, and Marpe, his expression forever immutable, tentatively cradled a machine gun in his damp hands.

But the Ebon slowed, and then failed, as Michael stepped towards them. The dark warriors looked upon him and stumbled, afraid. Michael continued his approach, and the ranks flailed in unpractised retreat, gripped with wordless horror.

"*Cowards!*" Charon screamed, and the ground shook. "Worthless spawn. Destroy the mortals!" But the army would not advance.

Michael shook his head. "Even they understand what you cannot, brother. What you have blinded yourself towards."

Another scream struck and cracked against the nearby pillars. Fire leapt from Charon into the night, and as Erae watched the moon and stars vanished beneath a swift gathering of dark clouds, bloated with hate and malice.

"This is my time!" the Peret declared. "My triumph! I am your fate!" The clouds broke, and raindrops thick and sour fell from the sky. The floodlights became obscured and dim as the torrent fell into the water, drenching everything in a warm sound and substance.

"Blood!" Amarie exclaimed, and Erae turned to see her friend's face covered in dark red and set in disgust. Her hair was plastered to her head. "It's raining blood!"

The smell was as heavy as the rainfall and soaked right through Erae. She resisted the urge to vomit and peered past her barricade through the storm. She couldn't see ten metres beyond her barrel.

But even in the storm, she could hear the sound as Charon dashed through the night and thrust his blade at Michael. She heard the clash of steel and ivory, the roar of flame and the crack of thunder.

Erae felt the ground underneath them move with the impact, and she quailed. Her left hand seized into a fist, and she struggled to breathe for a moment. If this was the sum of Charon's strength, what hope did they have?

Who did they have hope in? Tomas had asked her. And she'd answered.

Eladdiyr. Only the King's strength would save them now. Erae closed her eyes and steadied her breathing, flinching as the duel of the Neiru sent another quake through the earth.

But this time, it did not fade. It rumbled on with all the ominous rhythm of a stampede.

It is a stampede. Erae opened her eyes. "They're coming!" she yelled, her cry carrying through the earpiece of every soldier. "Fire!"

Though they could see no targets, the soldiers fired into the downpour. And as they did, the charging Ebon fired back.

Tomas fired. He spun. He dove and climbed and fired and balanced his shields and pitched and fired—an endless sequence of actions with the barest opportunity for emotion. Emotions, even thoughts, took too long. Too many would get him killed.

"He's sticking to me, Flak," he grunted and banked sharply, trying in vain to get out from under his opponent's guns. It wasn't working, and though most of the plasma aimed his way was lost to the string of curves and dives, his rear shields were still dropping.

"Yaaii!" Slate Eleven cut in from the side with both cannons blazing, pummelling the clawcraft to molten slag. "That's three!"

"Thanks, partner. I'm coming around," Tomas put actions to words, lining himself up behind his wingmate as Flak jetted towards the first clawcraft he could spot. There were plenty flying about, tangling themselves amongst the Defiant squadrons, stealing individual fighters away for a dance from which only one would ever emerge.

Eleven and Twelve angled in on an enemy fighter, five streams of blue energy streaming from it into the shields of a War-Moth. The deflectors collapsed, and the craft was engulfed in flame. Tomas felt a stab of pain as the starfighter disintegrated, and cut his speed as Flak swept in and railed the responsible Ebon. He shoved the pain away. Pain took too long.

Two more clawcraft curved in from either side; the wingmates of Slate Eleven's latest kill. Ebon starfighters flew and fought in trios, and knew how to use their numbers to their advantage.

But Tomas had fought these Scourge-spawn his whole life. He was ready for them. A grim smile crossed his face briefly, and he launched his missiles.

The warheads spun and strafed after their target, who was trying his best to evade his fate. The outcome was certain, however, and Tomas had already pulled up to track the second fighter when the glow of the explosion met him.

"Hold still Eleven," he told him. "Try to look tasty."

Flak stalled his evasion, providing too tempting a bait for the last pilot to resist. The clawcraft levelled off and began to fire, but Tomas already had two thumbs on his firing studs. Azure bolts split the distance between them and crashed into the clawcraft's shields, and then the hull.

Tomas must have missed the engines, for the craft failed to explode as Tomas buzzed past it. Looking over his shoulder, he saw that one of the craft's claws had been severed, and the viewport had blown out. Where the Ebon's body was, Tomas didn't know. It would be impossible to spot amongst the stars.

"Dive, Twelve! Dive!" Tomas pushed forward in thoughtless trust and was rewarded when a Syphon-class frigate brushed past his engines, portions of its hull spouting red flame.

The doomed vessel was taking damage from one of the enemy dreadnaughts; a relentless stream of cannon fire that raked across the smaller craft's hull. Metal swelled and burst apart, sending kuwrium plates flying off into space. Only a trickle of fire returned towards the Ebon warship and was swatted batted away by the bigger craft's shields.

The Syphon's lights went out as an explosion rocked the forward end of the craft, and that was the end of it. In unison, the Plague turned its guns towards one of the other small ships battering its defences.

"Why has *Sunbird* stopped firing?" Slate Eleven demanded through the channel. "What is she waiting for?"

Tomas made sure there were no fighters headed towards him before taking a proper look at his monitors. Frigates clustered in groups, concentrating their fire on sections of their larger adversaries. *Security*, the Cyclone-class dreadnaught, was squared off against one Plague all by itself, and both ships registered significant damage. The dreadnaughts maintained a constant rotation, attempting to bring undamaged cannons and shields to bear.

But *Sunbird* was sitting still, the batteries that had opened the conflict sitting silent ever since. The Ebon forces were leaving her to herself, and Tomas knew why.

"She's got her auxiliary shields up," he explained. "Admiral Five is protecting the civilians."

"We'll be killed if she doesn't do something soon," Flak shouted in a panic. "We're outgunned without her!" His statement was punctuated by a half-scream across their squadron frequency, followed by a crackling silence.

A new trio of clawcraft sped in from the side, tearing their projectiles across Tomas' flight path. He and Eleven split and curved in different directions, and Tomas felt a jarring thump as a bolt found its way through his Wasp's shields.

He didn't have time to look out towards the shift gate, but the waiting vessels were fixed within his mind, Kithmakh chief amongst them.

We're outgunned anyway, he thought, banking so sharply that grey spots appeared in the corners of his vision. *Please Eladdiyr, you need to help us.*

31

The world was water, fire and blood.

Plasma bolts whizzed through the air, screaming from rain-curtained sources to targets equally obscured. Erae snapped off a few shots then ducked back behind her barricade as her clip ran dry. She ejected it and inserted a new one—her last one.

The Ebon assault was relentless. One ear filled with the whine of plasma fire, the other with the vein-freezing shriek of the Ebon warriors. Her eyes saw darkness, her lungs breathed fetid decay. Every sense was saturated with death.

A body grazed her thigh, face down in the swirling muck. She reached down and took the spare ammo from its belt, then swung around to fire some more shots. She aimed for the sources of light and noise.

"Save us, Eladdiyr," she pleaded. "Get us through." There could have been just ten Ebon left, or a hundred. The unholy downpour broke her truth and her will just as readily as her sight. She couldn't hear Michael and Charon anymore, but the ground still trembled with the rhythm of their duel, and every now and then a bolt of lightning or blast of ice would pierce the deluge.

Peek, aim, fire. A skulking shadow bent over its smoking chest and was lost in the flood. Peek, duck—peek, fire. Her shelter shuddered under the enemy salvo, and chips of hot metal struck her cheek. Peek, aim—

She jumped as a figure charged through the dark towards her, then another. She raised her rifle ready to defend.

"Captain!" Marpe shouted over the rain as he pushed in close, Amarie beside him. His colossal form was stained dark from the rain. A nearby flash lit up all but his eye sockets: a brief and haunting image. "The last group of survivors is stalled, stuck, trapped under the structure twice north of here."

"Where?"

Amarie pointed, but the gesture was swallowed in the storm. Erae gave her a visual once-over, and she seemed unharmed. She held up an empty pistol.

"We could use an escort," she explained.

Erae nodded and wiped gunk from her eyes. "On my mark."

Eladdiyr guide me now. She angled her head out and tried to note the sources of fire. There were too many.

"Go!" Amarie took the lead, then Marpe, who for once kept pace. Erae followed a few steps behind, returning any fire directed their way, hoping to scare the guns to silence. Shapes and forms lurked and screamed in the dark, but the three friends didn't slow. A few bolts caught Marpe in his chest, but he bowled through them, the energy shedding off his natural armour. Erae sent a bolt of her own, and no more plasma came from that corner.

It was a hard slog through the thickening sea. The water pulled at their legs, and hid the rise and fall of the ground. Erae had used another clip by the time the shadows of the settlement ring loomed above them. She followed Marpe through the waterfall at the ring's edge and stepped into a brief but welcome reprieve.

Further along, still in the protection of the ring, was a group of civilians. There were eight of them, young and old, huddled together beside a support pillar. Two soldiers stood by them, urging them on, but the group only pressed tighter.

"What's wrong?" Amarie waded over. Erae followed, keeping her attention on the cascade around them, watching for anything to break through.

"What do you think? They're terrified," one of the guards explained. A black scorch mark streaked across his chest plate. "They won't make the distance, not like this."

"And we won't make it if we wait for them," the other added. He resumed pulling on one of the women's arms, dragging her out from the others. The woman shrieked.

"*No!* Don't make me! They're waiting, they're waiting they'll *shoot* me!"

"Stop!" Amarie closed the distance in a heartbeat, pulling them apart and rounding on the soldier. "What do you think you're doing!"

Erae stepped closer, shifting her aim to the water pouring down just behind the group. A small adjustment would bring the angered soldier in line. She hoped she wouldn't need to.

"They have to move!" the soldier shouted, drawing up to Amarie. "They stay, we die."

"So, you're going to drag them one at a time?"

"If I have to!" The man gestured into the dark. "The Ebon are going to burst through any second, and then we're all dead. So *scorching move.*" He shouted the last words over Amarie's shoulder.

That much was true. They couldn't stand here fighting; they had to muscle through. Erae turned to call her muscle into the situation—

Where was Marpe? She looked around, but the Qua'seth had lumbered off without her noticing.

Amarie stood her ground. Her emerald eyes blazed at her adversary. "We're not dead yet."

"Not yet, but you know who is? Krezek, Farlane, Naharai. Riger's only alive because the bolt went through Greaser's heart first." He looked to his comrade, who lowered his eyes to his burned armour.

Fear swept over the soldier's anger. "We can't win." I dropped ten Ebon into that water. I could have dropped a hundred and they wouldn't know. They're still coming. The Neiru promised new life, but we're just being sent to die. For who? Them?"

"Yes!" Amarie yelled.

Erae stepped forward. "Am—"

"When the Ebon reach us, who are they going to kill? A coward, or a soldier?"

"Why does it matter?"

"*Because you'll know why!*" Amarie roared, forcing the soldier onto his back foot. She breathed and glanced at Erae, then spoke in a pleading calm.

"You'll know that you died to save people. Not to kill, not to save yourself. The why matters."

Am. Erae blinked and wiped her eyes. The soldier stared. Beyond the curtain, the sounds of war rolled on. A blast shook the ground, and dust fell from the curving road above.

The soldier shook his head. "I'm getting on that ship," he said. "Now."

"We all are." Amarie turned to the group of civilians. They were deathly quiet. "You've got the same choice. Wait for the Ebon under here, or take it to them out there."

To Erae's surprise, the group started to nod and move forward. But then something crashed through the wall of blood, and they screamed. Erae swivelled with her rifle raised.

Marpe stood, dripping red, visibly exhausted. His head canted as he examined the group, then he grunted and pulled his prize in from the rain. Erae smiled.

"Perfect," she said as she beheld the battered steel barricade Marpe had dragged through the water. "Now we've got a plan."

And with a plan came hope.

"Quickly now, let's go." She helped Amarie usher the group to the edge of the ring. The soldiers stuck close, eyes scouting through the torrent, preparing for what came next. As Marpe pulled the barricade close onto his back, Erae stepped through the veil.

The relief the shelter had given was ripped from her as a reeking, staggering weight slammed into her head and shoulders. It was difficult to see, but Erae continued forward, the shuffling, waterlogged steps of the group not an inch behind her.

They moved as a cluster, keeping Marpe and the barricade between them and the enemy, determining each other's presence by touch more than sight. It was a slow march, but it was working.

"Look out!"

Erae swung to meet an Ebon charging in from the side, his weapon raised to fire. His death whistle cut off as Erae speared a bolt straight through the centre of his featureless face. The body crumpled.

Plasma fire began to find Marpe's barricade, occasionally at first, then increasing as more Ebon locked on. The constant pounding drowned all other sounds in a deafening roar. A flurry of shots struck from the right, catching Riger and throwing him under the waves. Erae spared one grieving thought, then kept on. Each step felt like a lifetime, and there was no indication they were any closer to their goal, or even that they were headed in the right direction.

Fifty more steps, then Erae pitched forwards as her legs struck something. Face first, she plunged into the drink, pushing against the cold flesh that had given way beneath her. In fear she jerked away from the corpse, flailing as she tried to right herself.

A hand caught her by the collar and yanked her above the surface. "Go!" Amarie yelled into her ear. "I can see the ship ahead."

Wiping the soup from her eyes, Erae could make out the masked glow of the transport's lights, and the line of Defiant defending it. With renewed vigour, the party continued its trek. The ramp came into view, and she nearly cried.

"Captain Tamah to transport." she activated her comm as the civilians scrambled into the evac freighter. The soldier looked back at Amarie, then discarded his gun and followed them in. "All civilians aboard. You are clear to launch. We did it."

If there was a cheer, Erae couldn't hear it. Rain abandoned its vertical descent and was sent scattering as the transport powered its thrusters and launched into the night. The roar of its engines was exultation enough.

"Thank you," she whispered, and despite the death reigning around her, she felt an overwhelming calm and relief.

It was soon taken from her. "What now, Captain?" the nearest soldier shouted at her. "Do we pull out?"

She nodded, then realised the action would have gone unseen. "Yes. There's nothing more we can do here. It's up to Michael now."

"No!" Marpe bellowed from beside her. "We must stay, and give him every chance to end this war."

"How can we help? The Neiru are immortal: we are powerless against them."

Marpe ignored her exasperation. "We have *the same power*," he rumbled. "The same king."

"We can't even see them," Amarie pointed out. "This storm's too dense!"

"Then that is our first task," Marpe said and, stepping past them, lowered himself to his knees. Inky water broke across the stone of his chest and back, swallowing him.

"What are you doing!" Amarie stepped forward to rouse the giant, but Erae stopped her with a hand.

"Look, she said, pointing down at the water.

It was moving.

Tomas watched Flak's Wasp break apart, and despair took over.

A stray shot from one of the dreadnaughts had caught Slate Eleven dead centre, tearing through his already weakened shields and detonating the starfighter right before Tomas' eyes. Flak hadn't even had enough time to scream.

Tomas screamed, pulling away as the cloud of shrapnel expanded across his flight path. Fragments of what had just been his wingmate pinged and fizzled into his shields. It was just one more death amongst many, but it was enough for Tomas. The cost of this mission had climbed too high.

"Eladdiyr!" he shouted out, angry and afraid. "Where is your power? Is this what your son died for?"

The Defiant had known from the start that they wouldn't win without help. Erae and Marpe had repeated the sentiment to him a hundred times while aboard *Sunbird*. But what were they expecting? Eladdiyr hadn't shown up.

Or had he? The not-quite thought from earlier had never left him. As fear and grief boiled and broke within him, it remained one layer further down. It brought a peace that, while not loud, was not moved by the terrible death around him.

Tomas worked his controls and dropped behind a new target, blasting away until his bolts melted through to the other side. He kept his focus, but only barely. He was listening, leaning in.

We need you with us.

A familiar wind brushed against him, peeling back the layers of seven long years until he was staring at the stern of a weathered shuttle that would not flinch from his missile lock.

I am with you. This time it *was* a thought, one that struck his ears before it reached his mind.

"Eladdiyr?" Tomas asked. He armed his last pair of missiles, watching the distance scroll down. His question only felt half-right. His finger hovered over the trigger, ready to complete the memory. Last time it had made him a hero. It had also made him a villain.

I am within you.

The vision faded, and he found himself rocketing towards the bow of one of the dreadnaughts. The main guns were engaged with nearby frigates, but the point-defence cannons swivelled to bracket him in their sights.

Tomas wasn't afraid. He launched his missiles.

The candescent projectiles raced ahead, darting past the plasma fire that tried in vain to keep them at bay. They reached the boundary of the Plague's inner shields, but no explosion occurred.

The torpedoes flew on, hammering into the warship's bridge and shattering the front viewport. Tomas dove.

"Impact on the bridge. Bow shields have collapsed. Concentrate your fire on the forward hull!" A renewed barrage of energy assaulted the front of the Ebon vessel, buckling the plates and eviscerating the guns. Flames spewed out of breaches in the hull, and with a flicker the remaining shields collapsed, sealing the dreadnaught's fate.

Cheers rang across the comm, but Tomas was too stunned to add to them at first. His missiles had skipped *through* the shields. It was impossible, but Tomas had felt the power come from inside him, willing the warheads along.

"Ben did give us power," he said, and laughed aloud. "The king is here!"

The cry was echoed over the comm, pushing back against the darkness. The Defiant would not be defeated this day.

A hail from his comm cut through the noise. "*Sunbird* to all available fighters. Repeat all fighters. The last evac transport is away and needs an escort from the surface. This is your top priority."

Tomas rotated and pushed forward on his acceleration lever. A roiling storm churned over Kaluma's surface, right where the settlement was supposed to be. Tomas cranked his acceleration higher, watching his radar for the first hint of the evac transport, pleading that the *Silent Empress* was right behind it.

An explosion rocked the stern of his Wasp, throwing the yoke out of Tomas' hands. He cursed and searched over his shoulder, but his pursuer remained out of sight. Cursing again, he wrestled the yoke back to forward.

But the stick was useless; his engines were gone. Alarms ricocheted through the cockpit and Tomas' dashboard went dark. A burning smoke began to fill the cabin from behind.

"No! Not now!" His hand worked across the controls, but to no avail. Slate Twelve plummeted towards the storm-choked planet. Tomas checked the pressure seal on his flight suit, locked his visor in place, then grabbed for the ejection lever.

Not yet.

Tomas moved his hand away. Call it insanity, or call it trust, but something had come upon him. As long as it lasted, he would listen.

His cockpit began to shake as he scraped the first layer of atmosphere. Tomas took his yoke in both hands and continued to fall.

The tide was receding.

Erae kept one eye on Marpe. He was bent over in the water, his prayer inaudible as it travelled from his beard straight into the swell. A swell that swept past with a strong current that hadn't been there before. The water level had already dropped by half.

Erae didn't have the faintest clue where it was going, but she was pretty sure she knew the cause. Her heart in her throat, she kept watching.

Plasma fire continued to shoot out in all directions, reminding her that they were still in the middle of a fight. But the Defiant were holding the line. They'd had enough of running away.

The sounds around them changed as the rain struck bare, dripping rock and stone.

Marpe straightened and rose to his feet. He looked at them and slowly, deliberately, wobbled his head back and forth.

"We serve a wonderful, powerful, glorious, marvellous, radiant … " He stopped himself, then gurgled. "We serve a good king."

Erae grinned despite everything. She swore she could see a twinkle in Marpe's empty eyes.

Look," Amarie exclaimed. "The storm is fading!" Erae realised she could see further, making out shapes and figures in the fading dark. Soldiers began calling out enemy locations, adding precision to their fire. A few ran forward in the thinning rain.

"Not yet," Marpe arrested her shoulder. "Stay back, everyone. Ready your weapons."

"But the storm's stopping!" Amarie raised the carbine she'd taken to replace her empty pistols.

"The enemy's is, yes," he said. His head continued to sway. Erae felt a thrill of anticipation rise inside her. "Ours is about to begin."

The floodlights that had been obscured by the deluge shone across the battlefield once more, striking the silhouettes of the enemy, glittering off the ground. There in the centre of it all was Michael and Charon. Both Neiru stood tall, too far away for Erae to gauge injuries. Their attacks came slower, and no sparks or flame accompanied their jabs and strikes. The ground no longer shook.

At least, not because of them. Erae watched a group of Ebon run past the duelling immortals, the rage of battle forgotten. A lot of Ebon were running away, and a lot of Defiant were running towards her, scrambling from the cover they'd kept. Erae turned.

In the distance behind Marpe, the beams of the floodlights ended short. A wall of night-black water swept towards them, its rolling crest as high as the clouds. Erae tried to find the side of it but failed. There was nowhere to go.

"Brace yourselves!" she cried out, crouching and finding a crack in the rock to hold on to. Those around her followed suit. The wave continued to mount, but Erae wasn't afraid. It wouldn't harm her.

She turned to see Michael and Charon pause, both staring in wonder at the approaching tsunami. The space before Michael folded in, and he vanished from sight. Charon tried to do the same, but his energy must have been spent. Smoke grew and shrouded his legs, but no further. He raised his arms and roared at the rushing water.

Erae held her breath.

The water roared back, swallowing everything in darkness.

32

The wave's impact instantly took Erae's legs from under her. Her grip went next and she bounced along the ground, her arms curled around her head.

It wasn't a gentle ride, but it was brief. The tidal wave passed over her, and the water receded in its wake. Erae opened her eyes to a different planet.

Sunlight shone through the parting clouds. The eclipse was over.

She rose to her feet, water falling off her and playing around her ankles. It looked like glass, clear and bright in the noon sun. The basalt ground was hidden beneath its mirrored radiance, covering the rock in silver-white and bending Kaluma's settlements into majestic concrete islands that floated in dew and sky.

A cheer rang out, then more, each Defiant joining in as they helped one another to their feet. Eladdiyr had saved them. He had given them victory.

One sight quelled Erae's own shout of triumph. The current had forced her back towards the centre of the battlefield. Only ten metres beyond her, a lone shadow knelt in the field of light. Charon was still, his head bowed. His army had been washed away. With a graceful shimmer, Michael appeared before him. His mouth moved, but Erae didn't hear the soft words.

She heard the reply, though.

"No," Charon said. The voices surrounding Erae quieted. "No, it will not end like this."

"You are spent, brother," Michael replied. Numerous fresh wounds of white ribboned his body. "Your power is great, but it is your own, and it ends. I lean on my king, and his strength restores my soul."

Charon's head shot up. His eyes stabbed rays of light into Michael. "You think you know power? You could not even best me yourself!"

Michael thought, then shrugged. "That was never the plan."

"Pestiferous worm! I command legions! I possess and destroy worlds with a breath. With the flick of a finger …"

The rays of his eyes turned downward, illuminating an ornate ring and its dazzling white gem.

Michael took a step forward. "Kithmakh cannot strike quicker than my spear. I will kill you if you order it to fire."

"Order it? *Order it?*" Charon laughed long and low. While Michael and the rest watched, he struggled to his feet. Erae turned only long enough to find Amarie and Marpe and retreat towards them.

Charon growled loud. "This ring is no simple tool of command. It is a tether. It is a *hunger*. When I bore it, it swallowed me in its depthless maw. I was consumed, but I did not die. I would not yield *my power*.

"*I* am the conqueror. *I* am the endless night. You call me spent, brother. I am not spent." Charon grinned and bared his fangs. "I am hungry."

Michael leapt forward, spear in hand, but was knocked back by a shock-wave as Charon rammed his fist into the ground. The gem split open, and black fire shot out in all directions.

Charon roared in pain, and the sky shook as a second roar joined his, tearing across space. Erae ducked and covered her ears as the atmosphere shuddered. Charon punched down a second time, and the dark flame flashed large enough to engulf him. When it withdrew, he stood tall, eyes shining bright, and sucked a shuddering breath between his fangs. His fingers flexed as he summoned a crimson blade into each hand.

The sound of many cracking whips filled the air. Kithmakh was blinking in and out of existence, blindly launching across space, stuck halfway between the Shift and reality. The ship was out of control.

On some of its nearer passes to the planet, Erae saw explosions dot the behemoth's hull as it collided with the battling Defiant and Ebon forces. Dreadnaughts were sent flying, and the others turned away from the fight and hurried to engage their point drives.

On the surface, Michael steadied himself, weapon at the ready.

Charon sprang like lightning, faster than Erae had ever seen him move, and his blades struck with a peal of thunder that shook Kaluma down to its core. Fissures split the ground, and the water poured into them.

Michael had blocked the assault mere inches from his face. Charon leaned in.

"*I am power!*"

Steam burst from the rifts in the rock, and Charon exploded into his attack. His blows were as swift as they were powerful and battered the Celah from every angle. With each strike, the earth split and moved.

"To the ships!" The cry went up and was swiftly raised in chorus.

"Run! The planet is tearing apart!"

"Get on board before the ground falls from under us. Launch, launch!"

"The Ebon are fleeing for the gate. Kithmakh is everywhere."

"Will it hit the moon? The *planet*?"

"Erae?" Amarie and Marpe had turned to flee, but Erae hadn't taken her eyes off the battling immortals. There was nothing she could do to help.

A ravine yawned open on their right, rocks tumbling and colliding in its maw.

"*Erae?*"

Michael was forced back, barely keeping his weapon before him as again and again Charon swung. The power of Kithmakh's ring coiled around him. It leapt out in whips of dark flame, and Michael gasped as a tendril lashed his leg.

It can't end like this. Erae looked on with mounting fear. *Not after everything we've done. Run, Michael!*

The tip of Michael's spear dropped.

With a roar of triumph, Charon wrested the weapon from his foe's hands and flung it away, then struck out with a wave of pure force. Michael was knocked flat, his back hard upon the ground. Charon dove on top of him, driving both blades through the flesh of his splayed arms, shattering bone and sinking them into the rock until the hilts burned his ghostly skin.

Erae and Amarie screamed in unison.

Michael cried in pain as white blood pooled around him. The ground stopped its quaking, leaving the last of the water to boil within the cracked landscape. The raised settlements were all in ruins.

Charon roared again, and Kithmakh roared with him. The Peret stood over his fallen prey, panting. Power engulfed him in waves, demanding release, striking the air. He straightened and reached into the ether to draw one last, gleaming blade. He paused at the apex and turned his face suddenly to the sky. Erae did the same, and her eyes widened.

Trailing smoke, the front end bright as a meteor, a starfighter dove from the heavens. It was one of the Defiant's Wasp fighters, and it was coming in fast.

Her comm crackled. "Get … clear … can't …"

Erae's heart stopped. "Tomas? Eject!" The craft wailed as the atmosphere tore at its integrity, threatening to rip off the wings. The smoke blackened as the paint job burned away, but the craft continued its ballistic course. Blue plasma shot out from its mandibles: lightning without rain.

In a burst of motion, Charon swung his blade, unleashing an arc of black flame, a scythe larger than the *Empress*. It overwhelmed the incoming bolts and chased them to their source.

"*Tomas!*"

The Wasp exploded in a cloud of smoke and fire, debris raining down. Erae took off, sprinting towards the Peret Neiru. Rage, loss, determination boiled within her veins as rocks and ravines disappeared underneath with barely a thought for where her feet were landing.

"Rae stop!" Amarie cried into her commlink as Erae leapt over a gaping cleft, rolling as she hit the far side. Charon was still watching the explosion, but her time was running out. Her footsteps were like cannons blasting through her bones.

"Erae, he's unstoppable!" The words scraped against the red haze in Erae's mind. "Erae please!"

Amarie was right. Erae didn't even know if Michael was still alive, but he must have been, for Charon had turned back to the prone Neiru, his blade high.

Eladdiyr I need you, despair overtook her rage, a last reaching hope. *I can't ...*

Charon inverted his blade and plunged it towards the heart of his prey.

With a wordless cry, Erae leapt forward and deflected the attack to the side. Metal sang along metal, piercing the air, shimmering along the length of Erae's glinting blade. Time paused, and both she and Charon stared.

A radiant sword was in her hand. An elegant rapier, not white like Michael's but silver-blue. The guard was in the fashion of two wings, and a brilliant moonstone was set in the pommel. *How ...*

"Impossible," Charon snarled. For a moment he seemed small, mortal.

Then his anger overcame his surprise, and power shot from him like a cloud of shadow. Erae stepped back, but she did not quail. Light burned within her, and she raised her blade to the ready.

Tomas felt like he'd been through death and back.

He'd waited until the last moment to eject from his Wasp, clearing the arc of supernatural flame by a hair. Then his fighter had exploded, and he was sent soaring on the edge of the blast. Intense heat swallowed his lower body, burning through his suit. Smoke and fire confused all sense of direction.

But he knew he was falling. He tugged on the cord under his flight chair, and his organs crashed against one another as the parachute deployed, righting Tomas with a jerk.

His breath escaped him, and he coughed as hot smoke burned his lungs and stung his eyes.

An echoing clash pierced the fog; the sound of steel striking steel, and then Tomas fell below the cloud. Kaluma rose towards him, closer than he had thought. He had pulled the chute with little time to spare.

There was Erae, standing protectively over Michael, but a terror dwarfed them both. It looked like a Peret Neiru, but barely, for dark power leapt from it on all sides, erupting around a head of horns and two brilliant eyes. Flame and shadow pooled at his feet as he raised himself up, and with a wide swing of his arm Charon struck out.

Erae caught the attack on her blade. Her feet dug into the ground as she was pushed back, but then she spun away, out of reach of the lashing darkness that followed. The next slash was accompanied by an arc of black lightning, and she threw herself to the side.

"Erae!" Tomas shouted, and pulled the pistol from his belt. He fired, but the shots vanished in Charon's growing storm. The Peret didn't even notice, blasting shards of ice towards Erae. She dove beneath them but stumbled on the loose rocks. He brought a sword down to crush her head, but she diverted the blow just in time.

She can't keep this up. I have to do something! Tomas had nearly reached the ground and began to search it with his eyes, desperate for anything, *anything* he might use. His body felt like it was on fire. His legs were the worst, but he shunted the pain away. He couldn't give in now.

There! A glow of silver-white amongst the grey, lying between him and the battle. The same light was in the blade Erae wielded. But could he even make it?

Please, Eladdiyr. She has to hold on.

Charon's fury surrounded her, blocking out the sun. It surged like water, lifting Erae off her feet. She landed and twisted out of the way of the next attack. There was no space for a strike of her own. Her weapon seemed no bigger than a needle against his, but it did not break as she held it above her head and caught another downstroke on the shaft. The impact shuddered along her bones and drove her into the ground. Her blade might withstand the assault, but her body couldn't take much more.

Eladdiyr. Though all her concentration was needed to stay alive, she spared a thought to focus on his name. It might be the last thing she ever knew. *Eladdiyr.*

Charon stepped forward and space began to shift, but teleporting appeared to be too precise for his empowered rage. He was no longer roaring as he slashed forward again and again. He was *screaming,* Erae realised, tortured by the same dark nexus he drew power from. Kithmakh and Charon were eating each other alive.

She dodged again, and he bellowed. *"How dare you stand before me!"* His voice shook the planet, and Erae staggered as the ground moved beneath her next step. She kept moving in a circle.

"I am the Master, I am the Lord. You will kneel!"

Erae cried out as Charon brought his fist down like a hammer before her feet, splintering the ground into molten fragments. A few of them caught her legs as she sprinted around, her eyes wide as she tried to track the next attack. Every muscle was on fire, and every breath shredded her lungs. Her rapier was lead in her hands.

Eladdiyr. She cycled the word in her mind, clinging to it. *Eladdiyr Eladdiyr. Eladdiyr Eladdiyr Eladdiyr.*

The storm around Charon continued to grow, and through the smoke his sword came, snaked in lightning. She twisted away, but a fork of energy caught her in the back, curling her spine. Stars burst before her eyes as she hit the ground, and she coughed up blood.

"Eladdiyr, Eladdiyr, Eladdiyr," she pleaded, each note numb and trembling.

"Silence!" Charon's rage doubled, and Erae screamed as a coil of flame snared her shoulder, searing the flesh. She pulled the arm away, fighting as pain greyed her sight, trying to bend aside as he stood over her, a colossal shadow. His eyes, terrible-white, blazed down.

"Eladdiyr ..." She willed her sword to move, but her arm was lifeless at her side.

The flaming blade lifted, and through a part in the darkness behind Charon she saw ... *no!*

Charon turned as Tomas charged into the vortex, Michael's spear braced at his hip. With a bellow of hate the Peret wheeled, his sword poised to fall as Tomas ran closer, fighting the black wind of the storm.

Wrenching her body around, Erae took the rapier in her other hand and plunged it into Charon's leg, collapsing the knee. The storm faltered as Charon cried out.

Tomas let out his own tearing howl as he drove the spear straight through the Neiru's heart.

33

Sound caved in to silence. Mortal and immortal stood for a moment, frozen before each other, joined by a shaft of white. Then exhaustion overtook Tomas, and he fell back from the spear. Erae was folded at Charon's feet, motionless.

The Peret Neiru tried to speak, but as his mouth opened his head snapped back, and a primal shriek was ripped from him. Red lightning burst from the ring, pulling on the surrounding air. Scarlet lines webbed and ruptured across and within his flesh—a flame far brighter than his scars.

The crack and shriek of whips grew to a crescendo as Kithmakh launched through the dimensions, ripping itself between spaces over and over again. With a final ear-splitting blast, it disappeared.

Tomas looked down. Charon was gone, leaving no mark on the shattered ground. A body lay crumpled below where he had stood. Tomas looked at her; at her clothes, scorched and torn, the pewter coat drenched in red. The black stripes that scarred her shoulder, carving into the sapphire scales.

"Erae ..."

Her eyes fluttered open, and she brought her head up. Tears were caught in her eyes. He felt them in his own, and they began to run freely down his face.

The burns on Tomas' legs were a blinding torture, but he pulled himself up. Using his arms, he scraped himself over the rocks. He grunted at the pain each movement brought, but he didn't stop. He reached out.

Her left hand took his.

They lay there. Apart. Together. He didn't know for how long. Eventually he began to feel a rhythmic vibration through the ground. He heard running footsteps.

"Erae!" Amarie dropped to her knees as she arrived. "Erae! Tomas! Don't move, either of you. Driz is bringing the *Empress* around."

"We're … okay," Erae said, dropping Tomas' hand to take Amarie's. It's … it's over."

"For now."

Tomas angled his head, seeing Marpe lumber up to them with Michael limping at his side. The Neiru's body was riddled with fresh scars. A huge gash went through each arm, thick and white.

"Nicely done Captain, Commander," he coughed. "Nicely done."

"It seems the day has been saved," Marpe sloshed, his face as unreadable as ever. "The Ebon fleet has fled into the Shift, and now it's time to go home."

Home. The word wasn't as uncomfortable as before.

"Is Charon dead?" Erae asked. Tomas looked back to where the Peret had been, searching again for some stain or mark. But nothing remained.

"Yes, he is dead," Michael said sadly. His eyes were dim.

"And Kithmakh?" said Tomas.

He shook his head. "I do not know. But don't worry about tomorrow, my friends. It will keep. We have much to be thankful for."

The distant roar of engines met Tomas' ears, and he laid his head back. The pain was fading, which was nice. His vision was going with it, but that was probably fine, too. A shadow swept over him, followed by the curving silhouette of the *Empress*.

He'd saved people today. It hadn't been many, and his part had been small. Even in his own Wasp, he felt like he'd watched someone else fire the guns and conquer the darkness.

But what a sight it had been. He could see the missiles launch from above him, oblivious to the enemy's shields, detonating upon the bridge. Maybe he'd dream of this from now on, free from the mistakes that had clung to him for seven years.

He'd destroyed his Wasp again. That seemed to happen when he saved people.

As unconsciousness finally took over, Tomas thought he heard Dan laughing at him. "Crashed? Again? And you say my flying's terrible," he guffawed. "Are you sure about that, Lead?"

"Yes," Tomas whispered. "Yes I am."

He woke up in *Sunbird*'s medical wing. The air was filled with the scent of burn gel, healing stims and plaster. Deep breaths summoned the taste of ash from his lungs and wracked his body with painful coughs. He kept his breaths shallow once he learned that. Most movements hurt, but his legs definitely had the worst of it. He restricted his motion to his head and eyes.

Most of the casualties near him were pilots who had ejected mid-combat, or frigate crew members who had been caught in ship fires on their way to escape pods. Burns, vacuum-exposure, smoke inhalation. If she was injured, he didn't see her. If she was healthy, she didn't come to check in on him. If she was dead …

Sometimes he closed his eyes, and when he opened them there were new casualties in the beds next to him. He didn't talk to them. There wasn't much to say, and when there was he couldn't focus on the words. He suspected it was due to pain medication more than injury, but trying to tell the difference was one more thought that wouldn't stick. Most often, he closed his eyes again.

Once he opened his eyes and saw Marpe standing next to his bed. The Qua'seth wasn't moving, and his face was turned away. No information, no news. He could have asked, but talking hurt, and Marpe seemed to be asleep. It was a comfort nonetheless.

Eventually Tomas opened his eyes to a different view, and a much clearer mind. The walls and floor were white tile. The ceiling was a cross-hatch of kuwrium girders and snaking illumination tubes. The strip of yellow running past the foot of his bed left no guesses as to where he was.

Presently, an elderly nurse pushed through the privacy curtain and checked on him. She smiled warmly on seeing he was awake. Her face was wrinkled and spotted, and a pale pink band held grey curls away from her face.

"Good morning, soldier. How're you feeling?" she asked.

Tomas pulled himself up and gingerly moved his legs. Then, when not much happened, he reached out and patted them through the sheets. The contact sent hot electricity along his nerves, but only briefly.

"Pretty good," he said, still inspecting. "I don't know if that means I'm healed or medicated."

The nurse laughed politely. "A bit of both, you'll find." She crossed to a monitor and looked back and forth between it and her tome-tile. "The synthetic grafts have done you wonderfully. How about your lungs?"

Tomas breathed, waited, breathed deeper. "The cough's gone, but I still taste a bit of smoke."

"Ah, being a living fireball will do that to a person," the nurse's eyes twinkled. "Can't do much for it now, but I can give you something else to chew on. How's that sound?"

"Lovely," Tomas said.

"Alright then, soldier. I reckon you can have a short walk after a meal, and all going well I'll get you out of here tomorrow. Is there anything else I can get you?"

"No—wait yes, actually. Can I send a message out? Off the Shard, I mean?"

The nurse canted her head. "You're new, aren't you?"

Tomas looked down briefly. "Yes ma'am."

She patted his arm. "You can record a message, no quibbling from me. But we don't shoot them to Fal-Comm from here. The next supply run will send them from a common port. So don't be waiting for a reply."

"Ah. That makes sense." Tomas looked down again.

"Do you still want it?"

"Yes, I think. If that's okay."

"Of course," she glanced once more at the monitor. "I'll have a device sent with your breakfast."

She left through the curtain, and Tomas relaxed and closed his eyes. He could almost imagine he was in a substandard military hospital on Kaldea's rings. But even as he thought it, he realised he didn't want to. Being here was so strange and unknown. But it was better.

The breakfast arrived half an hour later, but not in expected hands. Tomas opened his eyes when he heard the curtain being pulled to the side. Remiel stepped through first, followed by Amarie.

"Uh, hello?" Tomas greeted them, bewildered.

Remiel laughed and placed a tray of food next to Tomas' bed. "Greetings, master pilot. I seem to have been pressed into the catering service." He laughed again, a bright, dry rustle of noise.

"But why? I don't understand."

"Peace, child. I was already coming to see you and saw the opportunity to lend a hand. There isn't an empty bed here, I think."

"Ah." Knowing the old Celah Neiru was here with a purpose gave Tomas less peace than if he had been here on a whim. He turned to Amarie, who was doing an excellent job of looking everywhere but at Tomas. "And you?"

Amarie's eyes settled somewhere above Tomas' head. "I just thought I'd check on you quick. I'm on my way to see …" she trailed off.

"Erae?" Tomas suggested.

Amarie shook her head. "Michael." Her cheeks flushed. "I, uh … you're fine, right?"

Tomas shook his head and smiled. "I'm fine, thanks Amarie."

"Great. Bye." She was through the curtain before Tomas could respond. It wasn't much, but she'd begun and ended a conversation without threatening him. Maybe she cared more than he thought.

He regarded Remiel quizzically. "Can our medicine do anything for a Neiru?"

Remiel smiled. "Unfortunately, no. Michael will heal quickly on his own, but a great wound requires great rest. I'm sure the long hours will be shortened by pleasant company."

I'm sure it will. Tomas sighed, mentally preparing himself. "But you aren't here for pleasant company."

"No, though I hope I provide it nonetheless. I'm here to answer questions." Remiel focused his half-lidded gaze on Tomas. "If you still have any, that is."

"Plenty." Tomas paused to consider where to begin. He barely knew anything about the Neiru, good or bad. He had a vague grasp of who Eladdiyr was, but were there rules or tenets in this kingdom of his? What if, after all this, he didn't belong?

The thoughts orbited in his head, but distantly. He knew what he really wanted to ask, what he wanted to know.

"What happened at the battle of Tachillah?"

Remiel's eyes shone like white rainbows. "The truth is a tricky thing." He held up a hand as Tomas huffed. "But I shall tell you the answer.

"The Ebon are not a sentient species like Humans or Yiishi or Dabans. They have intelligence, but they were created with purposes. They were made to kill and to conquer and, surprisingly, to lose."

"To lose?" Tomas didn't believe it.

"Yes, child, at least to begin with. Because as you kill them again and again, as you master them and think you have control, you find yourself not so different from what they are. A shadow, dark and empty. A vessel for death. Either way, when the fighting is done, the Peret will stand atop a Cluster that no longer contains life."

Tomas stared. "But we've just *been* fighting them! That's what you sent us off to do!"

Remiel nodded. "A foolish endeavour save for one thing. Your vessel isn't empty. Ben-Eloah filled you with something that makes the Ebon shudder, something that persists against the corruption of war."

"What did he give me?"

"Once again, the truth is a tricky thing. But for now, think of it as your sword against the darkness. Think of it as light."

Tomas closed his eyes. He thought of what Erae had shown him in his apartment. Even at the memory, a warmth and colour seemed to fall gently upon his mind. "I think I understand."

"An understanding that will only grow with time. Did you have another question for me?"

Tomas looked at him. "Do you know what I've done? What I did that day?"

"No," Remiel said. "But I think I can guess."

Tomas turned away from the luminous gaze. "And what does that mean for me?"

"What do you want it to mean? Your misguided choices caused great harm, but from it Eladdiyr and his son planned great good. This does not make your action right, but it makes their gift all the more wonderous."

"But he's dead, Remiel!" Tomas said. "He gave me light, and I killed him. What do I do now?"

Remiel's eyes sparkled. "The truth is a tricky thing, my child. For now, let us say he died."

"That's what …"

Again, Remiel held up a hand. "As for what you should do, I suggest trust. Trust our king. Trust yourself. And trust me, as I'm trusting you now." He reached into the folds of his cloak and pulled out a tome-tile. He placed it on the table beside the food.

Tomas looked at it, then back at Remiel. "Thank you."

"I can guess who you want to message. Do you know what you want to say?"

"Not yet. That I'm alive, I guess. That I'm safe. I wish I could know the same about them."

Remiel closed his eyes and smiled. "I trust you'll know soon enough."

34

Erae wasn't supposed to be discharged when *Sunbird* returned to the Shard. Her burns, bruises and fractures were all responding well to medical treatment, but the combined sum of them drained her energy. Her right shoulder continuously throbbed beneath its wrapping.

But one arm couldn't stop her from flying her ship, planning runs or resourcing refugees. The war hadn't stopped with Charon's death.

The problem she found was that no one *let* her help. They all told her to rest, to take time for herself. She couldn't even get a refuelling order for the *Empress*. The whole station seemed in on the plot, conspiring to get her to slow down.

Slowing down had hurt in the past. It allowed thoughts and whispers to come creeping from the corners of her brain. Thoughts about the missions she'd failed and the people she'd killed.

Erae wasn't so worried about that now. They had taken losses at Kaluma, but each life had been given to protect something greater. Even now, the miners and smugglers from Kaluma were settling into their new apartments, organising furniture and tucking children into bed. It was everything she'd fought for.

So why was she scared to stop?

If the nightmares weren't waiting for her when she slowed down, then what would be?

She continued the battle for two days until Amarie found time between visiting Michael to pass her a message. Tomas was getting discharged from the hospital and wanted to see her. She instantly agreed.

For Erae, it was something to do. It was a step down that didn't quite leave her alone with her thoughts. For Tomas, well, she couldn't imagine it would be very heartening to leave the hospital and go back to his empty, unfurnished apartment. She picked him up and led him to the West Park.

They sat on the cliff edge in Erae's usual spot, overlooking the dewbark trees that spread below their dangling feet. A soft breeze conspired against her hair and cheek. They talked through a few unimportant topics. Ships they'd flown, planets they'd seen, things like that.

"Where are they going?" Tomas pointed beyond the dome to a string of ships, both large and small, that were gathering together in a loose convoy.

Erae had noticed that there had been more people moving around today, and at the same time less and less. Now she saw the reason. "They're going to Beriah," she told him. "The system Boaz mentioned at the meeting."

"That's right. He said there was no shift gate for that system. Is it inside the Cluster?"

"I think so," Erae shrugged. "The Neiru were the ones who told us about the system, and Raguel guides the pilots on their way. I won't know where it is unless I join them."

Tomas looked more intently at the line of vessels. "They're running away," he said. "Even after we won."

"The Cluster is breaking, Tomas. Even if we beat the Ebon, there is plenty to run from. Some want to get away from the Core. Others want to get away from themselves."

Tomas smirked. "You sound like a Partisan."

"Have you ever met one?"

"Well, no …" he trailed off.

A honey-coloured leaf fell from one of the trees overlooking the cliff, and the breeze carried it out over the edge of the rockface. It glided, lingered and almost returned on an unlooked-for draft. Inevitably, though, it found its way between the golden treetops and to the ground below.

It was beautiful, but it was brief. Life was no different.

Stop it. This is what slowing down gets you. She forced her thoughts elsewhere. "The crew can help you get your apartment sorted tomorrow. Do you have any thoughts for decoration?"

"I think I can put something together," Tomas chuckled. "I did spend a few days imprisoned in storage. I found potting mix, statuettes, girder brackets. No knives though. I looked everywhere for a knife."

Erae laughed. "We aren't *completely* incompetent, you know."

"I've gathered." Tomas laughed again and shook his head. "There's one thing I still don't get, though. Why do you have key cards?"

Erae inclined her head. "We don't want people running all over the station. The children especially. If they could access the armouries …"

"That's not what I meant." Tomas interrupted. "I understand the need for security."

"Then I don't understand."

"Your I.D. chips," he explained, holding his right palm toward her. "Every place I've ever visited has used chip access on their doors. That is, except here."

"Ah." Realisation snaked along Erae's right arm, and it felt suddenly heavy. Her hands took turns in closing, tensing and then falling open again.

The hesitation was natural, but her shame surprised her. She closed her eyes, staring at herself for a moment. *I don't have to show him,* she thought. *Words will work just as well.*

She wanted to show him, and she didn't, and both decisions tugged at her, strung to reasons both known and unknown, good and bad, one sometimes stealing the points from the other.

"When ..." she stopped, tried again. "We found that ..."

The words knotted. With a resigned sigh, Erae held out her right hand. With a final hesitation, feeling like she was as transparent as a Neiru, she tugged off her combat glove.

The silver-cream of her prosthesis' unfeeling skin did not shiver as it touched the cold. Slowly, she turned her palm to the sky, then back again. She bent her fingers, imagining the tug of pistons and the turn of motors lying unseen beneath the alloy. Her thumb ran the length of her index finger, testing it, but she could not feel the sensation on either digit.

Tomas tracked every movement and leaned in unsettlingly close as he beheld her robotic hand. His eyes slid from the nail-less fingers to the line-less palm, then to the wrist guard that hid the moment the device ended and the woman began.

"Why?" he asked her.

"It's an ugly, primitive thing, isn't it? I thought about painting it, but that just seems dishonest."

"Why?" he repeated.

Erae sighed. "So we could hide," she said, "and so we could be free. Every door you open, everything you buy, it's all traceable. And the chip is wired into your nervous system, so just cutting it out fries your whole arm. For Defiant who work in the field a lot, it made sense to get rid of the problem altogether."

Tomas looked her in the eyes. She gazed back, drawn again to the thin gold edge of his brown irises.

"May I?"

She nodded, and his sight was once again on her hand as he brought his own towards it.

A finger grazed her own, its pad barely deforming against the anogite-bonded surface. Erae watched as he increased the pressure, feeling nothing as she always did, and yet feeling each touch now for the first time.

The finger became three as he moved to her palm, and then the edge of her wrist. What he was looking for she didn't know, but there was no compulsion to end the study. She kept her eyes on his fingers, which were shaded from the park lights by the shadow of two heads.

"You really would do whatever it takes." It was half a question and half a statement. "It's beautiful."

Erae had to swallow before she could respond. "It really isn't," she insisted. "If it was a proper prosthesis you wouldn't even know it was there."

He lingered at the edge of the metal, then gently placed his hand in hers. Their eyes met again.

"I still think you're crazy, Erae," he said. "And I don't know how this war will end. But I trust you." Then the hand was gone, and Tomas was on his feet, walking away.

Erae nearly let him, but her brain finished rebooting. "Wait," she called, and he turned. "Do you know the way back?"

"Nope." He smiled. "Will you show me, Captain?"

Electricity hummed in Erae's wrist. She picked herself up.

"Of course, Commander. Follow me."

EPILOGUE

It was all such a waste.

An age ago, the Cluster had been full of large, old stars. Planets had been few, and mortal life a distant dream. A fragile order destined to return to chaos.

And chaos returned. A number of stars near the Cluster's centre died within years of each other, throwing their components out amongst the neighbouring masses. One explosion induced another, then another, until chains of destructive supernovae swept through most of the Cluster.

The inferno lasted for centuries, and when it slowed, gravity resumed its tireless work. New stars, planets and nebulae formed. And at the centre of it all, the remnants of chaos drew together in an immense, lightless amalgam. A black hole.

Abaddon.

It was the name of the dark star, and also the name of the spire of black glass suspended above it. The structure sharpened to a point at the base, and was spoked just before the summit, like a dagger of ten sides. It glittered in the warped light of Abaddon's accretion disc, the captured remains of those long-dead stars, eternally falling, eternally consumed.

This spire was the Master's standard. His flag of dominion skewered into the heart of the Cluster to claim it as his own. As it hovered above the inescapable singularity, it promised that all the disparate, divided systems and stars would one day be whole. Drawn together, all would join in a destiny of darkness and death.

Plasma and lightning erupted from the top of the spire, lancing across the brilliance of the accretion disc, sharp and pure against the black hole's maw. The windows blew out, then the walls on one side, shattering into countless flickering shards, each so small and with such force that they managed to escape the event horizon. Three of the ten walkways split and fractured, tumbling away from the rest of the structure.

Remiyyah shielded her eyes with her hands, stepping back from the source of the detonation. Orexis cowered behind her throne, or most of it. The left edge was spinning through space along with the walls and floor. Brother Charon's throne was nowhere to be seen. It had been the target of the attack, after all.

This room will have to be entirely rebuilt. Remiyyah thought. *Rebuilding takes time. It takes resources. Resources I could have used on grander things.*

She might have told him to stop. But it was far safer to let him spend his anger on the empty throne of their brother than to spend it on her.

Charon was a waste, too, and he wasted our finest weapon.

The onslaught ceased. Remiyyah's thoughts were interrupted as Krateo turned towards her, lightning still slithering along his fingers, arcing at the tips. Broken glass crunched underfoot as she took another step back. It made no sound in the vacuum, but she felt each snap as if it might be her own neck.

But that would be another waste. Krateo knows this, right?

"Brother?" she ventured, and this sound did carry through the void of space. It was her voice, and it would go where she willed it.

Krateo growled low. "This war is still ours."

Remiyyah bowed her head in assent. "What do you command?"

"The fleet is still ravaging the Cluster, and the Ruin is still of use, though we control it no longer." The Kin Lord stalked back to his throne—which had barely escaped being thrown into the void with Charon's—and sat down.

"With every victory the mortals gain, their fear lessens, and their hope festers. It is an infection, an abhorrence, and I will not tolerate it." His head was locked towards her, and she felt pierced by his scarred, sightless gaze.

"Do not repeat Charon's mistakes, sister. Give the mortals their wishes. Give them their lusts, their desires, their dreams. Give them happiness, even, if it suits your deceptive ends. But do not give them hope."

Krateo crushed his hands together, and electricity was exchanged for seeping darkness. "We must extinguish their hope."

He opened his hands, and there within were three rings. Cast in black metal and shaped with spiralling arms, they murmured with power. Each had a jewel: one an onyx, one a ruby and one a diamond stained with mists of pale green.

"*Orexis*," Krateo growled, and the small Neiru slinked out of her throne's shadow.

Cautiously, Remiyyah lifted a ring from her brother's palm and held it aloft. Its red gem glinted as it reflected the bright rays of her eyes. Her hand tingled with anticipation.

When Orexis had taken hers, Krateo joined them both in standing. "Our Master is waiting," he said, and slipped the last ring upon his finger.

"In darkness let him come."

ABOUT THE AUTHOR

Luke A. Winter is a document controller, preacher, and theology student living in Western Australia. He holds a Diploma of Theology and is working on his Bachelor's. Writing has long been a hobby, but it became a priority after miraculously surviving a cardiac arrest in 2020. In his spare time, he enjoys reading, gaming, and playing the piano.